I0590409

ENTHRALL
SHADOWS

ENTRALL SESSIONS
BOOK TEN

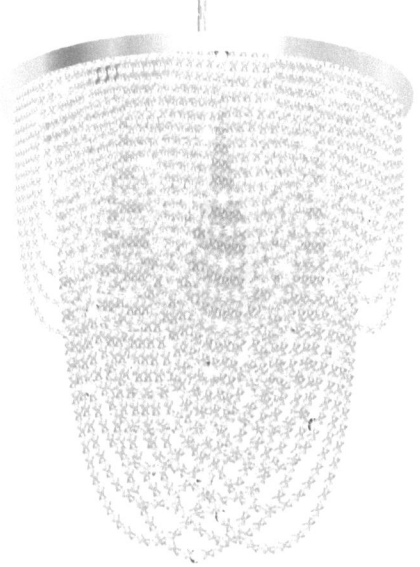

USA TODAY BESTSELLING AUTHOR
VANESSA FEWINGS

FBI Anti-Piracy Warning: The unauthorized reproduction or distribution of a copyrighted work is illegal. Criminal copyright infringement, including infringement without monetary gain, is investigated by the FBI and is punishable by up to five years in federal prison and a fine of $250,000.

Enthrall Shadows
Copyright © 2022 Vanessa Fewings

All rights reserved.

No part of this book may be used or reproduced in any manner whatsoever, including Internet usage, without written permission from the author. This story is a work of fiction. References to real people, events, establishments, organizations, or locales are intended only to provide a sense of authenticity and are used fictitiously. All other characters, and all incidents and dialogue are drawn from the author's imagination and are not to be construed as real.

Cover Design by Hang Le

Formatted by: Champagne Book Design
Editor: Debbie Kuhn

"I think we ripple on into others, just like a stone puts its ripples into a brook. That, for me, too, is a source of comfort. It kind of, in a sense, negates the sense of total oblivion. Some piece of ourselves, not necessarily our consciousness, but some piece of ourselves gets passed on and on and on."

—Irvin D. Yalom, MD

For my cousin, Steve

ENTHRALL SHADOWS

ENTRALL SESSIONS
BOOK TEN

CHAPTER ONE

Henry

LOS ANGELES IS PRONE TO EARTHQUAKES.

Yes, thank you, brain, for offering that reminder every time I enter my executive glass elevator on the 79th floor.

I patted my thigh to get Dex to follow me in. My black Labrador settled by my feet, peering up at me with affection.

From the loftiest level of Cole Tower, I had a panoramic view of the city. Twinkling lights and snaking roads appeared beyond the skyrise, a bluish nightscape of vibrant life.

The streets below were snarled with the usual Friday traffic.

Dex's interest grew as the elevator descended. He knew what came next—a run around the park. After that, a bowl of Pedigree for him back at the suite. And for me, a glass of Macallan as I watched the news.

Alone.

Although Dex did keep me company at the Bel Air Hotel. I'd stayed there since arriving on the West Coast. The suite was comfortable enough. The staff spoiled Dex. Spoiled me, too, to be honest.

To them, I must have seemed eccentric—a billionaire who could afford his own place but preferred a more reclusive lifestyle.

For now, anyway.

Dex missed those long runs around Central Park. Or maybe it was just me feeling nostalgic for Manhattan.

This eclectic metropolis and I were still getting acquainted.

As were the staff with my mercurial reputation, which apparently had preceded me.

If you wanted to test my nerve, just ask me what I did to my brother. He'd saved our company with his usual acumen. Before the dust had even settled, I had claimed my rightful place as the head of our family empire.

Cameron had acquiesced with his usual compassion.

This crisscross of dark glass and steely architecture reflected the heart of the man who now ruled from within.

My father had named C. R. Cole Tower after Cameron because they'd abandoned hope of me ever taking over.

It had taken courage laced with grit to rise again. Once I'd taken over the leadership, I'd sliced through their preconceived ideas about what I was capable of. I'd made hard decisions that ensured profits continued to soar—my personal brand of control proving effective.

The remarkable skill set I'd brought back from the Navy SEALs usually kept my enemies at bay.

Right up until it didn't.

That's why I'd brought in a crack team of investigators—led by Shay Gardner—to root out our apparent corporate spy. Once we found them, I'd throw the fuckers to my shark lawyers and have them devour the bastards.

A blood bath awaited.

Metaphorically speaking, of course.

I turned to face the elevator doors in anticipation of hitting the ground floor, feeling our slowed descent.

The elevator stopped on the fifth floor.

Which should never happen. It should take me right to the subterranean parking garage.

Sliding doors pulled back to reveal a pretty stranger, her complexion a golden brown. As she stepped inside and joined me, uninvited, I guessed her age to be around twenty. Her brown hair fell neatly down her back. She glanced over at Dex and then spun around to face the door.

"This is the executive elevator," I informed her.

The doors slid closed.

She rested her palm against the door as it shut. "Sorry."

"It's fine," I said. "This time."

She dropped her hand and kept her back to me. I noticed she was holding an envelope.

An intern, maybe?

But she had severely missed the mark on business attire, wearing jeans and a red FSU sweater that hinted she hailed from out of state.

She'd also missed the *Executives Only* sign on the panel beside the call button.

Pivoting to face me, she asked, "You're the CEO?"

"I am."

Her face seemed familiar. "Have we met?" I said.

"No."

I tried to place her.

"Where do you work?" I asked.

"Just visiting."

I was making this girl nervous, so I pulled back on the light interrogation.

The elevator slowed to a stop—stuck between floors.

I leaned forward and jabbed the DOWN button.

Beyond that sliver of glass lay a sheer drop.

I stabbed the G button again. "It'll be fine. This is a state-of-the-art elevator."

"Thank goodness." She faced me and reached out to shake hands in an act of boldness. "I'm Lilly."

I stared down at her hand, refusing to take it.

She dropped it back to her side.

Touching a stranger in close proximity was a bad idea.

Unless…

She'd infiltrated us as a spy to get closer to me.

My patience was wearing thin. Having to use extra caution with every interaction was getting tedious.

Even this stranger, who at first appeared too young to be given any kind of great responsibility, could be a hazard.

Paranoia had been thrown into the mix.

That's where I'd landed since Shay had delivered the news about a threat to my company. I needed it dealt with.

I needed out of this elevator.

I punched the red button and it lit up.

Then went out.

"Oh, God," she said, sounding panicked.

"Give it a second."

Pulling out my phone, I shot off a text to inform the main desk. Then I sent one to my executive assistant, Jen.

Lilly reached out to push the button again.

"Let's not touch anything else," I said. "I've alerted my team."

"Okay."

Even her voice reminded me of someone.

A cold chill washed over me. "Are you interviewing here?"

"No."

"Could you stand back, please?"

She moved to the other side of the elevator.

I remained against the glass wall, a sheer drop behind me. I drew in a steadying breath.

An awkward silence loomed.

Squeezing the bridge of my nose, I tried to center myself.

"You served in Afghanistan?" she asked. "That must have been terrifying."

What the fuck?

I remembered that my bio could be found on our website.

Only a young person would be brash enough to bring that up with the timing reserved for the naïve.

I suppressed my annoyance. "Who are you visiting?"

"You."

I felt a sting of regret for not asking her to get out when I'd had the chance. "All appointments go through my executive assistant."

"She wouldn't set one."

"Then how did you get in?"

"Visitor's pass."

Still, she shouldn't have gotten access to the fifth floor.

"You got in here with me on purpose?" I said quietly, my jaw flexing.

She reached out and offered me the envelope.

I chose not to take it.

A million thoughts crowded my mind. "Who's it from?"

"Reese."

My heart missed a beat. "Who?"

"Reese Papadopoulos."

"She wrote it years ago?" I said flatly.

"No."

I felt the shock of an invisible defibrillator.

"Are you okay?" The girl's voice found me in the darkness.

I'd barely been twenty when it happened.

Reese, a few months older.

I'd been too love struck to believe my girlfriend had a reckless edge. The victim blamed for the sins of others. I'd refused to bow to that theory.

I'd loved Reese so damn much.

A fissure struck my soul.

"The last time you saw her was at the beginning of her gap year?" she asked, her voice soft.

The last time I saw her?

At the airport.

Where I'd kissed Reese goodbye.

For the last time.

Reese had set off like so many before her on an expedition to build homes and teach English in Chile. Months in and she'd disappeared without a trace in Patagonia.

What followed had been worse than hell.

The ones left behind carried the guilt for what we should or could have done.

We'd searched for her tirelessly at the campground in Chile, including the surrounding areas. Some of us had hiked further into the wilderness.

We'd halted our lives for months.

Eventually, and reluctantly, I'd returned to the States. I'd had to face my parents, who'd found it hard to believe that I'd risked my life trying to save hers.

Grief from those years had been carved into my DNA.

Even as I'd finally made peace with her being gone.

This young woman—this stranger—was now asking me to reopen old wounds.

She could never understand the seriousness of this interaction.

The outcome of that college trauma had me hurtling into a different future than the one I'd first imagined for myself. Giving up my dream of becoming a Navy fighter pilot, I'd been jettisoned into the extreme life of a Special Forces Officer.

A trajectory that had proved every decision mattered, both Reese's and mine.

The consequences of such a change in my career path had landed me as a prisoner in an enemy camp in Afghanistan—suffering unceasing torture.

Some part of me had never left that cell. My mind had fractured like shards of glass never to be made whole.

"Henry?" Lilly's soft voice drew me back.

She offered me the letter again. Seemingly innocent, yet containing a secret.

I felt a stab of doubt. "*When* did she write it?"

"A week ago."

Impossible.

What the fuck is this?

Denial raged against reason. "Who are you?"

Her expression softened. "Her daughter."

CHAPTER TWO

Henry

I'D GUESSED THE YOUNG WOMAN'S AGE CORRECTLY.

She was insinuating that Reese hadn't died in Chile. Reese would have given birth in her early twenties—if it was true. She must have become pregnant after arriving in Patagonia. Lilly's radiant complexion hinted at her father's origin.

That type of revelation would have hurt me to the bone. Missing out on my child's life would have destroyed me.

"She's really still alive?" I held my breath, waiting for her response.

Lilly glanced down and then raised her gaze to meet mine. "Yes."

A rush of emotions swirled through me at Reese's betrayal.

This can't be true.

As much as I need it to be.

Nausea welled up inside me and I tasted dread.

The elevator jolted, resuming its descent.

Uneasiness slithered down my spine. The hazard of this lofty height had been replaced with something worse.

I leaned over to pat Dex, my fingers brushing through his warm fur. He rested his head against my palm, soothing me a little.

The elevator doors opened.

I stood there mulling over whether to step out and take our conversation into the foyer where others could observe us—or deal with this in private.

This felt like drowning and rising to a high altitude at the same time.

I gestured for Lilly to exit the elevator first.

Years of military training had taught me how to control my heart rate.

But all of that meant nothing in this moment.

They can't train you for this.

"You don't want the letter?" she asked.

I went with, "Let's grab a coffee."

Having witnesses to our conversation seemed like a smart idea. I knew well enough not to accept envelopes from strangers for legal reasons.

She stepped out of the elevator and then turned back to me. "Are you allowed to bring your dog into the café?"

"It's my café."

"Right." She gave me an endearing smile. "Can we have tea?"

"Sure."

I could see it now, her resemblance to Reese.

Or maybe this was a cruel hoax on a man too blinded by emotion to see it, who wanted to find similarities in her mother.

I led the way and patted my leg. "Dex!"

Obediently, he stayed close.

"He's cute," she said.

Dex was so much more. Cameron had given him to me as a puppy upon my arrival back in the States. Dex had been with me through the hardest times. Now, I intended on spoiling him through the good.

Lilly seemed calm considering the news she'd imparted.

Maybe I appeared uncommonly reasonable.

Or maybe her mom had told her she'd be meeting with a

decent man, a dangerous assumption. I'd radically changed from the college student she'd once known.

Had I once loved a woman who had disappeared of her own volition?

None of this made sense.

In the café, a barista scurried around preparing two cups of Earl Grey.

I considered texting Shay, but thought better of it. I was already keeping my head of security super busy. If I messaged Cameron about this, he'd tell me to walk away.

That would have been the wiser choice.

Two venti Earl Grey's were set on the counter. Lilly carried hers over to the condiment table and added a dash of milk.

I joined her, pouring a packet of sugar into mine.

My hands were surprisingly steady.

I directed Lilly into a corner booth.

Dex scurried beneath the table and promptly lay on my feet. I let him; we both needed the reassurance.

I ignored the curious glances from the staff and zeroed in on my visitor.

Running through all the possibilities of what someone would gain by doing this, I scanned Lilly for traits similar to Reese's. She had her mother's features—the way her face brightened when she talked. Her earthiness. The same lithe frame.

Reese had been into running track—as had I.

We'd met in college on the field, with her sprinting counterclockwise and me chastising her for going the wrong way. I'd found her rebellious nature alluring.

I glanced at the envelope. "What's in it, exactly?"

"To be honest, I don't know." Lilly surveyed the marble foyer. "I was instructed to hand it to you, then leave."

Yet here she sat having drinks with me.

I recognized her stubbornness. She had Reese's temperament. Lilly appeared just as curious about me.

"What does she want?" I said, playing along.

"To see you."

"Why isn't she here?"

"It's complicated."

Exhaling in frustration, I sat back and pretended to answer a text. "Give me a second," I said, discreetly taking Lilly's photo.

Even though we must have security footage of her visiting the Tower, I wanted a close-up.

"Is your mom in L.A?" I asked.

"No."

Disappointed, I said, "Put her on the phone."

Lilly slid the envelope across the table. "Mom believed if you saw her, you'd walk away."

Would I have?

I wasn't sure.

I tried to imagine how she'd look now. Would I even recognize her?

"How did you plan on meeting me in the elevator at the right time?"

"There's a café opposite Cole Tower."

"You've been watching me?"

I'd skipped the usual drill of consistently choosing a different time to both arrive and exit the building. This week, I'd been distracted with a new brand, spending more time in the office than usual.

Lilly lowered her gaze. "She understood this would be difficult for you."

Where had that compassion been when she'd written that damn note, or when she'd slipped away like a ghost?

Reese had been The One.

Or so I'd believed.

The wisdom of dredging up all that grief was questionable.

I'd never actually believed this day was possible.

"Why has it taken her so long?"

All this time...

"Mom threw herself into her work. She's dedicated her life to it."

"What does she do?"

"She'll tell you."

"So your mom wasn't kidnapped?"

"No."

A million more questions raced through my mind.

"You were born in Chile?" I asked, lifting the cup of tea to my mouth. I blew on the black, aromatic liquid to cool it before taking a sip.

"Yes."

"Does she have any idea how many people searched for her? All the suffering that followed her disappearance? How much her family grieved?"

"She's suffered too," said Lilly. "She had to give you up."

I failed to rally any sympathy.

She hadn't needed to give me up—she'd chosen to.

But I'd made my own mistakes.

Like hiding away in a cabin in Big Bear after returning from the Middle East—the reason my brother had gifted me a puppy, my beloved Dex. Those who'd mattered to me had known my location. I wouldn't have tortured my family like that.

"Where did your mom go after Chile?" I asked.

Lilly reached out and rested her hand on mine. "She's promised to answer all your questions."

I dragged my hand away and stood up.

I was done with this game.

"Do you live in L.A.?"

"No, but I'm hoping to attend UCLA. Thought I'd check out the campus while I'm here."

I didn't care about her college plans. I wasn't there yet.

"Do you have somewhere to stay?" I asked.

"I booked a room at The Belmont Crescent Hotel."

An interesting choice, hinting she really was from out of town.

"That place is notorious," I said. Its reputation was as fascinating as its once prominent location.

She gave a shrug. "The room seemed nice when I booked it."

"You flew in just to see me?"

"Yes."

"What's your last name?"

"I'd rather not say."

My jaw tensed. "How long are you in town?"

"One more night."

"Let me move you to another hotel."

She shook her head. "No need."

The first thing I'd do when I saw Reese—if I saw her—would be to tell her to take better care of her daughter. It should have been her who came to see me.

"I'll send my driver to move you to another hotel. It'll be on me."

"I'm fine, really."

"What's your phone number?"

She hesitated and then offered me the envelope. "Our contact information is inside."

"Convenient," I said bitterly, accepting the letter.

Holding the seemingly innocent envelope caused a visceral response.

As though I'm touching Reese.

"Thank you for seeing me, Mr. Cole." Lilly pushed up and slid out of the booth.

"You didn't give me much choice."

Glancing down at Dex, who was still sprawled near my feet, she gave him a pat on the head.

"I like my hotel," she said. "I don't want anything from you. Just so we're clear."

Lilly left her cup of tea on the table and walked away.

I watched her stroll through the foyer and leave through the lofty front entrance.

Once outside on the pavement, she turned left and disappeared from view.

Loosening my tie, I inhaled sharply, filled with an equal measure of hope and anguish.

CHAPTER THREE

Henry

TWO SHOTS OF A TWENTY-ONE-YEAR-OLD MACALLAN FROM the hotel bar and this is where I'd ended up—outside the doors of the grandest property on Bel Air Drive.

It was a ten-minute cab ride from my hotel.

The driver dropped me off before reaching the main gate. Even with a high blood alcohol level, I knew to be discreet.

I didn't usually drink this much, but then again, it wasn't every day you received a letter from someone presumed dead.

The gate opened for a silver Jaguar to enter. I slipped in, walking the rest of the way up the winding path.

Well, I was here now.

The grand palace—the best description for it—was perched above a canyon with a dramatic view of the city, encompassed by tall palm trees and other fancy lush foliage. There were no other properties nearby.

I saw a blur of movement to my left.

A fucking peacock, prancing around like it owned the place.

A red Mercedes-Benz slowed down to avoid hitting the bird

and then pulled up to the front door. A young, well-dressed valet sprang into action, taking the car keys from the passengers as they got out of the car.

The couple wore cocktail attire and masquerade masks. I watched them stroll through the front door.

I hung my head, thinking I might not be able to get in.

It's better to be here than back at the hotel.

With that unopened letter.

Before reading Reese's words—if they were indeed hers—I needed time to consider the risk.

Maybe finding out I was a successful businessman had lured her back into my life. She'd spoken out about me joining the Navy. Now, though, I had been hailed in the press as a billionaire worth nabbing.

Getting away from reality seemed like the best escape.

This impressive mansion used to be my younger brother's secret haunt—before he'd handed over the reins to Richard Booth, another bad boy who excelled at whatever they got up to here.

Those two Harvard grads were incorrigible.

Cameron had named this place Chrysalis. Apparently, it was like Enthrall only grander in scale.

Within this mysterious setting was one of the most profound treatment centers in the world.

I wasn't so sure about that.

My Savile Row suit would have to do. I'd not changed since leaving work.

I went on inside and was greeted by opulence.

The lavishly decorated foyer elicited awe. An impressive chandelier hung low from the ornate ceiling as a central focal point, its magnificence capable of stopping you in your tracks.

Beyond the enormous glittering display of crystal droplets was an elaborate marble staircase with iron filigree banisters. It swept up dramatically to the first floor and headed in opposite directions.

On the ground floor, extravagant décor welcomed guests into

a world of indulgence. Marble flooring shone beneath my Oxfords and lavish textures and bright colors made the luxurious furniture stand out. A soft blue light set an ethereal tone.

Hell, even I was aroused, and this grandeur served merely as the entrance.

"You can't come any farther, sir," said the fast-approaching guard.

"This is my brother's place," I said. "Cameron Cole."

"Sir!" He blocked my way.

Bulky and gruff, the guy could have been a professional wrestler.

Still, no way could I leave now.

Traces of my brother's personality were everywhere, contrasting imperialism meshed with a welcoming openness.

Cameron had always been a complex man, drawn to simplicity. Yet his taste was extraordinary. Even the stairway offered an alluring mystery, making one wonder what lay beyond.

"Henry!" Richard Booth swept through the foyer appearing suave in his black tuxedo.

He strolled toward me with one hand tucked into a pocket, showing that familiar confidence. His dark blond locks were tousled with the ease of a distracted hand.

"So, this is it!" I glanced around at all the mysterious glamour as I greeted my brother's best friend.

"Cameron's not here," said Richard.

I hadn't expected him to be.

As far as I knew, Cam had left this behind and had thrown himself into philanthropy.

Richard waved the guard away.

"Henry, how are you? This is unexpected."

"It certainly is."

Richard took my arm and led me left, down a hallway. "You didn't see anything," he said, upping the intrigue.

Despite all Richard had endured because of his corrupt father, he did not appear jaded. He had dropped his real last name—Sheppard—to hide the fact he was the son of the man who had brought down Wall Street.

Everyone here adored Richard. They called him Booth.

He'd played a major role in saving Cole Tea. For a while there, he'd even dated Mia Lauren before she'd married Cameron.

And they called me complicated.

A flurry of ten young barely clad women wearing masquerade masks scurried in the opposite direction, a sexual fantasy unraveling in real time.

I found it challenging to look away.

It would probably be frowned upon if I tucked one of the submissives under my arm and ran out the front door, trying to save a lamb like Clarice Starling in Thomas Harris' novel.

I staggered, feeling dizzy.

"Steady there," said Richard.

He led me into an office that contained sophisticated remnants of when my brother had owned this space. A framed photo of Carl Jung was one of many items decorating the walls.

Richard fished out his iPhone, threatening to text Cameron.

"Not yet," I said.

"Not yet?" His tone held a hint of amusement.

"Let's not bother him."

"Right." He arched a brow. "Because what could possibly go wrong?"

I stepped forward and eased the phone out of his hands, setting it on the desk.

"What are you doing here?" he asked.

I mulled over an explanation we'd both believe.

He leaned over the desk and pressed a button on the office phone. "Coffee. Soon as you can."

Sobering up was not on my agenda.

I thought about Reese's unopened letter.

Open it and that old pain will spill out.

"I'm not ready," I whispered.

"What's going on with you?" said Richard softly.

"How about a tour?"

He gripped my shoulders as I swayed. "Talk to me."

I couldn't say it. That my life had been stained with an incident I still blamed myself for. Maybe had I gone with Reese to Chile, she'd have remained safe.

I'd learned to live with my past, but it hadn't learned to live with me.

I hated all the uncertainty.

What Lilly had shared with me in the foyer café seemed inconceivable.

"Come sit down." He led me toward a couch.

My spinning head was making me feel nauseous.

I slumped on the sofa. "This is all very nice."

A glass of water appeared before me. I took it, swallowing the refreshing drink, only now realizing my thirst.

Richard eased the glass out of my hand and lifted my feet up, tipping me over on my side and forcing me to lie on the couch.

"Rest." He dragged a throw over my body. "I'll come back for you."

I closed my eyes, shutting out the light, the world.

Shutting out *her.*

The door opened and closed.

I felt myself drifting off in a haze.

A dark room.

I could hear yelling, the language Pashto. Another man screamed at me in Farsi.

I am the man of the hour. The focus of their hate.

Starved.

Weak.

Fatigued.

The scent of filth and sweat—mine.

I tasted blood from my cut lip.

Blurred vision, but I had memorized every fissure of these walls of captivity. Every scratch left by previous prisoners. Those who'd left their mark on each brick. Some had signed their names in the hope that loved ones might find out what had happened to them.

This. This is what had happened to them.

I forced my swollen eyelids to open.

"Any chance I can get an upgrade?" I asked in French to spite them.

Another strike to my face.

Strange, how you once had everything a man could want and yet it slipped away.

How long had I been a captive? Three weeks?

Death's stench filled my nostrils.

I'm never getting out of here.

CHAPTER FOUR

Henry

I SPRANG AWAKE, SHAKEN FROM MY NIGHTMARE.

Dragging air into my lungs, I shoved a throw off me and sat up straight as the stark memories began to fade.

Overwhelming relief flooded my senses. I wasn't *there,* in that fucking cell.

I could hear music beyond the door.

Chrysalis?

I reached out for Dex.

That's right. I'd left him back at the hotel to rest. I needed to get back to him soon.

I'd not had one of those nightmares in a while. They were triggered by stress; triggered by the ghosts from my past.

Glancing at my watch, I saw that I'd been out for thirty minutes.

I poured coffee into a mug from a silver pot. Somebody had brought in that tray. Richard, maybe? If not, the stranger would have observed my current state.

I hoped they'd be discreet.

Waiting for my coffee to cool, I scanned the office.

An impressive book collection neatly filled the floor-to-ceiling shelves. With the plush high-back chairs at the back of the room, it reminded me of a gentlemen's club.

I chugged the delicious, cooled coffee and poured myself another cup. Caffeine rushed through my veins.

They had served me the Cole brand, of course.

I stood and walked over to the wall mirror, straightened my tie and ran my fingers through my ruffled hair in lieu of a comb. My reflection wasn't too bad, considering.

I noticed a golden Venetian masquerade mask resting on a nearby shelf and picked it up, examining its craftsmanship. An enigmatic disguise—just what a distinguished gentleman needed.

Placing the mask over my face, I tied the silk straps at the back of my head to secure it.

Stepping out of Richard's office, I blinked to clear my vision as I considered which way to go.

I went left, ambling through the sea of well-dressed masquerade guests. I avoided the guard who'd stopped me on the way in—just in case.

I nabbed two flutes of champagne off a silver tray as though I meant to offer one to another guest and then followed a group of tuxedo-clad guys into a noisy room.

Inside, a cocktail party was in full swing, the women in elegant gowns and the men in formal wear. Nothing scandalous going on here—other than striking submissives in fine strips of latex with pasties over their nipples. A few of them were topless.

An arousing vision to behold.

To my right, a man wearing a masquerade mask knelt loyally beside a dominatrix. He was being a well-behaved male sub—she literally had him leashed.

To each his own, as they say.

Two scantily dressed submissives approached me and bowed their heads.

"No," I said firmly.

Their faces lit up with mischief and then they ran off, vanishing into the crowd.

How any warm-blooded male managed to walk around here without a boner was beyond me—it would take a small miracle.

At the end of the great hall towered an impressively carved double doorway. Well-guarded, it made me wonder what went on in there.

I handed one of the champagne glasses to a petite blonde and reached for the chain dangling from her collar, hoping I wasn't stealing her from anyone.

I led her across the ballroom, trying to blend in, and stopped in front of the intriguing doorway.

"Password?" asked the well-dressed doorman.

Getting thrown out of my brother's place was an embarrassment I didn't want to endure.

"Elite members only," he said. "Sir?"

"Rosewood," said the pretty blonde.

"Rosewood," I parroted, without breaking eye contact with him.

This submissive was a gem.

She lingered close to me, her perfume light and youthful. Her obedience assured by her quiet demeanor.

We were permitted to enter.

Holding tightly to the fine chain, I led her into another enormous ballroom.

Tall pillars were spaced throughout the chamber. In a tipsy haze, I succumbed to the vision.

Red lighting lit up the room, the heady space alive with movement in every corner—and on every piece of furniture. Against every pillar, men and women were fucking, sometimes with a third partner.

"Wow." The audacious hedonism made me grin.

The submissive studied me. "You've not been in here before?"

I took a sip of my champagne instead of answering.

She suddenly appeared out of the ether—a sexy dominatrix

with an alluring figure and blonde waves tumbling over her bare shoulders. A glamorous masquerade mask covered half her face and she wore a spray of black feathers like a crown.

"Henry?" she asked in a sultry tone.

Cover blown—even with me wearing this masquerade mask. Richard had probably sent her to retrieve me.

She pried the submissive's chain out of my hand and handed it back to the girl. "Run along," she ordered. "Now."

The submissive scurried away.

"Impressive," I said.

The dominatrix came closer and whispered, "You're not allowed in here."

"Who do I have the pleasure of meeting?"

"Put your drink down."

Of course she was bossy, too.

I set my champagne flute on a nearby table.

She wrapped her arm around mine. "Walk with me."

Seduced by her serene authority, I allowed myself to be led away.

As we walked through a doorway, she added, "Don't say anything else until we're alone."

This woman's smoky brown irises were mesmerizing, and a striking contrast to her wavy golden hair. Her shiny lips were something to behold—or kiss.

She had the confident, sexy stride of a supermodel, her hips majestically swaying with the lure of feminine rule.

We continued down a staircase and along another hallway.

"This area is closed off tonight," she said. "No one will bother us."

I gave a nod as she led me through an impressively large door.

Music greeted us on the way in, an exquisite operatic aria; a soprano's voice set the scene with a mood that caused chills.

Wow, again.

With my back towards the only exit, I surveyed the dungeon, recognizing a few pieces from a brief Internet search I'd done back in the day. To my left was a St. Andrew's Cross, and interesting looking instruments hung on the walls, as varied as they were stylish.

The blonde stood in the center of the room. Light from the crystal chandelier above danced over her figure, magically flickering like fireflies kissing her slender body.

Wearing only a bodice and a fine thong and stockings, she looked ready for a hot night in the bedroom.

For a man worthy enough.

"You're lovely," I said. "But this is not why I'm here."

She placed her hands on her hips. "I brought you in here for *your* safety."

I noticed a dangerous-looking contraption in the far corner—a metal cage.

Fuck that for an experience.

Becoming trapped in a dungeon was not my best idea.

I eased up the masquerade mask and rested it atop my head. "If anyone locks this door—"

"No one's locking the door." She blinked and her expression turned to one of admiration now that she could see my face.

"Who are you? Clearly you recognize me."

She removed her masquerade mask, revealing features of an iridescent beauty.

I drew in a sharp breath. Her complexion was luminous, her wide chestnut eyes hypnotic. High cheekbones made her look youthful, but I guessed her age to be around thirty. My gaze was drawn to her full, red lips.

I would have remembered her if we'd met.

She didn't blink. "Yes, I know who you are. You're Cam's brother."

I slid my hands into my pockets, assuming a casual pose. "You've been tasked with keeping me here until Cameron arrives?"

"Maybe."

I could leave now.

Or wait and enjoy the pleasure of seeing his face when he found me in one of his sacred dungeons.

"Your security leaves a lot to be desired," I jested.

"Don't flatter yourself. Being a Cole bought you time. No one could touch you because of him."

"Other than you?" I stepped away from her. "Want to give me the grand tour?"

"I'm going to spank you if you don't behave."

"Not into it."

"You would be by the time I finished whipping your ass." She broke into a grin.

Her adorable expression lit up the room.

"We should probably start over again on a better foot," I said.

"If you like."

"And you are?"

She hesitated and then said, "Charlotte, but please call me Lotte."

"Last name?"

"Chamberlain."

"Lotte, I don't want to see news about my visit here plastered across the front page of the *L.A. Times* tomorrow."

"That's not what we do."

"I wish I believed you."

She reached up and ripped off the blonde wig, revealing her stunning pixie cut beneath. The style highlighted immaculate eyebrows over large brown eyes. She'd transformed into an attention-grabbing bombshell.

God, a raven-haired beauty.

A weakness of mine.

Had she not worked *in this place* I'd have asked her out for dinner. This woman was mesmerizing.

She threw the blonde wig onto a nearby chest.

"This is where it all happens, then?" I asked, trying to shake the hypnotic effect she had on me.

She looked amused. "Where what happens?"

"Shenanigans."

"We offer therapeutic exercises."

I chuckled.

She raised her chin defensively. "Cameron is a genius."

"He's many things to many people. To me, he'll always be my younger brother."

"He saves lives."

"I can see you like him."

"Our relationship is professional."

"Of course."

Everyone crushed on Cameron, with his easy charm and uncanny gift to read a room. He'd be a dangerous enemy if he lacked compassion.

"I never thought I'd see *the* Henry Cole here."

I was the conservative brother who frowned upon my sibling's ventures.

All these amateurs playing torture when they had no idea what humans really do to each other in the name of war.

My body ached as the memories swirled.

No one can hurt me.

Not now.

And never again.

She must have read my expression. "You're safe," she said softly.

An uncanny gift, not unlike Cameron's.

She'd clearly been trained to decipher people's thoughts and moods.

I walked across the room, trying to distract myself from this enigmatic woman. "What's this for?" I picked up a small, spiked wheel.

Lotte came over to me and took the item out of my hand. "A Wartenberg pinwheel."

"What do you do with it?"

"May I?"

"Sure."

She nudged my jacket aside to reveal more of my shirt and rested the pinwheel against my chest, and then rolled the spikes over my pecs, causing a jolting sensation in my nipple.

I didn't flinch.

Wasn't going to give her the pleasure of trying to shock me. Even if this felt agreeably arousing.

I arched a brow, amused.

She studied me. "I thought you might be open-minded."

"I'm not like my brother, if that's what you mean."

She patted my chest. "You look similar."

"That's where the similarities end."

"You're more ruggedly handsome."

"Broke my nose playing rugby for the Navy."

She studied my face. "I can't see where."

"Plastic surgery. My Navy buddies got a huge kick out of that."

"Was it frowned upon?"

"It's not exactly a warrior move."

"But it is a privileged one."

God, this brash woman didn't care to say what she was thinking.

I found it surprisingly refreshing.

Usually, the moment someone discovered I was a Cole, they began to act differently.

Not her, though.

Lotte's nature was beguiling.

"You and I don't move in the same circles. Let's put it like that." I reached for an enormous dildo and waved it like a wand.

"A handheld electric massager."

"Oh."

"The head rests on the clit." She pointed south. "You pound it until you come. And you come hard with this."

"Good for you." I handed it back.

"Want to try it?"

"You plug it into an outlet?" I smirked. "If the lights go out in L.A., I'll know you're using this."

She giggled and it sounded so damn sweet.

Lotte set it back on the shelf.

"Might have to get me one," I quipped. "Fire it up and see where the evening takes me."

That made her face brighten.

I smiled, thinking that probably nothing could shock her.

Lotte turned to face me. "Anything else you'd like me to demonstrate? Or have you finished making fun of us?"

"I'm intrigued. This is all new to me."

"Respect your brother's work."

"It's enlightening."

"He's helped so many."

"What happened to cause you to end up here?" I asked.

"Don't be condescending, Henry. You may be Cameron's brother, but you don't get a pass." She stepped closer, staring up at me with an unexpected fierceness.

So damn pretty—and fiercely confident.

Her soft perfume wafted right into my tipsy brain.

"I like helping people. You can talk to me." She'd purred the words as though reciting an incantation.

Her lips were dangerously kissable. It would be easy to lean forward and press my mouth to hers, draw her breath inside me.

Standing so close to her caused my arousal to peak; my cock responded at the thought of touching her.

I imagined she inspired all kinds of obsession.

I gave myself a mental slap to break her spell. "You're watching over me like I'm a problem."

"Being here is totally out of character for you."

"You don't know me."

"I'm aware of your history."

"What do you care?"

"I'm part of your extended family."

"Don't I get a say in that?"

I regretted the words as soon as they left my mouth.

Cruel, but I'd mastered the art of pushing women away, of refusing to let love find me.

But if Reese was still alive, what did that mean for us?

My heart still pined for those years with her.

"Tell me about you." I broke the unbearable silence.

"I started out as a pharmacist," she said. "Went on to study psychology."

"And came here?"

Her gaze narrowed. "You have no real idea of the kind of work we do."

"True." My focus drifted over Lotte's curvy bodice.

Her breasts pushed up to reveal an enticing décolletage, inviting a kiss. Her stocking tops were devastatingly sultry, her pussy barely covered by her thong.

"You don't get embarrassed dressed like that?" I asked.

Lotte's jaw flexed as though I was trying her patience. I knew her type—she was more than capable of delivering a clever retort.

Instead, she whispered, "This is my armor."

"How do you fight off the men?"

"With my sharp wit."

Drinking in the intoxicating vision before me, I considered how she'd taste if I nudged aside her thong and licked along her sex.

She probably had every man in here fantasizing like that.

"I'm sorry," I said, realizing it was obvious I was ogling her.

"My bodice is designed to elicit a reaction."

I shot my hand up. "I'm the consummate gentleman."

"I can see that."

She continued to study me—or maybe she'd already profiled me.

"Something triggered you," she asked softly. "That's why you came here?"

"No." Denial came easy.

"Share the reason with me?"

"Does therapy with a mistress even work?" Because, as far

as I could tell, all the blood had drained into my cock. It was a struggle for me to remember my problems.

"I wear a suit with clients." Her tongue ran along her plump lips.

Alone in a room with the sexiest woman I'd ever met—probably not one my better decisions.

I strolled over to the St. Andrew's Cross. "This one is interesting."

She followed me. "It's where I secure my submissive."

"You're gay?"

"You don't get to ask me that."

"I thought we're extended family?"

She leaned forward and lifted the metal cuff at the top. "This is total surrender."

"They can't fight back?"

"Everything I do is consensual. There's an arousing aspect to being tied down."

Reaching up, I examined the silver cuff. Everything here was expensive and classy, emanating sophistication—even the more restrictive pieces.

A game within a game.

My fingers accidently brushed Lotte's forearm and an invisible electric spark had me snapping my hand away.

She tapped the cuff. "Put your wrist in here."

I let her lift my arm and place my wrist in the cuff. She clamped the catch down and secured me in steel.

I gave a tug.

A jolt of dread rushed through me.

Her voice trailed off.

A crawling sensation ran through my arm. "Unclip it!"

Her fingers fiddled with the catch.

"Now!" I tried to do it myself.

"Let go," she ordered. "Let me do it."

Finally, the metal cuff unlatched, releasing my wrist.

Freeing me.

"Henry, I forgot. I'm sorry." She sounded distraught.

I took a few steps back, perspiration spotting my brow. I drew in a deep breath, trying to gain some semblance of self-possession.

Caressing my wrist, I brought myself back to the present. "Not into it."

"Of course not," she said, with a guilt-ridden expression.

I wasn't into loud bangs either. Or anything that brought pain. Even the kind of pleasure that might render me vulnerable was frequently avoided.

"That one?" I pointed to a velvet throne that would fit right into the Metropolitan Museum. "Very regal."

I wasn't such a bastard that I couldn't make someone feel better about their mistake—or mine—by changing the subject.

"Fit for a dominatrix," I said. "The queen of Chrysalis."

"I'm flattered."

She knew I needed her not to make *a thing* out of my thing.

She raised her chin with pride. "This is where I get to lord over the chamber."

"We worship at your feet?" I grinned to lighten the mood.

She made her way over to the throne, elegantly turning to sit on the velvet cushion and resting her hands on the carved wooden armrests.

I folded my arms across my chest. "That's the tamest thing in here."

"You think so?" She waggled her brows.

Okay then.

I got its significance: her lover would kneel on the cushion before her and pleasure her with oral sex.

I imagined myself kneeling between her thighs doing just that. I felt drawn to her, captivated by her soft scent. It was like a drug was being piped in to render her victim powerless—the mood all kinds of erotic.

Seeing my stare, she pouted, her mouth dangerously inviting. It would be easy to wander over there and kiss her. Maybe

I would if she gave me a signal that she wanted me to. My body ached with the desire to bury myself inside her.

I wanted to inhale her scent, kiss her pale throat, and then glide downward between her thighs to taste her *there.*

She threw her head back and moaned as though she was in my fantasy; whimpering as though I'd made her come.

The mesmerizing fantasy was just out of reach.

Falling for a woman like her would be a disaster. I had my reputation to protect. She'd be a scandal in the making. But, God, how I wanted her.

I'd had too many drinks to make this kind of decision.

"I should go." I stepped back towards the door.

Lotte snapped her thighs together. "Too much?"

"No, very educational." I gave her a formal nod. "You've been the consummate hostess."

"Henry, this is nothing compared to the party you crashed!"

"Totally agree." I raised my hand. "I can find my own way out—can't exactly be seen with you."

Her face fell.

I'd offended her.

Clearly an extraordinary woman, but this was the kind of addiction I didn't want in my life.

One taste of her and I'd be lost.

All this sensuality had me rethinking why I was here. The point, I suppose. This room had been created with an atmosphere to invite surrender.

To her.

This dazzling dominatrix owned each second of every breath.

"You're not who I thought you were," she said.

It sounded like an insult.

I lashed out. "Yet you are exactly what I expected."

I pivoted and walked toward the door.

When I reached it, I silently chastised myself for retaliating.

Turning toward her again, I said, "You remind me of Audrey Hepburn."

She looked thoughtful, and her calm demeanor made me want to stay.

"Thank you for your service, Henry," she said with sincerity. She'd heard all about me from Cameron.

Stay.

Give yourself more time with this goddess.

It would be hazardous, entrusting my happiness to someone like her.

"You're too good for this place, Lotte."

I pulled down my mask to disguise my face and stepped into the hallway.

Retracing my steps, I made it back to the foyer beneath the landmark of that extravagant chandelier.

With a polite nod, I strolled past the guard and exited through the front door.

Once down the hill and through the gate, I drew in a deep breath of air, trying to resist the urge to go back inside and search for that mysterious woman.

Charlotte Chamberlain.

Reason kicked in and I shut that desire down.

A match with her was impossible.

I headed out on foot, needing to come down from the high of Chrysalis. Touching my face, I realized what I'd done.

I'd left wearing the golden Venetian mask.

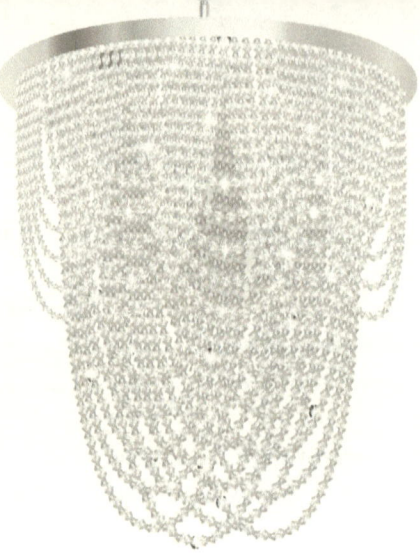

CHAPTER FIVE

Lotte

RICHARD AND I HAD MADE IT TO SHUTTERS ON THE BEACH at the same time—both of us running late to the Cole charity event.

He'd driven over from Paramount Studios on Melrose, where Andrea was filming her latest TV show. I'd taken side streets from Encino to Santa Monica to avoid Saturday night traffic.

"Andrea will be joining us later," he said. "Filming wraps around nine."

"Can't wait to see her," I said cheerfully.

Richard looked gorgeous in his tuxedo—in anything, really.

I wore my favorite vintage-styled chocolate satin gown with a plunging neckline, a dress from the Mia Lauren summer collection.

Cameron's designer wife knew how to flatter a woman's figure. She'd come so far from the innocent girl I'd once interviewed at Enthrall.

My pixie-cut bangs hung low on my forehead in a sultry style, my makeup subtle with a hint of sparkle.

Cole events were coveted tickets, their auctions famous for raising millions for charity.

The evenings were filled with so much fun, and it was always a joy to see everyone again.

With a show of our invites and a check of our names on the guest list, Richard and I were permitted entry into the ballroom.

Sweeping drapes were pulled back to reveal the striking view of the Pacific Ocean. Laughter and chatter from the hundreds of guests seated at the lavishly decorated tables carried around the room.

My kind of music was playing—Adele's exquisite voice surrounded us, the song about finding a lost love.

I jolted to a stop, startled by the vision of a dashing American aristocrat—Henry Montgomery Cole.

The man who'd helped the Tea Cole brand become a household name.

Smolderingly handsome features collided with his complex persona. He looked like an intimidating figure in his black designer tuxedo and pristine white shirt, a bowtie twisted into perfection. It seemed like the tailor had carved the suit around his tall, muscular frame. Flawless bladed eyebrows arched over intelligent chestnut irises.

The way he studied everyone around him probably was a residual habit from when his life depended on that kind of alertness.

Last night, I'd been tasked with containing *that* gorgeous man after he'd trespassed into Chrysalis.

The same man who would be sitting at *our* table. I cringed at the thought of Cameron's elitist brother seeing me wearing fetish fashion.

I huffed my frustration. "What's he doing here?"

"Who?" Richard followed my line of sight. "Henry?" He grabbed my arm and pulled me toward the table. "He has something of mine."

When Henry caught my eye, he visibly jolted.

Both of us had been shocked by the same voltage.

A little hate never hurt anyone.

He ran his fingers through his perfectly styled short waves, looking like a prestigious older version of Cameron. They were only a couple of years apart in age and yet there was a light year's difference between them.

I gave a warm greeting to everyone at our table.

Except for him.

At Richard's request, I spun around so that everyone could coo over the dress from Mia's fashion line, the straps delicate and the silky material feeling luxurious against my skin.

Cameron and Mia pushed out of their seats to give Richard and I warm hugs, as did Scarlet and Ethan. Shay and Rue waved from where they sat.

Oh, God.

The last seat available was directly opposite Henry's.

Richard pointed at him. "You have something of mine!"

Henry's gaze locked on to me as though he were thinking up an arrogant quip.

"Isn't this wonderful," said Mia. "Everyone together."

The response was a rumble of agreement.

Mia looked radiant in her blue satin dress. It was one of her own designs with a signature dip between her breasts. Scarlet and Rue were both stunning in their long black gowns, and each of the men cut a suave presence.

"How's Dex?" asked Richard.

"He's great," said Henry. "I took him for a run earlier. He's asleep back at the hotel."

Just the thought of Henry sprinting around a park made me shiver in anticipation, as though I might get to observe that sight one day.

Ridiculous.

We were destined to never spend another second alone together.

As though sensing I was ogling him, Henry gave me a heart-stopping grin. Maybe he was recalling his time at Chrysalis.

"When are you gonna buy a house?" asked Richard. "Give Dex a big yard?"

Henry glanced over at me. "Trying to find the right location. Anywhere but Encino."

"I live in Encino," I said, annoyed.

After an awkward silence, Cameron said to me, "That dress is beautiful."

I'd been staring at his brother. But in my defense, he'd been staring at me.

Maybe Cameron had picked up on how uncomfortable I felt.

"You all look divine," I said, making eye contact with everyone—except *him*.

Henry acted like the ultimate snob. That encounter with him in the dungeon had been enough to last a lifetime.

His intensity was unnerving.

Cameron piped up, "Let's address the elephant in the room."

Henry bristled. "You better not be talking about me."

"Yes, Henry," said Cameron. "I am."

Henry gave me a reproachful look, as though he blamed me for the awkwardness. "I apologize for turning up at your den of iniquity."

"You mean Chrysalis?" Richard seemed offended. "What did you do with my Venetian masquerade mask?"

Cameron glared at Henry. I wondered if they'd talked about him visiting our private sanctum.

Mia punched Henry's arm playfully. "Give it back."

"Of course," Henry said calmly. "I have no reason to keep it."

And I had no choice but to sit opposite this pompous ass for the entire evening.

Sipping my drink, I continued to make polite conversation, trying to avoid that devilishly handsome face across from me.

"It's good to see you, Charlotte," said Henry, during a lull in the conversation. "You appear…different."

Yeah, he really had gone there.

Richard leaned forward to get his attention. "What can you tell us about the new brand you're working on?"

Henry's brow arched. "It's under wraps."

"I saw the billboard campaign for Dandelion Diva," I said brightly. "Have you seen it?"

"Our competitor's campaign?" Henry sounded peeved.

"Not the usual stuffy promos your company runs with," I teased playfully.

Henry frowned at his brother. "Some classless campaign, I imagine."

"Where did you see it?" asked Cameron.

"Can't remember now," I said. "Maybe near the Grove."

"If you could wrack your brain and recall where you saw it," said Henry, sounding annoyed, "we'd appreciate it."

"As the CEO," I quipped back, "I'd have thought you'd be on top of that."

"Who runs the advertising at Chrysalis?" Henry asked, taking aim at me.

Cameron didn't flinch. "Did you enjoy your time in one of our dungeons?"

"It was enlightening," Henry answered, his gaze focused on me.

I opened my mouth to defend myself and Cameron's hand covered mine, silencing me.

We changed the subject with lively banter. I sat back and enjoyed the discussions between friends—the smart conversations around politics, current affairs, and some more philosophical subjects.

I enjoyed revisiting the fun stories that found their way around the table.

And then there was Henry.

Most of the time, he sat there quietly, seemingly in a judgmental mood.

He preferred Mia's company, it seemed. They had a special bond. You could see the respect they had for each other, their shared whispers and the way he gravitated to her. He felt safe with Mia.

Not that long ago, Mia had pried Henry out of a secluded cabin in Big Bear. The consequences of that were sweeping. Henry had taken over the running of Cole Tea. But Mia understood Cameron had never wanted to be a CEO.

Everyone seemed happier now.

Everyone except me, I suppose.

I felt unsettled lately, with a desire for change. But at the same time I was fearful of it.

I hid it well.

The menus were presented, and we each took one.

I chose the lobster tail from the menu and paired it with a crisp chardonnay. When it was time for dessert, most of us chose the chocolate mousse.

I counted the minutes until it arrived.

Finally, the waiter set a dish of delicious creamy mousse before me. My mouth watered as I savored the pudding.

While licking chocolate off my spoon, my tongue rimming its edge, I suddenly realized that Henry had become fixated on me.

Quickly, he pushed up from the table and excused himself.

Discreetly, I watched him stroll away.

My heart sank.

I finished my dessert and glanced his way, pretending to scan the room.

At the bar, he had struck up a conversation with a stunning blonde with a neat chignon—a flawless representation of the ruling class.

They appeared to be hitting it off.

That kind of pompous male species were set on finding a woman they could take home for their family's approval.

Henry reflected sophistication in or out of his tuxedo, this one a little less crinkled than the one he had worn last night at Chrysalis.

He leaned on the bar, impressing the mystery woman with his casual yet controlled demeanor.

I focused on my friends once again, convincing myself this was one of the nicer evenings I'd had in a while.

I admired how romantic Shay behaved with Rue. His frequent gestures of affection to reassure her she belonged.

Mia and Cameron were so damn beautiful together—the "It" couple of every event. They always made everyone feel comfortable around them. Scarlet and Ethan were at that stage in their marriage where they finished each other's sentences. Richard appeared relaxed as he waited for Andrea to join us.

My attention was again drawn to the bar, where Henry was ordering them two more drinks.

Two fancy cocktails soon appeared, set down by the discreet barman.

Henry's body language proved he was enjoying the pursuit. Leaning in, he whispered something into Chignon's ear.

Something seductive? She bit her lip, seemingly intrigued with him.

It didn't make any sense.

How could I be obsessing over a man I hated?

When I turned back, Cameron's focus had shifted to me. I'd been caught admiring a Cole—his older brother.

It was impossible to get away with anything when this man was in the room.

I needed a few seconds to center myself.

"Will you excuse me?" I said.

Cameron sprang up and helped me with my chair.

Strolling through the partygoers, I made my way onto the balcony where the sound of music was muted. A warm breeze washed over me. Beyond the endless palm trees was a dreamy view of the Pacific Ocean.

It was a view I never took for granted because I'd been born and raised on the opposite coast—the daughter of a housekeeper.

I wasn't so naïve that I'd reveal my modest childhood to a snob.

I only trusted a few close friends with that knowledge. Moving in elitist circles, I knew well enough to protect my heart, but I was proud of my mother, who'd worked two jobs so that I didn't have to clean alongside her, so I could study.

"I miss you, Momma," I whispered.

Those memories of her were sacred.

I tried not to reminisce.

But my ex came back in a flood of memories—the Dom who'd broken my heart. Austin Lee, with his enigmatic New York attitude, had brought a unique vibrancy to our relationship.

It had ended painfully five months ago, when he'd returned to New York. I had continued to live in the home we'd built together, but after he left, I'd redecorated. I was still searching for the energy to sell the property and start over.

We'd been ill-matched from the start.

He liked to party hard and I preferred clean living. Simplicity brought the peace I had always cherished. I savored the quieter moments of a day, curling up on the sofa with a good book or hiking Laurel Canyon on the weekends. And I savored owning a home for the first time in my life. I'd had fun decorating my Encino house, in a neighborhood located in the heart of L.A. Family-friendly and safe, its previous reputation was no longer relevant.

I heard the screech of a microphone from inside.

Henry's deep voice rang out, sexy as hell, his speech flowing loudly with his usual panache as he thanked everyone for coming. Laughter rippled through the ballroom in response to some joke he shared.

The man would no doubt be swarmed by every single woman afterwards.

"Quite the view," said a male voice.

Pivoting, I turned to see Cameron.

He stood beside me. "We can't both be trying to avoid my brother?"

"I'm not avoiding him."

"He likes you."

I wasn't sure about that.

"Henry appears pensive," he said. "I sense that something happened at Cole Tower. He won't talk to me. Maybe he'll open up to you."

I pulled a face. "We didn't hit it off, to be honest."

"I thought you did."

"He's hard to read."

Cameron nodded in agreement, and then said, "The event's going well."

"I might bid on one of the auctions."

He shook his head. "If you see something you like, I'll buy it for you."

I hung my head at his generosity. "No."

He studied me. "How are things?"

"Fine."

"You miss him?" said Cameron.

"Who?"

I'd loved him—how could I not? Austin had been fun and charismatic. But he drank too much and could be cruel.

"You know who," Cameron said, gazing at me with sympathy.

Our love had been a lie that had torn its way free. I proved how strong I'd become by ending us.

I straightened. "I prefer not to talk about him."

"Okay, how have you been?"

"I've missed you," I said softly.

"I chose to leave Chrysalis," he said. "But I respect that decision didn't land well with everyone."

"Richard shines in your position. But he's no you."

"You're ready for a change, too."

I turned to face him. "How do you do that?"

He shrugged. "You have a solid background in psychology. If you want to join my practice in Beverly Hills, you'd be welcome."

A rush of hope hit me—it was a possibility I'd not even considered. "Go mainstream?"

"Life is change." He patted my arm. "The only certainty."

"True."

"Opportunities can come from anywhere. Be ready."

I tried to read his meaning. It was as though he knew something, or sensed it. Or maybe Cameron merely detected my melancholy.

"You're looking beautiful." His eyes crinkled as he smiled with affection. "I'm not the only one who noticed."

He meant Henry.

For some reason that thought brought a wave of giddiness.

"It's because I'm wearing one of your wife's gowns," I said. "Mia is talented."

"I'm biased, but she is." He beamed with adoration for her.

The great Cameron Cole was still love-struck.

"Oh, pretty." I pointed down at the beach, at a bride in a lace gown who was gliding ethereally along a strip of red carpet laid upon the sand. A nervous groom awaited her beneath an arch covered in flowers.

I hummed dreamily. "A beach wedding."

As though reading my mind Cameron said, "You'll find him."

I nudged his arm playfully. "It's perfectly acceptable to be single and happy."

"I agree." Cameron continued to observe the wedding party.

Following his line of sight, both of us checked out the guests who'd turned to watch the bride make her way down the "aisle."

The bride stood close to the groom beneath the flowery arch, their faces lit up with happiness, the groom finally relaxing because she'd joined him.

I felt enamored by their romance. "They're cute."

Cameron's expression turned dark.

"What?" I glanced back at the couple.

"Look." He pointed farther down the beach at the small rockets embedded in the sand. "Fireworks."

Cameron had to be afraid they might trigger Henry's PTSD.

My pulse quickened at the sight of them.

Cameron's brother could still be heard talking at the podium in front of hundreds of guests.

"We have to warn him!" I said, grabbing Cameron's arm.

We sped back into the ballroom.

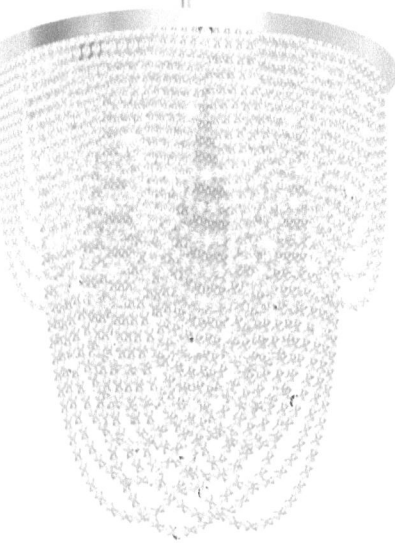

CHAPTER SIX

Lotte

A PLAN CAME TOGETHER QUICKLY.
Cameron hurried ahead and took the first door that would lead him to the reception desk in the foyer.

I went to warn Henry.

Standing a few feet from the podium, I discreetly tried signaling him to get his attention. He glanced over at me with a frown and then peered down at his notes, continuing to woo the audience.

I moved closer. "Henry."

Subtly, he gestured for me to wait.

"You have to come with me," I whispered. "It's important."

My iPhone buzzed and I read the text from Cameron: *Get him to room 407.*

Continuing to ignore me, Henry addressed the audience. "The Cole family would like to thank all of you for everything you have done—and continue to do—for our foundation. Your dedication to our causes never goes unnoticed. You're making a difference by helping save lives."

He threw a salute to the audience, and I could feel their collective stares burning into my back.

Henry came away from the podium. "This better be good."

"This way." I led him around the tables toward the back of the ballroom and onward through the foyer toward the elevators.

"Where are we going?" he snapped.

I punched the elevator button a few times. "You have to trust me."

"You're not the only one who can give a good spanking," he joked.

I faced him. "The hotel next door is about to launch fireworks."

He glowered. "And your point?"

"Cameron and I thought..." I swallowed hard. "We got you a room—number 407—if you want to use it."

"Is this Cameron's idea?"

"Both, really."

"Fuck!" He shoved open the door to a stairwell, leaving it open for me.

"The elevator will be here any second," I said.

He headed up the stairs. "You interrupted my speech for this?"

"You go on. I'll be slower in these shoes!"

He came back down the steps. "Isn't it four floors up?"

With a tug of my hem, I showed him my six-inch heels.

"Want my help?" he asked casually.

"Sure."

He quickly lifted me up and threw me over his shoulder. Within seconds we were flying up the stairs.

I should have had him clarify the type of help he was offering.

"Henry!" Being upside down, I had a nice view of his ass.

"Your idea, Charlotte."

We continued through another doorway onto the fourth floor.

Henry set me on my feet. "Which way now?"

How the hell was I the one who was out of breath? "That way." I pointed to the wall showing the descending numbers.

We checked the doors as we went.

I knocked on 407.

Cameron opened the door. "Hey."

Henry stormed inside.

"We wanted to get you somewhere private," explained Cameron.

"You had Lotte interrupt my speech?" he snapped.

"We get it," said Cameron kindly. "Take a breath."

The living room was decorated in a modest but sumptuous fashion, with calming yellow walls, lush plants, slatted windows and handcrafted furniture in soft palates.

It would have been pleasant if not for the tension.

"Stay in here until they're over," Cameron said.

"Anyone else involved?" Henry asked, sounding annoyed.

"Just us," said Cameron.

"There wasn't much time to warn you," I said in our defense.

Henry cupped his ear as though trying to hear those elusive fireworks.

I went to leave.

"Stay," said Henry. "It's just PTSD. Nothing mysterious. Loud noises trigger it."

"Can I get you anything?" I said, trying to ease the awkwardness.

Henry strolled out of sight into a bedroom.

"Wanna stay with him?" asked Cameron.

I blinked at him. "You're not?"

"I'm crowding him."

"You're better suited to help with this," I whispered.

Henry's voice piped up from the other room. "Please don't argue over me!"

Cameron squeezed my shoulder reassuringly as he strolled past me toward the door. "Text me if you need anything."

He exited the suite.

I set my purse down onto the entry table. "Want a drink?" I called out.

"That's not a healthy solution," he called back.

"Right, of course." *I knew this.*

Only he made me antsy.

Bang.

I jolted in surprise.

Zing.

Whistling fireworks were now lighting up the night sky.

"They've started," I blurted out, and then cringed at how stupid it sounded.

More bangs and whistles and sparks broke through the quiet.

I entered the bedroom and found it empty. Walking past the king-sized bed, I approached the bathroom en suite.

I discovered Henry sitting on the tile floor with his back against the generously-sized bathtub. "Shut the door."

I closed it and joined him on the floor, sitting opposite him.

The beach-themed décor was continued in here, with cream-colored cabinets mixed with ocean designs and a seashell-framed mirror. A cabinet held lotions and towels and an invite to the spa. Cameron had thrown money at this—booking a room no one would sleep in like it was nothing.

But this was him being the best kind of brother for Henry.

"Just breathe," I whispered.

He inhaled sharply, his gaze on me. "You don't have to stay."

"I want to."

"You don't even like me," he said sourly.

"I thought the same about you."

He scoffed and hugged his knees, perspiration spotting his brow.

I slipped out of my heels, glad to be free of them. My painted toenails peeked out from beneath my long hem, and my diamond toe-ring and ankle bracelet were on show.

He stared at my feet.

Hard to tell if he approved of the way I'd adorned them.

"When you first saw me tonight you looked horrified," he said.

A ferocious series of booms rang out again, muted a little through the door.

He squeezed his eyes shut.

"Can I do anything?"

He wiped a trail of sweat from his temple.

"You're safe, Henry. Remain present. Remember where you are."

He pointed. "Give me your foot."

"Why?"

His brows knitted together. "Your feet hurt."

Cautiously, I stretched my leg toward him.

Henry positioned my foot on his lap, his large hands feeling warm and inviting. His fingers began working the tension out of my arch. The pressure felt good—blissfully relaxing considering the circumstances.

"Anything I can do for you?" I said, lulled by his kneading. "I should be massaging yours."

"That would be weird."

I chuckled. "Why?"

Silence once again settled over our hiding place.

"Thank you for all you did." I said it before thinking.

"When?" His puzzled expression disappeared as he realized I'd referred to his time in Afghanistan. "Let's not go that far."

"I shouldn't have mentioned it." I silently chastised myself for bringing up his past.

But this man had sacrificed everything for his country. He couldn't even enjoy an evening we all took for granted.

"Talk," he coaxed.

"About?"

"You."

"Nothing really to say."

"You're not married?"

"I should hope not with my foot in your hands."

"Good point."

"I broke up with my boyfriend a few months ago."

"I'm sorry."

"Don't be. We weren't compatible."

"Why?"

"Long story."

"We have time," he said.

I shrugged. "Austin could be a little sadistic."

"How can you tell in your line of work?"

"Consent."

"Did he hurt you?"

"I told him to leave."

"Good for you." He breathed in a calming breath when the sound of more fireworks cracked in the air.

"Are you dating?" I asked.

"No." His hands stilled on my foot for a few seconds, and then his strong fingers began kneading again, easing the ache.

More fireworks went off.

I tried hearing them the way Henry did, as a cacophony of blasts.

Seeing me flinch, he said, "Imagine how birds and animals feel."

"True."

"Keep talking," he coaxed.

"Do you like being CEO?"

"It's what I was born to do."

"But do you enjoy it?"

"Do you enjoy what you do?"

"Yes. I do. I change lives for the better."

His gaze narrowed on me. "It's not just some kinky clients getting their rocks off?"

"Play nice, Henry."

He smirked, looking devilishly gorgeous. "Keep talking."

"I graduated with a bachelor's at USF."

He seemed impressed.

"Started out as a pharmacist and switched careers."

"Why?"

"I felt closed in when I worked in the pharmacy."

"You figured out how to take away mental pain without a prescription," he reasoned.

I loved the way he seemed to understand my change of heart over my career.

Henry studied me for a beat. "Give me your other foot."

The one he'd massaged felt warm and tingly from his touch. The other one relaxed as he began kneading my toes.

"You seemed to be having fun tonight," I said.

"Not really into public speaking. But there you go."

"I meant the blonde."

He scrunched up his nose. "She didn't recognize me."

"That a problem?"

"She acted standoffish."

"As soon as you stepped up to the podium she realized who you are?"

He gave a nod. "Her expression changed when she realized she'd missed her chance to snag a billionaire."

I chuckled at that.

He exhaled sharply. "I've been undergoing noise sensitivity sessions. Been making progress."

"Exposure?" I said. "You're doing great."

He tilted his head as though listening. "Sounds like they're over."

Henry leaned over and reached for my shoes. He held one up and eyed the impressive length of my Valentino heel, giving me an amused look before easing my left foot into the strappy shoe, clipping it in, his fingers gliding over my sensitized skin, sending a shudder through me.

Then, he secured my right foot into the other shoe and stood, holding out his hand to me. I took it and he pulled me up, our bodies standing close.

An invisible current zipped between us.

A frisson went down my spine.

He reached out and eased the strap of my gown up my

shoulder from where it slipped, his fingers trailing, setting alight my skin with his touch.

"You're the best kind of friend," he said softly, breaking my trance.

I'd been staring at his mouth.

"We should get back." I hurried out of the bathroom and pressed my hand to my chest, trying to calm the beat of my heart.

Henry followed me into the sitting room.

I picked up my purse from the entry table.

He strolled over to peer out the window. "Thank fuck that's over."

"You'll come back down?" I asked.

"Sure." He kept his back to me.

I hesitated to leave, wanting to bridge this gap between us.

He turned to see me still standing there. "Do I make you nervous?"

"You're a little intimidating."

"In what way?"

In every conceivable way.

He opened his palms. "It's just me."

The confident stance was back along with the dashing charisma. The vulnerability was once more hidden behind a steely exterior.

He scanned the room. "The right decision."

"I'm glad you think so."

He tucked his hands into his pockets. "How do you think I view myself?"

"How do you mean?"

Silence settled over us, but it wasn't uncomfortable.

He looked thoughtful. "You edge pleasure?"

"Yes."

"I've edged death." He shrugged.

"Terrifying."

"Terror is the kindest thing they do."

"Henry—"

His hand snapped up. "The experience made me an astute businessman."

"I believe that."

The experience had also profoundly changed him. Cameron had revealed little, except that his brother was hardly recognizable when he came back.

"You're beautiful." Henry gave me a kind smile. "I should have told you before."

"So are you. I mean, you're very handsome in a tuxedo." And out of one, too, I imagined.

He strolled toward me. "Give me your hand."

"Why?"

He reached out and took my wrist. Lifting my palm to his lips, he kissed it tenderly, his mouth grazing my fingers with soft caresses.

It left me breathless with my world spinning.

When he let go, my hand shook.

I quickly tucked my purse under my arm.

Reaching up, I worked at his necktie to neaten it. His cologne wafted around me and stirred my core, arousal washing over me.

Being this close felt dangerous.

Maybe he also sensed it—this magnetic force shimmering between us.

I saw the immediate change in him, the moment he recognized our chemistry.

"It's a pity," he said softly.

"What is?"

"We come from such different worlds," he said, his tone filled with regret. "Otherwise, you and I could be more to each other."

"Different worlds?"

"You're…"

"Working class?"

"I meant the other situation."

He meant me being a dominatrix.

I stepped back and then elegantly strode for the door, bursting out of the suite in a show of self-respect and pride.

The door slammed behind me.

The atmosphere felt different, the air breathable.

I'd gone from breaking up on entry in his hot stratosphere to descending into zero degree chilliness.

The adrenaline was wearing off.

I needed to put some precious space between myself and the man with all the power—the kind that could hurt me without him even knowing.

Halfway down the hall, I turned to glance back at Room 407.

I'd dominated presidents, had other men of influence on their knees—spanked kings, for God's sake.

Henry Cole shouldn't faze me.

Calling the elevator to the fourth floor, I mused over the contradiction of being enthralled by Henry and at the same time sensing I'd never be good enough for a man like him.

I'd never felt that way before.

The elevator doors slid open, and I stepped inside.

Hanging my head, I remembered that Henry had come back a war hero. He'd been to hell and back and deserved some slack. What he'd just gone through was stark evidence of how much pain he still carried. My frustration with him returned to respect.

I'd enjoyed tonight, never expecting to be magnetically drawn to him and then feeling as though I'd burned up on entry.

The elevator landed on the ground floor with a small jolt.

The doors slid open and I hurried out, making my way back to the ballroom.

I paused when I saw our table was swarming with guests who wanted to see actress Andrea Buckingham. The Hollywood starlet had arrived. She sat beside Richard, who held her hand as they greeted her admirers.

Suddenly, I felt very ordinary.

Without being noticed, I slipped out into the foyer and left Shutters on the Beach as quickly as possible.

CHAPTER SEVEN

Henry

I NEEDED FRESHER AIR—NOT THIS RECYCLED CHILLED OXYGEN from my chauffeur driven town car.

The traffic was moving painfully slow, even for a Monday morning, the cars bumper to bumper.

The towering architectural designs of the financial district reminded me a little of the city I'd left behind. With Cole Tea moving its head office here, I'd had no choice but to relocate. Luckily, many of our staff had transferred to the West Coast along with us.

I had loved New York—its vibrancy, its people, and its architecture. I'd called it home. But my life was still being lived on someone else's terms.

"Unlock the door," I said.

"Sir." Griffin, my young driver, held my gaze in the rearview. "The last time I let you walk you gave money to a homeless guy. You can't do that here."

Did he just refuse to let me out?

I could fire him. That option was still available.

Cole Tower rose in my sights, the dramatic sleek architecture ruling over the other skyscrapers.

Not going anywhere made me antsy. It threw me back into thoughts of the past—never a good thing.

Besides, seeing someone go hungry pained me. Privilege carried a burden. No amount of charity could solve the worlds' problems. Still, if we all did something it would make a difference.

I rubbed my brow, remembering how my weekend had been derailed.

The event on Saturday at Shutters had gone downhill fast. In Room 407, I had offended one of the most intriguing women I'd ever met—right after Lotte had sat with me through a potential crisis. She deserved better. I shouldn't have been brash to someone as exceptional as Charlotte. Our interaction was a rare occurrence in my otherwise dull life.

I pointed straight ahead. "The tower is within walking distance."

Why the hell was I explaining this to my driver?

"I see it, sir."

Griffin Tomlinson appeared to be in his early twenties and was apparently too young to recognize an order, still refusing to pull over and let me out of the car.

I gazed out my window and focused on the electric billboard lording over the district.

The garish display had caught my attention. It was Dandelion Diva's movie-style advertisement for a new brand of tea—the one Lotte had mentioned last night.

The fuckers were going after the younger crowd.

Stretching across the screen, a half-naked blonde woman sat in a sultry pose, peering over her shoulder with a lustful expression. Her left hand barely covered her breast and in her right hand she held a mug of tea, our competitors tag hanging over the side.

"Who the fuck approved that?" I mumbled. It was a total misfire of branding.

"Sorry, sir?"

"Someone's getting fired."

Or maybe that same someone just got promoted. Many of the pedestrians and surrounding drivers were staring up at the tea-porn.

"Everything okay, sir?"

"Open the fucking door!"

I heard a sharp click.

I got out of the car and shut the door behind me, stepping onto the sidewalk and drawing in a breath of pollution.

Snow was falling now in New York, covering Manhattan with a picturesque powdery blanket of white. Here, the climate persisted in being hot and dry and the air was full of desert smog.

I missed riding the subway and visiting my favorite museums. I missed the restaurants and theatres, pining for time spent with good friends.

My focus returned to the billboard, to the alluring features of the striking model. Her rosy cheeks reminded me of a renaissance painting.

Though she had nothing on the attributes of Lotte, she reflected the mystery of a worldly woman.

Lotte. I'd send her a gift basket to soothe my guilty conscience.

When I reached Cole Tower, I walked through security with a wave of thanks.

With my head down, I made my way toward the coffee shop nestled in the corner of the main foyer. I picked up an Earl Grey from the upbeat barista and then rode the glass elevator to the 79th floor.

The ride was thankfully unremarkable compared to the way my weekend had begun.

Three days ago, I'd learned that the love of my life was still alive. Yet I carried on like nothing out of the ordinary had happened. Like her mysterious letter wasn't sitting on a table in my hotel suite waiting to be read.

I'd waited decades for answers. *What's another day?*

Work would take my mind off Reese.

When I stepped out of the elevator, my assistant Jen greeted me, hurrying forward in a cloud of rich perfume and competence.

She seemed anxious. "Charlotte Chamberlain is in your office."

I didn't hide my surprise.

"Is it a problem?" she asked.

I glanced at my Rolex. It was 9:00 A.M.

"Lotte doesn't have an appointment." Jen kept up with me all the way to the office door. "But she did have a VIP pass."

I felt a rush of anticipation and drew in a sharp breath.

"I'll take it from here," I said.

Jen opened the door to my office.

I went in and shut it behind me.

Charlotte sat seductively on the edge of my desk, gorgeously chic in a pencil skirt and a golden blouse. Her coat had been discarded on one of the armchairs, along with her Prada handbag. The only hint at her profession was a pair of knee-high boots.

"Good morning," I said, refusing to be thrown by the woman who outshone the sun.

Her striking grace made me forget myself.

Lotte slid off the desk and strolled by me like she owned the room. In this moment, she did.

A waft of delicate perfume brought back memories of our time together at Shutters two days ago—both of us sitting on the secluded bathroom floor, the conversation flowing naturally despite the circumstances.

I recalled over-compensating for my embarrassment by being an ass.

Lotte's presence was alluring. Mesmerizing, really.

And she hadn't even spoken a word.

I shook off my trance. "Hello, there. This is a nice surprise."

"So this is where the great Henry Cole reigns supreme?"

I smirked at her brashness.

"You have a great office."

"I like it." I walked over to my desk. "Cameron called you in a pass?"

"Shay." She lowered her gaze. "We had breakfast."

"Good. Why?"

"We're friends."

I wondered what they'd talked about. Hopefully not me.

She stepped closer. "I wanted to see how you're doing."

"Oh," I said, wishing we could both forget Saturday. "I'm fine."

"I left without saying goodbye," she said.

"You were missed. It wasn't because of me, I hope?"

"Of course not."

"Once Andrea Buckingham arrived, our table had a constant flow of visitors."

"That's why she arrives late," she said.

"I planned on sending you a gift basket," I admitted. "To apologize."

That brought a sparkle to her eyes. "No need."

"We ended on a bad note."

"Because you told me I wasn't good enough for you?" She waved that off. "I found myself in the area and thought I'd visit to clear up the awkwardness."

"That was decent of you," I said, biting my lip. Annoyingly, she'd interpreted my comment just the way I'd meant it.

She peered up at me from beneath long eyelashes. "I promise you I'm discreet."

Hiding from fireworks didn't exactly inspire hero-worship, but my shoulders relaxed at her reassurance. Caressing the bridge of my nose, I tried to shake off this private sense of shame.

"It's okay," she said softly.

Her words brought me back to the present.

I stared at her rouged lips, so pouty and kissable. Her tongue flitted to the corner of her mouth.

I tried to fight the urge to drag her in for a kiss.

I met her gaze. "We have another event coming up soon."

"I'm probably busy," she said, her voice clipped.

"Right."

She grabbed her coat and purse off the chair and then strolled leisurely with her hips swaying toward the door.

"That's it?" I said.

The memory of her in a corset and not much else graced my mind, making my cock stiffen. "You don't want to stay for a drink?" I gave her a dashing grin. "You'd be welcome."

She turned back to face me. "No, thank you."

"Sure?" I coaxed.

"Quite sure."

"Back in that hotel room, I shouldn't have told you you're—"

"I'm what?"

I shrugged. "It's that I saw what you do at Chrysalis."

"You didn't see me doing anything, Henry. I escorted you to safety, remember?"

"Let's start over," I said sincerely.

Her eyes sparkled with mischief. "Give you the chance to apologize properly?"

"Well, it's the least I can do."

"What do you have in mind?"

Have you kneel before me and take my cock in your mouth, I mused darkly.

A smile played on her lips. "Take me out to dinner. Tonight."

"I've discovered a few great places. I'll book us a table."

"I'll choose the restaurant."

"Of course. It was good seeing you again, Charlotte." I gestured to her outfit. "Very chic."

She studied my face. "You're going to have to work harder to impress *me*."

"How about you're the most beautiful woman I've ever met."

"Be honest, Henry."

"I am being honest."

She took a few seconds to process my words. "That's third date material."

"I'll make a note."

"Tonight is *not* a date." She held her head high. "It's just dinner."

"Point made."

"I'll leave my address with your assistant. Pick me up at seven." She strolled out of my office in a delicate waft of perfume and feminine elegance.

I found myself staring at the place she'd been standing seconds before—totally mesmerized.

I was having dinner with *her*.

My body was charged with an electric pulse that felt obscene—and dangerously addictive.

CHAPTER EIGHT

Henry

I WAITED IN THE EMPTY CONFERENCE ROOM FOR SHAY, USING my phone to answer emails and thinking I'd never see an end to my inbox content—even with Jen tackling most of them.

Glancing over at the window, I saw Dandelion Diva's featured billboard.

More specifically, the half-naked model peering over her shoulder, enticing me to drink their tea.

I was mulling over whether the advertisement might actually inspire me to try their brand when Shay walked into the room.

He threw a wave at me before whipping out a small device and circling the table with it held up in the air, checking for listening devices. Reassured he hadn't detected any bugs, he tucked the scanner back into his pocket.

I walked over and slapped his back with affection, glad to see the man who could resolve our nightmare situation.

A few weeks ago, he'd discovered we had a corporate spy in our midst.

We needed Shay to unravel this mess. With only months to go before we launched our new product, time had become precious.

Our mutual experience of serving in Afghanistan meant I could trust Shay. I knew no other man who could get this done fast.

"How's Rue?" I asked.

"She's great." He beamed at me.

Seeing how important she was to him filled me with envious warmth.

Rue was perfect for him, too.

"Rue loved Saturday," he said. "You had fun, right?"

"Absolutely," I said.

"Those fireworks were a surprise." He watched my reaction.

"I stepped out for a second."

He studied me some more, polite enough not to push it.

Instead he said, "You have to host another party again in a couple of weeks?"

"One event after another," I said, nodding.

Shay had been to hell and back dealing with emotional residue from our deployment. He'd withdrawn from that fog and my brother had been partly responsible for helping with Shay's recovery.

This man deserved the best kind of happiness.

"Okay, so what's the plan?" I got to the point of our meeting.

"Time to find, fix, and finish this," he said.

A SEAL strategy.

His confidence was inspiring.

A knock at the door had us both facing that way.

Jen strolled in with her notebook. "Sorry I'm late. You had a meeting?"

Shay and I swapped a wary glance, and I said, "We're just catching up."

"Oh?" She hesitated, trying to read us.

"Just a social visit," said Shay.

"Isn't your office more comfortable?" she asked. "I can have drinks sent in."

From the way Shay straightened his back, I could tell he sensed the same thing.

Or maybe I was over-thinking it.

"We're fine in here," he said.

We waited for Jen to back out and close the door behind her.

"Her background checks out," he said.

"That's a relief."

"But don't trust her completely." He leaned against the conference table. "Someone could have gotten to her. Just because she has a clean past doesn't mean she's not bribable."

I rubbed my brow. "I need this to go away."

"I respect that."

"We have a new product coming out soon. I need it protected at all costs."

"My team is on it."

I noticed his pained expression. "What?"

"Avoid dating for now."

"Sexpiange?" That made me smirk.

The thought of a woman trying to get close to me was amusing.

I'd been too busy with work—and too uncomfortable with the idea of commitment.

I hesitated to tell Shay about dinner with Lotte tonight. No real point in sharing this with him. She'd made it clear this evening would be romance free.

I wasn't sure how I felt about that.

Cameron had let her into his inner circle. That meant she could be trusted.

"Did you have breakfast with Charlotte?" I asked.

"Yeah, she swung by with some questions about Chrysalis."

I was intrigued. "She visited me, too."

"She's fun, right?"

"What did you talk about?"

Shay became guarded. "The usual. My life. Hers. She filled me in on how Enthrall and Chrysalis are doing."

"Did she mention me?"

He lowered his gaze. "What happened between you two at the party? You disappeared at the same time."

"Nothing."

He studied me with the respect of an old friend.

"Will you please focus on our corporate spy?" I said.

"You're the one who mentioned her."

I glanced toward the billboard. "Dandelion Diva's making a point with that."

He made a dismissive gesture. "They made sure we could see it from here."

Taunting us.

I met his gaze. "If I spend billions in developing a product, throw in research dollars and market testing, and our spy steals our plans, they could create a similar product. Beat us to market."

"Which would be a financial catastrophe. I get it."

"I want this handled."

He gave a patient nod. "By the way, I'm going to switch out your driver."

"Griffin?"

"His background check revealed his dad died in Afghanistan."

"He didn't mention it."

"Hired before my time," he said. "I wouldn't have missed it."

"What have you found out?

"Staff Sergeant Tomlinson died at the beginning of the war."

I rested a hand on Shay's shoulder. "Let me keep him as my driver for now. I'll get him to talk."

"I've ascertained he's a risk."

"Give me a week."

He gave a reluctant nod, understanding why we should take care of Griffin. We took care of our own—even the sons and daughters of the fallen.

"I have to go," he said. "I'm meeting with Cameron. We

need to secure every aspect of the business, including the Cole Foundation."

"What else can I do?"

"Don't accept any gifts. Have them dropped off at security so we can assess them first. They put listening devices in credit cards these days." He read my expression. "You've not been given anything have you?"

"Nothing significant."

Other than that envelope Lilly handed me on Friday. The one I still needed to open.

I'd not considered it might be pernicious.

I'd have to deal with it soon—deal with the ghosts from my past, lying in wait to ruin my soul all over again.

My priority was my friend here. We'd been busy, with him at Enthrall and me in New York. We had so much to catch up on.

"How are sessions with Cameron?" I asked.

"Good."

It had been hard going for him for a while there. Shay had blocked a memory so severe it had impeded his life. I recalled the terrible day he took out a young enemy soldier. The boy had been pointing his weapon at me. Shay saved my life that day. But in doing so, he had scarred his own.

Before his breakthrough, Cameron had warned me that Shay's mind had fractured from the incident, preventing him from re-membering the truth in order to protect him. I was told not to bring up the subject.

Now Shay could talk about his past. His life had done a 180 since then. He was in love and building a home in Malibu—and working for us with a generous package.

He'd been given a second chance.

Our war, the one we'd fought together, had changed us both.

"Your brother's a remarkable therapist," said Shay. "Have you considered talking with him about your PTSD?"

"I've been busy."

"Like you told me, we should live life to the fullest, Henry. That's the best way to honor the lives lost."

"I agree."

He nodded. "Okay, I'll dig around and discover everything I can about Dandelion Diva."

I turned to stare once more at the billboard. "Soon as you can, please."

CHAPTER NINE

Henry

L ATER THAT MONDAY EVENING, I DIRECTED MY DRIVER, Griffin, to park the town car outside Lotte's home on Oak Lane Drive, a cozy corner of Encino.

I'd changed from one of my usual tailored ensembles and upgraded to Dormeuil Vanquish—a bespoke suit blended with six fabrics to provide suave comfort. I also wore a pair of Alessandro Galet Oxfords.

Though I hoped it was my cultured sophistication that Charlotte felt more drawn to—as well as my devastating charisma. I couldn't help but smile at that thought.

We were early so I decided to wait a few more minutes.

This seemed like a great neighborhood. Maybe I'd have my realtor check out some homes here, too.

I recalled that asshole statement I'd made at the gala about buying a house here. Between the two of us, Lotte and I were gathering one cringe-worthy moment after another.

The woman was still annoyingly alluring.

For now, I was fine living at the Bel Air Hotel. A mansion

would exacerbate my loneliness. One of these smaller properties seemed like a reasonable option.

Dex deserved a spacious yard.

My thoughts returned to that dreaded envelope. I'd secured it in my hotel room's safe. If it contained a listening device, the safe walls would block it.

Not opening it could be considered passive-aggressive behavior. That's what you got for trying to mess with my head.

Reese didn't deserve to be a priority.

I half expected it to be a hoax anyway.

Focusing once again on my chauffeur, I asked, "Where's your family from, Griffin?"

"Santa Clarita, sir. Not far from here."

"Tell me about them."

He hesitated. "Not much to say."

His words made me pause. Shay's gut reaction weighed heavily on me.

Something was amiss.

Griffin exited the car and hurried around to open the rear door for my guest.

I'd have to continue this line of questioning later.

With sophisticated elegance, Lotte walked down her driveway, long legs highlighted by strappy heels. Her red halter-neck dress emphasized her slim shoulders and sexy curves.

A breathtaking vision.

She walked with the authority of a woman who knew how to bring a man to his knees.

Her Burberry coat was thrown over her left arm and she held a small clutch and car keys in her right hand.

I leaned low to see her face better.

"I'm driving." She pointed to a silver Jaguar parked in front of her house.

It wasn't a question—I'd been given an order.

She headed off towards her car.

I slid along the seat and climbed out. "Griffin, take the evening off."

"I'll follow, sir."

"Not necessary." I closed the door behind me. "Thank you, though."

I joined her in the silver Jag and pulled on my seatbelt. Taking a few moments, I admired the woman next to me.

"Everything okay?" she asked.

I suppressed my boyish grin. "Wow."

She glanced my way. "You'll do."

Her temerity was refreshing.

Lotte's delicate perfume smelled like a fusion of serenity and sensuality.

Using the passenger rearview, I glanced back at the town car.

Griffin remained parked behind us.

"Can you lose him?" I joked.

She started the engine. "I can try."

We navigated away from the curb and soon reached Ventura, a primary thoroughfare in San Fernando Valley.

We went one way and I was relieved to see the town car go the other. Griffin had followed an order for once.

I recognized our Mulholland route. I'd traveled this shortcut with Cameron numerous times.

When Lotte pulled her Jag over and parked at the curb, I gave her a curious glance. She'd chosen a residential area.

She held something in her hand.

I glanced down at the strip of material.

"It's a blindfold," she said.

"I can see that." I gestured a polite refusal.

"Humor me."

"You put it on."

"I'm driving."

"I can drive."

"You want this," she purred.

"I thought we were having dinner?"

"We are."

The taste of sin.

Unfamiliar and yet alluring.

"Don't be boring," she said huskily.

She wouldn't have considered the possibility that *they* had kept me blindfolded.

I kept my calm façade in place.

Even the seemingly mundane made me flinch.

Fuck them.

Fuck their ability to ruin my *now.* So much had been stolen from me.

So damn much.

I snatched the material out of her hand. "Fuck it."

"That's the attitude."

She pulled away from the curb and continued to navigate the neighborhood.

Reaching up, I secured the blindfold to my face.

The car took several turns as though she was trying to shake off my sense of direction.

Her perfume and the way she reached over to squeeze my arm to reassure me made this intriguing.

We course corrected.

Another fact she wouldn't guess: I had an innate instinct for direction.

She blasted music—some modern pop tune she knew the words to, having fun being wild and free.

When the car began its ascent up an incline, I suspected where we were going—because I'd been here before.

My memory was both a gift and a curse.

The car came to stop.

"Can I take this off?" I tugged at it.

"Yes."

Dragging the blindfold away from my face, I blinked at the restaurant we'd pulled up to, and noticed the fancy insignia on the awning.

She flashed me a mischievous grin. "We're here."

"I guessed that."

"You do look very handsome," she said, drawing my focus back to her.

I might have taken extra time to style my hair, paying more attention to the cologne I chose and wearing cufflinks that carried the Cole crest—because I was trying to impress her.

I met her gaze. "You look absolutely stunning tonight."

"Well done."

Her patronizing remark made me wince. "Stop that."

"I'm just messing with you."

I reached over and brushed a strand of hair out of her face. "I'd prefer you treat me with respect."

Her eyelids fluttered as though she'd been affected. A fleeting moment passed between us—intimacy, a rare connection.

"Let's get this over with," she said, her voice sounding breathy.

"Wait here."

I climbed out of the car, strolling around the front of the Jag to get to her side and then opened her door.

"Thank you." Lotte took my hand and climbed out.

She peered up at me, maybe wondering why we were standing so close—but neither of us moved. We merely lingered as though we'd been magnetically drawn to each other.

I wanted to reach out, wanted to brush my thumb over her plump lips as though we'd already become more.

Finally, I stepped back and gave her space.

Atop this high canyon, standing regally in all its majesty, was that familiar Bel Air mansion—though we were seeing it from the side view.

Sparkling lights shone from the sprawling hills beyond.

If I strolled around the corner, I'd arrive at the entrance of Chrysalis. If I went inside, I'd again be entranced with their impressive chandelier.

Lotte didn't seem to realize I recognized where she'd brought me.

Three nights ago, I'd visited this sanctum.

Her sanctum.

I wasn't annoyed, merely amused.

A valet hurried from around the corner and took Lotte's car keys. Her Jag was quickly driven out of sight.

Together, we strolled beneath the dark green awning.

Entering the restaurant, I admired the French-styled theme that blended luxury and intimacy into an art form.

"What's the name of this place?" I watched her reaction.

"Imperial."

"Of course it is," I mumbled. "How's the food?"

"Delicious."

She led the way over to the concierge, who greeted us with aplomb to show we were expected and he in turn led us through a double doorway into a busy restaurant.

Lotte's fingers slid naturally into my grasp, sending an unnerving tingle through me.

Unwittingly, I snapped my hand away.

She glanced at me with curiosity.

With a nod of apology, I took her hand in mine again, weaving my fingers through hers.

No one seemed to notice us, which didn't make sense to me. This woman was clearly stunning, her presence even prickling the hairs on my nape.

The restaurant appeared normal enough. Luxurious high-backed chairs were placed around generously-sized tables where elegant guests dined.

The restaurant at Chrysalis could pass as any fine-dining experience.

Little minx.

I caught our reflection in one of the surrounding wall mirrors, surprised at how good we looked together.

Like a power couple.

We settled in a private booth and our waiter quickly brought us two glasses of sparkling water.

I ordered bourbon.

Lotte declined a beverage. "It's a weekday," she explained. "I'm driving precious cargo."

"You certainly are," I quipped. "How did you discover this place?"

I had decided to play along with her little game.

"A good friend was hired to decorate here."

"They have great taste." I accepted the menu from the waiter all the while watching his interaction with us.

He appeared reserved.

"What do you recommend?" I asked Lotte.

"Their Lobster Bisque is to *die* for."

Her expression immediately turned regretful and she reached out, resting her hand on my thigh as though to apologize for her thoughtless comment.

We locked gazes for a long moment.

The waiter set my bourbon before me, breaking the spell.

She whipped her hand away. "Order for me."

"I'm not a Neanderthal." I read the menu, pleasantly impressed.

"Convince me," she chided.

I smiled at her. "Tell me more about you."

"I'm just a dominatrix, Henry. Nothing more."

"I'll ask Shay to tell me all about you." I took her napkin and laid it over her lap. "Anything you particularly like to eat?"

"I love everything they have here."

A quick gesture to the waiter had him returning to our table. "We'll begin with the mussels in white wine sauce, please, followed by Tarragon Chicken."

The waiter nodded. "Good choice, sir."

Lotte frowned. "That's a lot of food."

"What you don't eat you can take home."

"Is that you appealing to us working-class types?"

I reached for my tumbler of bourbon. "I respect the value of food."

"I didn't mean—"

"You see me as privileged."

She bowed her head. "That was rude of me."

"Apologizing?" I said. "Thought I'd never see the day."

She elbowed me playfully.

"Do you miss Big Bear?" she asked.

"Now and then."

"Were you lonely?"

"Dex kept me company."

There were lonely times, I suppose, but I kept myself busy. I enjoyed hiking along wooded trails with Dex and painting landscapes—generally letting the days pass by without circumstance.

"You left Big Bear because Cameron needed you?"

I studied her. "You've heard my story?"

Cameron had faced prosecution for his relationship with Mia because he'd personally taken on her complex therapy. She had saved him during that difficult time.

"Why don't you stay with Cam?" she asked.

I leaned back. "I've caused enough problems."

Guilt still lingered over my actions.

Over a year ago, I'd inadvertently sent Mia hurtling off to Europe into the center of a potential disaster.

Being kindhearted, Mia had forgiven me—but I would never forgive myself.

"Your brother adores you," said Lotte, as though reading my mind.

The plate of mussels arrived and the delicious aroma of fine wine and garlic wafted around us. The waiter placed a few onto Lotte's plate and then mine, setting the dish between us.

Having to give up fine-dining had been hard during deployment. We'd lived off ready-to-eat meals.

I savored each mussel with gratitude. There was no doubt I was a foodie.

"At the party, you mentioned house hunting." She dabbed her mouth with a white linen napkin. "Any particular neighborhood?"

"My realtor favors Bel Air."

"So very you." Her face cracked into a smile. "And so close to Chrysalis."

I was polite enough not to mention that Encino had once been known as the porn capital of California. I'd done my homework, too, when I'd received her address.

Still, the impressive area had shaken off that reputation.

"What do you like to do when you're not enthralling?" I asked playfully.

"I'm learning to paint."

I flinched. "Who told you?"

I guessed it was either Cameron or Mia. They were the only ones who knew I'd used that addictive art form to quiet my mind.

"Told me what?"

"I painted often when I was in Big Bear. I've worked on some smaller pieces since, but when I moved to L. A., everything in my life was packed up—including my brushes."

"No one shared that with me," she said earnestly. "We're both allowed to be artists."

"How long?"

"I've drawn and painted since I was in school," she admitted. "Some of my work hangs at Enthrall."

"Favorite artist?"

She lit up with joy. "William-Adolphe Bouguereau. You?"

"Same. I mean, I'm a fan of his work. I'm also drawn to Rothko."

I watched as a half-naked subservient strolled elegantly by our table, led through the dining room on a chain by a tall gentleman in a dark suit. The blonde was being escorted to a table of guests.

"You don't see that every day," I whispered.

The vision was mesmerizing.

I'd only glimpsed a scene like this once before—last Friday at Chrysalis. There had been wall-to-wall beauties in another part of this great house where the visual display of servitude unfolded spectacularly.

Lotte was staring at me.

The voluptuous young woman with large breasts obediently followed the orders given by her master. A crisscross of latex adorned her figure, her lace underwear a touch of normality.

The only normal thing about this scene.

Staff appeared out of nowhere.

The central dining table was cleared of all cutlery, plates and glasses, leaving only the table linen shimmering white beneath the dimmed lights. The striking couple seated there pushed up from their seats, their expressions surprisingly calm.

Obediently, the sub sat on the edge of their table and laid back flat against the surface, her plump legs splayed, not caring that the entire restaurant was observing her.

A stark quiet had fallen over the regal dining room.

I shot a wary glance at Lotte and saw defiance reflected in her demeanor. *This is her world.*

If I pushed aside my preconceived attitude, I could understand the remarkable nature of what was unfolding close to our table.

But I felt self-conscious, even though no one noticed me.

I sat back.

The confident Dom eased his sub's thighs apart, offering what lay between. The couple had circled the table and now stood before her.

I took a swig of my drink and then put it down.

The couple's fine-dining experience was morphing into a salacious event. Both were enjoying taking turns performing oral sex on the chained blonde, devouring her pussy with a frenzied passion. Their willing victim writhed with pleasure, arching her back, her moans rising into a cry for more.

The live action scene was poetic and yet forbidden—and erotically addictive.

Lotte reached over and took my hand as though sharing the moment, her touch soft and inviting, the brush of her thumb on the back of my hand lulling me.

My cock twitched; I couldn't tear my focus off them.

The star of this display seeming tranced out, her blonde locks spilling over her pale nakedness, breasts swollen and prominent nipples desperate for suckling. Her body trembled, her back arched as she experienced a blinding orgasm.

Her Dom became aware of us.

"Isn't it hypnotic?" Lotte's hand squeezed mine.

Richard Booth burst out of a door to our left. He strolled up to the couple's table, where the action had become even more heated, offering a few words to the Dom.

The handsome couple glanced our way and then sat back down.

The submissive was quickly ushered away.

Guests resumed their conversations, the clink of cutlery again striking porcelain plates.

Richard appeared to take a few seconds as though gathering his thoughts before making a beeline to our table.

"I would say 'what the fuck?' but this time I'm going to go with 'what the fucking fuck?'" he said quietly.

"Hey, Richard," said Lotte.

He bit his lip in frustration. "Always good to see you, Henry. But this is not the place for you."

Calmly, I folded my napkin and rested it on the table. I enjoyed seeing him riled up.

Lotte watched me carefully.

She'd tried to shock me, apparently.

Richard looked at her. "What's going on?"

She glanced my way. "We're having dinner."

"I can see that," he said. "How's the meal?"

"Perfect," I said.

Richard gave Lotte an intense glare. "Can I have a word with you alone for a moment?"

She huffed. "Whatever you have to say you can say in front of Henry."

Richard let out a sigh. "Explain this idea of yours."

"I'm not ashamed of my profession," she said.

Dragging his fingers through his hair in frustration, Richard was no doubt trying his best to grasp why Lotte had invited Cameron's stuffy brother to eat here.

She turned to face me. "Let me guess, it's been fun but I'm not your type?"

"Don't you put this on me," I said sternly.

Admittedly, I came from an impressive legacy. I'd had a remarkable military career. Was I superior to her? *Yes.* Did I come from American royalty? Again, a resounding *yes.*

Open to new and exciting experiences like this? No, not really.

Still, I went with, "I'm unshockable."

Lotte pointed at me. "You certainly like to watch."

"Hard to ignore."

"Seeing you here is somewhat traumatizing," joked Richard. "Though what's more disturbing is seeing you two together." He stood up straight. "I don't want to be around you both to see how this hell fest turns out."

I folded my arms. "I'm good company."

Lotte spoke up. "We're just friends."

"You brought him to Imperial!" Richard waved his hand through the air. "Breaking protocol."

"Doesn't Cameron's brother get a pass?" I reasoned.

"No." Richard folded his arms. "Lotte, you're banned from Chrysalis for a month."

She inhaled sharply.

"Take a vacation." He gave us a gracious nod. "I'll have the chef prepare your food to go. The meal is on us."

When Richard walked away, Lotte sighed.

"What am I going to do with all that free time?" she mumbled.

"Pull back on the recklessness, I imagine?"

She faked a sulk.

"Actually, I'm flattered you invited me."

"You don't hate me?"

"Hate's a strong word." I arched a brow. "Let's just say this place would make the Smithsonian proud."

"You're taking it very well."

I turned in my seat to face her. "I'm attending a garden party on Wednesday. Join me."

"Whose party?"

"Some private bash."

"Why would you want *me* there?"

I slid out of the booth. "But if I see a peacock in a leather vest, brandishing a paddle—"

She laughed. "Not to worry, you have to pay to see that."

The waiter brought out our boxed and bagged food and I took it from him.

"My hotel's close," I said. "I'm at the Bel Air. Can you drop me off there?"

She slid out of the booth and grabbed her purse. "I imagine you can't wait to buy a home somewhere. You can't stay at a hotel forever."

I smiled, preferring not to answer.

Right now, I didn't need to exacerbate my loneliness in a house big enough for all my ghosts to find me.

CHAPTER TEN

Lotte

T HE BEVERLY PARK TERRACE MANSION WAS EXACTLY where I'd expect to find someone like Henry Cole.

It was Wednesday, which gave away the nature of who else might be attending the party—the kind of people who could easily escape the office midweek.

The neighborhood was beyond real. I'd driven past other multi-million dollar properties, but this was easily the most distinguished, with dramatic Roman pillars and an endless driveway to reach them.

Flashy parked cars confirmed I'd be mingling with the super-rich.

Intrigue had brought me here, doubt held me back.

Maybe this wasn't such a good idea.

A middle-aged man dressed in a black peak tailcoat appeared and with the panache of a British butler checked my name off the guest list, permitting me to enter.

I'd chosen the perfect outfit for a garden party: an embroidered cream lace mini-dress with delicate pumps and a silk shawl to wrap around my shoulders.

A member of the staff pointed down a sunlit hallway. "That way, madam."

"Thank you." I offered him a warm smile.

Several maids scurried by and I observed them with affection. My momma had dressed in the same black and white uniform. She'd worked tirelessly for us so we could have a better life. A familiar ache found me and I longed to pick up the phone to speak with her.

I peered up at the heavens. "Momma, you'd get a kick out of this."

On my way down the hall, I passed a six-foot cobalt blue vase that screamed extravagance. When I reached the vast terrace, I had to walk around a statue of Venus, again proving this over-the-top mansion belonged to the ruling class.

I stepped onto the perfectly manicured lawn.

High brick walls covered in crawling ivy framed the expansive lawn and gardens.

Intimate groups had gathered here and there. To my left, a sparkling swimming pool set the scene for a more casual party at another time.

"Ma'am?"

The server offered me a glass. "Thank you."

I didn't hesitate to accept the glass of Pimm's, garnished with slices of cucumber and strawberries.

My heart fluttered when I saw *him*.

Henry stood alone in the middle of the lawn, hands tucked into the pockets of his beige linen pants, seemingly daydreaming. His matching jacket reflected a causal mood, the flawless linen cut to perfection and highlighting his broad shoulders. He dragged his fingers through his dark locks as though caught in a thought.

Not that far away, the guests chatted with the vibrancy of family.

This was a Cole family event.

Had he invited me so I'd endure judgment from his peers as revenge for taking him to Imperial?

It certainly seemed so.

His parents—who I recognized from the most fashionable magazines—were hosting the bash. Standing with them was an impressive circle of high-society types. A leggy brunette appeared deep in conversation with his mother.

The woman glanced my way and then quickly became disinterested. She turned her back on me.

I wondered if it was too late to withdraw.

A black Labrador with a tennis ball in his mouth bounded up to me wagging his tail. Kneeling, I patted his head, laughing at his cuteness. The dog's sweet welcome had immediately disarmed me.

Henry strode toward me, quickly closing the space between us. "Have you lost your mind?"

I pushed up. "What do you mean?"

A nauseating wave of doubt washed over me.

"Can't believe you came." He smirked as he reached for my hand and planted a kiss on my wrist. "You accepted my invitation. Bravo!"

His touch made my skin tingle with pleasure.

"I see you met Dex," he said warmly.

"He's cute!"

"He's a rascal." He knelt to grab the tennis ball and threw it across the lawn. Dex scampered off to retrieve it.

Henry looked me up and down. "You'll blend in nicely."

"Is this a family event?"

"Not a problem, is it?"

"You could have warned me!"

"Don't be dramatic."

"What's the occasion?"

"Mom arranged everything. We're merely pawns in her world."

"I intend on having fun," I said confidently, rallying my playful side.

"That's the spirit."

His parents turned their focus on us, which caused others to look our way, too. I felt another wave of discomfort.

Henry seemed to sense it. "Need anything?"

"An escape hatch," I mumbled.

"Don't mind the show."

"What show?"

"You and me." He guided me across the lawn. "I need you to deflect someone."

"That's why you invited me?"

"You're perfect for this mission."

"Is this revenge for me inviting you to Imperial?"

He chuckled. "This is far more perverted."

I held back.

"I'm kidding." He tugged me along. "Cameron will be here soon. Everyone loves him."

I couldn't wait to see him.

Henry studied me. "You're not nervous, are you?"

I recognized a few public figures. "Just don't introduce me to your parents."

Henry wove his fingers between mine and led me across the lawn. "You mean like this?"

Oh no.

Henry let go of my hand. "Mom, this is Charlotte Chamberlain." He nudged me forward a little. "Lotte, this is Victoria Cole."

"An honor to meet you," I said.

"And this is Dad," he said, dropping the formality. "You can call him Raif."

"Pleasure, my dear," said his dad warmly.

The way his mom glanced awkwardly at the tall brunette beside her made me believe she hoped for a match between them.

Still, I gave them my brightest smile.

Introductions continued with Henry's father leading the way with their other friends.

The conversation weaved around current affairs and other subjects. Including attending the *usual* events like the Met Gala.

I did my best to pretend I belonged.

The stunning brunette offered me her hand to shake. "Chantelle Addison."

"A pleasure," I said, wary of the coldness she emanated. "I'm Lotte."

Her false eyelashes exaggerated her discreet contempt. I could see why Henry needed a wing woman.

I felt a tap on my shoulder.

I turned to see Cameron behind me.

"Hey," he said.

I felt a rush of relief. Cameron's presence always warmed my heart.

"Is Mia here?" I asked.

"She'll be arriving soon. We live fifteen minutes away."

I took a few steps back from the group. "Do you disapprove?"

"Of what?" He led me over to a drinks table, out of everyone's earshot.

"Of me being here."

"Don't be ridiculous," he said. "You're too good for my brother. Speaking of Satan, I need to get a message to him."

"Sounds ominous."

"You really did hit it off with each other," said Cameron, amused.

"I like him."

Inwardly I was cringing that Cameron might have heard I'd invited his brother to Imperial. I should have given the consequences more thought.

"You were wonderful on Saturday." Cameron exuded gratitude. "Thank you for staying with him during his episode at Shutters."

"He did great. Anyway, he's fun to be around."

"Don't get too comfortable." Cameron let out an exasperated sigh. "He can be unpredictable."

"Does he ever talk to you about the past?"

Cameron lowered his voice. "He has a therapist."

"You?"

"Goodness, no. My advice, stay away from his past." Sadness shone in his eyes. "If you knew what they did to him, you'd see him differently."

"How do you see him?"

Cameron went to answer, and then stopped himself.

"What are you two discussing?" Cameron's father called us back over to rejoin them.

"Ask Mom about the Cole Foundation," said Cameron. "She loves that subject."

"Thank you," I said, grateful for the insight.

I tried to get Henry's attention, let him see that his brother wanted to talk with him, but he didn't notice. He was too deep in conversation with Chantelle.

I discreetly watched for any sign of chemistry between them. They were discussing another Cole function planned in a few weeks. Henry had another speech to prepare.

He gave me an intense look to remind me I'd ruined his last one. His focus remained unnervingly on me.

"How do you know each other?" asked Chantelle.

Henry moved closer to me. "Lotte is one of our dearest friends."

I waited for the punch line, the moment of humiliation to follow, but none came. Henry rested his palm on my spine.

"What do you do for a living?" asked his mother.

"I'm a psychologist," I replied, prepared for that question.

His mom appeared impressed for a second and then turned her attention elsewhere.

"I hear you do a lot of good work for the Foundation," I caught his mom's attention. "I'd love to hear more about it."

Victoria brightened as she proceeded to share her passion for fund-raising to support their charities. Our conversation flowed and Mrs. Cole even laughed at my jokes.

"Do you work in a clinic?" asked Chantelle.

"Lotte's an old friend of Cameron's," Henry interjected. "He's been keeping her hidden. Now that I've discovered her, I'm reluctant to let her out of my sight."

"I can imagine," said Chantelle with a forced smile. "By the way, I love this house. Who owns it?"

"It's beautiful," I agreed.

Henry nodded, appearing curious about this, too.

We all turned toward his mother for the answer.

"Don't you just love it, Henry?" his mom asked, her eyes sparkling with delight.

I felt a sinking sensation in the pit of my stomach.

I looked at Henry to see his reaction.

His mom raised her hand in defense. "You can't stay in that hotel indefinitely," she said. "It's not respectable."

Cameron tapped on his mom's arm, his expression frustrated. He'd tried to warn his brother of Victoria's meddling.

This was a surprise housewarming party.

"The pool is twenty feet deep," said his dad. "Earthquake safe."

Henry pivoted toward the manor as though seeing the home from a different perspective. "You should have spoken with me first, Mom." He glared at his father. "Are you in on this?"

"Well, it's done now," said his mom. "You're moved in."

Henry scowled at Cameron as though it was partly his fault.

Cameron raised his hands to declare his innocence. "Dex seems to like it."

"Will you please excuse me?" Henry gave a polite nod and turned, walking across the lawn.

He disappeared inside the house.

"He's gone off to explore?" his mother said. "He likes it, right?" She directed that question to Cameron.

Cameron hesitated, seemingly searching for an answer that would appease her.

Chantelle broke away from us and followed Henry inside.

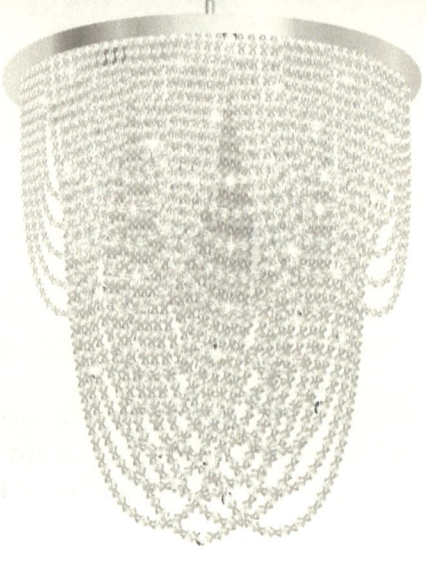

CHAPTER ELEVEN

Lotte

CHANTELLE WOULD HAVE TRACKED HENRY DOWN BY NOW. That's if she had found him in this maze of hallways. With no insight on their friendship, I only had my instincts to go on. She seemed a little hard-natured for Henry. He'd need a woman less intense—someone worldly but with softer edges.

His family had thought he'd taken too long to buy a house. His reaction proved he'd found his mother's generosity overwhelming. For anyone else, being gifted a home would be remembered as the happiest day of their life. But not for him, apparently.

I peeked behind doors, searching for him, breathing in the familiar, refreshing lemon scent that lingered in the air. I could also smell fresh paint.

My momma had once told me that hardly any of the rooms were ever used in these big old houses, the kitchen being the most popular, followed by the sitting room. The others were usually left for guests or staff.

A door banged.

Chantelle stomped toward me.

"Did you find Henry?" I asked.

He'd brought me along to block her from moving in on him—something we both seemed to sense.

"He's impossible," she snapped.

"Is he okay?" I asked, as she hurried by. "Henry's been through a lot."

"Haven't we all?" Chantelle paused, turning around to face me. "What are you to him?"

"A friend." Her iciness was unsettling.

"Is that an old Prada?" She gestured at my clutch.

"This?" I held the delicate bag tighter. "It's sentimental."

She's already made up her mind about me.

"You don't have to stay," she said, raising her chin. "If it's all too much."

"What do you mean?"

"You're behaving like a fish out of water!" Chantelle turned and stormed off.

I was beyond needing anyone's approval. Or having my ego bruised by a cruel socialite. Jealousy came in many forms. It wasn't a mood I found helpful.

"How is he?" I called after her.

"He wants to be alone!"

Shaking off her frazzled energy, I approached the door, rapping it with my knuckles.

No one answered.

Gingerly, I turned the handle.

I saw Henry's tall figure standing by a bay window overlooking the courtyard. He was posed in his familiar sexy stance, with one hand tucked in a trouser pocket.

A somber oak desk had been placed in the center of the room and books lined the shelves against the wall. A lone armchair sat in a corner.

This formal office wasn't him.

"It is better for Dex," he said without turning around.

I wondered if he could see my reflection in the glass.

"He seems really happy here," I agreed.

Henry turned to face me with a quizzical expression.

"But you have to be, too," I added.

He pointed outside. "The courtyard doesn't face south."

"Because then it would get the sun for most of the day," I said. "It'll stay cooler in summer. Bring in Cameron's decorator. That'll spice up the place."

He smirked at that.

"What did Chantelle say?" I asked.

"Nothing, really." Sadness settled in his expression. "A house is one thing."

I cringed at his insinuation. Clearly his mom had set him up with her.

He shrugged. "Exit stage left. I certainly would."

I moved closer and reached up to straighten his tie. "This mansion is spectacular."

"My staying in a hotel is a disgrace. Who knew it's better to have a collection of naked statues?"

"I only saw one."

"I'll give you the grand tour."

"I'd love that. Anyway, they add intrigue."

"I'll have one delivered to your home."

"I wouldn't go that far."

He laughed, but then his expression turned dark. "This house is their way of saying I'll never be able to go back to New York."

I processed that. "Why did they move Cole Tower here?"

He frowned as though mulling it over.

I tapped his arm with affection. "You'll be missed at the party. Come on."

He towered over me. "Not yet."

I felt that familiar tingle of chemistry stirring in my belly.

He and I could never be more than friendly acquaintances because the great Henry Cole dating a dominatrix would shock the world.

I didn't want to guess how his mom might react.

"Why do you have to be so fucking beautiful?" he whispered.

"Being friends is good," I reasoned.

"You're still here. You must be doing something right."

I raised my chin. "Turn off the arrogance, Mr. Cole."

"Turn off the sassy, Ms. Chamberlain."

"Thank you for letting me in," I whispered.

"How's the view?"

"The view?"

"I may have left the war, but it's not left me."

Silence screeched louder than words.

His face contorted in confusion. "I'm not the same man I was before I was deployed. There are times when I don't even recognize myself."

"These things take time. I see a lot of clients who've endured the worst of humanity."

He reached over and tucked a strand of hair behind my ear. "What if I don't want you just as a friend?"

I hesitated, trying to read his meaning.

"What if I let you in permanently?" he said, his face reflecting a multitude of emotions in that moment.

I smiled up at him. "I'd like that."

He cupped my face with his strong hands, his touch magnetic, as our lips drew closer and closer, his minty breath enticing.

Before his lips met mine, I rested my hand on his chest.

"No," I whispered against his mouth.

"No?"

"Kissing me is a reflex, an act of rebellion. A response to regain some semblance of control. It's advisable we don't."

"What if it's just a kiss?" he said huskily.

"It's not."

"Maybe it will solve all our problems?"

"We'll never know." I reached up and caressed his cheek. "Good friends don't take advantage."

He leaned in again and our lips brushed lightly.

It was a preview of all that could follow if I let myself go there. Let myself have this moment of intimacy with him.

"Lotte, the best thing about this house is you standing inside it."

"Henry, that's romantic, but..."

He stepped back. "You're right, of course."

"I want you to be happy."

He blinked as though hearing that word for the first time.

Then he walked briskly over to the open door. "Ms. Chamberlain." He motioned for me to leave. "Go get something to eat. The entrees are about to be served."

"This is me protecting you," I said. "It's not a rejection. I'm the kind of friend you need."

"Thank you," he said, giving me a thin smile, "for letting me experience what it is to be ordinary." He drank me in for a long time and then said, "Go."

I wasn't ready to give up my self-respect.

Taking advantage of that open door, I strolled out without glancing back.

I retraced my steps to the terrace, where I saw Cameron standing at a table covered in fancy food platters.

I made a beeline for him—ready to bask in the presence of the brother who always knew the right thing to say.

CHAPTER TWELVE

Henry

FUCK.

When I'd used the word "ordinary," what I'd meant was "normal." It had come out wrong.

Charlotte made me feel there was a place for me in this world. Why did she have to be so infuriatingly attractive? She'd come to check on me and I'd rejected her kindness.

It had taken all my strength not to possess her in that moment. My body screamed with the desire to go after her. My mind, however, remained painfully logical.

It was the reason why I'd let her walk out.

I regretted my harsh response to a woman who deserved so much more—the kind of worship I'd never felt capable of—until now.

Cameron had been able to marry Mia because as the youngest son he had the privilege of choice. Our sister, Willow would have the same freedom. She was still in New York living her best life.

I'd been the one destined to marry well and suitably into a

family of equal social standing. My children—if I ever had them—were also expected to continue the Tea Dynasty.

My response to destiny was to refuse to marry anyone. My mother had failed to set me up with Chantelle, a woman who came from money and acted like it.

These rules were just another kind of prison.

Correcting my attitude, and rallying gratitude, I returned to the party.

Across from me, Cameron chatted with Lotte. They were laughing at something and seemingly having fun.

I watched them, recalling our near kiss.

I'd been close to tasting the forbidden. Lotte had drawn me toward her like a magnet, her authentic nature enhancing her natural beauty. She looked so pretty in her short dress, a shawl falling off her left shoulder, leaving it bare. She had an aura of self-assurance.

Bewitching.

She had held her own with my family. It had been impressive to observe.

I headed over, feigning that nothing was bothering me, that I was unaffected by a mere moment of intimacy. The lie was a saving grace.

Until Lotte walked away.

It hurt, even as there was no reason for it. We were friends and, as she'd pointed out, that could be enough.

At the other end of the lawn, she knelt down and petted Dex. My dog always drew the best kind of attention.

Avoiding me was probably a wise move on her part.

She was running away from the sexual tension because I was a Class-A asshole.

Cameron stood before the linen-covered table stacking an ungodly amount of Beluga caviar onto crackers.

"Hungry much?" I asked, amused.

"Eating becomes a spectator sport if you have a baby."

"You need a nanny."

"Babysitters do just fine for now."

"You are inspiring," I admitted.

We had rarely seen our parents during our childhood, having been raised by nannies. Most of my memories consisted of boisterous days with the staff. We'd stayed in touch with many of them. They were our surrogate family within a family.

"Have you recovered from the shock?" He popped a loaded cracker into his mouth and chewed.

"The house?" I glanced back at it. "Why does it have to be so fucking big?"

"Because you're a Cole."

"Did Lotte say anything about me?"

Cameron's quizzical stare burned through me.

"What?" I snapped.

He glanced over at Lotte. "You like each other. A lot."

"She's—"

"Don't bother denying it. You have lipstick on your collar."

I dipped my chin, trying to see it. Of course, I saw nothing there. And that was how my brother set a trap for the truth to spill.

"Fuck you," I said.

"I approve. If you need to hear that."

I bristled at my annoying brother. "I don't."

"Caviar?"

"Sure."

He used a ridiculously small spoon to scoop fish eggs on top of crackers.

My mouth watered at the saltiness I was about to enjoy. "Thanks."

He handed me the plate. "Lotte's a good person. Don't hurt her."

"I'm not getting involved." I shoved a cracker into my mouth and hummed over the delicious tang.

"Involved?"

"Nothing happened."

Other than the fact I'd never wanted a woman so damn much.

Dex scampered back to Lotte with the ball in his mouth. She must have thrown it countless times for him already.

She patiently threw it again.

I thought hard on how many faults she'd revealed, trying to make this easier to accept.

None, as far as I can see.

Cameron followed my line of sight. "She's your type."

"You have no idea what my type is."

He arched a brow. "Well?"

It was useless trying to get anything past him. "She's perfect except for her profession."

"I hope you didn't say that to her."

"Of course not." *Not in so many words.*

Maybe a secret affair was in our future.

Aunt Rose joined Lotte at the edge of the lawn. They appeared to be getting along well, sharing a laugh over Dex's tireless enthusiasm for his ball.

"Stop staring," said Cameron.

"You should have warned me about this house," I said, changing the subject.

"I tried."

I scanned the towering walls. "What am I meant to do with all these rooms?"

"Invite us round."

If they visited, there would be laughter here at least some of the time.

He ate another cracker and chewed thoughtfully. "If you want to sell it, I'll support you."

"Thank you," I said. "I appreciate that."

His expression turned serious. "Something else is bothering you. Share it with me. And it's not just the house."

The only way he'd realize Lilly had visited Cole Tower was if he replayed the security tapes of us talking in the café.

I wasn't going to share that—or the reason for Lilly's visit. Not until I felt ready.

"Our advertising campaign."

He studied me for the longest time, clearly not believing me. "Not my department."

"Seriously?"

"Yes, Henry, that's on you now."

"Your feedback would be appreciated."

He brushed a crumb off his lip. "If you want my honest opinion, Dandelion Diva's ad is striking."

"They're a new brand. Have a way to go before they're a threat."

"What's the plan with them?"

"Observe. For now."

"Let them be an inspiration. See it as positive."

"They placed a billboard opposite Cole Tower."

That got his attention.

"We're in their consciousness," I said. "In their sights."

He mulled that over. "Either a healthy competitor or perhaps they placed our spy?"

"My thoughts, too. Shay is digging around."

Cameron tapped my arm. "I want to get your take on something, too."

"Sure."

"Our Foundation has planned an expedition. I'm tagging along."

"Why?"

He gave a shrug. "Feels right."

"What does Mia say?"

"I wanted to ask your opinion first."

"You're a father now."

He grimaced. "A predictable answer."

"Searching for excitement?"

"I want to make more of an impact."

"You realize how many people depend on you?"

"They depend on you, too, Henry."

"I'm sure Mia will support whatever decision you make."

I turned to scan the windows of the manor. "It's the total op-posite of what I like."

"I'm afraid you're all moved in."

"Who checked me out of my hotel?"

"Your butler, I guess."

"I don't have a butler."

He cringed. "You met him on the way in."

"The English guy? I hardly spoke to him! He's going to think I'm an asshole."

"You are an asshole."

"Yes, but at least give me some credit for civility." I glanced around at the guests surrounding us. "Who are these people anyway?"

"Friends of Mom." He narrowed his gaze. "I'm guessing Chantelle is a hard pass."

I ignored that banal topic. "Did you see the statues?"

"Mom likes them. She's trying to make your life easier."

All the blood suddenly drained from my face when I recalled I'd placed *that* envelope in my room's safe at the Bel Air Hotel.

"Are you okay?" He tried to read me.

"Why did Dad move Cole Tower from New York?" I asked, swiftly changing the subject. "It meant a lot of upheaval for ev-eryone involved. Dad's vague when I ask him."

Cameron started to answer, but couldn't find the words.

His way of spilling the truth.

I set my plate down, the insult shocking my system.

The answer had been glaring. This man, my brother and a brilliant psychiatrist, had been tasked to watch over me. They'd moved an entire company across the country to make sure I didn't fuck up.

The broken son who had barely survived hell.

"Where are you going?" Cameron called after me.

I left him standing there as I strode across the lawn, making my way in and through the house.

Halfway down a long corridor, I almost bumped into a member of the staff, a friendly maid.

I offered a nod of apology. "And you are?"

"I'm not allowed to talk with you, sir."

"Why ever not?"

"Rules."

"The rules have changed. What's your name?"

"Diana, sir." She blushed. "Di, to my friends."

"Nice to meet you, Di. Let me know if you need anything. Where's our butler?"

"Kitchen, sir." She pointed back down the hallway.

Turning, I said, "I'll circle back later and we'll chat some more."

She scurried away.

Was I really that intimidating?

I followed the hallway until I reached the kitchen.

Staff buzzed around preparing entrees and setting them on trays.

I'd lost my appetite.

The middle-aged man dressed in a black suit was easy to distinguish as the butler.

"We've not formally met." I stepped forward and offered him my hand.

He shook it. "Hello, sir," he said, with a highbrow British accent.

"I'm Henry, and you are?"

"Alstead, sir."

"Great to meet you finally." I glanced around at the Downton Abbey crew.

My childhood on replay.

"Let's set a meeting so you can all tell me what you need," I said.

"What you need is more important, sir," said the butler.

My focus returned to him. "First name?"

"Conrad, sir."

"You can call me Henry." I motioned for us to move toward a more private area. "Conrad, were you tasked with checking me out of the Bel Air Hotel?"

"Yes, sir."

He'd have found the suite pristine—a habit from my military days.

"There was a personal letter, in the safe."

He thought on it. "The safe was empty, sir."

Feeling uneasy, I asked, "How did you get in it?"

"I found the safe open upon my arrival. I had the manager check the room afterwards." Conrad thought on it some more. "I packed up all your personal items. Nothing was left behind."

"You're sure?"

"Yes, sir. Quite sure."

Yet I was the only one with the pass-code to the safe.

"Call the hotel. Double check for me, please." My throat constricted with dread.

Lilly would have checked out of her hotel by now. Maybe the chance to trace her had gone cold. Just like her mother, she'd disappeared into the ether.

It had been ridiculous of me to wait so long.

I faced the awkward quietness of the staff. They stared back, waiting for me to share some insight or offer some wisdom.

I must have appeared off-kilter.

"Thank you," was all I could say.

I hurried out of the kitchen, fighting off memories of growing up in a house like this.

My seclusion was now compromised.

I easily found the back stairs, and after making my way up to the spacious roof, I surveyed the crowd mingling below. Everyone seemed to be having a good time and enjoying the housewarming party I'd not been warned about.

I couldn't see over the walls of my neighbors on either side, which meant they couldn't see over to my side either—a level of privacy I'd like if I stayed.

I scanned the crowd for Lotte, but couldn't see her. Maybe she'd had enough, and if so, I couldn't blame her.

Ironically, I was forbidden to be with the only woman who soothed my psyche. The one woman who I sensed was perfect for me.

I reached for my tie and pulled at it until it hung off my neck, inhaling sharply to regain some sense of control, some sense of balance.

Ripples of laughter came from all around, the chatter of complete strangers.

I was in L.A. and for all the wrong reasons.

The truth was crushing my ego.

I'd come so far in my recovery and yet had so far to go.

Letting out a long breath, I tried to figure out why the hell Reese's letter wasn't where I'd left it.

Because there are too many people interfering in my life.

All of them are suffocating me.

I should drive over to the Bel Air and search the room myself.

Or maybe destiny had also had its say.

This year was panning out to be one of my worst so far and the baseline had already been low.

Peering over the wall, I assessed how easy it would be to jump from here into the over-sized swimming pool. I'd trained for more daring pursuits. And if they expected a show from the damaged son, I should mix things up a bit.

After removing my shoes, I pulled off my shirt and stripped down to my boxer shorts.

I was ready to climb the wall and leap right into the sparkling pool.

Because today, rebellion felt fucking fantastic.

CHAPTER THIRTEEN

Lotte

I F YOU TELL ME I CAN'T DO SOMETHING, IT MAKES ME WANT it even more.

Which explained why I was back at Chrysalis four days after being banned.

Lately, I'd found myself rebelling a little more than usual.

Richard would have forgotten my faux pas by now. He wasn't even here. It was business as usual as far as I could tell.

In the hallway outside the Harrington suite, I leaned against the wall with whip in hand, taking my time with this punishment.

Three submissives were on their knees in the grand hall, all of them assuming the submissive pose, all of them eager for my return.

I waited for the strain of uncertainty to work its magic on them.

I felt comfortable being back at Chrysalis where I belonged— not at some stuffy garden party. Yesterday, I'd met karma head on when Henry had taken his revenge out on me for inviting him to Imperial.

I'd fallen for it. Henry Cole's alluring air had captivated me.

But dating was the last thing I needed. I'd grown restless, unsure of what lay ahead, and this inner voice was warning me that change loomed.

Henry's arrogance repelled anyone who got close. He had reminded me why I remained single. We were playing a game of cat and mouse with our differences. Our chemistry wasn't an issue—unless you counted that near kiss.

Men don't realize they are just as much as a trap for us.

I'm too fiercely independent to become someone's trophy.

There was no capturing a woman this erotically inclined and profoundly aware of her worth.

Henry had always been a mythical character we'd heard stories about from Cameron. I couldn't remember ever having such a visceral response to someone.

Time to forget him.

Time to dive right back into the luscious world of Chrysalis.

I glanced at my wristwatch and saw that ten minutes had already passed. I shouldn't be wearing this TAG Heuer. It had been a gift from Austin. I promised myself I'd never wear it again.

The submissives waiting for me had just been caught spying at the Imperial restaurant's doorway.

They'd broken the rules.

Elite submissives like these usually excelled within the walls of Chrysalis. Though clearly there was room for improvement.

Usually, I'd have given them over to Richard Booth or other senior Doms such as Greyson Grantchester or Atticus Sinclair—or even de Sade if he promised to go easy on them.

My testy mood came back around more frequently than it should.

Opening the door to the vast room, I ordered the submissives to rise and told them to follow me. I led them back down the hallway and through the grand foyer, where we strode beneath its remarkable chandelier.

Cameron had once told me he considered "the human psyche

to be much like a chandelier, the splintering of the mind also re-flecting shards of light and mysterious shadows."

To me, the chandeliers bathed us in their light as a blessing.

They were a symbol of our freedom.

Our work here was enthralling—the reason Cameron had named our sister manor Enthrall. As for Chrysalis, its meaning was easy to decipher. Each one of us had experienced what it felt like to break free of our societal husk to transform into a brilliant version of ourselves.

I pivoted to make sure my subs were obediently following in silence with their heads down.

We only allowed the best at our world-renowned center. We only accepted one application in ten thousand.

These trainees were undergoing emersion. For them, I gave extra time and attention.

I had a treat in store for my beauties.

Our destination for today's lesson was the exclusive pony club, where young men underwent strict fetish training. The most beautiful were often chosen.

Usually, Master Dominic lorded over this specialty.

As an elite mistress, I had authority to outrank him.

Just outside the stables, I ordered the three subs to place their hands against the wall and to push their buttocks out.

I slapped their ass cheeks, one sub at time. They each whim-pered with an equal measure of discomfort and pleasure, their rounded flesh reddening as my palm heated from the strikes.

Already I could see that tell-tale sign of their arousal glistening.

I used the whip to take them further into a trance—spiking their dopamine.

I knew how to punish these little minxes.

I ordered them to be silent and had them follow me inside the luxury stables, where I had them kneel on the hay.

They watched fervently as I led three ponies out of their stalls—tall, lean young men whose appetites for play were as frisky as you'd expect. These thoroughbreds had donned black latex that crisscrossed their firm chests and thighs.

I removed the bits from each of their mouths and led the fine specimens of manhood into the center of the stable, lining them up. I demanded they straighten their spines and stand ready for my inspection.

One by one, I eased off their cod pieces, allowing each thoroughbred's phallic greatness to rise free.

Gently, with my whip, I teased each erection, tickling, stroking with the curled strap. Soon, the well-bred male submissives were swooning and shuddering against my leather strokes, desperate for relief.

I continued to gently trace their balls with the end of the whip, using the same pressure to tease their nipples—deriding them when they moved or twitched or shuddered.

"Move again and you'll be put back in your stalls!" I scolded.

It was the surest way to turn everyone on—the kind of showmanship worthy of the manor.

Stepping back, I gestured to my subs. "Kneel before each pony!"

My pretty subs rose from where they'd been kneeling and obeyed, hurrying over to bow where I directed them.

Each pony had a sub kneeling before them.

They were all trembling with need, holding it back with the same tension as an arrow being held taut in its bow, poised for release.

"You may begin," I said. "Show us how well trained you are. I expect the best performance."

My ingénues gratefully lapped at the balls of their chosen one, masterfully taking their precious gift in their mouths, a cock for each.

Sensual moans and groans rose in the air, blending like an erotic symphony. The men's erections received lavish, feverish attention, tongues gliding over each tip until there came a perfect rhythm of each submissive delivering a topnotch blowjob.

The ponies were striving to obey and not move.

They were being used and played with like the toys they were.

The erotic scene exploded into a frenzy of want.

"Time to fuck," I said. "Stay with your partner at first. Then you may share."

Observing from a corner of the stables, I savored the way they maintained their pleasant forms. Training ensured the orgy unfolded in a somewhat organized fashion.

I saw toned bodies interwoven with flashes of silver harnesses, the rising and falling of pounding buttocks. The females had their thighs spread wide to encourage deep penetration from their lovers.

Male and females intermingled in a sea of fucking.

Some rode their pony cowboy style, and others wildly pummeled the other into the hay.

One couple formed the sixty-nine position as they exquisitely devoured what lay between their partner's thighs.

A tableau of wanton lust and greed unfolded before me as an exchanging of partners came next, the couples writhing in a prism of colorful, erotic pleasure.

I felt my own arousal pleasantly stirring.

Richard Booth suddenly appeared, standing beside me.

I'd not heard him enter over the din of moans.

He watched the exquisite scene with quiet intrigue.

Finally, Booth whispered, "I told you to take time off."

I gave a shrug, still observing the fantastical orgy.

"Can I have your attention, please, Mistress Lotte?" he said. "Outside."

CHAPTER FOURTEEN

Henry

"**D**O YOU THINK YOU CAN STICK IT OUT?" CAMERON seemed extra testy today.

I threw a chopped potato into a pan of cold water. "I'm more than capable of handling this from here."

He watched me move around Charlie's Soup Kitchen; seemingly unconvinced I could complete the task he'd assigned.

This entire escapade was being watched by Shay, who was sitting on a countertop munching on a carrot. He knew not to interrupt brothers throwing shade on each other.

It felt good to be out of a restrictive suit—my usual attire during the week. All three of us were casually dressed in jeans and T-shirts.

The place was empty, other than the three of us. Charlie's Soup Kitchen was my brother's labor of love.

Yes, he once ran kinky clubs that were meant to help people—I wasn't sure who exactly—but he also had a big heart.

This soup kitchen was dedicated to the homeless. It was

nestled between two stores in Santa Monica and could feed up to one thousand homeless men and women a day.

At 9:00 A.M. we were the only ones here in this state-of-the-art kitchen. The place opened at 11:30, so we had plenty of time for the staff to prepare the food.

I continued to chop vegetables—repetitive work, but it was for a good cause.

This wasn't my usual Saturday routine. Usually, I'd be reading the paper in bed and maybe even answering emails while working from home, before taking Dex out on a long run around the neighborhood.

I already felt the benefit of helping others instead of focusing on my own woes—and I was feeling more settled after Wednesday's near catastrophe on the roof of my new home.

Damn Cameron and his annoying habit of being right.

I regretted not coming to help at Charlie's sooner, but I wasn't going to tell my brother that and give him the satisfaction.

He'd told me that Mia still worked at Charlie's from time to time.

"The chefs get here in an hour," he said. "They're going to appreciate you helping them out."

I threw my hand up in a salute. "My pleasure."

Cameron glared at Shay. "Are you seriously eating the produce?"

"This one is gnarly." Shay held up the crooked carrot he also happened to be munching on. "Anyway, what's the worst that can happen? You've already fired me from Enthrall."

Cameron cracked a smile. "Why are you even here? You should be off with Rue."

"She's working. Anyway, I like to hang out with my buddy, here," Shay mumbled, his mouth full as he pointed at me. "You're not supposed to cut broccoli that way."

"If you think you can do better," I offered him the knife, "have a go at it."

Shay declined with a wave.

Cameron finally seemed confident enough to leave. After my last escapade, I'd gotten off lightly, I suppose.

Shay continued to criticize my sous-chef talents.

It was good to have company. Gardner was the kind of buddy who could sit quietly in a room with you. It wasn't necessary to talk.

"I'm impressed with your efforts, at least," he said.

"If you want to make yourself useful, you can chop carrots," I said.

Shay leaped off the counter and washed his hands at the sink. Then he came over and joined me in cutting up the rest of the vegetables.

"I met your butler, Jeeves," he piped up.

"Alstead?" I glanced at Shay. "I should have asked Cameron if he needs a butler. He can have him."

"Has Jeeves done something wrong already?" he joked.

"He checked me out of my hotel without asking my permission."

Shay grimaced with sympathy. "No one says no to your mom."

"It was a violation of my privacy."

"I swept through your hotel suite before he packed up your things," he said nonchalantly, as though it wasn't a big deal.

I stared at him. "You went through my things?"

"I wanted to scout ahead for anything important." He studied me. "Found an envelope in the safe."

I felt a wave of relief. "How did you guess my code?"

"I have a gadget. Didn't open the letter, obviously."

"What gadget?"

"Need to know basis." He chuckled at that.

"What did you do with the envelope?"

"Put it in the safe in your home office." He gave a nod of re-assurance. "Jeeves let me in—nice new pad, by the way."

I kept my annoyance hidden. "Same code?"

"Yes," he said flatly.

The guilt I'd been feeling lifted. I hadn't let Reese down.

Shay read my reaction. "Gonna tell me what's in it?"

I took out my frustration on an innocent potato, slicing with vigor. "Wish someone would have asked me about the house first."

"I heard about the surprise." He cringed. "She means well."

I glanced out the window at the crowd forming by the side of the café. Shay followed my line of sight.

We swapped a glance.

The people out there were living a hard existence. I wanted to go outside and hand them all money, but Cameron had told me such things needed to be handled carefully here to make sure no one got mugged.

Being here reminded me of my privilege.

"About the envelope, I get it—it's personal," said Shay.

I grabbed a cauliflower and peeled off the leaves. "An old girl-friend's daughter gave me the envelope."

"Who?"

"Reese Papadopoulos." Saying that name out loud never got easier.

He stopped chopping and looked at me with a surprised expression. "Wait! I thought she'd died."

"Exactly," I said. "Slightly terrifying."

I knew he'd react like this, grilling me.

The answers were still out of reach.

He glowered. "When did you meet her daughter?"

"Last Friday at Cole Tower." Mentioning that I had become trapped in an elevator with her could wait until later. "Her name is Lilly."

"How did she get into the building?"

"Not sure."

"You do realize who you are talking to?"

"How could I forget?"

"Have you called Reese? Confirmed it's her?"

"No."

"Henry!"

"I wanted to deal with it later."

Only I wasn't.

"Does Lilly live in L.A?" he asked.

"She flew in."

"And where is she staying?"

"At the Belmont Crescent." I acknowledged his frown. "She's probably checked out of there by now."

"Have you got her phone number?"

"Reese's?" I said the rest with a shrug. "Maybe it's in the envelope."

"I meant Lilly." He wagged his finger. "You need to update me on these kinds of events."

I sliced another cauliflower in two.

"I need to be notified whenever you have an anomaly," he added.

"And I need to be notified when you move my shit."

"Does that envelope not strike you as weird?"

"It could be a hoax."

"We'll face it together. How about that?"

I conceded with a nod of thanks. "Don't share this with Cameron."

"Well, he's the best person to talk with about this."

"Maybe. But not yet."

Shay conceded with a wary nod.

"Opening that letter will open up old wounds," I said.

I ceased chopping and turned to face him with a somber expression. "I flew out there and gave up months of my life searching for her. I trekked over the mountains, searching for a body."

That ordeal had destroyed me.

"It's probably a hoax," he said softly. "Keep the envelope in the safe. If it's a listening device, it's blocked."

"My thoughts exactly."

"We'll open it together," he said softly. "Just say when."

"Can you take Dex for a couple of days?" I said, changing the subject.

"Sure. Always a pleasure."

"I appreciate that." I smiled at him. "I head out to Geneva tonight."

"That's right. You're taking the new formula to show your dad."

"Exactly, I need to be dialed in." *No distractions.*

"Welcome to the party!" announced Shay.

I glanced up.

Lotte stood in the doorway, a confused expression on her face.

I held my breath for a long moment, slowly taking in the vision of feminine beauty.

She wore jeans and a jacket over a John Lennon T-shirt, her naturally rouged mouth looking kissable. Even with no makeup she was still striking. Her short dark hair was tucked behind her ears.

"What are you doing here?" she asked.

CHAPTER FIFTEEN

Henry

RICHARD APPEARED BEHIND LOTTE IN THE DOORWAY.
"Whoa!"
I mirrored Lotte's sentiment with an expression that said *what the fuck is she doing here?*

I never expected to see her at Charlie's.

Chopping vegetables wasn't exactly on brand for me, and letting someone else see that my younger brother had ordered me to work here felt humiliating.

"Did you both pick the same day to volunteer?" Richard glanced from Lotte to me. "Seriously, I had no idea."

Lotte glared at Shay, and he held up his hands to indicate he'd had nothing to do with me being here.

Lotte tucked her Smartphone and car keys into her jacket pocket. "Well, I'm here now."

Shay quickly washed and dried his hands and then walked past Richard. "I'll see you later, Henry."

Richard stared at Shay's back as he strolled out of the place, his expression revealing they'd messed up with having Lotte volunteer today.

"Did Cameron plan this?" I asked Richard.

"I don't run things by him." Richard surveyed the kitchen. "Have the customers been warned it's you cooking?"

"Fuck off," I said.

Richard grinned. "Impressive."

"When was the last time you helped out here?" I shot back.

"Boys, boys," said Lotte. "Can we lower our testosterone levels, please?"

"So why are *you* here?" I asked her.

Richard excused himself and left us to it.

We watched him go as though seeing our last lifeline slip away.

"I'm just here to help out," said Lotte.

I couldn't hide my frustration that this beautiful woman was in my space. I didn't need to complicate my already complicated life.

"You volunteer here often?" I asked.

"Now and again." She raised her chin. "You?"

"First time."

"You'll fall in love with everyone."

That was something a hippy would say.

I waved a hand over the chopped food. "Once this is done, I'm leaving."

"What's your crime?"

"For Cameron inviting me here?" I hesitated to tell her. "Didn't need to commit one."

Her smile told me she knew Cameron's M.O. only too well. I doubted she'd let the issue go.

"You go first," I conceded.

She shrugged. "I hosted an orgy in the pony stables."

"I'm sorry, what?"

"At Chrysalis."

What the actual fuck?

She sucked on her lower lip, and it looked devastatingly seductive.

Then a thought hit me. "Do you dress up in that fashion?"

"No."

I tried it out for size in my imagination. Nope, definitely not into pony play or anything close to that crazy.

"I thought Richard placed you on leave from Chrysalis?"

"He did."

"You're here for disciplinary action?"

"Yeah." She glanced around. "Something like that."

I gestured to the baskets stacked in the corner. "A fruit salad is on the menu."

Lotte walked over and got to work.

Both of us kept glancing out the window at the queue of guests. We were on the clock to get this done.

"An orgy, huh?" I said finally.

"It was spectacular."

I raised my hand to stop her, afraid to hear the details.

"What did you do to have Cameron bring you here?" she asked.

It wouldn't hurt to tell her. Not after *her* major revelation. Mine seemed insignificant compared to an orgy.

"A momentary lapse in judgment," I answered.

"In what way?"

"I almost jumped off the roof of my house into the pool."

Her jaw gaped in horror. "When?"

"At the garden party." I let out a sigh, not wanting to share that losing a precious letter had set me off—not to mention finding out how far my family would go to help correct my life.

"Why did you want to do that?" she asked softly.

I shrugged. "Cameron stopped me."

Our hilarious struggle on the roof with him trying to manage my momentary crisis would only serve as ammunition for him in the future.

"I'm glad he did. Too dangerous," she said, stating the obvious.

"It felt good."

"Out of character for you, Henry."

"You don't know me."

"Same here," she jabbed back.

My feet wobbled and I felt the sensation of being on unsteady ground.

"Huh," she said casually. "Earthquake."

I grabbed her arm and hurried her across the kitchen. Shoving her into a storage closet, I followed her in and shut the door behind us.

"What are you doing?" she asked, flipping on the light.

"We have to shelter." Instinctively, I pulled her into a hug to shield her, waiting for what came next.

Which I assumed would be the end of us—or at the very least the ceiling collapsing and burying us alive.

"Hmmm. I'm guessing a three."

It took a moment, but then I realized what she meant. "On the Richter scale?"

"You'll get used to them." Her body was still pressed to mine.

"We had a few in Big Bear," I admitted. "They can get loud."

"It's disconcerting."

Our continued embrace felt natural.

Her body fit mine, her curves and softness melding perfectly. My chest was against her breasts, and my arm was wrapped around her body like our lives depended on it.

I refused to let go in case the big one came next. "Let's wait a few more seconds, just in case."

The infamous San Andreas fault-line could still give way beneath us.

Her cute reaction made me cringe at my mistake.

But the hug felt nice.

I allowed her to stay there with her arms wrapped around my body. Or was she allowing me? Her head rested on my chest, her heart beating as though the earthquake had scared her, too.

"Sorry," I said sheepishly. "I overreacted."

"No, you saved me. Thanks."

"Anytime."

She paused and then asked, "Why did you want to jump off your roof?"

"You make it sound like I wanted to end myself. That wasn't it at all." I shook my head. "I was just pissed off."

"Because of the house? I think the Venus statue is so you."

"William Randolph Hearst come and get your décor," I mumbled.

"It wasn't just the house that upset you?" She squinted at me. "Something else?"

"I'd lost something important," I admitted. "Or I thought I had, anyway."

I'd not only admitted it to her but to myself as well. The letter really meant something to me and playing it down was impossible.

"Then I'm glad you didn't lose it," she whispered.

I felt a flurry of excitement in my chest—not unpleasant but certainly uncommon.

We were still crushed together. It felt right. Like a connection that went soul deep.

She looked up at me, trying to gauge how I was doing. "We're okay now."

I held her gaze, enjoying this feeling of rightness.

She reached around me and dragged something into my line of sight. "Mistletoe."

Lotte held a sprig above our heads.

I frowned. "Christmas is over and that's parsley."

A playful expression flashed over her face.

I snatched the parsley out of her hand and threw it down. "If I want to kiss you, I don't need some old-fashioned custom to entice me."

Telling her I'd wanted to kiss her since our time in the dungeon wasn't going to happen—because *this* wasn't going to happen.

My ability to resist the darkest temptations was legendary.

"Just a bit of fun," she whispered.

"I don't do fun," I growled.

"Then you should try it."

"Not sure you can handle me," I teased.

"I can handle anyone."

My hands rose up and cupped her face.

God, how I wanted to taste her, press my lips to hers and have her mouth widen in response to mine.

A spark of electricity marked the moment with a secret language, an unknown sensation rippling through me. This woman was a force of nature.

My lust for her felt darker than any truth.

I leaned down and crushed my lips to hers, kissing her hard and fast. It felt like the most natural thing in the world, my tongue searching her mouth and lavishing affection—silently sharing my secrets.

Time left us alone.

Perfect and raw and real, our chemistry was impossible to deny.

No matter how I tried, I couldn't find an answer or any good reason to stop this from happening.

It was more about what we would do afterwards.

How we would move forward after a kiss *like this.*

I nipped her lip as I considered my options.

She moaned in response.

Maybe I should kiss her throat and ease back a little, break this spellbinding experience.

Only, it felt so damn good.

I couldn't recall the last time I'd felt anything quite like this. Our intimacy was equal to that first breath taken after surfacing from a deep dive in the ocean.

Had I been good friends with Lotte before my capture, it would have been so much more bearable, because I sensed her even when we were separated.

Our bodies harmoniously swayed together, my heart oscillating between exhilaration and fulfillment. She moaned against my mouth again, opening hers wider and inviting me to continue this unmatched affinity.

What was I doing?

I headed up one of the most successful businesses in the world.

Yet deep down I knew this was an insatiable desire that was completely unquenchable. This woman was exquisite in every conceivable way.

Breaking away from this, from her, felt impossible.

If it took an earthquake to get us here, it would take a seismic shift to tear us apart.

Lotte made me so damn needy. My cock was rock hard and bulging against my zipper, my flesh ignited with lust for her.

But my conscience told me that if we were going to do this, I needed to treat her with more respect and not fuck her in a storeroom.

Breaking off the kiss felt wrong, but I knew in my heart it was the right thing to do.

"Charlotte," I whispered, my mouth brushing her neck. "Not in here."

She shivered against me and then pulled away. "Of course not."

I smiled at her to ease the tension.

"That was fun, right?" she asked, smiling back at me.

I hesitated.

She reached up and smoothed my T-shirt across my chest as though it needed it. "Don't worry, Henry. No one will hear we snogged at Charlie's."

"Snogged? So European of you."

"We need to get back to work."

Tipping up her chin, I said softly, "I don't want this to be the last time I see you."

"That's adorable. And so very gentlemanly of you."

She thought I was being polite.

Could a woman like her really want to be around a man as mercurial as me? As gruff and bold and seemingly damaged?

The truth hit me in the heart like a dagger, embedding into my soul: She deserved a man who wasn't so torn up on the inside.

Lotte deserved to be happy every day of her life.

If we spent any more time together, she'd come to see that humanity was damned and I was an experiment gone wrong.

Maybe my parents were right. Maybe Cameron had been kind enough to make me believe otherwise.

No shaking the truth that life had struck too many hard blows my way.

Lotte was simply too beautiful a person to have to endure me.

I leaned in and kissed her forehead.

The tender act was needed to hide the shocking revelation that I'd fallen for the woman from the dungeon.

After nudging the storeroom door open, I followed Lotte back into the kitchen while brushing my fingers over my mouth, the ghost of her kiss haunting my soul.

"I'll head to the dining room out front," she said. "I need to prepare the cutlery and tables."

"Sounds like a plan," I agreed. "Want some help?"

"No, thank you."

I watched her leave the kitchen, feeling the awkwardness caused by a kiss that should never have happened. Or maybe it hurt because of my fear we'd never kiss again.

But today wasn't about me.

Hundreds of hungry people were lining up outside.

Get a fucking grip.

If I rolled up my sleeves and began cooking before the chef arrived—something I was more than capable of doing—then the guests would get to eat sooner.

I continued to prepare the food, all the while trying not to grin over the best kiss I'd ever experienced.

When Lotte reappeared, she acted in a way to convey business as usual—bright and bubbly at first and then, as she settled in to prepare the fruit salad, she became introspective. Her serenity was a thing of beauty as she chopped the ingredients and pre-pared the dessert.

When the usual staff arrived, they dived right in, joining us with friendly enthusiasm.

We fed over one thousand guests that day. Their expressions of gratitude melted my ice-cold heart.

Afterwards, when the guests had left and the café had been cleaned, we thanked the staff for letting us take on such a signif-icant role in their soup kitchen.

It meant so much to us that we both promised to return soon.

Lotte and I left Charlie's in our separate cars after giving each other a courteous wave goodbye—as though our kiss had never happened.

CHAPTER SIXTEEN

Henry

I MANAGED TO GET A FEW HOURS OF SLEEP ON THE COLES' private jet during the flight to Switzerland.

We landed early Sunday morning.

Cameron and I had left the States in the dead of night. Clandestine, but if one needs to prevent corporate spies from guessing what one is up to it's the only way to travel.

Dad welcomed us back to his impressive estate.

Decades ago, he and Mom had added this villa in the center of Montreux to their property portfolio. Nestled between steep hills and Lake Geneva, the mansion afforded spectacular views of the water and boats from its many windows.

This was the country where we had all learned to ski, sharing plenty of happy memories. We had enjoyed our time on the family yacht and our visits to local towns. As kids, we'd been lucky enough to go off exploring.

Dad had waited patiently for us both to mature to take on the business. Right up until he demanded Cameron leave medicine so he could rule the empire.

Eventually, I had taken over; ironically due to the patience and expertise of the man who I had grabbed the power from. As the eldest, this had always been my destiny.

In many ways, I'd set my brother free—and we both realized this fact, ensuring our brotherly bond remained strong.

Today, I'd present a remarkable new flavor to the grand master of teas. The brand would give us a competitive edge. Companies like Dandelion Diva could never hope to match it unless they played dirty.

As traditions went, this was one of the more exciting. I'd personally created this formula.

It stood to make us billions.

Our company's objective had remained the same for over a century—continue to make a substantial mark in the industry. It pleased us both that our dad could see the business remained in good hands.

Cameron and I entered the temperature-controlled lower room. The setting was simple. A table sat in the center with three chairs around it. As conference rooms went, this one had an understated elegance.

The main star was always the tealeaves.

The sealed glass jar on the table contained its weight in gold. We'd guarded it closely all the way here.

My brother's proud gaze lingered on me. "He's going to love it."

"We'll see."

I began to pace, and then whipped out my phone. I logged into Instagram as a distraction. My page was kept private. I scarcely posted any photos, but it enabled me to follow a few close friends.

I checked out Lotte's page. She'd posted a selfie from Saturday afternoon, showing her on a hiking trail wearing a baseball cap. She appeared happy behind the sunglasses. The photo posted before that one had been taken by Scarlet at the Cole ball at Shutters on the Beach over a week ago. She was joyfully raising her glass of bubbly to the camera in a toast.

Yet again I was floored by her exquisite beauty.

The Enthrall crowd proved how close they were, being the best of friends. They'd all gone out of their way to make me feel welcome.

Being that close to someone as bewitching as Lotte was the only reason I'd left the table. I'd struggled not to stare at her alluring beauty. I'd walked to the bar to cool my head and had struck up a conversation with a blonde stranger—all the while resisting the urge to glance back at Lotte, who was licking chocolate off her spoon.

Yet fate had brought us together again in the Shutters bathroom later that evening.

And once again at Charlie's.

The memory of our kiss caused me to brush my fingers over my mouth, as though that would allow me to relive that exquisite encounter and somehow conjure her up.

Lotte had this uncanny way of soothing my melancholy.

"Ready?" Cameron asked, shaking me from my daydream.

Dad entered and turned to shut the airtight door.

After some light banter where we all caught up, Dad gestured to my phone.

"Everything okay?" he asked.

"Yes." I gave a nod, tucking my phone away. "Just checking on something important."

Thankfully, Cameron turned his back on me to prepare the sample. He did the honors, pouring boiled water over a sieve filled with tealeaves, filling a China cup.

Over the years, we'd observed Dad conduct this same formality in what was essentially a tea ceremony.

We'd both mastered the art early on, having fallen in love with its refined simplicity, the serenity of this sacrament.

Cameron set the teacup before our dad. The scent of honey, walnuts, and nutmeg wafted over us.

After a few minutes of breathing in the aroma while waiting for the liquid to cool, Dad tipped a small amount of the tea into a porcelain saucer, his keen eye examining its consistency and appearance.

Then he lifted the teacup and took a sip.

I studied his reaction.

"Tell me about this," he said.

"It's caffeine-free," I said. "And eco-conscious."

"Cameron, what are your thoughts?" he said.

"It tastes great."

"Maybe caffeine isn't such a villain?" Dad suggested.

I agreed with a nod. "We could add that back, yes."

"This could be an excellent brand to compete with Dandelion Diva," he reasoned, having read the literature we'd sent ahead. "What did you discover about them?"

"They're a start-up," I said. "Funded out of Silicon Valley. Two guys with a lot of ambition. They appear to be growing fast."

"We're watching them carefully," said Cameron.

I studied Dad's face. "What do you think about the tea?" I'd pondered how he might react since this journey began.

Dad seemed to mull it over.

I sensed what he was about to say.

"What are your thoughts, son?" he asked me, his gaze steady.

The crushing truth hit me in a moment of self-reflection. "It's missing an ingredient?"

"Cameron?" asked Dad.

"It's great," he said. "A new favorite."

This one would have my name on it. It would be a signature brand that was my offering to the art of the craft, and it was worth trying for perfection.

I rubbed my brow, admitting defeat. "We're not there yet," I said. "Thanks for your honesty."

Cameron studied me. "I'll support whatever you decide."

"This has the potential to knock Dandelion Diva off the shelves," said Dad.

"Dad, you've been at this a lot longer," said Cameron, clearly to reassure me.

"Will Dandelion Diva be a problem for us?" Dad asked, sounding concerned.

All we had to go on was what Shay had dug up so far.

"They play dirty with their competitors," said Cameron. "We suspect they are doing the same with us."

Dad turned to me. "Strategy?"

"We have a team investigating them," I said with confidence.

"Shay is leading the fight?" he asked.

I gave a nod. "We believe they're the ones who placed our corporate spy."

A troubled expression crossed Dad's face.

I hated him knowing that our beloved company was under threat. The thought of someone working against us from the inside hurt.

Cameron and I swapped a wary glance.

"It's just a matter of figuring out who it is," I said. "We're focusing on it night and day."

"Wily fuckers," Dad muttered.

Cameron and I both had to suppress a smile. Our dad hardly ever swore.

"We're offering a superior brand," I reasoned. "Our integrity gives us our edge."

Dad let out a heavy sigh. "And once you find out who's spying?"

I gave a shrug. "We crush them."

CHAPTER SEVENTEEN

Lotte

I'D CONTRADICTED MYSELF TOO MANY TIMES.

I kept telling Henry I considered myself a good friend, but that wasn't how I'd conducted myself back at Charlie's—teasing him.

Which was why I'd come here, to prove we were capable of having a platonic relationship, breaking the ice again before crossing paths at another Cole event.

Our kiss wasn't an issue.

We were just two people mature enough to help each other weather this life. Cameron had mentioned his concerns that Henry had appeared fraught over a personal issue.

Maybe I could help him with that.

The warm front had allowed me to wear my Ralph Lauren floral Georgette blouse with jeans. It was always fun to see the reaction of friends to my varied wardrobe of classic styles—and my secret passion for Uggs.

My fashion sense was as versatile as my nature.

At the front door, I used the lion head knocker to announce my arrival.

Surprisingly, Henry answered.

He looked astonished to see me. "Hello."

"Just wanted to drop this off," I said.

Dex popped his cute head out, panting with his tongue hanging. Henry grabbed his collar to prevent him from escaping.

"Hey, Dex." My hands were full so I couldn't pet him. "I thought you had a butler?" I said brightly.

Henry glanced at the paper bag in my hand. "I sent him home."

I raised the take-out bag. "Chinese food."

"Oh, nice."

"And—" I showed him the wrapped gift. "A housewarming present."

He gave me a thousand-watt grin. "Thank you, Lotte! Come on in. It's great to see you."

Sensing someone else was here, I second guessed my decision.

Henry looked devastatingly handsome in a white shirt that hung over his designer jeans, his causal style a refreshing change.

I stepped inside. "You have a guest?"

He hesitated. "Yes."

I held my breath, waiting for him to explain. "I don't want to intrude."

He quirked a brow.

"I wasn't sure if you…" I cringed, reluctant to say the rest.

He frowned as though mulling over how much to share. "I have to tackle something I've been putting off."

"I can go. Keep the food."

"I'd love you to stay." He gestured for me to follow.

"I can leave. I won't be offended."

"Stay." He eased the bag and gift out of my hands, our fingers brushing.

I felt that familiar tingle at his touch.

I was unsure if he was just being kind, but then I remembered that wasn't Henry at all. He could always be counted on to be honest.

I followed him through the house. "How are you settling in?"

"Fine. Considering." He shook his head.

"Do you ever get lost? This place is huge."

"Navigation is kind of my thing," he said, chuckling.

"Of course it is."

"Thank you for bringing me food."

"You have a chef, but I thought it might be fun."

"More ordinary." He winked.

"Ordinary coming right up!"

He gave an apologetic cringe. "You're far from ordinary."

"I knew what you meant. I'm your friend from the cheap seats."

"You're starting to become someone I can't live without."

I almost forgot to breathe, feeling a spark of something greater between us than friendship, our body language being familiar and intimate.

His cologne reached me in all its complexity; rich and heady and dangerously seductive.

"Who else is here?" I asked, sounding breathless.

I recognized the door to his office.

He gripped the handle and opened it. "Come see."

Dex scurried into the room ahead of us.

I entered, hoping this wasn't a private meeting.

Henry placed the food on the coffee table. "Lotte will be joining us."

Cameron and Shay were here, both dressed casually, too, in jeans and shirts—and emanating that dark and dangerous vibe I'd become obsessed with.

I felt that familiar crackling in the air from their presence. They were the hottest men I'd ever met, other than Henry, of course. He had his very own powerful aura of dominance and an awe-inspiring stature. His military background had given him an added confidence.

"Hey." Cameron came over and I stepped into his hug.

Shay threw me a wave. "This is a nice surprise."

I pointed to the take-out bag. "Dropping off some food."

"And a gift," said Cameron, taking it off Henry and giving it a shake.

"A small thing," I said.

"And so thoughtful of you." Henry glanced at his brother. "This is why we love her, right?" He smiled at me. "It's good you're here, Lotte."

"Your timing is perfect," said Cameron.

I tried to read the room as the atmosphere became tense, questioning if I should even stay. It appeared as though a personal revelation was about to be spilled.

I'd always held my own with the alphas back at Chrysalis, but the undertones here seemed solemn.

Henry reached for a pair of surgical gloves that were lying on the table and pulled them on.

Weird.

He picked up an envelope next and showed it to me. "I received this twelve days ago. It's supposedly from an old girlfriend."

"Why the gloves?" I asked.

"She was presumed dead," said Shay flatly.

My jaw slackened in surprise.

"Want me to open it?" asked Shay.

"No," Henry said adamantly.

Cameron glanced over at me. "It's already been fingerprinted. More tests to follow."

"What if it contains a dangerous substance?" I said.

Shay shook his head. "We've screened for that."

"How did it get to you?" I asked.

Shay leaned against the wall. "Reese's daughter handed him the letter."

Reese.

"Lilly accessed Cole Tower to get to him," explained Shay. "A breach in security had her finding her way to the fifth floor. She joined him in the elevator."

I hid my fear at knowing she'd gotten that close.

"The guard who let her through has been fired," said Shay.

Henry used a letter opener to slice the seal of the envelope, tearing it open.

Wait, did he say twelve days ago?

I wondered why it had taken him so long to open it, and if Cameron knew the reason. Perhaps this letter was a trigger for his brother.

All three of us watched Henry's expression.

He unfolded a piece of paper.

"Genuine?" asked Cameron.

Henry blinked as though in shock.

"Henry?" Cameron got his attention. "What does she want?"

"My help," he whispered.

I was immediately suspicious, but both Shay and Cameron were more than capable of guiding Henry regarding this potential threat.

"Is it her handwriting?" asked Cameron. "If you can even remember."

Henry tipped the letter sideways and a tiny object slipped into his palm—a silver *R*. It was a charm for a necklace or bracelet.

"You gave her that?" asked Cameron.

Henry closed his fingers around it and squeezed, the blood draining from his face.

"Does she say where she is?" asked Shay.

"Florida," Henry said quietly.

Reese had been living only hours away from New York, an easy flight when he'd been based there.

I felt compelled to snatch the letter from him and set a match to it. Burn it up and end this painful charade.

"What exactly does she say?" asked Cameron.

"She's sent coordinates for her location. Instructions on how to reach her base."

"Base?" asked Shay.

My heart ached for him.

"I'll take it," Shay said softly, holding out his hand for the letter.

Henry's tormented gaze met mine, the letter not leaving his grip.

CHAPTER EIGHTEEN

Henry

S AYING GOODBYE TO LOTTE THIS TIME FELT MUCH HARDER.
Our hug at the door lasted longer than expected, our
affection deepening. She was fast becoming the friend I
needed.

Our differences didn't seem to matter so much when we were
in the same room together. She was probably the most reasonable
human I'd ever met.

I felt grateful for her presence over the last few hours.

And I'd enjoy opening her gift—a kind gesture.

My mind turned back toward that letter. Shay had insisted
on taking it from me but not before I'd taken a snapshot with my
iPhone.

Was I being given another chance to save Reese?

If this ended up being a grand hoax, at least I'd have my
answer.

I threw my old rucksack onto the bed and started going
through my drawers, dragging out khaki pants and other clothes,

and searching my wardrobe for my hiking kit, checking off what I'd need for every type of terrain.

What gave me faith was the fact that the silver *R* had come from a charm bracelet I'd given to her before she'd left for Chile.

Cameron hurried into my bedroom, eyeing the kit on the bed.

Finally he said, "You've worked out the coordinates?"

I nodded. "Of course. Fakahatchee Strand Preserve State Park."

"You're not serious?" he said angrily. "It's an enormous preserve, and that whole area is rife with danger."

"I could do with some alone time in nature."

"Wildcats. Gators. Poisonous snakes. Not to mention what you'll face when you arrive at those coordinates."

I shrugged. "I'm going to grab some anti-venom on the way."

"I'm sure that will help in the middle of fucking nowhere."

"What if that letter had come from Mia? Same situation?"

He gritted his teeth in frustration. "Reese needs to come here."

"Apparently she doesn't share that sentiment."

"Send Shay."

"I need him here." I threw a couple of sweatshirts into the case and then turned to face my brother.

"This scenario has sinister undertones," he said.

"Could someone have found letters from her past and replicated her handwriting? Yes, totally possible. I've only my gut to go on."

"Reese choosing to disappear and never reach out to anyone is a travesty."

"I have to hear why she did it."

Why, after all these years, had she contacted me?

"It wasn't your fault," he said quietly.

"I was her boyfriend, Cam. The one meant to protect her."

"You can't blame yourself. You were young. She went abroad willingly. Taking a gap year is totally normal. Hell, it's encouraged."

"I get that."

"This is about you finding resolution for the guilt you've always carried around."

"I'm not disagreeing with you."

"We pay people to do this kind of thing."

"I have to find out the truth for myself."

"This is Shay's territory."

"I have the same skills." I stood my ground. "I outrank him, remember?"

"You're well-trained. Still, this could…"

"Go on. Say it."

"It could be the one thing that destabilizes you. Don't go through with this trip. The work you've put in to get to where you are now is profound. Don't forget where you once were."

"You believe the letter is a fake? Someone is trying to get me to break?"

"It's a convenient time."

"They might come after you, too."

"I'm used to it. Solving emotional obstacles is what I do."

He wasn't wrong. Even I'd challenged him to the point of madness. Yet he'd hardly wavered.

"How do you do it?" I asked. "How do you navigate life's pitfalls so calmly?"

He mulled it over. "I once punched someone in the face and tried to drown them when they hurt Mia."

I pointed at him. "See, you and I are rational."

"I'm usually more philosophical."

"Go on, share your wisdom." I folded my arms ready to be patronized.

"People like Reese are toxic."

I raised my hands. "Her disappearance has haunted me. She's in my dreams. My nightmares. I want a sense of peace. I want to quiet the…"

"Voices?"

"It's just one, and it tells me I need to be a better man."

"Let's talk more about that."

"I know myself, and how hard I can push myself."

"Don't go down this path, Henry. The last thing you need is to chase this. It's a trigger. It could cause a relapse and undo everything."

"Maybe this is about your guilt for what happened between you and me in Afghanistan." I raised a finger. "For which I've forgiven you."

Sadness flashed over his face. "That's not what this is."

He'd seen me destroyed by terrorists, seen me at my most vulnerable. He'd extracted the Intel needed to end a war—but in doing so he had started a greater conflict within me.

Would I have had it any other way? Hell, no, because of the lives that were saved—even though it had almost killed me.

"Why do we have to bring up these consequences?" I said.

"I'm your brother."

A long time ago, we'd both agreed we'd not stand behind the shield of privilege. That we'd enter the fight to make the world a better place; give our lives meaning.

"If I can't change your mind, then I'll come with you," he reasoned.

"I'm going alone."

"You're about to launch a new brand. Yet you're seriously considering going back onto the battlefield of your mind."

"I'm capable."

"You understand what the fog of war is like, Henry. You think you can sense who your opponent is, but you're opening doors you shouldn't. The truth could result in your self-destruction."

"Thank you for the vote of confidence."

"You're walking into danger."

I straightened. "If this is a hoax, they have no idea who they've unleashed on themselves."

He sighed. "Is Reese worth this?"

"How the fuck am I meant to heal when everyone assumes I'm already broken? I need to be trusted when I make major decisions.

I need people to stand back and let me do what I believe is right—I need to face this head on."

"You just avoided my question, Henry."

I met his gaze, deciding to share the truth. "She has a piece of my heart."

"And you need closure?" Cameron asked, a pained expression on his face.

"I need *you* to respect me and my choices," I said firmly. "I'm your older brother. Treat me with the regard I deserve."

Cameron sat on the edge of the bed and bowed his head.

"Bit dramatic," I teased.

He looked up at me, his expression saying *this won't end well.*

I smirked. "I did once save the free world."

"That's why we have to keep you safe."

I slumped next to him and stared dead-ahead. "Shay? Really?"

"He's not emotionally invested."

"I want to reclaim myself," I said. "Get back that part of me I lost in Afghanistan."

"Lieutenant Commander, stand down," said Cameron softly.

Silence clawed its way into our space.

Finally, I relented to a compromise. "Shay gets one week."

Cameron exhaled in relief.

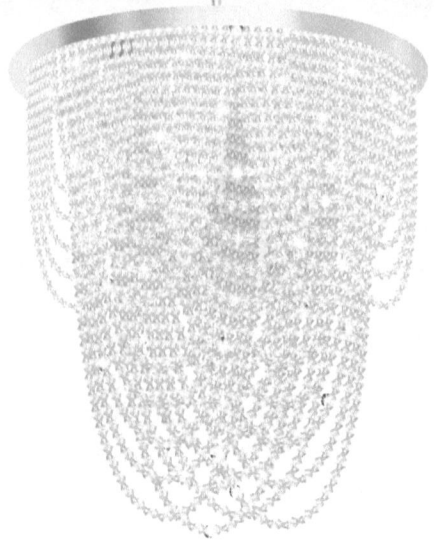

CHAPTER NINETEEN

Lotte

I WHEELED MY SUITCASE THROUGH THE TERMINAL.

This was my first time flying out of Santa Monica Airport, where the Cole jet was based. Usually, I traveled via LAX or even Burbank.

My ticket allowed me to proceed right into the VIP lounge.

I'd left home extra early to avoid Friday rush hour, so I had plenty of time to grab a drink and maybe read a little.

We were scheduled to arrive in Florida this evening.

None of us wanted to let Henry face this uncertainty alone. Cameron had briefed me on what to expect when we arrived at our destination, and Shay had ensured I'd be ready for anything.

I'd been tasked with immediately reporting anything suspicious. We were all uneasy about the strange communication from Henry's long-lost girlfriend. If genuine, Reese had caused him even more distress.

Being part of Henry's journey in any capacity felt right.

Having been suspended from Chrysalis—again—meant I had plenty of free time.

My secret crush wasn't an issue. I could handle myself, and I was confident that I'd already experienced most hurdles one had to face in life.

After entering the VIP lounge, I scoured the room for Henry.

He sat in a lounge chair in the far corner, reading from his phone, looking rugged in black combat pants and boots, a grey T-shirt stretched tight across his chest. A short jacket was thrown over his shoulder.

A former Navy SEAL prepared for anything—unlike me.

I was wearing jeans, a T-shirt and flats, because the adventure hadn't started yet.

Though clearly in *his* mind it had.

Mercenary Henry was a hot take on his more formal style. He seemed ready to tackle anything that might come his way with that familiar dark burn of alpha intensity. He pushed up from his seat and strolled toward me as he tucked his phone away, greeting me with an annoyance that bore deep into my soul.

I couldn't help but shudder with the roiling emotions of contained affection I was feeling for him. I drew on them as I delivered a friendly smile.

He'd again rendered me speechless.

"This is a hard *no*," he said gruffly. "Full marks on trying."

I rallied my courage. "Hello, Henry. How are you?"

"I'm guessing it's no coincidence you and I are at the same airport."

"I was born in Florida. The location you're going to is called the Amazon of North America. I grew up in similar terrain."

"You grew up in a preserve?"

"No, of course not. The Florida terrain—"

"This is too dangerous to include—"

"Say 'a woman' and I'll thump you."

"I was going to say someone I care about."

That caused me to pause before saying, "You told Cameron you were letting Shay handle it."

"He's the one who sent you?"

"Maybe."

He glanced down at my suitcase. "It would have been fun to watch you wheel that down the trails."

"My rucksack is in my suitcase."

"Makes sense," he said, sounding sarcastic.

"I'll leave my luggage in the hotel."

He glowered. "We should check out other tourist destinations while we're there."

"I'm on your side, Henry. You deserve answers."

He shook his head. "I'll have a car take you home."

"Cameron will ground your jet."

His jaw flexed in frustration. "I'll fly Virgin."

"They don't fly out of here."

"Thank you, Lotte, you're already proving indispensable."

I smiled sweetly. "This is what it's like to be loved."

"You love me?" He cocked a brow.

I rolled my eyes. "By your brother."

That made him smirk.

"I need to do this," I said softly.

"You'll slow me down."

"I'm trying to work out what I want in life. I've been offered a job, but I'm scared to leave Chrysalis. This trip will clear my head so I can see things differently."

He scratched the back of his neck, mulling over my confession.

I pointed a finger at him. "I'm your advocate."

He grabbed my finger and shook it. "Fine, but I'm in charge and you do exactly as I say. Understand?"

"Fine. If you want to believe that."

"Lotte, lose the attitude."

"Excuse me?" I gave him a frosty stare. "I saved you from Chantelle."

"How, exactly?" He glanced at my suitcase. "Do you even have hiking boots in there?"

"Yes, of course."

"Well, you're wearing lipstick."

"No, I'm not."

He hesitated as he studied my lips.

"This is my natural lip color. It matches down there."

"Yes, thank you, Lotte. You can be the light entertainment when the shit hits the fan."

"I doubt it will get that bad."

A female flight attendant gestured to us. Our plane was ready to board.

Henry lifted his rucksack with ease and slid his arms through the straps. Then he walked over and took my suitcase handle from me. I followed him as he rolled it through the exit and out onto the tarmac.

I couldn't stop staring at his butt, admiring how good it looked in combats. His cologne wafted back to me and I breathed in the masculine aroma.

This promised to be an incredible adventure—the kind you never sought out because it usually remained outside your realm of possibilities.

We climbed the metal steps up to the doorway of the jet. The familiar and impressive Cole family emblem was emblazoned on the side, resembling a royal crest.

The flight attendant took care of securing our luggage.

The carpet along the aisle was a soft blue and the lighting was comfortably dimmed. The fixtures were all chrome and silver—a sleek design for a fast jet.

I'd flown on a few in my time.

I sat in a luxury seat next to Henry. "This is amazing."

"Let's go light on the booze."

"No champagne cocktail?" I joked.

He raised his hand to get the attention of the flight attendant. "I suppose we can make an exception this once."

I rested my hand on his arm. "I don't want anything."

"Are you sure?"

"Well, I'd like to be treated with dignity."

He stared at me for the longest time. "You're making my life complicated."

"How?"

"Now I have to watch over you."

"I'm more than capable of taking care of myself," I said.

"You'll be a distraction."

"Henry, I'm carrying our medical kit. My pharmacy background could come in handy. I have anti-venom, an EpiPen and bear spray. Cameron prescribed emergency pain meds."

"Yeah, but if a gator grabs you, how do you get free?"

"Did you Google it?"

"Yeah." He smirked. "If that happens, we're fucked."

"What I do know from growing up there is that you avoid any body of water. Those prehistoric creatures lurk in the most unlikely places."

"We're literally going to be on a boat at some point."

"Oh, fun."

Henry reached into his trouser pocket and pulled out a map. "Want to see where we're going?" He unfolded it. "I have a copy on my watch but if that fails, we have a backup."

The jet's engine thrummed as the plane maneuvered to face the runway.

"The coordinates," Henry pointed to the center of a forest, "will lead us here."

The preserve's vast territory was made up of snaking waterways and dense woodland.

I shuddered at the thought of what we might come across.

"Can you not just ask Reese to meet you in Naples?" I said.

"Having regrets already?"

"There's no way of contacting her?"

"No." Henry turned to peer out of the window. "I'll be able to say everything that's been on my mind all these years."

I started to ask for details, but then thought better of it.

And if it wasn't her? What would he do then?

"One step at a time," I said softly.

I fastened my seatbelt, gazing past his hunky frame out the oval window as the plane glided down the runway.

"There's still time to back out," he whispered.

Reaching for him, I weaved my fingers through his. He considered our interwoven hands and clenched mine tighter.

He let out a deep breath, revealing his understanding of the special moment happening between us.

"Lieutenant Commander," I said. "Let's do this."

CHAPTER TWENTY

Lotte

A FTER ARRIVING AT NAPLES AIRPORT, A TOWN CAR PICKED us up on the tarmac and drove us to the Ritz Carlton Golf Resort, an exquisite beachfront hotel.

The concierge had been expecting us.

Henry refused any help with our luggage, telling me that being separated from our kit was inadvisable.

The man had morphed from sophisticated businessman into rugged explorer with the unmatched confidence of an adventurer. He'd commanded troops in the toughest environments.

I had never felt safer.

We'd been offered a suite by the concierge, but Henry had declined, preferring a more modest room. Considering he could have bought the hotel if he wanted, I admired him for that.

He threw his rucksack on the floor by the king-size bed. "We'll head out first thing."

"Great."

"Will the room do?" He arched a brow.

"Of course."

"You're used to the finer things."

I frowned at him. "I'm the daughter of a maid, Henry."

He stood there staring at me for the longest time. "I didn't know that."

"Well, now you do. My mother cleaned houses like yours."

"She's not with us anymore?"

"No."

"I'm sorry," he said thoughtfully.

Another good reason for us not to date, I mused cheerfully.

"Reese's father owned a Greek restaurant." He folded his arms. "I'm not the snob you believe I am."

"Yes, you are."

"Okay, I am." He relented with a nod. "Try not to clean anything here. We don't have time."

"Cheeky bastard."

"Are you like her?"

"Mom?" I lowered my guard. "Yes."

"She was beautiful, then."

"Good save."

"I meant it."

"Right," I said, hoping he would change the subject.

"Where in Florida did you grow up?"

"I was born in Miami, but grew up in the Keys."

"I need to visit there. Maybe you can take me one day."

I appreciated his polite reply. "My childhood was idyllic—even without a dad. Fishing on the weekends. Endless trips to the beach. Every day felt special to me."

"No father?"

I shrugged that off.

"I was born and raised in New York," he said.

"Total opposites," I agreed.

Not just our origins but our personalities, too. We stood there, both of us seemingly considering our many differences.

"We're camping tomorrow night," he said, breaking the silence. "I wasn't sure you realized that."

"I've camped before," I said, keeping a straight face.

Did my childhood backyard count?

"Good," he said, amused. "You're our resource."

I didn't want him to doubt my ability to support him.

Henry liked to be in charge. I felt comfortable with him taking the lead. Clearly, he had way more experience with these kinds of things.

"When we head out, you can leave your suitcase with the concierge," he said.

I looked around the room, and then turned to face him. "Why is there only one bed?"

He took a step towards me, his gaze on my lips.

If he tried to kiss me, I would let him.

Even though I'd still not recovered from our first kiss, and even though we both knew another might be inadvisable.

This version of Henry was mesmerizing. My body was thrumming as though he'd touched me in that familiar way; gentle at first and then taking command, taking what he wanted.

Taking me.

He grinned. "My room's next door. I thought having adjoining rooms might be best for security."

"I knew that." I tried to hide my embarrassment.

He picked up his rucksack and walked over to the other door, opening it and disappearing into the adjoining room.

I'd misread him, and he'd had some fun at my expense. I was still trembling from being so close to him.

He re-appeared in the doorway. "Hungry?"

"Yes." I was starving.

"Let's check out the restaurant."

The dining room was pleasantly quiet, with only a few guests having dinner. The vastness of the place meant we ended up at a table where we could talk freely.

The big room was decorated with airy colors and familiar lush greenery, the assortment of indoor plants making the space inviting.

Sitting opposite him, I took a few moments to process the fact we were really doing this—heading off into the wilderness tomorrow on what would most likely be the wildest adventure of my life.

But first, we decided to load up on carbs—both ordering Fettuccine Alfredo.

I imagined Henry had been this attentive to his men when he had served in the military, watching out for them and making sure they were prepared for what lay ahead.

Shay had told me Henry had earned their loyalty. His soldiers were willing to do anything for him, and when he'd been captured, they were distraught.

This had given me an entirely new reason for hero worshipping him.

"You've gone quiet." He rested his napkin on his lap. "You've ceased to give me your opinion on anything in the last five minutes."

I gave a shrug. "Without a personality transplant, not much can be done for you."

"Delivered with your usual aplomb."

"Henry, you're merely a result of your elitism."

"Yet you seem to like my brother?"

"He's unaffected."

"Unlike me?"

"When we first met at Chrysalis, you told me you didn't want to be seen with me."

He seemed to mull that over. "At least the chance of anyone seeing us together in the Preserve is unlikely." He winked.

Asshole.

The way he bowed his head looked so damn cute. "No one has ever dared to talk to me like you do."

"Get used to it," I said.

"Something tells me you'll always share the truth, Charlotte."

"I will, yes."

"How do you feel about tomorrow?" he asked, turning serious.

"Optimistic."

"It's a two-day trek." He studied my reaction. "You up for that?"

"Absolutely."

"At least you already hike." He quirked a brow. "I saw it on your Instagram."

"Yours is locked down," I replied, proving that we'd spied on each other's social media.

"I'll grant you access," he said playfully.

"Am I good enough to glimpse inside the secret world of America's most eligible bachelor?"

"You tell me." He grinned.

"I'm ready for anything."

"I can see that."

I hesitated and then just came out and asked, "Tell me about her."

"Reese?"

"Yes, if you like."

"We dated in high school. Met on the running track." His expression softened. "She wanted to be a veterinarian, even though her dad tried to convince her to run the restaurant. That's how I thought our lives would go. I'd join the Navy as a fighter pilot, and she'd follow her chosen career."

I leaned back. "You were going to be a pilot?"

"Fighter jets," he said. "After Reese went missing, I changed my mind. The SEAL Academy seemed like a better fit."

"You were angry?"

"Reese's disappearance had me spiraling off my axis for a while there. We loved each other," he said solemnly. "I thought we did, anyway."

"Tell me about her personality."

"She could be aloof. I'd find Reese alone in the library, reading in a corner. Or swimming endless laps in the Olympic-sized pool. But she seemed to love me back."

"Did you discuss marriage?"

Henry looked away. "Before she went to Chile, I asked her to marry me."

"What did she say?"

His expression told me that she must have accepted.

"I'm sorry," I whispered.

"We planned to become officially engaged on her return."

"And of course you were part of the search party."

He nodded. "Searching for someone for months on end takes a toll."

Oh, Henry.

"If it's not her, I'll deal with it. The mystery of what happened will still be out there."

Our waiter appeared and set down two plates of creamy Fettuccini Alfredo.

Henry gestured his thanks.

The waiter seemed to sense his awkward timing and walked away quickly to give us privacy again.

I twisted my fork to wrangle the pasta, my mouth watering at the delicious aroma.

"What is Reese doing in the middle of a preserve?" I said.

"From what I can tell, she's at a base camp." His frown deepened. "Maybe she's working there?"

"Were you able to get hold of the itinerary for the staff?"

"Not yet."

"I admire your strength," I said, pausing between mouthfuls of chicken.

"I'm sure you've had your own misfortunes."

"I suppose."

"Tell me more about you, Lotte."

I took a sip of water. "I've worked at Chrysalis and Enthrall for years."

"You mentioned you grew up with no father?"

"He left us when I was six."

"I'm sorry."

"We were both relieved," I said. "He beat Mom up a few times.

I was too young to do much about it. Eventually, we moved from Miami to the Keys and started a new life."

"Your mom ever remarry?"

"No, she was over men at that point."

"Is that why you became a dominatrix? To maintain some semblance of control?"

"You sound like your brother."

He studied me carefully. "You're ready for a change in career?"

"Cameron invited me to join his Beverly Hills clinic."

Henry seemed impressed "He still consults there from time to time."

"It will be a good fit for me."

"You mentioned having doubts?"

"It means giving up being a dominatrix. It's who I am. My whole life has been built around my alter ego."

"You'll miss the excitement?"

"I know I will."

"I envy you," he said, sighing.

"Why?"

"My destiny has been set since birth."

"From what I hear, you're a fabulous CEO."

"Cameron is biased."

"He would do anything for you."

"I've fucked up in more ways than I can count with him." He waved that off. "I have to be honest with you about something."

"Sure."

"Ever since I've met you, I've tried to fathom why you're not married. You're so damn gorgeous."

"Thank you."

"You turn heads wherever we go."

"My last relationship became strained. I need to stay away from men for a bit."

"I hope he didn't ruin you for the rest of us," he said. "For other men, I mean."

That made me giggle.

"He was an orthopedic surgeon," I said. "Alcoholism is not uncommon in that profession."

"A lot of stress."

I shrugged. "I'm willing to be a fuck buddy for now."

"You just came out and said it."

I smiled at him. "Not with you."

"Of course not."

"I enjoy sex, obviously."

"Is there anyone in your life you're hoping will fulfill that privileged role?"

"Not right now, no."

He blinked at me.

"It's been months," I admitted.

"Since you've had sex?"

"Since I broke up with Austin."

"I'm asking too many personal questions."

"We're at a place now where we can be open."

He gave a slow nod. "After this, let's stay in touch. Have dinner from time to time, that kind of thing."

"I'd love that."

"We get each other."

"We really do."

We took a brief break from conversation to finish off our meal.

Finally, Henry pushed back from the table. "Let's get some sleep."

"Great idea."

After he signed the check, we headed up to our rooms.

We agreed to wake at seven and head out immediately afterwards.

He followed me into my room and then walked through the adjoining door, disappearing for the night.

I stood next to the closed door with my hand pressed against it, listening for him. My gut was telling me that he might change his mind about taking me with him.

"Lotte?" said a voice behind me.

"Jesus!" I jolted and pivoted to face him.

He swallowed a smile. "I thought it would be less invasive to come in this door."

"I was just…"

He closed the gap between us and rested his palms above my head, trapping me between his firm chest and the connecting door. "I want to thank you."

"For what?"

He pressed his chest to mine, setting my body alight and sparking all kinds of responses from his proximity.

"For the housewarming gift," he clarified. "A snow globe of New York."

"My pleasure," I said, sounding breathless. "It's to tide you over until you can fly back and get your city fix."

"I'll treasure it."

"I thought you might hide it away."

"It has pride of place on my desk."

His words warmed my heart.

"Lotte, I'm restricted in many decisions," he said, "as you've personally witnessed." His lips turned up. "But you, you're beautiful and kind and funny. Everything that's good in this world. You'll choose the right path. Trust in yourself."

My lips brushed his. "I do. I mean, I will."

A prayer slipped through my mind that the world would change, and society would allow us to be together.

But I didn't really want that to happen with *this* man?

Did I?

He brushed his fingers up my arm causing the skin to tingle. "Someone needed to say it to you."

"I appreciate it."

He tilted his head in thought. "Offering to accompany me despite the danger reflects on who you really are."

My core ached for him, my body desperate for him to press his chest harder against mine, against my pert nipples, soothing their need.

Take me.

Enter me.

Right here against the dividing door. Bang me into oblivion. He pushed away. "Get some sleep."

I started to protest but he was already reaching for the door knob behind me.

I stepped aside and let him open it.

He walked into his room and closed the door behind him, leaving me alone again.

I contemplated the perilous chemistry between us.

I'd always been the strong one, the woman who knew her boundaries. But for some reason, with him, I surrendered to the point of disorientation—conquered merely by his presence.

CHAPTER TWENTY-ONE

Henry

I T WAS A DICK MOVE TO LEAVE WITHOUT LOTTE.

But she'd be safer at the Ritz Carlton. She could take a dip in the hotel pool, drink cocktails and relax. Swim in the ocean.

She could stay the weekend and fly back with me late Monday, taking advantage of an all-expense paid trip.

Hell, she could even go shopping if she wanted to, using my credit card.

I'd call her later and explain.

With that decision made, I lifted my rucksack and headed out, exiting the hotel, hoping she'd see this from my perspective.

I had the best intentions.

The early morning humidity was barely tolerable. The temperature would heat up as the day went on—not the typical suffocating climate at this time of year, but I'd have to watch my hydration.

The forecast for rain didn't sound good, either, and I'd be on foot by then, heading into the wilderness. I'd trained and trekked in every climate, though, so this should be pleasant in comparison.

My intrigue grew with the possibilities of what lay ahead, of experiencing the freedom I'd pined for while looking out my office window at Cole Tower.

I needed a weekend away.

A Land Rover Discovery was out front, delivered earlier by the rental company. I'd arranged everything in secret in case my well-meaning family decided to scupper my plans.

The four-wheel drive would handle the terrain into the park. I rarely drove these days, so this was my chance to recapture some independence.

I threw my kit onto the backseat and climbed in.

This is it.

I punched my destination into the GPS, quickly orientating to the controls.

A hand slapped against the passenger window.

"You were leaving without me!" Lotte shouted.

I'd failed the first part of the mission—to ditch Lotte.

She tried the locked door handle, and then slammed her palm against the window again.

With a press of a button, I unlocked the door.

She threw her backpack next to my rucksack and then joined me in the front. She'd changed into khakis, a T-shirt and hiking boots and had a pair of designer sunglasses propped on her head.

Lotte huffed in annoyance as she pulled on her seatbelt. "I can't believe you really did that to me."

"Don't take it personally," I said, navigating the Rover onto the road.

"How would you feel if I did that to you?"

I bit down my frustration. "Keeping you safe is my top priority."

"Same."

"I've been in combat situations. You haven't."

"This isn't combat—unless we're talking about the war going on inside your head."

"That's unfair."

She turned in her seat to face me. "You left me stranded."

"In a five-star hotel. How you'd suffer."

"Not the point."

"Forgive me for trying to protect you."

"You're capable of going alone. But why can't you see the benefit of me going with you for support?"

She fell silent.

"At least you left your suitcase behind," I jabbed. "Are you sure you're fit enough to carry your kit?"

"Are you?" She glanced over. "You've been living the high life since you left the military."

I glanced at her. "The occasional yoga class hasn't prepared you for this kind of endurance test."

"Occasional yoga?"

"How else do you achieve your hot body?"

She folded her arms across her chest, appearing quietly amused.

"Not P.C. enough?" I said. "You haven't heard my full repertoire. Settle in, the show's about to start."

"How about we just get this experience over with?"

"Cameron put you up to this. I bet part of your bargain is to report back to him."

"Not true."

"I need total transparency."

"I may send a text to keep him updated."

"Until we have no Internet."

"He told me you'll have SATCOM."

My wristwatch was reliant on a satellite. I'd have to show her how to use it later if anything happened to me.

A sudden crack of thunder startled us both.

Rain pelted the windshield, a deluge of water blurring the view. It was as though the sky had opened and dumped an entire cloud.

"It will pass quickly," she said.

With the windshield wipers on maximum, I could just about

see the road ahead. The other cars were also slowing to accommodate the low visibility.

My gut wrenched at having to slow down.

I was committed now—a tenuous connection was flowing between me and Reese.

Maybe she'd be disheartened that I'd not dropped everything the moment I'd received word she might be alive. Maybe she thought I wasn't coming at all.

My heart squeezed at the thought of finally seeing her again.

A thousand questions crowded my mind.

"See, the rain is lifting," said Lotte, bringing my focus back to her.

This growing affection for my sidekick felt refreshing. The isolation I'd become accustomed to was now lifting.

I wasn't going to share that with her though.

"Tell me you packed for this," I bit out.

She reached up and grabbed the handrail. "I brought my bikini."

"I'm serious."

"Have some faith in me," she said.

"Stay close."

"Close? With you? Deal's off."

"We have one tent." I glanced her way.

"Which is practical," she said.

"We're a team. We need to maintain open communication and stick to our objectives. Remember to stay hydrated."

She threw a salute. "Sir, yes, sir."

"Obedience," I said. "It suits you."

"Ha! This is going to be good for us."

I reached over and grabbed her hand, squeezing it. Her fingers curled around mine and I felt a jolt of excitement for what lay ahead.

"We'll do this together," she said softly.

"Together it is."

I intended on protecting her with every cell of my being.

CHAPTER TWENTY-TWO

Lotte

T HE LAND ROVER HAD TAKEN US INTO THE FAKAHATCHEE Strand Preserve as far as it could possibly go—we'd now have to leave the car behind and set off on foot.

It had taken us just over an hour and a half to get to this point.

We exited the vehicle and stretched our legs, standing on the verge of a subtropical landscape with pinewood flats and endless mangroves. We would soon explore the lush marshes and wilder terrain.

Beyond where we'd parked there stretched a pathway we would soon take. Somewhere, in the middle of these everglades, Henry's ex-girlfriend was living her best life.

Or someone had set one hell of a trap.

Either way, I felt ready.

Thankfully, the humidity in the air felt bearable. The moisture had already flattened my short hair, my bare nape keeping me cool. It wasn't my best look, but I loved the freedom of not caring about my appearance and going makeup free. No need for pretense. No need to impress.

It was like Henry and I had always been good buddies and that felt right.

He folded the map over and inserted it into the left pocket of his pants. "Let's check your kit."

He leaned into the backseat and unzipped my backpack. "We have to throw this away," he said, holding up a packet of mixed nuts like they were radioactive.

I went to grab it.

He held it out of my reach. "We can't have anything that'll attract bears."

"They can smell that?"

"Yes." He strolled over to a trash barrel and threw them in.

I envisioned a bear diving in there later for a snack.

After he appeared satisfied I wasn't carrying any other peanut-like contraband, Henry set our kits by the side of the car and handed me a two-way radio.

"In case we get separated."

It was small enough to clip to my buckle.

He tucked a water filter into a khaki pocket. "We have flares," he reassured me. "If anything happens to me, everything you need to survive is in my kit."

"What might happen to you?"

"Be prepared for everything."

I realized the magnitude of what we were setting out to do.

It was fascinating to be a part of the mystery that was driving Henry.

"Come here," he said.

He proceeded to smear lotion all over my face, his firm fingers gliding over my skin and making it tingle. He also spread it over the back of my neck, even covering my hands.

I beamed at him, feeling nurtured.

Next, we sprayed ourselves with insect repellent. He shoved the can back into his kit.

"I'm glad I came here," I said sincerely.

His frown deepened. "You're not regretting this?"

"Not one bit."

"This is a lot different to hiking in Cali."

"I believe it."

He rested his hands on my shoulders. "If you're tired, thirsty or need a break—or anything else—you tell me."

"I will."

I had to fight the urge to lean in and rest my cheek against his chest and breathe in his masculine scent.

Henry lifted my backpack onto me, making sure the straps were comfortable on my shoulders before swinging his on with the same ease, slipping his arms through the hefty straps.

"Walk ahead of me." He slid on his sunglasses.

I put my shades on, too. "In case a bear tries to eat me?"

"Exactly. That way I'll know which way to run."

"Funny."

He locked the car with the key fob.

Holding up his high-tech wristwatch he said, "We'll use SATCOM for as long as possible."

"That's some watch."

"Everything is on here. But tech fails so we must be prepared either way."

We followed the signs guiding us deeper into the park, eventually falling in step side by side.

"Of all my friends," he said. "You're the most eccentric."

"Me?"

He probably meant my profession.

I glanced at him. "I could say the same about you."

"Are we more alike than we realized?" he joked.

I smiled and we fell quiet for a minute.

"This must seem easy to you," I finally said, referring to his military background.

"The secret is to stay alert. Not let your guard down."

I scanned the towering trees on either side, feeling uneasy for the first time since setting off.

I wasn't sure if I should ask the next question that had been on my mind, but I couldn't hold back. "Do you think you'll be able to forgive her?"

He hesitated for a moment. "Maybe, when I get answers."

"This could be cathartic."

"Let's pick up the pace."

Now and again, we paused to take a drink, admiring the scenery along the way and the awe-inspiring variety of birds. The oppressive heat was bearing down on us as midday neared. Dry bracken crackled beneath our boots and the sounds of tropical birdsong accompanied us.

Occasionally we felt unnerved by rustling leaves or sudden movements in the brush as small animals scurried about.

We were also wary of coming across a mountain lion or panther. The plan was to make ourselves appear as big as possible if we saw one.

I really hoped we didn't.

After several hours of following the uneven foliage-covered pathway, we came across a wooden hut.

I tried to hide my relief when Henry told me we could rest here. If he'd been alone, he'd probably have kept going.

But I desperately needed to pee.

After setting my kit on the front porch, I went inside, instantly hit by a musty, damp smell. I threw my sunglasses on the central wooden table, which was surrounded by rickety wooden chairs. The hut was basic and bare-boned. In the corner, I saw two wooden bunk beds with lumpy mattresses.

Other hikers had left some cans of food and a few bottles of water. Or maybe they'd been left by the park staff.

To my relief, there was an outhouse behind the hut. I used it quickly and held my breath for as long as humanly possible, sucking in air through my mouth as though it would help me deal with the pungent scent of ammonia. This might be the last time I'd get to use a toilet—even one as bad as this.

I washed my hands with a rainwater container. Roughing it

was a new kind of experience. To be honest, the only person I'd do this for was Henry.

Returning to the main hut, I found him peering over the map he'd spread over the table.

"How's our progress?" I asked.

"Making great time."

I wondered if he was just saying that.

On the left side of the table sat a wooden box. Instinctively, Henry lifted the lid and peeked inside. His face went pale and he flipped the lid over, exposing what lay within.

I joined him. "What is it?"

His expression turned hopeful.

I peered inside and read the words on a strip of paper:

"Only those who will risk going too far can possibly find out how far one can go."

"Sounds familiar," I said.

"A quote by T.S. Eliot."

"Hikers left it to encourage us?"

He swallowed hard. "When I dropped Reese off at the airport for her flight to Chile, she was wearing a T-shirt with this exact quote."

As I processed that, I reread the profound words.

"They got hold of old photos, maybe?" he reasoned.

"It's not a coincidence."

"No," he said softly. "I agree."

I blinked at him, stunned he hadn't seen that her wearing this on a T-shirt had been a foreshadowing, an indication that Reese had an adventurous spirit, that she was the kind of character who might just up and disappear on a dangerous exploit.

Henry might not have seen this in her back then because he'd been young himself, unable to sense this woman might fly off without considering those left behind.

Only to turn up years later in a place like this.

With his memory now jarred, I wondered if more clues might become apparent.

Outside, a rustling startled me.

Henry didn't seem to hear it. He just kept staring at that piece of paper like he'd seen a ghost.

I felt a sinking sensation in the pit of my stomach as I hurried outside to retrieve my kit.

It was gone.

I bolted back inside. "Did you bring in my backpack?"

Henry straightened and shook his head.

"I left it on the step."

"You're sure?"

"Of course!"

"Stay here."

"Where are you going?"

He flew out the door without answering.

Fuck.

So stupid of me.

I followed him outside. "I'm sorry!"

The medical kit is gone, too.

Something sinister had just happened.

Throat tight with dread, I waited in the doorway.

If anything happened to Henry, I'd never forgive myself.

I should help him.

But he'd told me to wait.

I stayed put, keeping an eye on his rucksack inside.

Reaching in my pocket, I checked for my iPhone, and then my hand slid down to grab the two-way radio, unclipping it and holding it before me with my finger poised to press the button. This was my lifeline to him.

Please be okay.

"Henry!" I called out.

I heard only silence.

CHAPTER TWENTY-THREE

Lotte

P RESSING MY HAND TO MY CHEST, I TRIED TO SLOW MY breathing and calm my racing heart.

A mosquito buzzed my face. Annoyed, I waved it away frantically.

Sweat trickled down my back and my brow was spotted with perspiration. My entire body felt damp from clamminess, causing my clothes to stick to my skin.

Henry suddenly emerged from the trees and I sucked in a deep breath of relief, securing my two-way radio onto my belt.

He nudged me back inside. "Well, it's gone."

Feeling crushed with embarrassment, I covered my face with my hands to hide my shame. "Someone stole it."

I uncovered my face as Henry came closer. "You okay?" he asked.

"Not really."

"I have enough supplies for two." He gave a shrug. "This is one of the many unforeseen situations to prep for."

"What about the medical kit?"

"I have one, too, including anti-venom. We're all good."

I stepped back. "Why didn't you mention it?"

"Didn't want to steal your thunder."

"Well, my thunder just evaporated." Another realization hit me. "My sleeping bag!"

"I've got you," he said.

"How are you so calm?"

"I'm used to degradation."

"What's that?"

"The enemy fucking with your head."

"They'd steal your kit?"

"Might try. More of a concern is when a sniper takes out your buddy."

"Oh, God."

"They try to weaken your resolve. Breed fear."

"Are you trying to comfort me?" *Because that shit isn't working*. "You don't think someone is trying to sabotage us?"

"Probably just a hiker who ran out of supplies," he suggested. But he didn't seem too convinced.

Uneasiness slithered up my spine. "At least I had nothing personal in there."

He reached around and felt my butt. "There's your phone."

"Right." I tapped my side. "Radio."

The thought of a stranger rifling through my things made me feel violated.

"We'll move faster now," he added. "Your kit slowed us down."

"How are you not pissed off?"

"Losing your luggage is a test of character."

I'd just become the weakest link.

Henry squeezed my arm. "The last time I carried a ruck, grenades were flying over my head. This is a walk in the park. Just remain vigilant."

"Do you have a gun?" I whispered.

"Can't stand them."

I hated them, too, but we were super vulnerable out here.

"What do you call a SEAL who hates guns?" he asked.

"What?"

"A former Navy SEAL." He gave me a tired smile.

I sensed he'd had to endure the stigma of what his PTSD had wrought. I wished I could take all his suffering away.

"Who would do something like this?" I said, changing that gnarly subject.

"Dickheads." He handed me a bottle of water. "Drink."

I took a few swigs. "Could whoever stole it be a part of why you're here?"

"Crossed my mind." He took the water bottle back and sipped from it himself. "Best keep moving."

"Regret bringing me?"

"Never." He hoisted his rucksack onto his back. "I've almost forgotten what the objective is." He gave me a heart-shattering grin.

I grabbed my sunglasses off the table.

He glanced back at that strip of paper containing one of T.S. Eliot's most compelling quotes.

We headed out, both of us scouring the area for the thief, listening to every sound and hardly talking until we were clear of the hut.

Losing my backpack did make it easier on me. Still, I'd never get over the embarrassment.

As though sensing my reticence, Henry said, "We don't blame the victim."

"I take full responsibility."

"If life gives you lemons, make some hard lemonade."

"I love that." He had this calming effect on me.

"Wait here."

"Where are you going?"

I waited for Henry beneath the shelter of an enormous Banyan tree, the kind I'd climbed as a child.

He'd circled back to make sure we weren't being followed, checking for footprints in the dirt and recently broken brush, using the skills he'd once mastered.

I gripped my two-way radio in my sweaty palm, poised to talk with him if I heard or saw anything.

Henry reappeared on the path, offering me a big thumbs-up to indicate we were in the clear.

He continued to competently navigate us onward.

As the day drew on the heat peaked and the temperature began to cool.

Just before sunset, we found a clearing where it seemed safe to set up camp overnight.

Our hideaway was surrounded by tall mangroves, well off the beaten track.

"Stand back," said Henry, who had lain down a square of canvas.

Jaw gaping, I watched as the square was transformed into a state-of-the-art tent. He'd pressed a button on the canvas and a ready-made shelter had sprung up.

The generous height and width allowed two to fit comfortably. This was the kind of luxury camping I'd not expected.

I glanced over at him, impressed.

"Why not?" he said, reading my expression. "I'm over having to sleep rough."

"This is still sleeping rough," I said.

He pointed at the tent. "This is a palace."

Still, we only had one sleeping bag. The thought of having to lie down on the earth wasn't something I had even considered.

Henry set his rucksack close to the tent's entrance. Neither of us was letting it out of our sight.

With a steady hand, he shoved a post into the ground with a camera set on top of it. He pressed a button and the device began slowly spinning.

"It detects all movement in a 360 degree radius," he explained. "Constant monitoring."

"Does that include animals?"

"Any warm-blooded creature." He turned his wrist to show me his high-tech watch. "I'll get a notification."

This man really did have the best gadgets.

I hid behind a tree to clean myself, staying alert for anything that crawled, crept, or attacked. I used refreshing wet wipes to wash off. Henry did the same but he wasn't as bashful.

Before the last drop of light faded, we settled down to eat. Henry handed me a ready-to-eat meal, demonstrating how to pop the packet's sides. The food within heated up. Peeling it open, the inviting scent made my mouth water.

I couldn't remember being this hungry.

Tucking in with a fork, I found the contents tasted like a delicious homemade stew. Afterwards, I handed the degradable package back to Henry.

Exhausted from all the walking, I gladly ducked down to enter the tent. He followed me in and made himself comfortable in a corner.

Henry unrolled the sleeping bag. "There's room for two."

"I'm fine."

"Get in," he ordered. "I'm going to read."

He wasn't crashing like me.

"You're trained to go without sleep?" I asked.

"I only get a few hours usually."

"Really?"

"My sleep pattern never returned to normal." He started to elaborate but then thought better of it.

He was talking about the time he'd been captured. His torturers no doubt kept him awake for days.

I shared a moment of empathy with him, and from his expression I knew he felt grateful that I didn't pry, that I respected what he'd gone through.

I pulled off my shoes, relieved to be free of them.

"Get some sleep." He quirked a brow. "That's an order."

The things he did to me with just his voice would become the stuff of legends.

Gratefully, I slid inside the sleeping bag. I tried to fight sleep, to stay awake to make sure Henry would get some sleep, too.

He peeled back a small square in the roof, revealing the night sky and all those stars. Then he clipped a mosquito repellent to the side of the open flap, making sure we weren't meals for insects as we slept.

"Lotte," he said. "A shooting star."

I caught it just in time. It made me happy, since I had only seen one once before back in L.A., years ago.

I fell asleep to the view of the galaxy.

If I dreamed, I don't remember it.

I stirred awake as dawn was breaking, and saw that Henry was still reading from his phone.

Wiping the sleep out of my eyes, I sat up. "Please tell me you didn't stay awake on my account?"

My heart stuttered with the realization that no one had ever done something this remarkable for me.

Leisurely, he stretched.

Had I just witnessed Henry's compassionate side?

"Get some sleep," I said. "I'll keep watch."

He gave a nod of gratitude.

I eased out of the sleeping bag and we swapped positions. I sat where he had been a few moments before and he lay down on top of the sleeping bag.

"Are you comfortable?" I asked.

"Absolutely." He rolled up one of his sweatshirts and created a pillow out of it.

"I'll watch over you now," I said.

"Still have an adrenaline rush." Because Henry was moving closer to answers that he'd needed for decades.

"At least try."

"I know this seems futile to everyone else," he reasoned. "But I need to do this."

"It's not futile."

With his head resting on his hands, he glanced over at me. "Comfortable?"

"Yes, totally. I haven't had this much fun in years. And I bet it's nice to get out of the office."

"And a dark dungeon." He winked.

"I'm keeping you awake. Sleep."

"It's hot." He sat up and peeled his shirt up and over his head. *Oh, God.*

He'd revealed his chiseled torso, the low V at his lower abdomen. This man was ripped and so damn fine.

Being trapped inside this small space with him was almost too much to handle. I diverted my gaze, trying not to stare, my flesh ignited by the vision of the perfect alpha male laying a few feet away.

He settled back down. "I'll keep my pants on."

My heart fluttered and I tried to think of something to say. "I'm a sleep monster," I blurted out.

He grinned. "Hadn't noticed."

"Tell me I didn't snore."

"No, you're definitely in the sleeping beauty category."

I shook my head, amused, trying to hide my arousal.

I bit my lip to inject some pain into the mix, hoping to distract my mind from going *there.*

"If anything happens to me," he said. "I died happy."

"No regrets?"

"One."

"Are you comfortable sharing?"

He turned his head to stare at me for the longest time. "At Charlie's."

"Oh?"

"I get in my own way sometimes."

"What do you mean?"

"In the storage room."

Where we had sheltered from the earthquake.

I smiled at him.

He frowned as though he regretted saying it. "I've made this awkward."

"You've made it interesting."

"I have every intention of keeping you safe. Even from a man like me."

"I would never want to repeat what happened between us at Charlie's."

Disappointment flashed over his face. "Understandable."

"Given the same opportunity, I'd not end it with a kiss." A frisson rushed through me.

"Careful, or I'll—"

I moved quickly, cutting him off by pressing my lips to his. Not thinking, only reacting and trusting this moment was ours.

Then I eased back a little to make sure I had read him right.

His intense gaze met mine. "Say you want this."

"Shall I show you what I wanted to do the first time I met you?"

"At Chrysalis?" He broke into a grin. "Don't spank me."

I laughed at that.

"You have a smart but very kissable mouth." He moved closer, pulling me on top of him.

His tongue darted into my mouth, exploring and conquering, conveying a once hidden affection, creating sparks of arousal between us.

I straddled him, easing his hands above his head and crossing them at the wrists. "Like this," I said softly.

"I could stay like this forever."

Henry Cole was a dangerous romantic.

Shuffling down his body, reaching his thighs, I unzipped his pants and then glanced up at him for his nod of permission.

Once given, I eased his hefty girth out of his trousers, his impressive erection enlarging in the grip of my palm.

I dipped my head between his legs to taste his tip.

He exhaled in a rush.

Stroking his substantial shaft, I ran the tip of my tongue along his frenulum, circling the head of his cock and moving down to its base before rising to his tip again.

Taking him all the way into my mouth, I suckled, bobbing

briskly to give him the best blowjob he'd ever experienced—crafting pleasure with licks, laps, and a taut mouth to deliver endless sensuality.

He lowered a hand to cover his eyelids as he endured the erotic bliss, breathing heavily, and peeking between his fingers now and again with an expression full of wonder.

This meant more than sex. It was connecting with him on a whole different level using a language beyond words, a transcendent stirring of emotions.

I had seen the real Henry, the man who dealt with situations with an impressive calmness. A man who had endured deep pain. A man who had been kind and patient.

Those shockwaves from our first meeting had never worn off. Ripples of silence meshed with our sighs and murmurs.

Soothing him was a rare gift that felt good.

While stroking his cock as my mouth suckled his shaft, I witnessed a tremble surge through his body.

He exhaled sharply. "Lotte!"

I glanced up and saw he was close to release.

"The first time I saw you in the dungeon," he said huskily. "This is what I wanted to do to you."

"To me?"

He sat up and lifted me onto him. "Let me show you."

His right arm slid behind my back before rolling us both over with the strength of a gladiator—and the physique of one, too.

His body rose above mine, and then he moved down to reach my waistband, tugging my pants down to reveal my panties.

"I should shower first," I said, feeling self-conscious.

"I need to taste you."

As he pulled off my underwear, I lifted my lower half to help him remove them.

He dipped low, his hot breath shimmying over my sex as his tongue swept along my clit with brilliant precision.

I shuddered beneath him, gripping the sides of the sleeping bag as I watched the erotic vision of his mouth possessing my pussy with a passionate frenzy. The tickle of his hair on my inner thighs sent a shiver through me. With large, gentle hands, he parted my labia for better access to that wetness.

I moaned, arching my back with pleasure.

With his face buried between my thighs, he guided me into oblivion his wicked kiss there driving me wild.

My climax felt so intense I struggled to breathe.

His flicking tongue circled faster, the electrifying sensations making me swoon.

Another climax owned my soul.

Oxygen refused to refill my lungs as I gasped through the dizzying waves of ecstasy, soaring ever higher.

"Hands above your head," he ordered, mimicking what I'd made him do.

My arms flung upward and I obediently crossed my wrists one over the other. My legs were raised and widened by a man intent on staying between my thighs, wanting to deliver yet another heart-racing orgasm.

"I've wanted to make this mine since we first met," he growled.

"It's yours," I whispered.

My body shivered with delight, and I barely had the strength to respond to the control he'd taken.

He was like a Viking storming the shores and claiming his lover.

"Want me inside you?" he asked gruffly.

"God, yes," I pleaded, needing his fullness.

I felt that delicious sensation of his tip tapping my pussy.

His hips rose as he entered me with a gentle persuasion. He declared ownership with a deeper thrust inside me, stretching my channel wider and wider until he was fully inside. His ripped body was poised above me, supported by muscled arms to protect me from his full weight.

A conquering Adonis.

He began pummeling into my sex, my own hips meeting him halfway in a show of desperate need. I wrapped my legs around his back, clutching him to me so that his hips ground against my clit deliciously as we rocked together as one.

The sensations that surged through me were familiar and extreme.

Because of *him.*

I nuzzled into his neck, inhaling his scent.

"Fuuuuck," he said harshly. "You're so damn sexy."

I unabashedly scratched his back with an unquenchable desire.

The cold-hearted aristocrat surrounded by a wall of steel had finally let me in.

We were like fire; red-orange molten lava spilling over endless rocks, a dizzying passion that had finally been unleashed.

He rolled his pelvis to massage my clit, slowly at first and then faster as he ground me into the sleeping bag. I pounded him just as hard, his hips a welcoming piston inside me.

I quivered beneath him, both of us soaked in sweat and slickly shimmering as our bodies crashed into each other, breathless from this unstoppable passion—locked in an embrace that neither of us wanted to break.

He slowed his pace a little and stared down at me. "We were inevitable," he said huskily. "You see that, right?"

"Yes," I gasped.

Even if we'd denied ourselves this, destiny had a way of proving itself right.

Raising my T-shirt and bra, he cupped my breasts and squeezed my nipples, pinching and tugging them until I groaned. Then he lowered his head, his warm breath saturating my nipple, nuzzling there, his flickering tongue delivering strokes as he suckled.

"We were always going to fuck," he growled.

I cupped his face with my palm. "We were."

"We fought it for as long as humanly possible."

"We needed this." *I needed him*, but I shouldn't say it.

I refused to try and tame this explosion of chemistry that had sparked free.

Henry resumed thrusting with force, my legs spreading wider

to aid his plunges as I gave myself entirely to this man wild with want, reveling in the way he overpowered me.

There was only room for one dominant, and he demanded it be him.

The rush of pleasure surged like a tidal wave carrying me away, carrying me under.

Henry stopped moving, his heat spilling into me, my pussy filling with the sin of him, my heart and soul lusting for more.

Finally, when we'd fucked ourselves into exhaustion, I lay beside him, gathering my thoughts on how far we'd come in our friendship.

I still felt an unquenchable yearning.

We lay close together, both of us staring up at the breaking dawn, feeling the pulsing rush of lovers.

"You need to sleep," I whispered.

"You feel safe enough?"

"Yes."

He slid his watch off his wrist and then slid it onto mine, giving me access to his perimeter tracking app.

I felt glad for the responsibility, for the trust he had in me.

Henry rested his head on my chest, his breathing growing quieter.

Finally, he fell asleep in my arms.

Our passion had burned brightly, and what had just happened between us was as rare as one of those shooting stars.

Pressing my lips to his forehead, I braced my heart for when he awoke, fearing he'd regret what we'd done.

Or worse, seeing he had conflicting emotions.

Because that would mean hope for an *us*.

And that scared me more than anything.

CHAPTER TWENTY-FOUR

Henry

I AWOKE TO SEE LOTTE HOVERING OVER ME, OFFERING ME A cup of coffee that she'd just brewed. She had apparently found what she needed in my rucksack.

A delicious aroma of beans wafted in the air around us.

Her bright face and enduring kindness were something new to crave.

I felt different about everything—that underlying dread was gone.

Wrapping my hands around the warm cup, I sipped the invigorating drink that reminded me I had a purpose back home.

The familiar taste of quality beans quickly buzzed me awake.

Together, we packed up the tent and the rest of the equipment, neatly placing it all in the rucksack—including the infrared tracking system.

We set off along the trail with that familiar comfort level between us, words not being necessary. She wasn't afraid of the quiet—didn't need to fill the spaces between our conversations.

Watching this mystifying raven-haired woman walk ahead pleasantly distracted me from the threat of a downpour.

Dark storm clouds were gathering.

Lotte had no idea how easily she'd broken down my defenses and reached me—reached that part of my heart that had once lain dormant.

Ironically, just before seeing my old love I had found a new one—but Charlotte was so much more.

Fate had conspired to keep me and Reese apart. For the first time, I saw the wisdom in it. This brief encounter was a buffer to potential pain.

The goddess walking ahead had bewitched me.

Going back to what Reese and I had once was simply impossible. Moving forward with this fresh relationship, however, filled me with hope.

She'd metaphorically de-fibbed my heart back to life, causing my pulse to quicken and enabling me to relish my existence once more.

My company would see a CEO returning with a healthier attitude. Being a Cole carried a heavy responsibility. Now, I could envision not having to endure that future alone.

Still, we needed more time before the press discovered Lotte—or, more specifically, her profession. I could protect her from that only to an extent. Keeping her a secret for as long as possible was the wisest decision.

I paused for a second, considering whether to discuss what had happened between us a few hours ago.

She glanced back at me with concern. "Everything okay?"

Let her say it first.

Say that it meant something to her.

She came closer and rested a hand on my forearm. "We're here to reunite you with a good friend. Let's get you there."

"I've waited decades," I bit out. "Now we're on my clock."

"Good for you," she said, glancing back the way we'd come. "Tell me what's on your mind?"

She hesitated, looking uncertain.

"Say it," I demanded.

She let out a sigh, "The thought of never kissing you ever again…"

I lowered my shoulder to rid myself of the rucksack. It slid off my arm, landing heavily on the ground.

"I respect that's how things need to go," she said. "I'm mature enough—"

"No, you don't." I nudged her backwards toward a tree.

She was visibly shaking. "You have this way of making me say things."

"Need me to show you what that meant?" I towered over her, pinning her against the tree. "You and me, back there?"

She peered up. "Being here is not about me."

"It is." I rested my hand against her throat possessively. "It is now."

We could navigate anything because we were smart enough to make this work.

We could hide our affair.

A woman like this could handle secrets.

She met my gaze. "I hate wanting you this much."

Sliding my hand down her pants, I cupped her pussy, pressing that delicate nub, massaging it with the tip of a finger.

Her jaw slackened and she moaned softly.

She gripped my forearms, her fingernails digging into my sleeves and sending another surge of arousal coursing through me.

"We have something that deserves to be protected," I whispered.

"Yes." Her tone sounded uncertain.

Leaning in, I nuzzled into her neck and breathed in her soft scent before gliding my lips along her jawbone and cheek until I reached her mouth, hers opening wide to greet mine.

I claimed her soft lips, both of us demanding more from

each other in a frenzied kiss, tongues sharing what useless words couldn't convey—that we were fast becoming more.

So much more.

Seconds ago, she'd shared her fear that we may never kiss again.

I answered her with truth. "You miss me kissing you like this?"

"Yes."

"Let me rectify that." Gripping her chin, I took possession of her mouth again, our tongues clashing with passion fused with desire, leisurely fighting her lips with mine. Our need for this, for us, was frenzied and real as we both responded to this yearning.

She undulated against the tree as I continued to play with her clit.

"Henry," she stuttered. "I'm close."

"I want to watch you come."

She glanced down to witness the movements of my hand bringing her closer.

"Eyes on me," I demanded.

"I'm going to…"

"Does your cunt feel nice?" I growled.

"Oh, God." She half smiled and then shivered in pleasure.

Leaning low, I suckled her nipple through her shirt. She tugged the material down with her bra cup to give me access to bare skin. My mouth clamped her pertness, and I suckled her breast rhythmically until she gasped for air.

"What if someone sees?" she said breathlessly.

"Let them."

We were in the middle of nowhere.

And surely, voyeurs didn't faze her.

"This is impossible," she said. "I can't fall for you." Lotte searched my face. "This doesn't make sense."

"Want me to stop?"

She shook her head. "No."

I leaned closer to her ear. "Say 'my cunt is yours.'"

"It is."

"Say it," I demanded.

"My pussy is yours." Her jaw slackened.

Dominating this fiery woman was easily one of my finest achievements. I took pleasure in seeing her become weak and wanton in response to my ministrations.

Slowing the circular motion of my fingertip, I focused on her expression to gauge her desire.

I gruffly ordered, "Not yet."

"What you do to me."

With my other hand I reached for her wrist and grasped the other, lifting them above her head and pressing them against the bark, holding her captive like that. My other hand was still beneath her waistband, fingers flicking her in a leisurely circle.

"Eyes on me when you come," I demanded.

Her moans grew louder.

A bird took flight, seemingly startled by our heated passion and my taking of this precious woman.

The defiant look in her eyes was fading fast.

Her clit throbbed beneath my touch, an orgasm sweeping over her.

Her eyelashes fluttered, her body writhing.

"Seeing you come is the most beautiful thing I've ever witnessed," I said huskily, my throat tight with arousal.

She shuddered as her climax shimmied over her.

"Henry," she whispered.

Letting go of her wrists, I reached around to the back of her head to protect it from the tree. Still cupping her pussy with my palm, I leaned in and again stole another kiss, our tongues lashing, mouths clashing, her body weakening as she fell against me.

Finally, I broke away and kissed her forehead.

She reached for my zipper.

"No." I coaxed her hand away. "We keep moving."

She softened her tone. "I don't expect anything to come from this."

I tipped her chin. "We've crossed that line."

"It's impossible," she said breathlessly. "You and me."

"Don't."

"But—"

"First, we need to get out of this alive."

"When we get back—"

"When we get back, we'll make it work," I said, trying to control my roiling emotions.

CHAPTER TWENTY-FIVE

Lotte

WALKING ONWARDS, WE CONTINUED TO NAVIGATE THE overgrown pathway.

Henry Cole had always seemed out of my realm. Now, it felt foolhardy to even go there.

"Let's not be intimate again," I suggested. "Until we're home."

He gave me a heart-stopping smile to lower the tension, saying so much with that one gesture—we were having trouble keeping our hands off each other.

The afternoon humidity felt sticky on my skin. The sky's overcast grey clouds were threatening to break.

We sheltered beneath a waterproof tarp Henry held above our heads, with me huddling close to his towering frame. Rain pelted the plastic sheet, the air turning cooler as we waited for the storm to pass.

We weren't meant to get *this* close.

Henry would soon reunite with his lost love. Their future together remained uncertain. My desire had to be quenched. I didn't want to complicate this situation and make it more difficult for him.

But the chemistry between us was so intense.

I told myself our brief affair would end after this expedition. Peering up at Henry, I caught dark desire in his expression, contradicting my concerns.

"You okay?" he shouted over the rain.

"It's cooling us down," I yelled back.

He looked up and flinched, spotting something above us. Yanking the tarp off our heads, he grabbed my hand and pulled me off the trail.

I tried to see what was threatening us, but falling rain was soaking my face.

"What's wrong?"

"A drone," he said.

"What? Out here?"

Finally, he led me beneath a cluster of mangroves and we paused.

He caught his breath quickly. "Not sure if it saw us."

"Someone is tracking us?" I was panting from the exertion.

"The question is who."

"Reese?"

My clothes were soaked and sticking to my body, threatening to slow me down.

"If it is hers, and she failed to make contact," he said, equally soaked, "I'll be pissed."

He studied the map on his watch, wiping rain droplets off it.

"We'll cut through here. It's dense but we'll avoid being tracked. The drone won't make it through the trees."

Trying to hide my dread, I followed him through the dense forest, scouring the area for dangerous animals—or anything that might spring up and bite us.

I hated being engulfed by foliage.

"Are you sure this is the right way?" I called out.

He turned back at me. "Our next stop is less than a klick away."

"What?

"We're close."

"What if the boat's not there?"

"We continue on foot."

The thought of seeing anything slithering or crawling close by freaked me out.

I tried to keep doubt and fear at bay.

Calm. Down.

This is good for me.

Without my previous suffering, I'd never have striven for a better life—turning to gratitude to see the brighter side. Things hadn't always been easy. So many welcome lessons had been imparted during my time working at Enthrall and Chrysalis.

Maybe this helped with my decision to move on—because it was so damn scary to leave all that behind.

Leave them behind.

This, though, was scarier.

I was grateful for the experiences that had made and unmade me, forging me into this woman.

Whatever happened now, my time with Henry would always be cherished. I'd have that, at least.

Let him go.

Let him reunite with his lost love if that's what he wants. Give them both the second chance they deserve.

The chance he deserves.

What we had shared was no more than a moment in time between us.

Letting Henry know my thoughts might even reassure him.

Still, parting wouldn't be easy.

I tripped and he caught me as I felt against him, grinning back at me as though he was proud to see me keeping up.

I gave him a big smile back.

The sound of a gunshot ricocheted around us, causing birds in the brush nearby to soar up into the sky.

Bang.

Another gunshot.

I bolted left, sprinting forward several paces and then glancing back, not seeing Henry. I crouched, waiting for him to catch up, my mouth dry with panic. I was terrified of being mistaken for a deer by a wayward hunter.

Rain poured down my face, obscuring my vision. I blinked, still unable to see Henry. I scanned the trees, my heart pounding in fear.

More shots rang out.

Henry!

I heard leaves rustling as creatures scurried for cover.

Pivoting, I realized I was alone with no idea how to find Henry.

My breathing grew ragged as I stepped through the brush and out of the dense trees, halting next to a slow running river, feeling wary of alligators that might be basking on the edge.

With relief, I saw a small motorboat tethered to a tree.

But then I noticed movement near the boat and froze, unable to breathe.

A slim, weathered man stood near the water, pointing his rifle at me.

CHAPTER TWENTY-SIX

Henry

TERROR BIT INTO MY BONES, TURNING MY BLOOD COLD.
Whiteness blurred my vision as I crouched low against
the base of a tree, palms pressing against the rough bark.
Fear erased my ability to think.

Cowering, I felt for my weapon, reaching for my Heckler &
Koch, precious hardware that would help me fight my way out
of this.

It's not there.

I took off my rucksack and patted it down for my pistol. I
had no flak jacket.

What the fuck is going on? Where am I?

I dropped my rucksack and reached for my two-way radio,
staring down at the plastic gadget.

A piece of crap? Doesn't make sense.

I stared at my shirtsleeve, camouflage material—not my
uniform.

I buried my head in my arms.

Nothing made sense.

Capture was certain if I didn't break free from this position. I had to pull myself together.

Breathe.

Orientate.

I scanned the area for clues, my flesh crawling and uneasiness saturating each breath. My stomach threatened to spill my last meal.

Wrong terrain.

Dex?

No. He's not here.

My skin felt cold and clammy, sweat slithering down my spine.

Count to ten.

Dig deep.

With trembling hands, I reached out for *her.*

"Let me take your foot."

I was in a luxury bathroom, a woman in a silk dress sitting opposite me. She was saying something. *"Just breathe."*

I can do that.

A shimmering beauty.

I was remembering—envisioning Lotte.

"Henry!" Her voice broke through to me.

I sprang up, hurtling in the direction of the threat—desperate to find her.

CHAPTER TWENTY-SEVEN

Lotte

"DON'T SHOOT!" I SAID, RAISING MY HANDS IN THE AIR. Terror made me tremble. I had to force myself not to run. I couldn't make any sudden movements and give the man a reason to pull the trigger on his rifle.

I needed this guy to stay calm.

And I needed to find Henry, who could be anywhere. My heart ached knowing that he was suffering alone.

The man's weathered face showed his age to be around sixty. He had on a bright orange jacket, so a hunter, maybe?

"What are you doing out here?" he said with a Floridian lilt.

"Hiking."

"Alone?"

"No. Please lower your gun."

He lowered the weapon but kept it ready.

"I appreciate that," I said, letting my arms fall to my sides.

"Was that your drone? 'Cause we shoot drones around here."

"No, I—"

"Where's the rest of your party?"

Telling him we'd gotten separated wasn't a good plan. Making him believe someone else could have a weapon trained on him might make him reconsider shooting me.

I glanced at the motorboat, hoping it had been left for us. "Are you hunting?"

He was defiantly quiet.

Those gunshots had clearly been a warning.

He followed my line of slight. "Going down river?"

A gut feeling told me to be honest. "At some point."

"What's your business?"

"What's yours?"

He glanced at his rifle as though to say, "I'm the one with the gun."

Fucker.

Sucking in a deep breath, I said, "We're meeting up with someone."

"Who?"

"Her name's Reese."

His expression darkened.

"I've never met her," I said, reading disgust in his expression. "I'm from L.A. I can't wait to get back, to be honest. I'm a city girl, though I'm originally from Florida."

"Where?"

"Miami." I stepped forward. "You?"

"Naples." He looked impatient. "I gotta get back to work."

"What kind of work?"

"Security for Community Development."

"I've not heard of them."

"Your friend Reese has."

I shrugged. "We're just here for a couple of days. My partner has a SATCOM. Everything we do is being tracked and traced."

He scowled. "What's your business with Reese?"

"You know her?"

"Know *of* her."

I shuddered. He had confirmed that Reese was alive and well and living in this terrifying place.

"I haven't heard anything about what she does out here," I said. "I'm just here for the weekend."

"How are you finding it so far?" His sinister grin revealed missing teeth.

"It's a once in a lifetime experience. But I miss my shower. I'm Charlotte, by the way."

He grimaced and then said, "Tony."

I stared at the boat, guessing it had to be for us.

He studied me. "Hoping to use that to get to your friend's camp?"

"I'm not sure." I took another step forward. "We don't want to take someone else's boat by mistake. This trip wasn't well organized, to be honest."

I hoped this made us sound close to incompetent and less of a threat.

"You can see I'm unarmed," I added.

His expression relaxed a little.

"Did you fly a drone over us earlier?"

"That's them," he said flatly. "Spying on us."

I shook my head in feigned disbelief. "An invasion of privacy."

That seemed to appease him. "They make our lives hell."

"I'm sorry."

Tony rested the butt of his gun next to his feet.

"That for bears?" I asked.

"Protestors." He narrowed his gaze, looking past me. "He with you?"

Turning sharply, I saw Henry emerge from the trees. "Everything's okay," I called out to him.

I watched him for any sign he might act rashly. I didn't want him to spook the man, and I didn't want Tony to make Henry go rogue.

My pulse quickened as I watched Henry's response. He didn't even raise his hands as he casually walked over to stand beside me. Perspiration spotted his brow, and I could see he looked pale.

"This is Tony," I told Henry. "He's protecting his employer's land."

"That's right," said Tony.

"If you'll excuse us," I said. "We need to get going."

Tony stared at us for a moment before offering a nod of approval. Then he turned and headed off into the trees.

I turned to face Henry. "Are you okay?"

He gave an uneasy nod.

"This is for us." I pointed to the boat.

In a daze, he followed me toward the motorboat. Both of us climbed inside and kneeled to cope with the rocking. He sat near the engine and set his kit down beside him.

I sat opposite him. He appeared to be shell-shocked, caught in a state of panic.

"You need something sweet." Kneeling before his rucksack, I rifled through it.

Henry shook his head, as though he were trying to escape the waking nightmare.

"We're safe." Pulling out a chocolate bar wrapped in silver packaging, I ripped it open with my teeth and held it up for him. "Eat."

He blinked as he took the candy from me, biting into it and chewing.

He declined the second bar I offered.

"With your height and weight, you need two of these. I need to get sugar into your bloodstream. Eat."

He looked at me with a pained expression, his eyes pleading for my forgiveness. None was needed. I hoped my kindness conveyed that.

In time, the adrenaline in his system would lessen, and the fight-or-flight response would diminish.

"We don't have to continue," I said softly. "We can turn around. Go home."

He shook his head, likely believing we had already come too far to give up.

Cupping his face, I said, "You came to find me."

A gentle but strong hand brushed me away.

I sat back to give him space.

He accepted the water container I offered. After taking a few swigs, he offered it back to me.

I took a few sips myself, realizing how thirsty I was after that scare.

"We're a team," I reassured him. "Watching out for each other is what we do."

Calmer, he took another bite of the chocolate bar and offered me the other half.

"No, thanks." I smiled at him. "You finish it."

Henry gave a nod as though coming out of a trance.

"Reese came through with the boat." I waited to see his reaction. "That man back there told me he knows a woman named Reese who lives out here."

With each passing second, answers were drawing nearer.

Henry's gaze softened. "That's good news."

I hoped it was her. Witnessing Henry's disappointment would be a new kind of pain if it wasn't.

On the opposite bank, a tropical white bird squawked and flapped its wings. We shared a glance filled with awe.

"Reese," he whispered.

The way he'd spoken her name felt like a strike to my heart.

But this had always been the plan.

This boat would take us to *her*.

The woman who'd believed all this was a good idea. Maybe some part of her clung to him like he clearly did to her.

I'd support their reunion. I'd do anything for this man.

I had to push through this gut-wrenching dread that I was about to lose him forever to a ghost from his past.

I'd fallen deeper into love than I could ever remember, and I would soon be ripped apart when this river delivered him into the arms of his lost love.

I hid my inner turmoil and gave him a rueful grin. "I'm hoping you know how to pilot this boat."

CHAPTER TWENTY-EIGHT

Henry

A s I navigated the boat down the river, I fought
for some semblance of self-respect.

Right now I couldn't bring myself to make eye contact with her.

I wanted to stare at Charlotte's beautiful, flushed and trusting
face. Both of us were baking in the sun.

And we were both showing the strain of this trip.

I couldn't help but think about the remarkable way Lotte had
coped with the crisis back on land, her impressive calmness in
dealing with those gunshots.

She deserves a better man.

Guilt for agreeing to bring her along had soaked into my
bones. Yet having her here with me made it feel as though I had
an anchor in this sea of chaos.

This futile journey had me second guessing myself.

At least this motorboat was not dissimilar to others I'd mastered at BUDS. Each one of those training days was proving valu-
able even today.

With a careful hand on the rudder, I directed us down the center of the river so as not to run ashore.

An array of tropical birdsong filled the air. On the right bank, a deer drank from the water. Lotte observed it with equal wonder. The thought of predators lurking beneath the water made me shudder. The fearless animal watched us watching him as we floated by.

Tall trees were surrounded by the lush marshland, with palm trees lending a tropical flair. From the swaying sawgrass came constant sounds made by crickets and other insects.

My blood sugar had been low and eating a snack had lifted my brain fog, helping clear my thoughts and ensuring I could focus. I kept a constant watch for alligators—along with all the other critters that lived on or beneath the marshland.

"Henry," Lotte called to me.

She waved a can of insect repellant to remind me we needed to reapply it. I let her spray it over my neck and hands, covering my exposed skin. She gently smeared it over my face.

"Not the forehead," she said. "We don't want sweat dripping into your eyes."

I've dealt with worse.

She studied me carefully. "How are you doing?"

"Fine."

Her gaze was filled with sympathy.

"Don't." I turned away.

"Oh, shut up." She sprayed herself with the repellant. "This is my resting bitch face."

She always had a way of lightening the mood.

But what had happened back there had to be brought into the light. "I'm sorry."

"You were letting me deal with the guy because you knew I'm more capable of dealing with assholes."

"Maybe Cameron was right."

"Not true. You've gotten us this far."

"That man could have killed you."

"You came for me!" she said. "You found me."

"After you'd disarmed him."

She grabbed my arm, and repeated softly, "You came for me."

"I put you in danger."

"You can't control the world, Henry." She gripped my fore-arm tighter. "You're doing your best and so am I. That is all we can ask of each other."

The boat rocked and I caught her as she lost her balance.

Instinctively, I hugged her.

"I'll always come for you. If anything happened to you, I'd never forgive myself." I pressed my lips to her cheek.

"I'm right here."

"Oh, God," I muttered, grimacing at the taste of the repellant she'd dabbed on her face. "My lips are numb." I released her and wiped my mouth with my sleeve.

Her laughter rippled around us.

Nature came alive to the sound of her amusement, but quieted as we progressed through the marshland. I slowed the engine and our gentle drifting down river disturbed little of the wildlife.

Overwhelmed by the enduring heat, I wanted to rip off my sweat-soaked shirt and toss it. The moist, heavy air saturated my lungs. "I'd pay a million bucks for an air-conditioner right now."

Lotte nodded in agreement. "A cold glass of sparkling water with ice and a slice of lemon."

"Is it me or is it getting hotter?"

"Let's take a few minutes. Turn off the engine."

"We'll keep it idling, just in case."

"Good idea."

Sweat poured off me.

We passed the bottle of water back and forth, exhaling in long breaths as though that might help.

"When they captured me," I said, recalling how I'd felt this kind of heat before, "I used to envision myself walking along the beach and setting foot in the ocean. I'd peer down and imagine waves lapping my ankles. That symbolized freedom—standing in the Pacific Ocean one last time."

"That's beautiful."

"Mia persuaded me to leave Big Bear. It was Cameron who helped me take that first step to the ocean." My eyes broke hers. "I just never went back." I gave a shrug, finding my thoughts drifting to the memory of that suffocating cell in the Middle East.

Lotte remained quiet.

A flutter of wings caught my attention.

A tall white bird spread its feathers and flew over our heads. We watched in awe as it ascended.

"An egret!" Lotte called out.

"Of course, you should recognize much of the wildlife."

"I've lived in L.A. a long time. I'm familiar with many of the birds, though."

"This is certainly an interesting place," I said.

"It really is special."

I glanced at the SATCOM—the connection was understandably down. We were surrounded by trees shading our signal.

"A once in a lifetime experience," Lotte piped up.

"Never to be repeated." I shook my head. "This place. Not you, obviously."

"That's lovely of you to say."

I searched her eyes for the truth that she felt the same about me. "You've seen me at my worst."

She reached up and cupped my face. "There is a crack in everything, that's how the light gets in," she whispered.

"Hemingway?"

"Leonard Cohen. See." She pointed her fingertip. "I can teach you something, too."

The ever-changing scenery offered up a brilliant backdrop of mystery.

"I wish you'd known me back when I was in the military. I had some neat skills."

"Still do."

"Let's get you home first."

"I see you, Henry," she said, her tone sincere. "I love what I see."

"I couldn't have done this without you."

"Friends always take care of each other."

I studied her face. "We've gone beyond that, right?"

She fixed her attention on the dense forestry. "We find her, then regroup."

Reese had become a complication that needed resolving.

There'd be no romantic reunion. No sparking of passion between me and the woman I'd once sworn to protect.

She had destroyed me.

I'd been tortured beyond recognition, twice in my life. I wasn't about to self-inflict the same kind of pain.

No more drama.

No going back.

I continued to navigate us effortlessly down the river.

We flowed beneath the low hanging arches of a wide mangrove tunnel, branches strewn over our heads like nature's cathedral, crickets accompanying us with their vibrant mating song.

Occasional ripples appeared on the surface of the water.

Lotte took it all in.

I watched her closely, beguiled by her serenity, her rosy face framed by short hair as she leaned back in the boat, trying to endure the sticky heat. Now and again she would catch my eye, her face lighting up to show her enchantment with every passing second.

The canopy of plants stretching over our heads eventually cleared as the river widened.

"I forgot to ask," said Lotte. "Who is watching Dex?"

"Shay," I said. "He takes him running. Nothing changes much in his routine."

"I can watch him." She brightened. "If you ever need a dog sitter."

"I'll take you up on that."

Her expression turned dark. Following her line of sight, I saw what had changed her mood.

A wooden dock.

"This is it," I said.

Slowly, I guided the boat towards it and then killed the engine.

"Back there," said Lotte, "that guy called Reese a protestor."

She was only mentioning this now, probably waiting for the right time. My episode had kept her cautious around me. I'd have to earn back her trust.

"That drone wasn't his," she added.

"They're expecting us."

I turned and looked at an opening in the trees that led inland, camouflaged by towering trees.

"Stay here," I said.

"We should go together."

I shook my head. "If something happens to me, find your way back." I pointed to the rucksack. "A copy of the map is in there."

She sat up. "No, Henry. We should stay together."

"This is how it's done." One of us had to set off on reconnaissance to make sure the way was safe. That someone had to be me. "If I'm not back in twenty minutes, leave."

She gasped. "What if they have guns?"

"If you hear shots, turn the boat around. Understand?"

"No, I won't."

"That's an order."

"Fuck off."

"It'll be fine," I said.

My gut was telling me this was it—these coordinates had led us to this exact checkpoint.

After securing the boat to the wooden post, I stepped onto the jetty and gave Lotte a reassuring nod.

"Wait!" She handed me a bottle of water. "How do you feel about seeing her again?" she blurted out nervously.

How did I feel?

Seeing Reese after all these years would feel surreal. Seeing her alive would be cathartic.

All the guilt I'd held on to could finally be released.

Familiar memories flooded my thoughts.

Lotte would be safe. She was my priority. Moving forward, I would make this up to her, prove I could protect her.

Going on alone was my way of letting her see that.

Her compassion, kindness and strength were all remarkable gifts I'd not take for granted.

She gave me a thumbs-up, face bright with understanding.

I strolled along the wooden slats toward the opening in the trees.

CHAPTER TWENTY-NINE

Lotte

I WAITED FOR A FEW MINUTES—WHICH FELT LIKE A LIFETIME—for Henry to reappear to tell me we were safe.

I'd never been good at following orders, and I refused to let him walk into danger alone. We'd come too far for that to happen. He'd be pissed off if I disobeyed, but he'd have to get over himself. I'd always listened to my intuition.

And right now that small, quiet voice was telling me to follow him.

Huffing with exertion, I hoisted Henry's rucksack and threw it onto the wooden slats of the dock, straining my back.

Gripping the wooden pillar, I climbed out of the boat.

I slid my arms into the straps of the rucksack and shrugged it on, immediately staggering backwards.

Whoa!

I almost tipped over into the water.

Great. Getting eaten by a gator would be totally embarrassing at this point. And taking his kit with me would literally doom my spirit to purgatory.

Leaning forward to tolerate the weight of his kit, I huffed at its weight. Henry made lifting it look so effortless.

I trudged after him, walking face first into a cobweb.

I frantically brushed the sticky strands out of my face, hoping nothing fell on me.

And then I saw Henry.

He was at the edge of a clearing, standing before a crowd. He stood stock-still, staring at them. None of them had weapons, as far as I could tell. Taking a leap of faith, I moved toward him, closing the gap between us.

I stopped beside Henry, showing solidarity with him. Leaning over, I let his ruck slide off my shoulder. It landed with a thud near his feet.

He hardly noticed.

He remained stock-still, staring at an earthy beauty with blonde-white hair who was staring right back at him. She was thirty-something, with a deep tan that made her devastatingly pretty.

I could feel the thick tension between them.

The tall, lithe woman emanated pride. Her cheekbones were high and sharp and her eyelids were softly lined, her expression one of stark intelligence. Her beige khakis and T-shirt were creased and her boots were covered in dirt.

Henry appeared bewitched—staring as though hypnotized.

"Is it her?" I whispered.

He didn't seem to hear me, so I repeated my question.

"What?" he said.

His gaze finally broke away from hers briefly to meet mine, his expression anguished.

We'd found her.

Reese's tanned face revealed so much about her lifestyle and her home—this wilderness.

About twenty people stood behind her, all dressed like her, prepared for the elements.

All of them protestors, maybe?

From the five huts scattered here and there, I assumed we'd

found their base camp. A jeep was parked by one of them, along with a couple of tents.

Reese walked toward us.

Henry's back straightened as he braced himself.

"You came," she said. "I wasn't sure if you would."

Words formed on his lips, but he seemed too shaken to say them. I reached up and caressed his back to ground him in the moment.

"Sorry to bring you all the way out here," she said.

"Why did you?" he asked, his tone scathing.

"I understand this is difficult."

He glowered. "All these years you never reached out, never told me you were alive?"

"You have every right to be angry."

His jaw flexed as he worked on his response.

"I need to pee," I said. "Sorry."

Some truth in it, but I also wanted to get Henry alone with her. This experience had thrown him off balance. Henry was still a public figure. Anyone with a phone could film him.

"Forgive my manners." Reese held out her hand to me.

I stepped forward and gave it a firm shake. "Lotte."

"Nice to meet you, Lotte." She seemed to sum me up.

"This is Reese," said Henry, resting his palm at the base of my spine. "Reese, this is my girlfriend."

Her mouth twitched with jealousy.

I found it super weird, considering she'd given him up.

"Over here." She pointed to the furthest hut.

"Great." I wanted them to have privacy.

Reese led the way.

The crowd watched us carefully.

We walked up a few steps and entered a modest hut. Posters and maps were pinned to the wooden slatted wall. This was probably where they held meetings.

"Is this place safe?" I asked her.

"How do you mean?" she asked, though her focus remained on Henry.

"We met Tony," I said. "He used his gun to intimidate us."

She gave a weary shake of her head. "I'm guessing he works for Community Development."

A thousand more questions loomed but right now their private reunion was more important. They needed a few minutes alone.

I excused myself and went through the door marked "Restroom." I intended to listen in case Henry raised his voice.

The mirror was blurry, but I managed to catch my reflection. My face had been slightly burned, despite the sun block. I had a red nose and my hair was caked to my scalp.

Next to the serene Reese, I was a hot mess.

The toilet was basic, but it felt good to be around some normality. I navigated the small space as best I could to pee.

My thoughts turned back to Henry, trying to imagine what he was thinking.

After a few minutes, I rejoined them.

Reese stood on the other side of the hut with her arms folded across her chest in a defensive pose.

It was hard to tell who needed space from whom.

"Could we have some water, please?" I asked.

"It's on its way," said Reese. "We'll get you fed, too."

Her expression turned kind, her blue eyes showing compassion for our ordeal.

Henry glanced at me. "Give us a moment, please?"

"Of course," I said.

Reese glanced at me again. "I'll explain everything. Why it was important for you to see this place yourselves."

I directed the answer to Henry. "It's been quite the adventure."

I let him know with a glance that I would be just outside should he need me.

Stepping out, I breathed in the thick evening air, trying to shake off that glimmer of undeniable chemistry I saw passing between them—the way they'd stared at each other upon first sight.

They had a bond so strong it had seduced Henry into coming all the way out here.

After the dust had settled on their reunion, after they'd rejuvenated a lost friendship, what they'd once had might be ignited by a spark again and become something more.

Maybe their love could survive all those years apart.

Compared to their history, ours felt fragile. Soon, all I'd have left of Henry would be the memory of him—an indissoluble part of him that I would always cherish.

CHAPTER THIRTY

Henry

THE WALLS OF THE SMALL HUT SEEMED TO CLOSE IN ON me, the midday heat suffocating.

I shook my head to center myself.

The Reese Papadopoulos—or whatever name she went by now—literally stood right in front of me.

This wasn't a dream. It was more like a nightmare—the kind you can't wake from.

She'd put us all through hell back then, in that past I'd never acclimated to.

Here, now, her influence over me remained startling.

She'd lured me back.

Yet, at the same time, it felt good to see her again.

Damn confusing.

My shoulders relaxed as I realized I'd finally be able to get closure.

I'd once prayed for this—the moment when questions were answered and hope won out.

Glancing at the far wall, I got my bearings. A map of the area had been stuck to the wooden slats. Another beside it appeared to be of the enemy base a few klicks away.

Reese and her team were up against a goliath of a company. It made me wonder what kind of tactics they were using to stop them. Sabotage, maybe? That would make their endeavor illegal—no matter how morally justified.

Reese had stared at Lotte as she'd left us, clearly fascinated with her.

Now her attention had returned to me. "She's lovely."

"She is." More than Reese would ever comprehend.

"Lilly gave you the letter over two weeks ago," she said.

Of all the words she could have uttered, she had chosen those?

"This could have been a phone call," I said flatly.

A familiar vision from the past was standing before me—the same, but different. The years had been fairly kind, though the sun had loved her, leaving her with a golden complexion set off by her pale blonde hair. Her beauty had not been ravaged by time.

"The T.S. Eliot quote?" I said. "In the hut?"

"I thought you'd like it," she said. "You were always one for clues and deciphering puzzles."

My liking for the mysterious had burned out with her.

"And the drone?"

She seemed surprised. "We spy on the developers. We've lost a few. They crash in the Everglades."

"Have they harassed you? Is that why you need to spy on them?"

She gave a shrug, hinting her team might be just as bad.

"We lost a backpack along the way," I said, studying her. "Someone stole it."

"Wasn't us."

"What last name are you going by these days?" I asked.

"Vergara."

"Your married name?"

"We're divorced."

"I met Lilly. Is that her dad?"

"Yes. She liked you." She considered her words. "You brought her tea. Made her welcome."

"Is she here?"

"No."

"It should have been you who delivered the letter." I raised my hand. "Correction, delivered the coordinates."

"I doubted you'd agree to a meeting with me."

"You just had to keep the mystery up."

"I knew you'd come," she whispered, "*if* I made it intriguing."

"We searched for you all those years ago," I said coldly.

She looked away. "Want a drink?"

"I want answers."

"I respect that—"

"I thought you were dead. You led me to believe that. Do you have any idea how much pain you've caused?"

"Let me explain."

"Did you even suspect I was searching for you?" I bit out. "Night and day, relentlessly—even after I came back to America."

"You had a different path."

"Don't make this about me."

She raised her hand to calm me. "I wanted to work with the Peace Corp. You were heading off to the military. We were opposites. You just refused to see it, Henry."

My name sounded like poison in her mouth.

"I need a better explanation," I said. "The way you disappeared is unforgivable."

"I went off exploring. I only planned to be gone a few days. But the days turned into weeks. I started by hiking Mount Cerro Castillo, and I became obsessed with helping the people there."

"And you never once thought of coming back to base camp?"

"I became too scared to face everyone."

My shoulders slumped in frustration. "You met your husband there?"

She nodded. "Julian. We married a few months after meeting."

"You began a new life—and forgot us."

That truth stung worse than it should after so many years.

"I never forgot you," she whispered.

"Did your husband hear about your origin?"

She shook her head. "Not at first."

"A marriage based on lies?" I said bitterly.

"You have every right to be angry."

"I just can't wrap my head around why."

"You may never forgive me. But at least you can see I've dedicated my life to important work, continued to sacrifice everything for important causes."

"You could still have done all of that, Reese. I would never have stood in your way."

"My father would have." She shuddered. "He would never have let me stay in Chile. He wanted me to run the restaurant. I would never been allowed to follow my dreams."

"You could have told him no and refused to work there."

"He would have forced me, guilted me into it. I watched what that place did to my mom. She worked tirelessly to keep our restaurant going, dedicated her life to my dad's dream. In the end, it killed her. She worked herself to death. She died in her forties. I never forgave him for that."

"Her death was hard on you. I get that."

"Your family would never have let me marry you," she reasoned. "I was the girl from the wrong end of town. You're American royalty. It would have been impossible."

"I fought for you."

"Your family didn't approve."

And in the end they were right about her. This woman *had* destroyed me but in an entirely different way.

She moved closer. "You've accomplished great things."

What she didn't seem to grasp was that experience had sent me spiraling on a totally different trajectory.

"How did you like the Navy? Was it everything you wanted? Did you change your mind about becoming a pilot?"

She'd read up on me, unsurprisingly.

I shrugged, because that was all she deserved as an answer. She'd already stolen so much.

"Why now?" I bit out.

"I needed you to see how beautiful this location is. See it up close. The wildlife. The setting. The ecology."

"Well, now I've seen it."

"I didn't know who else to turn to."

"Well, I'm here now, so let's hear it."

"The company is Community Development. They don't care about anything other than profit. They're going to build a hotel in the center of the preserve. It would end up destroying the vegetation. The consequences will be terrible for panthers and other wildlife."

"And what do you think I can do?"

"We need your influence and wealth. They've gotten around several laws protecting the park. They've already begun leveling an area of land to start building."

"Surely that's not possible?"

"They're bringing money in, saying it will ensure the future of the park. They've paid off politicians."

I stayed silent, realizing she had only summoned me because she wanted to use me.

"I'm desperate, Henry. We've done everything in our power to fight this with no success. You're our last hope."

That explained why everyone had studied me with such intensity. "Two weeks ago, you upended my life with a vague invitation just so I could fix this for you? With no regard for all you did decades ago?"

"This isn't about me," she pleaded. "This is bigger and more important than both of us."

"I need some air." I turned and walked toward the door.

She called after me. "If I could go back in time and undo all the damage I would. I was young. Foolish. I wanted to save the world."

I reached the door and turned to look at her. "I would have saved it right alongside you."

Her face contorted with pain. "Tell me how to make it up to you?"

Impossible.

I stepped outside and a rush of heat hit me. After descending the steps, I walked away, putting distance between us.

Sucking in a breath of dry heat, I cursed myself for believing this trip was a good idea. She'd knowingly hurt me. All those years I'd wasted on guilt seemed so futile.

Lotte closed the space between us and reached for my hand. "Henry."

I pulled away, not wanting her to sense my anger. My relationship with Lotte felt like the only good thing that had come out of this escapade.

She let out a sigh. "What should we do now?"

CHAPTER THIRTY-ONE

Lotte

HENRY PULLED HIS HAND AWAY.

I pretended it didn't matter, but it did. We'd built a connection and, in that moment, I felt it slipping away.

Glancing back at the hut, I wondered what words had been exchanged. He had every right to be angry with her.

I could understand why he'd be distraught with this whole situation.

Henry stalked over to his rucksack and lifted it easily with one hand, again showing his impressive strength.

I'd not let our kit out of my sight.

I wondered how he'd seemed to Reese, this gorgeous, brilliant man who ran a billion-dollar empire. A contrast to the young man she'd once dated.

His ex-girlfriend was equally mystifying.

With conservation as her banner, she had given up her life in America for what she believed was an important cause. But the way she'd done it had left others suffering in her wake.

A fresh-faced male volunteer approached us. "We're grateful you're here."

A huff of annoyance came from Henry.

"I'm Lotte." I held my hand out and shook his.

"Michael." His frown deepened as he continued to stare at Henry for reassurance.

Henry's jaw flexed. "We need to take a shower."

"Right," said Michael. "I'll show you the staff quarters."

We followed Michael across a sparse wasteland into the largest hut on the premises, and he led us down a wooden walkway. The staff bathrooms were primitive, but I'd never been so relieved to see makeshift showerheads.

Michael grimaced, apologetic. "They're unisex."

I showed enthusiasm. "I'm guessing everything is eco-friendly."

"Once we're done, we break everything down and leave a minimal ecological footprint."

"That's good." I watched Henry's reaction.

He set his rucksack down in the corner.

"How was your trip here?" asked Michael cheerfully.

"Go away." Henry gestured for him to disappear.

I gave Michael a sympathetic glance. "This is perfect. Thank you."

He bowed his head and left us alone.

"You could have been kinder," I said quietly.

Henry shrugged. "He's part of the conspiracy that got me here."

"He's probably just following orders."

"Orders that pissed me off."

"You have every right to feel that way."

I was desperate to hear what he'd discussed with Reese—and hear her side of things. This felt like a film documentary in the making.

A multitude of questions stormed my brain, but I knew not to push him for answers.

He kicked off his boots and stripped off his clothes, dragging his shirt over his head and pulling off his pants, revealing six-pack abs. His chest looked ripped and his thighs were toned and muscular, his ass perfectly round. I stared at the impressive cock hanging between his thighs.

It was impossible to look away. Everything was on display like a statue in an art gallery—a masterpiece you wanted to touch but knew you couldn't.

Or shouldn't.

I struggled to hide what his incredible physique did to me. I took in the small space around us, but my gaze was unwittingly drawn back to him, my striking gladiator. I had an entirely different perspective of him standing there naked, compared to when he'd been laying down in the tent.

He stared back at me, that one sensual eyebrow lifted as though my reaction amused him. I turned away.

I guessed everyone else here just got on with it, showered with the opposite sex like they were just one friendly team.

We'd been intimate, but this felt different. Had he not pulled his hand away a few minutes ago, I wouldn't be experiencing this feeling of distance between us.

I heard the sound of running water.

"Fucking hell!" Henry grumbled.

I turned to check on him.

His face was contorted in agony as he stood beneath the running water.

"Maybe it will warm up?" I said, trying to be optimistic.

"Assuming anything will improve around here is asinine."

"Well, the view's improved." I smirked.

"Get naked," he said gruffly.

I dragged my shirt over my head and then slipped off my shoes, climbing out of my pants and throwing everything into the corner. I tried to forget how bad everything smelled from us sweating all day.

And great…my change of clothes was in my stolen backpack.

"A cold shower is good for your immunity," I reasoned.

"You always see the bright side."

"Can I borrow something to wear while I wash those?" I pointed to my discarded clothes.

"Sure." He stared at my nakedness, his lips quirking in approval.

Taking the shower next to his, I stepped forward and twisted the faucet on, bracing myself.

Cold water hit me, my teeth clenching as I endured what felt like falling icicles.

"The water's pumped in from the ground," he said. "I'm not so sure it's ecologically friendly."

I continued to inhale sharply as the frigid water splashed over my flesh, goose bumps forming on my arms.

We'd gone from intense heat to arctic temps.

I finally acclimated enough to the cold to press the pump dispenser for a glob of creamy gel, lathering my body.

Henry glanced over, seemingly just as fascinated with my nakedness, raking his teeth over his bottom lip as he admired what he saw.

Both of us kept stealing glances.

I rested both hands against the wall. "What can I do?"

"About what?"

I straightened. "You don't get to resurrect your wall just because you're hurting. You need to let me in."

"Honestly?" he said.

"Yes, I want honesty."

"You deserve better than a revenge fuck."

"Is that what it would be?"

He went quiet.

"Henry, talk."

"She wants money to help save this place from property developers. Reese brought us all the way out here to see their work."

I faced him. "I figured."

"She went into detail about why she disappeared. Gave a lame excuse."

I gave a nod to encourage him to keep talking.

His gaze lingered on my breasts and then took in the rest of me. "You're the only good thing in this hellhole."

"This is a nature preserve. They're doing good work." I turned off the faucet.

"On their side so quickly?"

"It's terrible what Reese did, and most people wouldn't forgive that. But she was much younger. She's not the same person now."

"It's like the Reese I once knew is gone."

"That's me, too." I moved closer to him, my self-consciousness gone. "I hardly recognize the girl I once was."

He twisted off his faucet.

"You've changed, too," I added. "You're honoring what it is to be a Cole."

He held out his arms. "Body warmth?"

I padded closer, leaning into him, trying to keep our hips apart for decency's sake. His arm curled around my waist and he yanked me against him, his heat welcome as I surrendered to being crushed in his strong embrace. I was pressed against a wall of pure muscle, his erection hard at my belly.

"Something good has come out of this," he whispered. "Getting to know you better."

"I want to protect you."

"Don't need protecting."

I pressed my palm over his heart. Warmth saturated my hand and I kept it there to make my point.

"I've survived worse," he said.

"I'm sorry."

"I've lived with this a long time, always wondering, feeling that same guilt. This is liberating." His mouth curled at the edges. "For so many reasons."

"We're still getting acquainted."

He let me go and stepped back. "You're allowed to have doubts."

"What I mean is that I really like you, but I respect how complicated this is."

"It's you I want." He studied my reaction.

This felt supersonic fast, and it scared me.

He gave a ghost of a smile. "You wish that wall would come back up?"

"Never."

He walked over to a stack of towels and picked one, unfolding it. "Come here."

I stepped forward into the towel that he held open for me. He dried water droplets off my body with long sweeps of the towel.

"I'm still up for a revenge fuck," I teased.

He grinned. "Or something decadent."

"Oh?"

Henry's finger slid over his wristwatch. He pressed his fingertip to an app. "How about this one?"

Familiar notes rose from his watch.

Neil Diamond's sultry baritone singing "Holly Holy" echoed around us, the song's emotional lyrics conveying the precious love a woman gives a wounded man.

As if we'd rehearsed it, we both tossed our towels aside.

With my hand in his palm and my other around his shoulder, we slowed danced in a tight circle. Rocking together, both of us naked and yet warmed by each other's bodies.

A classic song for a classic man, though way before his time. I knew there was a story there. He'd share it one day.

The sticky heat from outside was finding its way in here.

"They might hear," I whispered.

"Fuck'em." He tilted me backwards and then brought me up quickly to kiss my cheek.

Around and around we went, stealing precious time just for us, a slow pattern of togetherness. My heart soared with this precious connection.

Healing has a strange way of finding you. Sometimes it storms its way into your life and forces you free. Other times, it quietly whispers you were right all along.

All of this offered him vindication. I sensed the profoundness of that fact.

"This is our song," I whispered.

"This is our song," he repeated softly.

As the music faded, we stepped apart.

"Let me nurture you," I offered.

Kneeling, I took his erection in my hand. "We can make the rest of this stay about you."

His eyelids looked heavy. "About us."

Leaning forward, I pressed my lips into a tight pout against his cock, easing the head inside my mouth, taking him deep to the back of my throat.

He growled as his erection grew.

This closeness, this intimacy flowing with ease, was a connectedness that felt as sacred as this place.

Glancing up, I admired the way his tall frame hovered over me, like a proud king ruling over his consort, his dark hair framing that stark intensity as he watched me.

Pressing my hands to his thighs, I massaged his taut muscles, making a memory of this.

Time dissolved as I proved how much I cared for him, lowering my head to take his soft sacs into my mouth to suckle, their texture a contrast to his hefty, rock hard shaft in my grasp.

If only I could reach back into time with this special connection and prevent him being hurt, betrayed or harmed.

In my mind I saw flashes of us rolling around the tent at dawn, his passion and strength in the way he maneuvered me, giving me the sense he could protect me from anything.

He peered skyward as though disappearing into the pleasure. I exulted in the fact it was me freeing him, bringing him this blinding pleasure. I was unable to understand how anyone could let this man go.

I worshipped him as my throat closed around his shaft, drawing him in and out with a sleek bobbing, deep-throating him.

This was unlike any connection I'd ever experienced. Our unique chemistry felt profoundly rare and yet unfathomably familiar.

Falling and falling and falling *for him.*

"I'm gonna come."

I coaxed him into a climax.

As he stilled and his heat filled my mouth, I swallowed him down, grateful that we had this, at least. I held onto these precious seconds of an "us"—as fragile as they were beautiful.

CHAPTER THIRTY-TWO

Henry

I NEEDED TIME ALONE.

Time to process how a situation this dire could end up liberating me, all thanks to Lotte's insight. There was no pressure there, which made me want to spend even more time with her.

Reese was right about one thing: I'd once loved puzzles and, ironically, Lotte had become the missing piece.

I stole a few minutes to walk the perimeter, maintaining a visual on Lotte and the rucksack. She sat at a picnic table, drinking a bottle of water, seemingly comfortable talking with Michael.

I'd given her fresh boxer shorts and one of my T-shirts to wear. Someone else had given her a pair of socks. Mine were far too big. Reese had leant a pair of khakis. Lotte was a little shorter than Reese, but she managed by rolling up the cuffs. Her boots were holding up well.

Showering with her had felt as natural as breathing. What happened afterwards—us dancing to one of my favorite songs—had felt dreamlike.

I was meant to be miserable, *goddammit*.

Every time Lotte stepped into my line of sight, I felt victorious. As though everything I'd experienced had been profoundly worth it because I had found her, leading me toward potential happiness.

But did I have her, really?

Or perhaps my imagination was running wild with this need to believe I could find love again. Hurting her wasn't an option. But her hurting me, it hadn't even figured into my equation.

I'd gone into battle many times. But this was a brand-new risk.

"A battle of the mind," as Cameron had succinctly put it.

I couldn't refuse Charlotte anything.

Getting her out of here safely had become my number one priority.

With my SATCOM back up, the clearing helping with the signal, I sent a brief text to Shay to inform him we'd reached our destination.

The screen flashed his answer.

Shay: Sitrep?
Me: All clear.
Shay: Casualties?
Me: None.
Shay: Target?
Me: Located.
Shay: Wow. Extraction?
Me: TBD.
Shay: Thumb's up emoji.
Me: All good there?
Shay: Yes. You good, buddy?
Me: Thumbs up emoji.

We'd reverted to shorthand because in situations like this time was of the essence and small talk was ineffective. There'd be plenty of time for that when I arrived home. Though the threat of danger had somewhat lifted, I knew to stay alert.

If I wasn't a billionaire, I would probably never have heard from Reese again. She wanted me again, but this time for my money.

If things went wrong now, there'd be no searching for her. She could get eaten by a fucking gator and I wouldn't grieve. Okay, an exaggeration, but it was close to how I felt.

With Lotte, however, I'd leap into the water to save her, allowing both of us to be swallowed up in the Everglades—our happily ever after as tragic as a Shakespearean romance.

I'd need to carefully navigate where we went from here to avoid invasive journalists who wanted a pound of flesh. Especially someone ruthless enough to ruin my reputation as their career highlight.

A sudden movement in the trees caught my attention.

I leaped to my feet.

A creature stared back at me. A baby raccoon. The little guy was peeking around the stump of a tree, looking so damn cute with his big round eyes and button nose.

"Hey, little guy," I whispered, not wanting to scare him. I scanned the leaves for his mother.

The hoot of an owl startled me.

Shielding my face, I looked up, admiring the majestic grey and white feathered owl who seemed equally as fascinated with the little fellow below.

My shoulders slumped at the realization that Reese had a point. These adorable critters were at risk. There was no doubt this location was precious to wildlife.

After I extracted my moody attitude out of the picture, I'd be able to give this issue more thought.

I glanced back one final time at the baby raccoon. Its family was around here somewhere.

I raised my watch and snapped a photo of the critter. Maybe I'd send it to Mia and Cameron, later. They'd get a kick out of it.

Discreetly, I watched one of the volunteers reappear at the

entrance to the campsite. He scurried off toward a hut and disappeared inside.

I followed a hunch.

Within minutes, I'd returned to the dock we'd arrived at earlier.

The boat we'd arrived in had vanished. It was probably just a coincidence; perhaps one of the staff was using it.

But what if there wasn't a reasonable explanation?

A chill shuddered through me.

They'd gone to a lot of trouble to get us here. Allowing our exit might not be part of the plan.

The hair on my nape prickled.

I made my way back through the trees in the direction I'd just come from.

No one seemed to notice.

Reese took unnecessary risks, and she didn't much care about the consequences. I knew people could change, but they also repeated patterns. It was impossible to separate her work here from what she'd done to me—and to her family, too.

It took a certain ruthlessness.

Her marriage had failed. There was more to that story. I suppose she had a daughter to make up for that failed relationship.

Would we have made it as a couple? Maybe not. We had grown into totally different people. Even now, Reese jeopardized my old-fashioned American values. Everything I did had to be within the law—scandals kept at bay.

I wanted to keep Lotte away from Reese's potential toxicity.

And goddamn if the chemistry between Lotte and me didn't create a white-hot passion that was undeniable. She had helped make this experience cathartic, healing old wounds and soothing my pain.

I headed back to the picnic table and sat beside her, giving Michael a respectful nod.

"How are you doing?" I asked Lotte.

"Fine," she said. "You?"

"I checked in." I showed her my watch so she could see I'd messaged Shay.

"I texted them, too," she admitted.

"That's good."

Reese came over and sat with us.

"We're grilling dinner," she said. "Vegan okay?"

"Of course," I said.

Michael gave me a lingering look best described as admiration. "Navy SEAL?"

I gave a nod.

"Thank you for your service."

I offered him a warm smile. "You were worth it."

His face lit up.

My kind response was borrowed from that time I observed a stoic veteran from World War II interacting with a young stranger.

Michael relaxed a little, unraveling a map on the table. Red markings delineated where the developers had dug in.

Straight to business.

"How have you been?" I addressed that to Reese.

She seemed startled, as though not expecting polite conversation.

"We don't stop," she said, glancing at Michael.

"But how are you?" I was making an effort to check in with her, see how her life had gone and how she had coped.

"I'm fine," she said. "Taking each day as it comes. Doing my best."

I had a thousand more questions but I went with, "Did you continue your education?"

"I studied anthropology." She watched my reaction. "At the University of Chile."

"You were happy there?"

"Yes." She was clearly uncomfortable.

I wanted to ask how often she saw Lilly, but that might appear as a dig at her motherhood skills.

The sounds of a helicopter reached my ears.

"That's them leaving," Michael piped up.

"Show me." I pressed a finger to the map. "Here?"

"Yeah," he said.

From the coordinates, it looked like it would be a reasonable drive in their jeep, perhaps crossing challenging terrain—or half a day on foot.

The location and clearance size for a helicopter had just been answered by that chopper. Shielding my eyes from the sun, I watched the yellow Bell 205A-1 fly off.

A Bell could perform high-altitude lifting missions, which meant they were about to commence building.

I broke my gaze away so as not to arouse suspicion.

"How far along are they with construction?" I asked.

"They've flattened the land," Michael answered.

"So, if they're stopped now, nature can reclaim it?"

I watched Michael swap a hopeful glance with Reese.

Reese gave a nod. "Minimal damage would have been done."

Making a note of the coordinates, I pointed in that direction. "Show me their base."

"You need to see it?" asked Reese.

I gave a shrug. "My team will need as much info as possible."

"You'll help, then?" asked Michael.

"I have a few ideas." I watched their reaction. "Do they have security overnight?"

"No," she said. "Not as far as we can tell."

I read her concerned expression. "A problem?"

She hesitated. "We were served with a restraining order. Can't go within one hundred feet of the outer rim."

"Your involvement is being litigated?" I asked.

Her team had probably sabotaged their base, or at least tried to make construction difficult.

"Lotte and I can go alone," I said.

"We can all go first thing tomorrow," said Reese, seemingly not willing to let us out of her sight. "Before they arrive in the morning."

"Can you stop them?" asked Michael.

"Possibly," said Lotte. "But whatever we do must be within the law."

I pushed up. "If you'll excuse me."

I felt Reese's gaze on my back as I walked away.

Lifting my watch, I sent off another message to Shay.

Shay: Ready.
Me: Helicopter extraction.
Shay: Clearance?
Me: Proven. 26°00'00"N 81°25'01"W
Shay: Got it.
Me: Tonight. 7 PM EST.
Shay: Confirmed.

That gave us less than one hour to arrive at the checkpoint.

We needed two thousand feet of clearance from the nearest landmass. The Bell had cleared it, but I'd need to confirm. We also needed to minimize disturbance of the wildlife.

I returned to the table and sat with the others.

Lotte would have no idea the boat was gone. I didn't want her worried.

"Everything okay?" asked Reese, watching me carefully.

I focused on her. "We're starving. Do you have veggie burgers?"

"On their way." She relaxed a little. "Let me show you where you'll sleep tonight."

"Actually, I want to see the site after we eat," I said. "That's non-negotiable."

"He wants to get right on it," said Lotte. "This place is breathtaking."

Reese sat back as she considered it.

Not suspecting this woman of foul play was challenging. She'd already proven what she was capable of.

Getting what she wanted would always be her end game.

CHAPTER THIRTY-THREE

Lotte

HENRY WAS SHOWING REMARKABLE PATIENCE. I'd learned to read him; the cadence in his tone, the way he held himself. The distinguished way he interacted with everyone.

I knew once he settled in a little, catching up with Reese would be good for him.

Visiting the construction site this late in the day meant we'd arrive around 7:00 P.M. Maybe he wanted to explore the area under the guise of dusk.

I hated the idea that someone here had something to do with my kit's disappearance. Even so, that sounded counter intuitive, since they needed Henry's help.

Searching for it here wasn't a good idea.

The fact Reese had left a T.S. Eliot quote for us in the hut felt like a mind-game.

Reading her was difficult even for someone like me who'd mastered the art of deciphering micro-expressions. In time, people like her revealed their true nature.

After a light vegan meal with the staff, Henry asked me to join him in the main hut.

He made sure we were alone.

Kneeling before his rucksack, he rummaged through it, pulling out the water filtration system and a bottle. After tucking those into his khaki side pockets, he did the same with the paper map and other essentials.

He handed me the medical kit. "Fill your pockets."

"Why?"

"We're leaving the kit." He handed me a few packages of food, too.

"Leaving it?"

"I need you to trust me."

I realized he didn't want anyone to steal his stuff. We could do without these items for a while. Leaving them behind would be fine.

I clicked open the medical kit and gathered up the contents.

He gestured to my pockets. "Don't let anyone see you have something in there."

"Okay."

Henry pushed to his feet.

I offered the medical items back to him. "Go with Reese. It might be good for you to spend more time with her."

His back straightened. "Not this time."

"I'll see you when you get back." I again held out the medical supplies. "I insist."

"Put them in your pockets."

We heard a knock at the door.

Henry took the items out of my hands and shoved them into my khaki pockets.

The door flew open and Michael motioned that they were ready.

Henry carried his rucksack out into the open. With a huff, he set his kit on one of the benches. "I'm going to leave this here."

I whispered discreetly, "You've waited all this time. Use this opportunity to talk."

He came closer so that we were face to face. "I'm asking for your total loyalty and devotion." He winked.

Hesitant, I said, "You're avoiding what we came for."

"Reese's ready to drive us," Michael called over, pointing to where she sat behind the steering wheel.

"It'll be more fun with you." Henry threw them a wave and then focused on me. "Anyway, you owe me."

"What for?"

"Imperial."

"You're still upset about that?" I asked, surprised.

"She can stay here," said Michael, coming over to see what the delay was. "That's fine."

I rested my palm on his firm chest. "Go."

CHAPTER THIRTY-FOUR

Henry

I'D NOT TAKEN INTO CONSIDERATION THAT HAVING A compassionate woman might threaten the plan.

I leaned in and whispered to Lotte, "Don't make me order you."

"I'm not backing down," she said.

"Remember that time with me at Enthrall?" I arched a brow.

She started to correct me and then blinked as she processed that I had gotten the name wrong. I'd never once stepped foot in Enthrall, but I'd met her at Chrysalis.

And I never got my facts wrong.

"I remember," she whispered.

Before she broke away from my intense gaze, I could see she now realized why I'd emptied the rucksack.

"It'll be fun," I said loudly enough for Michael to hear.

Lotte and I climbed into the backseat of the jeep.

Michael climbed in beside Reese in the front. I noted they'd brought two-way radios. Ours were secured to our belts but they were small enough to go unnoticed. If everything went well, we'd not need them.

We sped down a well-worn pathway.

Should anyone examine my kit back at base camp, they'd find the contents sparse. Though in my experience, when an object was left in plain sight in front of everyone, it didn't arouse suspicion if they'd observed its drop. Not right away.

We kept the conversation light.

Half an hour later, Reese pulled the jeep up to the edge of a vast area of land. Several earth diggers sat like prehistoric dinosaurs waiting to be put to work. There was a portable toilet for the workers and a cabin for them to convene, along with all the usual machines one found on a construction site.

All four of us exited the jeep and moved closer to the plot of land. Wary of us invaders, no animals could be seen or heard.

An eerie silence surrounded us.

"They're done for the day," said Reese.

Stepping forward, I studied the area to confirm we had at least two thousand feet of radius needed for extraction. Their pilot would be used to this. Ours would need reassurance that the landing site appeared safe.

I pulled the infrared camera out of my pocket and stepped forward.

"What's that?" asked Michael.

"I'm checking to make sure we don't have company," I said.

I scanned the dense brush and tree line, hoping our escape wouldn't be sabotaged by a renegade like Tony, whom we'd had the misfortune of meeting earlier.

"No one is here," said Michael.

The tech confirmed it, detecting no body heat within a mile. One thing was sure, if you needed a job done, you did it yourself if unfamiliar with your team.

I tucked the camera away.

If anyone shot at our pilot, I'd become the hunter out here.

Having a former SEAL go rogue amongst the Everglades would become everyone's nightmare.

So far, they'd all been spared my fury.

I turned to Reese. "I need to talk with you in private."

She swapped a wary glance with Michael.

We walked out of earshot of him and Lotte.

"Well?" said Reese.

I followed her line of sight. "We can get an injunction. Slow it down."

"You've been gracious." Reese let out a long breath. "Considering how I got you here."

"I'm a forgiving guy."

She focused on the mounds of piping ready to be buried. "They only care about money."

"Money's important." I towered over her. "If you had more, you could throw money at this. How many billionaires did you try before me?"

"None." She looked vulnerable then, as though my bluntness hit harder than intended. "Forgive me, Henry. You were the ultimate sacrifice I had to make."

"How honorable."

"It hurt me, too."

"Why did you send your daughter to tell me? It should have been you."

"Lilly?" She flinched. "I couldn't leave my team."

"She's just like you."

That made her relax. "Lilly's hoping to move to L.A."

"Where is she now?"

"Here, in Florida. She wants to study biology at UCLA."

"When did you get pregnant with her?" I asked.

"I don't want to talk about it here." She folded her arms protectively over her chest.

"I'm sure your dad would want to meet his grandchild."

"Don't." Reese looked away. "That part of my life is behind me."

All that time searching for her, and she'd moved on in another relationship. She'd gotten married, had a child, and even qualified as an anthropologist.

All while I'd been back in the States trying to pick up the pieces.

She rested her hand on my forearm. "I never stopped loving you."

"If you love someone you don't hurt them."

"Never intentionally," she said.

"We were young, I suppose."

"You never stopped thinking about me?"

She'd like that. To believe all this time, I had waited for her.

Her tone softened. "You're not married."

I glanced over at Lotte.

Reese noticed me staring at her. "We go back further. That counts, surely?"

The difference between her and Lotte was miles apart.

Charlotte's thoughtful nature was refreshing in all this drama.

Reese stepped closer. "Think about all the good I've done. Saved chimps in Africa. Manatees in Florida. The work we're doing here is crucial to save the panthers. I've put myself second in everything."

"You're doing good work," I said. "But there's another way to handle this."

Chopper blades cut through the air, echoing around the clearing.

Reese observed the bright landing light.

"That's my ride," I said.

"You're leaving!"

"Yes."

"You don't want to stay longer?" She was flummoxed. "We've hardly talked."

"I run a corporation." I waved at the pilot. "Work that can't be done from here."

"What's one more chopper disturbing the peace, right?" she said.

"Well, we would have gone by boat." I gave her a wry smile. She'd believed she'd outsmarted us.

"Come visit me in L.A.," I said.

"Why?"

"I'll give you my answer on your dilemma."

"Summoning me to California?"

I gave a nod and threw T.S. Eliot's quote back at her, "'Only those who will risk going too far can possibly find out how far one can go.'"

I motioned for Lotte to join me, grabbing her hand and pulling her toward the helicopter.

"Don't look back," I told her.

She followed my lead and bent over as we made our way beneath the spinning blades to reach the passenger door. I opened it for her and helped her climb into the back seat before quickly joining her.

I helped secure her seatbelt and slid a pair of headphones onto her head before placing a set on mine.

"Good to go," I directed the pilot.

Gravity pulled us down in our seats as the helicopter rose sharply, banking left as we flew up and over the Everglades. The dusky view of endless trees surrounding the marshland was spectacular. We went higher still, seeing the greenery blanketing the land below. To our far right, a flock of pelicans flew toward the sunset.

Lotte had an expression of wonder on her face. I returned a nod of understanding.

"Thank you for being here!" I called out to our pilot.

He gave me a wave. "Pleasure, sir."

Looking back at the clearing, I saw Michael and Reese grow smaller with every passing second.

"You should have told me this was the plan." Lotte's voice was in my headset. "I'm good with secrets."

"Need-to-know basis." I grinned.

She folded her arms across her chest. "Tell me we're not leaving because of me?"

"I did consider leaving your pretty ass behind."

She smirked at that. "Wait. What about the car?"

"I'll have it collected."

"You've thought of everything."

"We did good," I said. "You really shone out there."

"You did, too," she said warmly.

"Well, as far as missions go, I'd say it was successful."

This wasn't the way I'd imagined my reunion would go. I still had mixed emotions about seeing Reese again. She'd lived a full life without me. The kind we could have shared but that hope had been dashed on the rocks of a selfish decision. Yet despite this once roiling pain, Reese had given me a remarkable gift.

Precious time with Lotte.

Reaching for her hand, I drew it to my mouth and kissed it.

"Will you be able to help save this place?" Her voice sounded soft in my headphones, her authentic concern tugging at my conscience.

Even now, after all the complications of our experience in the preserve, Lotte saw through the disarray and set her sights on what was important.

I gave a nod. "Reese might not like my methods."

The view of the preserve shrank as we ascended toward the fading sky.

At one time, nothing could have soothed this void inside me. Now, the way forward was brilliantly transparent.

CHAPTER THIRTY-FIVE

Henry

OUR HELICOPTER MADE IT TO THE AIRPORT IN NAPLES in less than thirty minutes.

Cameron and Shay were on the jet, which was no surprise. Shay would want to talk about our experience and Cameron would be here for brotherly support. He knew well enough to keep his analysis to a minimum.

Our plane had been fueled and was ready for take-off.

Lotte and I cleared our pockets of the contents from the kit, and she settled in the private cabin where she could get some sleep. She looked exhausted.

Gently, I brought the blanket up to cover her. Pausing in the doorway of the cabin, I watched her sleep, entranced by her beauty.

I've fallen hard.

For the first time in my life, a relationship wasn't cause for apprehension—because it was her.

Closing the door, I took a few seconds to gather my thoughts. Both of us had lowered our defenses and trusted in the other.

That night we spent sleeping under the stars would become a cherished moment.

I made my way down the aisle and took the seat opposite Cameron and Shay.

"This is a nice surprise," I said.

Cameron met my gaze. "You're a stubborn bastard."

"We're both absolutely fine," I replied.

"How's Lotte?" asked Shay, handing me a bottle of water.

I accepted it gladly and took a gulp. "She's good."

"Hungry?" asked Cameron. "We can get you a meal."

"No, thank you." I looked at Shay. "How's Dex?"

"Great. Completely spoiled now. I'll have Rue drop him off later. Get some rest first."

"How did it go?" asked Cameron.

"Mission accomplished." I sat back. "Who sent Lotte?"

They swapped glances.

Cameron spoke up. "She wanted to go with you. And I permitted it."

I bristled at his arrogance. Though it was good to hear Lotte had wanted to be with me for this.

"Where's your ruck?" asked Shay. "I heard that Lotte lost hers. She updated me."

"I left it behind on purpose."

Shay held my gaze.

We'd both been in the kinds of situations where we'd learned to follow our intuition. But clearly my having to use a ruse didn't sound good.

Cameron's jaw flexed. "How's Reese?"

"She's well." I shook my head. "But she has an agenda."

"She knew we were searching for her?" he asked.

"Yes."

"Her excuse?"

"Believing she could change the world with her activist work. Leaving behind a life she didn't want, the life her father wanted for her. There's more to it, though."

Her comment about my family's disapproval had hurt the most—as though I would have had no sway.

"How did she seem?" asked Cameron.

"Older, but the same in many ways."

"Was her daughter with her?" asked Shay.

"No."

"The reason she's surfaced?" My brother's voice held a quiet fury.

"She wants financial support to stop a company from building in the preserve."

"That's a surprise," Cameron said sarcastically.

"It's a beautiful place," I admitted. "I've invited her to L.A. I'll deliver my decision in person."

"You're considering it?" said Shay.

"I'm in the consideration phase."

Shay studied my face. "I wonder what Lotte thinks about all of this?"

Both their expressions were filled with affection at the mention her name.

"Right now she's super tired. We did a lot of walking."

Cameron's fingers curled and then relaxed as he seemingly imagined the dangers we'd trekked through.

"I'd have given my life for her," I said softly.

Cameron leaned forward. "She felt the same, Henry."

Her coming with me had been both welcome and a responsibility. She'd made the entire spectacle tolerable.

The flight attendant handed us each a mug of tea.

I wrapped my hands around the heavy porcelain, sipping my favorite brew. All the other luxuries of home were a five-hour flight away.

Shay beamed. "Talk about building the tension. You and Lotte, I mean."

I stared back at him. "Yes."

My brother looked concerned.

I knew he'd want reassuring. "It was good spending time with her. Getting to know her—"

"Under difficult circumstances," he said.

We'd made love before I'd arrived at Reese's camp. Anyway, that wasn't any of their business.

And yet my brother seemed to pick up on that.

Cameron leaned back against the headrest. "Wow."

"Disapprove?" I bit back.

He smirked, but he seemed pleased. "I'm glad you finally saw what the rest of us have been witnessing."

"Yeah, finally," chided Shay.

"Charlotte's the grace none of us deserve," said Cameron sincerely.

"Thank you for covering for me," I said.

Prior to boarding on Friday, I'd emailed my brother and asked that he hold down the fort while I was away.

"There's a lot going on," I added.

"Just a small matter of corporate espionage," said Cameron.

"Any updates?" I asked.

Shay waved that off. "We have a few reports for you."

"I'll take a look." I shrugged. "I needed a weekend away."

"Much deserved," said Cameron. "Even if you had our head of security here tracking your every move on the SATCOM."

I'd assumed as much. "I'd have done the same."

Cameron peered out the window. "So would I."

"By the way, I left the rental car at the edge of the preserve," I told Shay.

"A Land Rover Discovery, right?"

They'd even kept tabs on my credit card activity. I'd hired the best so what did I expect?

"Consider it dealt with," said Shay.

I couldn't blame them. I was the golden child guiding a billion-dollar company through the twenty-first century. A lot counted on keeping me alive.

As the tension lifted, I felt the drag of exhaustion. Not even the tea could help me rally.

Seeing my past clearly for the first time, the shame I'd felt from what I thought I had done wrong back then was finally dissipating. My journey into the preserve had left me vindicated.

All this had also gotten me closer to one of the most remarkable women I'd ever met.

Charlotte.

"Get some sleep," Cameron said softly.

I chose not to disturb Lotte by sharing the bed. I stayed in my seat, eyelids closing, body relaxing, drifting into unconsciousness—my thoughts finding refuge in the only person who had ever brought me solace.

CHAPTER THIRTY-SIX

Lotte

B LINKING AWAKE, I PEERED OUT OF THE TOWN CAR'S window to see we'd arrived outside Henry's home.

When the jet had landed at Santa Monica airport, Cameron and Shay had headed off in one car and we had left in another.

"What time is it?" I asked sleepily.

"Three A.M." He gave me an endearing smile.

I stretched. "Can your driver drop me off at my place?"

"Of course," he said. "If that's what you want."

"You don't want some alone time?"

He lowered his voice. "I have an NDA on my desk for you to sign."

I blinked some more. "Oh?"

"Joking." He elbowed me playfully. "I thought it might be nice to have some breakfast."

"You don't have to do this," I whispered.

"I want to do this. Let's go in. I can drive you home any time you want. Or arrange a car if you'd prefer."

I sensed he was trying to be kind.

Also, he probably didn't want to discuss anything in front of his chauffeur. Maybe he wanted to debrief me.

And not the fun type of debriefing, either.

Even though I was still wearing his boxers.

"I'll carry your backpack in," he said, watching my reaction.

I thumped Henry's arm playfully.

Laughing, and surprisingly awake, he leaped out of the car.

The chauffeur opened my door. I thanked him as I suppressed a yawn.

Henry led me into the foyer.

I covered my mouth, yawning again. "I'm sorry."

"You slept on the plane!"

"Kept waking up."

He studied me for a while and then relented.

"Come on." He took my hand and had me follow him up the winding staircase.

He guided me along a marble hallway. It was fun seeing more of the house. I'd only glimpsed some of the ground floor the last time I'd visited during the garden party.

We walked into a dramatically decorated room. I saw nothing personal of his in this guest bedroom.

I pretended not to be offended. "This is pretty."

"Not my taste. That will hopefully change soon." He walked over to the duvet and patted it. "Better than a sleeping bag, though, right?"

"That depends," I said seductively.

His expression showed conflicting emotions. "Everything you need is in the bathroom."

Then it hit me—he'd brought me into the house so he could have *that talk*.

Right up until I appeared too tired for one.

He was going to tell me this weekend had been an anomaly. That we'd both crumpled under the pressure of extraordinary circumstances—nothing more, nothing less. The sex had been amazing but now we were back to reality.

"We'll talk later," he said, walking away.

Maybe he suspected I was too tired to discuss the end of our brief affair.

He paused in the doorway, watching me.

"The room is perfect," I said.

"Sleep well." He gave a nod and closed the door behind him.

I stood still for a second, a victim of his formality.

Anyway, I was too tired to get back in that car and drive home. Crashing here would do fine.

Taking advantage of his bathroom, I had to stop myself from falling to my knees and worshipping the open marble shower.

I felt grateful to pull off my boots.

After stripping off my clothes, I mulled over whether to keep Henry's boxers as a souvenir.

Cringing, I realized that I'd left wearing Reese's pants, and someone else's socks. I'd left my hand washed clothes back at the preserve, too.

But at least we were both home safe.

I stepped beneath the piping hot water, the force of it pummeling my aching limbs and washing off the grime of sweat and dust.

Eventually, I dragged myself out from under the blissful cascade and climbed into his king-sized bed, snuggling beneath the covers and drifting off to sleep.

And dreaming.

My feet sank into the swampy land as I searched frantically for someone.

"Henry!"

I jerked awake, my heart racing. I let out a long breath, taking a few seconds to re-orient myself and recognize my surroundings. I was sleeping in a strange bed—though not *his*.

My bad dream was not surprising considering the stress I'd put myself through. My subconscious had taken the hit.

And now I was starving.

Slipping out of bed, I peeked between the window blinds, seeing darkness. I must have only slept an hour.

I pulled on the luxury bathrobe Henry had given me and padded out to search for something to eat. He wouldn't mind if I investigated the fridge.

I soon found the kitchen, which was as big as my living room and a lot more luxurious. A pot of coffee was brewing, the scent of delicious beans filling the room.

That's right. I'd slept in the bed of a tea and coffee mogul.

How fun is that?

Had sex with him, too.

That story was reserved for the history books.

I opened his fridge.

Hmmm.

There was a generous collection of pasta dishes that could be heated up in the microwave. Olives in fancy jars. Pots of caviar. A selection of fruit. Chef prepared meals. Beneath a silver dome lay a selection of desserts.

And sugar was exactly what I was craving.

After washing my hands, I found a small plate and placed a large chocolate éclair on it. This was my reward for surviving an adventure of a lifetime in the untamed wilderness.

Taking a seat at one of the central island's barstools, I bit into the éclair and moaned as cream oozed out of my mouth. I licked my fingers.

"That's not erotic at all," said Henry.

I yelped in surprise—then laughed nervously.

He'd been sitting in the shadows all this time, seemingly comfortable in a high-backed chair with an iPad on his lap.

"You scared me to death!" I blurted out.

He set the iPad down.

"Hope you don't mind." I pointed to the fridge.

"I'm glad you're making yourself at home."

"What are you reading?"

He stood and stretched. "Catching up on work."

"This early?"

He strolled over to the coffee pot and filled two large mugs. Then he carried them back to the central island and slid one of the mugs over the counter to me, taking a seat on the barstool opposite.

"Thank you." I brought the mug closer to me. "You're not a sleep monster like me."

"No."

He was acting bashful again—an endearing trait that made me swoon every single time.

His intense gaze captured mine. "How do you feel?"

"Good, considering." I pushed the other half of the éclair toward him. "After all that walking we did."

"You're having that for breakfast?" He arched a brow, chastising me.

"Why not?"

He lifted the éclair and then bit into the pastry, immediately giving a nod of approval, his face lighting up with joy. Cream oozed out and he licked it off his fingers, lapping the side of his mouth with his tongue.

He caught me staring.

"Yummy, right?"

"Cameron's the one with the sweet tooth," he said. "But I can see this becoming a tradition."

I'd tried hard not to like this man so much, but now I was seeing another side to him, his authentic side. I was mesmerized by his boyishness, the part he kept hidden behind a steely facade.

I cherished access to his true nature.

"Can I cook you something more substantial?" He pointed to the plate.

"No, thank you. This is delicious."

He pushed off the barstool and stood. "Sure?"

That sounded like a social cue.

My face flushed. "I'm ready."

"For what?"

"To go home."

"Back to Encino?"

"Everything is fine. I'm perfectly capable of coping with a brief affair." I tried to read his stern expression.

"That's what it was to you?"

"You've been through a lot," I reasoned. "You need time to process."

"Do you?"

"I'm not going to make this difficult."

"You want to leave?"

"Don't you want me to?"

He waved his hand. "I'm blunt. You've learned that about me. I don't play games, ever. So, here's what I'm going to do. The Jacuzzi is on. I'm going climb in and soothe my weary bones. Turns out I'm not the fit stud I used to be. Need time to recoup." He smiled. "You're welcome to join me and I'd love it if you would. You and me under the night sky. Just like old times."

He headed out of the kitchen.

"You're going now?"

"No pressure. Leave if you want. I won't be offended. I'll have a driver take you home."

"Thank you."

He pivoted to face me. "I had this vision," he added. "Me in the Jacuzzi, watching you strip naked before me. Me with the best seat in the house."

Butterflies went crazy in my chest.

"But I'm fine with whatever you decide."

Watching him go, I tried to comprehend that he wanted more time with me.

"Henry!" I called after him.

He paused in the doorway.

"I'll join you, if you're sure?"

He came back for me, grabbing my wrist and leading me through the house like we were on another adventure together.

We strolled by a replica of a famous Roman statue and

swapped an amused glance. Farther down, a vast canvas hung boldly on a white wall, shades of gold set with lavish tones.

"Oh, I'm in love." I moved closer to inspect the masterpiece.

"One of mine."

I stared at him in awe. "You painted this?"

"We both have a thing for rich colors, apparently."

"We do!"

Although his dark carved frame was worth a small fortune. I felt the familiar persuasion of an art piece that tempted the voyeur to reach out and brush their fingers over the masterful strokes— the miraculous allure of fine art.

I smiled, feeling a flurry of contentment that we had a common passion.

Happiness—it springs up when you least expect it and finds its way to you when you've wondered for so long if you'd ever visit its shores again.

We continued onto the terrace.

Next to the swimming pool was a generously-sized Jacuzzi. And there, scattered around it and atop the bubbles, lay countless rose petals.

He was showing me that what we'd experienced in Florida meant something. We'd connected on a deeper level.

"Did you do this?" I asked.

He ran his fingers through his hair as though he was unsure how I felt.

"Henry, you planned this?"

"Came out here half an hour ago. Wanted to surprise you when you woke."

"This is romantic."

"You deserve it."

He began stripping off his clothes, again revealing his ripped chest and impressively muscular physique—a form sculpted by his days playing rugby.

The area was softly lit, the height of the walls ensuring no one could spy on us. Almost two weeks ago he'd hosted a party on the lawn—the day I'd been introduced to his parents.

The same day when we'd unwittingly revealed our magnetism.

I remembered how we'd almost kissed.

So many kisses had followed since—our affection was uncontainable.

Instinctively, my gaze rose to the roof. He'd admitted that, at the same party, he'd almost jumped from the highest point into his pool. Gauging it, I wanted to believe he'd have made it safely into the deep end. Glad Cameron had stopped us from finding out.

Henry had a vulnerable side, and I adored deciphering every part and facet of him. Naked now, he descended the steps into the bubbling Jacuzzi, slowly lowering himself into the blue swirling water.

I untied my bathrobe and opened it so he could view my naked body.

His eyes devoured me hungrily.

I shrugged the robe off my shoulders, posing seductively as it slipped down and pooled at my feet. "Like this?"

"Exactly like that."

I arched a brow suggestively. "What comes next in this fantasy of yours?"

He held out his hand, beckoning for me to join him.

CHAPTER THIRTY-SEVEN

Lotte

HEATED BUBBLING WATER ENVELOPED ME AS I SUNK INTO the hot Jacuzzi, surrounded by pure luxury, feeling grateful for every minute spent with Henry.

As he pulled me toward him, I admired his kissable mouth, savoring the sight of his handsome features.

Being with him like this, alone and intimate, was a rare privilege.

With his chest submerged in the swirling water, Henry seemed just as content.

"The staff doesn't arrive for hours," he reassured me.

"We can do anything we want."

"Anything." He reached up to cup my face with strong hands, his mouth closing in on mine. That first shock of our tongues touching sparked arousal, meaningful and passionate.

He crushed me to him and my legs wrapped around his waist easily in the buoyancy of the water. I threw my head back in surprised laughter as he spun me around and pressed me against the rounded tile wall.

"You're trapped," he said gruffly.

"Totally."

"I'm going to have to punish you for losing your rucksack."

"You left yours behind."

"I'm going to punish you for that, too."

"How is that one my fault?"

"I don't have to have a good reason to punish you."

"How will you punish me?"

"In a less painful way than your skill set." His kisses trailed along my jaw line, down my throat and along my chest, sending tingling sensations into my skin.

His cock pressed against me. With a tipping of my pelvis, he slid all the way in with ease, my pussy wet for him. His impressive girth stretched me wide and I held my breath as I acclimated to his growing size. He filled me entirely.

"Wait," I said. "I just want to be still."

"I've got you," he said huskily.

Caught between him and the wall behind me, I held onto him, embracing his body, wanting us to be one. Resting my head in the crook of his neck, I inhaled his delicious cologne.

Feeling him twitch inside me, I knew he was equally aroused but patiently letting me have this moment between us, my expression one of delight.

"I missed this," he said.

Never wanting to be separated from him, I wished I could stop time and stay in this peaceful, serene moment.

His kisses resumed along the shell of my ear, tenderly gliding to my throat, leaving tingles of sensual pleasure. I longed for more even as he showered me with affection.

"Beautiful." His palm caressed my nipple.

Sensitive, it beaded beneath his touch, sending a frisson of bliss through me.

"Every part of you is perfect," he added, his kisses trailing over to my other breast. "Charlotte, I can't see past you." He drew in a sharp breath.

"Take me," I begged, feeling breathless.

Swapping violent kisses, our bodies sank deeper into the water, into the rhythm, into each other.

He pulled his cock out a little then plunged back inside me, delivering delicious strokes, both of us craving this desperate friction. His palm slid down between us and found my clit, making me squirm.

The intense pleasure caused me to buck and ride him with verve, chasing my release.

"Come together," he said, his voice sultry.

Giving myself over completely I pounded him back, hips crashing against his as he reciprocated with fierce strikes.

We shattered together at the same time, hard and fast, water splashing as he thrust into me.

He was giving me everything I had been missing. We were lovers desperate for more of each other. My fingernails clawed his back as I rode his length, drawing out the delicious spasms from his cock, crying out at the pleasure and trembling from his frenzied fucking.

His body stilled as he came hard inside me, going rigid, eyelids closed as he endured his seemingly endless orgasm, spilling his heat inside me and burying his face in the crook of my neck.

We shuddered through the aftershocks of our release. Resting my head back, I let the waves of orgasm linger.

We moved apart after that, needing to recapture our decorum after revealing the truth of our mutual obsession.

Settling opposite each other, we continued to soak in the heated water while sharing the occasional glance of contentment.

After half an hour, we finally climbed out of the Jacuzzi.

Once we were back on dry land, he lifted me and carried me through the house. The shock of the air conditioning was stark against my skin, his welcome body warmth easy to crave.

We made love all over again beneath the generous downpour of his open plan shower.

Breathless, and with me boneless after another hard fucking, I felt grateful for the way he dried me off with a plush blue towel.

I took him up on his offer to borrow a T-shirt that swamped me and a pair of his shorts. I cinched it with a belt I also found in one of his bedroom drawers.

I needed to go home so I could dress in my own clothes.

We just weren't ready to be parted yet.

Or at least I wasn't.

We ate a heartier breakfast than those few bites of profiterole that I'd found previously in his fridge.

While I brewed more coffee, I had fun watching Henry scramble eggs and make toast, move around his kitchen like he'd lived here forever—and acting like this was normal for us to prepare breakfast together.

We tucked into the fresh food, grateful not to have to eat another processed meal like the ones we'd eaten during our adventure.

Every precious moment I'd spent with him at the preserve was playing in my mind like a movie, and I suddenly had a flash of inspiration.

"I want to take you somewhere special," I said. "Only I don't have a car."

"You're okay going out like that?"

"No one will see me wearing your clothes."

"Going to give me a clue?"

"It's better to show you."

He looked intrigued, and in less than a minute we were standing inside his impressive garage trying to decide which of his three cars to choose.

The Range Rover was so very him. There was also a silver Mercedes and a bright red Tesla Roadster.

I blinked at the choice. "I can't believe these are all yours."

"What are you in the mood for?"

"Any of them, and I'm driving," I said.

"Want to take the Roadster?" He grabbed some keys from a lockbox and threw them in the air.

I caught them.

The red Roadster would be the flashiest car I'd ever driven. It was like something out of the future.

Henry pressed his thumbprint against the car door to unlock it. "Want the roof down?"

"Yes, please." I leaped into the driver's seat, inhaling that new car smell. "This is flashy for you."

"I didn't buy it."

"Was it your mom?"

"Dad." He settled into the passenger seat beside me. "I was happy with the Rover."

With a press of his thumb, the engine started.

Carefully, I navigated the expensive car out of the garage and down the long driveway, turning onto the street. The car was responsive and the ride was smooth.

We took the 405 freeway.

Even at five in the morning, traffic remained heavy, but the outside lane allowed us to make good time to see the sunrise.

We made it to our destination in just over an hour.

Henry knew why we were here. His demeanor revealed the tension he was feeling.

I parked the Roadster against the curb.

"A beach," he said warily.

"Huntington City Beach." I watched his reaction. "It has lovely sand."

He gave a reluctant nod.

Reaching over, I rested my hand on his. "One step at a time."

His shoulders slumped as he stared past me toward the Pacific Ocean.

"Remember that time on the motorboat," I said softly, "and what we talked about?"

"I remember."

"You envisioned this." It had kept him going.

"Don't make me regret sharing that."

"It's important to feel safe enough to share our deepest memories."

"And hopes for the future?"

I shook my head because that wasn't relevant.

He turned in his seat. "You'd like to be a mom one day?"

I took a deep breath, my gaze meeting his.

"It wasn't hard to guess," he said. "You're very nurturing."

"This is about you." I replied. "You deserve to find peace."

"I know." He exhaled slowly. "Have you heard of the luminous?"

"Yes."

He smiled. "It's what Rudolf Otto, an eminent German philosopher, called the experience of being in a state of mysterious terror and awe—experiencing the majesty of the human condition at its most beautiful and terrible."

"Whether experienced close-up or personally felt," I added.

"A sacred privilege," he said softly, "like holding the hand of a dying man; beautiful and horrifying at the same time."

Something told me he'd actually had that experience.

"It's a privilege to see pain close up," I said with quiet respect.

Henry understood that, for me, this was both painful and profound, helping him fulfill this promise. Because he had shared the weight of what this meant.

"Let me be there for you," he said.

His words were absorbed deep into my heart.

We exited the car and, hand in hand with fingers entwined, we strolled the short distance to the edge of the sand.

Sitting on the short wall, we removed our shoes and tucked our socks inside them before picking them up to carry with us.

Standing back to give him space, I let him take that first step onto the sandy beach, trusting in this sacred moment—a milestone in his recovery.

He didn't need to say anything. We both knew what this meant.

He studied his feet in the sand and then gestured for me to join him.

The moment my bare feet sank into the sand, I relaxed. Something as simple as this was a conduit to calmness.

We trekked along the beach as waves crashed close by, enjoying the smell of the fresh air and the feel of the balmy morning breeze.

Glancing over at Henry, I saw he, too, was drinking in the view.

"The profoundness of the earth's creator," I whispered. "Soak it in."

"I am." He dragged in another lungful of air.

This time, I stayed back, taking a seat on the sand.

My view now was a man strolling toward the water's edge, fulfilling a promise to himself.

As though he was able to go backwards in time and say, *"I made it. I'm alive. I pulled through. Permission to live."*

Henry threw down his shoes and rolled up his pant legs to prevent them from getting wet. Then he bowed his head as if saying a prayer before finally peering skyward.

I said a prayer of my own, beseeching God to allow Henry to find freedom from his internal pain.

We had asked so much of him.

He'd been sent into battle to protect the world and keep us safe. He had fought willingly, aware of the ultimate price and the sacrifice that would be demanded of him.

His heart and mind had been carrying the burden.

Henry.

Holding my breath, I observed him moving closer to the rippling water.

Finally, he stepped forward, bathing his feet up to his ankles in frothy rolling surf, a tall silhouette of a man against the horizon.

As a healer, what I had hoped for him was this experience to serve as a way for all the fragments of his consciousness to come together to bring about a harmonious balance so he could find a peaceful, brighter future.

Cameron had begun this healing journey for Henry. Maybe I was the one who could lead him back to that path.

Only he could walk that stark passage out into the light. Words were not needed. Not anymore. These moments were dedicated to him with the hope that one day he'd heal from what had happened in the past.

I took a shaky breath, my gaze never leaving him.

Finally, Henry turned to me and smiled.

CHAPTER THIRTY-EIGHT

Henry

T UESDAY FELT LIKE A MONDAY.

I finally peered up from the file in front of me and pushed my chair back from the desk.

Jen stood on the other side, bright face greeting me as she set a coffee on a coaster. She wore one of her pristine suits, her stance reflecting business as usual here at Cole Tower.

Again, I thought back to yesterday in Malibu.

I thought about *her*.

Lotte's insight had us both visiting the beach; a simple yet profound gift I should have already given myself. It had helped more than I had believed it would.

After our tumultuous weekend, that visit to the ocean had also refreshed me.

I eased my constricting necktie away from my throat.

Reese, the reason we'd flown to Florida in the first place, had morphed into a memory that landed differently now.

Which felt insane.

The yearnings of a young man had been turned toward something greater.

"Sir?" Jen said, pulling my focus back to the present.

"Yes."

"Everything all right? You had a long weekend off."

"I needed a break," I said.

"Go anywhere nice?"

Yesterday, I'd buried my feet in the sand. It had felt cathartic. Our visit to Huntington City Beach was a memory I'd cherish.

But I didn't want to share that with anyone.

"Relaxed, mostly."

"Can I help you with that?" She pointed to the file.

"Not yet."

"You've had a meeting request from Lilly Vergara," she said.

"She's in town?" I was thoughtful. "Later this afternoon works for me."

"Who is she?"

I hesitated to answer. "An acquaintance," I finally said.

She turned to peer out the expansive window. "How did you pull it off?"

I followed her gaze. "You're referring to Dandelion Diva's ad coming down?"

"Yes," she said warily. "And Cole Tea's ad now in its place."

It was a more tasteful movie-styled billboard featuring the beauty of the tea leaf itself.

"Who told you I took it down?" Sitting back, I studied her, watching for any sign that might reveal she had inside knowledge of our rival.

"The team from marketing mentioned it," she said.

"We became a client of their ad company. Told them the deal with us was contingent on them dropping Dandelion Diva's contract."

"You made them drop their client?"

I gave a shrug.

It was a cold move—but necessary. If you poke a lion don't be surprised when it shows its teeth.

"What do you think of them?" she asked.

A reasonable question, her showing interest in a company that had flaunted itself within sight of the tower.

So far, Jen hadn't shown she had any insight into that situation.

A small business could reverse engineer a major company and learn how to evolve. Every company had to contend with idea theft. It wasn't new. It was, however, a royal pain in the ass.

"What are your thoughts on them?" I asked.

Jen started to answer, but then noticed Shay standing in the doorway.

"Now a good time?" he asked.

I motioned for him to come in. "Always a good time for you, Shay."

Jen reached for the file on my desk.

I rested my palm on it. "Give me a day on this."

"I'll scan it—or whatever you need me to do."

I shook my head. "Not yet."

I watched as she walked out of the office, closing the door behind her.

Turning to Shay, I asked, "How are you?" I gestured for him to take a seat across from my desk.

"Fine." He glanced at the file as he sat opposite me. "She seemed eager to get her hands on that."

I opened it again and scanned the summary of our fake brand. "The recipe tracks."

"If copied by Dandelion Diva, we have them."

"Jen's not involved," I said quietly. "She's been with the company for years."

"She relocated from New York. This is a good position. She'd be a fool to fuck it up. She has a pension here."

"Something bothering you?" I could read him as easily as he read me.

"Griffin, your driver. I've got some Intel."

"Go on."

"His father was a medic. Died in an explosion in Afghanistan." Shay leaned forward. "You want him to continue driving you but—"

"Until you have something more substantial."

Shay couldn't hide his frustration. "I'll work on the timeline from when we were over there. Check for any crossover with his dad's deployment."

"Good plan."

"Griffin has never once mentioned to you that his dad served in the military?"

I shook my head. "It's unusual."

Considering he'd been driving me around for months.

Shay crossed one leg over the other. "I've emailed you the report on Community Development. They're set to build on the preserve in three days."

"That doesn't give us a lot of time."

"What do you want to do?"

"Slow them down."

His frown deepened. "We can have a council member out there halt construction. Find an issue that needs resolving."

I raised my hands in the air. "Don't tell me any other details."

He nodded. "How's Lotte?"

I smirked at his subtle way of fishing. "Exceptional."

"You guys are getting along?"

"She stayed over last night."

Though we'd arrived home in the early morning, so it had made sense.

Admittedly, I hadn't wanted her to leave.

Shay studied me. "Seeing Reese didn't stir up any old emotions?"

His question was super private, but we'd been through a lot together.

"I've lived my entire life imagining what it would be like if I ever saw Reese again. I loved her once. Saw us getting married."

But after what she had done to everyone, and her reasoning behind it, even with all the good she has done in the world I couldn't get over it.

"Do you regret inviting her here?"

I shrugged.

"You're only human."

"Excuse me?" I said, grinning.

He smirked. "Superhuman."

"Exactly."

"What was it like? Seeing her again after all this time?"

"I felt nothing."

"Yet with Lotte?"

I raised a hand. "Can you let me work through our friendship first? I get that she's your dear friend, but we need some space from everyone crowding us."

"Of course," he said. "It's just that we're all blown away that you're seriously dating a dominatrix."

That hit harder than I expected.

"She left Chrysalis," I said. "She's not going back."

He blinked at me, and then looked away.

My stomach clenched. "Richard let her go, temporarily. But she's going to work as a therapist in Beverly Hills. Cameron offered her the job."

Shay chewed on his lip.

"She's not going back," I repeated.

"Okay, good." He didn't appear too certain.

"Are you making any progress on our spy?"

"I'll have my report for you ASAP." Shay pushed up. "Speaking of which, I have to get back to work."

He headed for the door.

I sat back, realizing Lotte had not clarified when she'd be leaving that Bel Air manor.

From Shay's reaction, Lotte might already be back at Chrysalis.

CHAPTER THIRTY-NINE

Henry

STANDING IN THE FOYER, I COULD SEE THE APPEAL OF BEING greeted by a half-naked submissive. She was on her knees before me, her slender figure hugged by a tight-fitting bodice, her expression full of adoration.

Totally hot, to be honest.

Maybe it was her comfort level or the fact I'd visited before, but I was no longer surprised by anything at Chrysalis.

Dex sat by my feet.

The submissive reached out to pet him. I didn't miss the fact that they were both wearing collars.

"I'm here to see Lotte," I told her.

"Sir, please wait here," she said, her voice soft and inviting as she pushed up. "Dogs are only allowed with permission."

"Rules are broken all the time here," I chided.

Richard strolled across the foyer toward me. "Cole!"

I cringed when I saw him.

"Twice in two weeks," he said, sounding snarky. "To what do we owe the pleasure this time?"

"Lotte's not answering her phone."

He rested his palm on the submissive's spine. "Thank you."

She gazed at him with worship in her eyes—a popular theme around here.

"Take the dog for a walk." He gestured for her to disappear with Dex.

Agreeing, I handed over the leash to her.

We both watched the erotic scene of the sub strolling toward a hallway, round ass on show, peering back at us seductively as Dex happily trotted off with her.

Richard noticed my expression of concern. "She loves dogs."

I still eyed her suspiciously.

Richard added, "She watches over Winston. She's perfectly capable."

"Andrea doesn't mind?" I asked, curious. "You touching other people like that?"

"That's a show of kindness. You should try it."

"Here we go," I said. "The mighty gatekeeper of Chrysalis on the defensive."

He visibly centered himself.

"Sorry." I drew in a calming breath. "It's been a rough day."

His sigh was infused with sympathy. "Come on, let's wait in my office. We can catch up. I'll message Lotte to meet us there."

Lotte *was* here.

"I thought you banned her?" I said.

"Not permanently."

"What is she doing?"

"Right now? She's in a session—"

"Don't want to hear it." My frustration was simmering close to the surface.

Richard changed the subject. "You caught the sun in Florida."

"Is Lotte with a male client?"

He raised his hand to clarify. "It's not what you think."

Really?

It sounded *exactly* like what I thought.

He motioned for me to go on ahead. "Walk with me."

"I'll find her myself." I headed off toward the door that led to a stairwell.

My imagination swirled with what kind of client I'd find her with, what kind of compromising position.

Had last night meant nothing? We'd literally made love for over an hour in my Jacuzzi and then continued to make love in the shower.

Then, we'd driven to Huntington City Beach. I'd shared one of my most precious moments with her.

Did all that mean nothing? Because it meant everything to me.

Yet she'd snuck back here.

I could feel Richard's glare on my back as he followed me, probably getting a kick out of me trying to find my way around.

We descended into the lower level. Learning my way around was relatively easy, but knowing what to say to Lotte was an entirely different challenge.

Eventually we reached the lower level and the scent of vanilla mixed with incense hit me. It was the familiar scent I remembered from when I'd visited over two weeks ago.

Just two weeks.

And I was already possessive of her.

Along the dimly lit hallway was a row of doors, lights above several of them. I guessed that meant they were occupied.

"Which one?" I turned to Richard, sophisticated enough not to interrupt a scene.

I just didn't want *my* woman touching another man in any scenario, which was fair.

"Allow me," said Richard, moving by me and walking up to a door.

He knocked lightly and then opened it just wide enough to slip through into the room, making sure I couldn't see past him. A few seconds later he reemerged, backing out.

"Who is he?" I barged forward.

Richard blocked me. "If she barged in on you during a meeting, how would you feel?"

"This is different."

Lotte appeared at the door, just behind Richard. "Henry!"

My jaw tensed when I saw the whip, words failing me.

She wore next to nothing—a bodice and panties with stockings and boots.

"Go next door." She pointed. "You can see through the window."

"I've seen enough."

Lotte disappeared for a beat and then stepped out into the hallway. "Follow me."

She was clothed as a seductive dominatrix, wielding that familiar riding whip in her right hand.

I hesitated for a beat and then agreed to follow her down the hallway. She opened a door and gestured for me to step inside.

I went on ahead, pivoting to peer through the window into the room she'd left. I was immediately mesmerized by the four submissives kneeling before another dominatrix. The erotic sight was extraordinary.

Lotte came to stand beside me. "It's a one-way mirror. They can't see us."

"Isn't that a breach of their privacy?" I shot back, feeling relieved there wasn't some hot-blooded male in there.

"They've been under my tutelage. I'm transferring them to Penny Lansbury."

"Do you really need to dress half-naked for that?"

"Excuse me?" She turned away. "You just interrupted a session."

"Might just stay for the entire show."

Her whip hit my ass. It stung like a motherfucker.

"Follow me," she demanded as she led me out.

We walked across the hall—right into an empty dungeon.

She appeared calm, but I knew me being here unannounced would piss her off.

I hated we were having this disagreement.

It was a sparse room with one familiar piece—a St. Andrew's Cross in the center. A high-backed velvet chair sat nearby with a gold-colored ottoman beside it. Long drapes framed the floor-to-ceiling windows. The fake Paris landscape looked extraordinary.

"No expense spared," I mused.

She moved closer to me with a sharp confidence. "Your behavior is unacceptable."

"Behavior?"

"I intend to leave Chrysalis, but on my terms."

"You have a job waiting for you in Beverly Hills."

"I'm still talking, Mr. Cole." She raised her whip. "The submissives you saw are under my supervision. Leaving permanently without an official transfer would compromise their progress. They are vulnerable."

"Maybe they shouldn't be here at all, Ms. Chamberlain."

"No, you're not going to intimidate me."

"Or is it Mistress?"

"Take off your shirt."

"You've got some nerve."

"I told you to remove your shirt."

"Remember who you're talking to!"

She pointed her whip at the St. Andrew's Cross. "Stand there."

"I'm not doing this with you."

"You need a taste of what I do. This is how we'll build respect. Now walk."

"No."

"Humor me."

Dragging my fingernails across my five o'clock shadow, I tried to find some semblance of normality to hold on to.

"Do it for me," she whispered.

Hanging my head, I decided I owed her a few minutes of my time because we'd already shared so much.

Our intimacy meant something. What we'd shared meant

everything. Only it was hard to dial down my jealousy when I was here in this place.

Blinking through the dusky light, I glanced at the St. Andrew's Cross. "I'm not into pain."

"I remember."

"This is a waste of time."

She snapped her whip against her high latex boot.

Her sternness was amusing and admittedly arousing, though I'd never give up control.

Stomping across the room, I turned my back and leaned against the Cross. "Same perspective."

Her hips swayed as she walked by me to get to the curtains. It was intriguing to watch her legs in those high-heeled boots glide by with elegance. Right up until I saw what she brought back.

"Here." She ordered me to raise my hand. "It's silk. You can break free anytime."

"Why?"

"You want answers. I'm going to give them to you."

"That's a hard pass."

"Really? Because I recall going all the way to Florida for you."

God, she was infuriating.

Resting my right hand on the side bar, I let her tie my wrist to the structure. A tug proved her theory. If I wanted to, I could break free. She did the same with the other strip of silk, securing my left arm.

"Now what?" I studied her annoyingly stunning face; cheeks flushed from her quiet fuming.

Multicolored lights danced over her figure, her curves emphasized by the sensual outfit that clung to her shape.

Lotte stepped back and then dragged a chair across the room, setting it in front of me. "Let's talk."

She sat like a therapist.

I considered breaking free. "You're not qualified to mess with my head."

"That's not what this is." She waved her whip at me. "Straighten up."

I straightened to my full height to appease her.

"We're going to calmly discuss your concerns about dating a dominatrix."

"I admire you for wanting to fight for this fragile relationship," I said bitterly. "But we can both see it's futile."

If my words hurt, she didn't show it.

I shook my head. "This isn't what I'm used to. It brings back memories of being forcibly restrained. I'm sorry."

She sat back, crossing one leg over the other, that pointed heel sharp and threatening. "You're not restrained."

True, but close.

"This is getting you to focus."

"Oh, I'm focused."

"What is the worst thing that would happen if the world discovered you were dating me?"

I gave a shrug at the obvious.

"Say it."

"Don't want to hurt you."

"Then you shouldn't have come."

"Me being here hurts you?"

"Turning up full of anger makes me uncomfortable."

She was right, of course.

"I'll be mocked in the press," I admitted.

"Let's explore that concern."

I hated the idea I might hurt her even worse. "I don't want people to believe I need to get whipped to get it up. Or that I like to be subjugated. I have more self-respect."

She nodded with the kind of agreement I'd seen in therapists. "Those in this community have plenty of self-respect. Enough to feed their desires, gift themselves whatever makes them happy."

"Fine."

"What if you leaked a different spin?" she suggested.

"Spin?"

She pushed up and closed the space between us. Her soft perfume absorbed into my psyche like a siren call. Close enough to touch, if only I could.

I considered her words. "I'd prefer to deny it."

"You could. Or you could share with the world that I've finally found the kind of man I can't dominate. Henry Cole—the formidable alpha who now possesses me. I've finally met my match. I've tamed oligarchs, princes, kings and presidents. But Henry Cole is the only man who ever tamed me."

I thought on it.

It might work.

But did I really want to be connected to this world?

She dropped the whip. Reaching around her back, she unclipped her satin bra. It dropped to the floor, leaving her pert breasts with beaded nipples.

Oh, God, what she did to me.

"It's my job to sense what you want," she said softly.

If she'd glanced down at my pants, she'd see my erection shoving against my zipper. What I "wanted" was her.

What I needed.

I longed to reach out and caress her pert nipples.

She leaned down and picked up her whip. "Your punishment awaits."

"I told you, I hate—"

"What if I told you I'm on the precipice of delivering blinding pleasure?"

"Just you and me?" I clarified.

"That's all you deserve."

That made me smirk.

"You're far too fond of being inside your own mind," she purred. "It's time to come over to my side. Experience my kind of freedom."

"The dark side?" I grinned at that.

She brushed the whip along my inner pant leg and moved it up farther to stroke my cock. "If you like."

The sensation made me ache, my cock roused to rock hardness by her seduction.

I couldn't shake this doubt.

No.

This wouldn't work.

Not now.

Not ever.

Breaking out of the silk ties, I twisted my wrists until they were free. I stepped forward and pressed my chest to hers, towering over her.

Maybe I should just fuck her in this room. Try out her theory for size. But I wasn't like the men who came here, the ones who bowed and gave over their power.

I needed her to see that.

Reaching around the back of her neck, I dragged her in close, dominating this scene. Proving I held *all* the power.

Her naked breasts were crushed against my chest, her mouth close to mine. Her perfume mixed with her secret lust, her expression open and trusting and full of desire.

God, I wanted her.

Wanted to see Chrysalis from her point of view.

I just couldn't get there.

Our kiss didn't happen. Couldn't happen—even when my body yearned for her.

For this.

A dark, delicious fuck that would have her signature all over it.

Eventually, I persuaded myself to let her go. "Excuse me, please."

She stepped back. "Henry?"

"I thought we had an understanding."

"What do you want me to say?"

"I'm sorry, Charlotte." I bowed my head.

This isn't working.

Her face wore a surprised expression.

I couldn't bear to see her heart wounded.

"I'll call you later," I said.

"This is goodbye?"

Better not to say it.

I walked fast toward the door. When I reached it, I paused, searching for all the things I could say, or should say.

I refused to look back at that striking beauty who was threatening to destroy me with a threat of love.

I stepped out of the chamber and closed the door behind me, shutting her out. Had I glimpsed her reaction, I'd be filled with doubt. Maybe that would have made me stay. A mistake I couldn't risk.

I retraced my steps through the manor.

Ending this, ending *us*, was already proving more painful than anticipated.

When I made it to the foyer, I paused beneath the impressive chandelier, staring into the prism of light glinting above.

Go back.

Tell her you need more time.

I stared at the brightly colored crystals as though searching for answers—looking to that light for confirmation that I'd made the right decision.

Dex scampered up to me, thrilled to see me like I'd been away too long. The submissive handed me back his leash.

I wondered if this submissive knew I'd fallen for her mistress.

Dex rubbed against me with affection.

"Hey, buddy." I caressed his head.

"I gave him a snack," said the young woman.

"Thank you." I headed for the door with Dex trotting beside me, glad to be escaping.

I'd sealed this break-up by doing it here, at her place of work. A cruel mistake.

One I'd have to reconcile later.

Walking away before the emotions I was feeling overwhelmed me was the best way to avoid pain.

I'd flown too dangerously close to this sensual world.

CHAPTER FORTY

Lotte

MY SHARP BREATHS ECHOED IN THE DARK CHAMBER AS I rested a hand on the St. Andrew's Cross to steady myself.

I just need a second.

Snapping my hands up, I covered my breasts like Henry was still here. For the first time in forever I felt vulnerable, naked and exposed.

Quickly reaching for my bra, I put it back on.

I'd served in this profession for over a decade. This was the first time I had ever doubted myself.

From the beginning, my intuition had warned me that nothing good could come from having a crush on Henry.

Yet I'd allowed *this* to happen.

The St. Andrew's Cross haunted my vision. What had I been thinking, tying him to it—even with silk binds.

Insanity.

I'd struggled to fight for something that was already a lost cause. Henry would never date a dominatrix. For me to have believed he could was crazy.

Yesterday, when we'd made love at his home, I hadn't known it would be the last time we'd ever be intimate.

My legs grew shaky at that thought, and I sank to the stone floor, sucking back tears. Kneeling, I clutched my stomach as I rode out this uncertainty, my body reacting viscerally. For a moment there, he'd felt like The One.

I felt someone touch my shoulder. Startled, I glanced back to see Richard. I hadn't even heard him enter the chamber.

"Come sit down." Richard helped me up and led me over to a high-backed chair.

He sat on the ottoman next to me, resting his hand on my leg.

"Has he gone?" I asked.

"He's gone," said Richard. "What happened?"

"Nothing."

"Henry looked surprised when he learned you were here," said Richard softly. "Did you tell him you'd left Chrysalis?"

Embarrassed, I stayed quiet.

He took a few seconds to process that information. "I get it."

"Not because of him. I'd already spoken with Cameron about working at his clinic."

"You'll always have everyone's support. We love you."

"I'd miss you all. It's hard to explain." Richard's kindness made me feel worse. "I should have told you."

"I could see something was troubling you." He brushed a strand of hair out of my face. "That's why I gave you time off."

"For a second there," I said huskily, "I thought we had something special."

"Lotte, anyone who has the privilege of meeting you experiences that connection."

"He can't date someone in my profession!" I blurted out. "I knew that."

"Load of crap."

"As much as I hate to say it, he's right. If the press found out about me, it would ruin his reputation."

"I don't see it."

"His breakup delivery was questionable," I said. "Only, the hurt in his eyes—"

"He's been through a lot." Richard squeezed my arm. "He's the only one I'd ever say this for, but Henry gets a pass."

"Because of Afghanistan?"

"It's a miracle he's made it this far."

"I know they hurt him."

"Lotte, what they did to him surpasses all comprehension."

"Did they waterboard him?" I whispered.

"Amongst other things," he said softly. "They pulled his fingernails out."

I squeezed back tears. "He never told me."

"They grew back. When he returned to the States, Henry was in bad shape."

"That's why he went to live in Big Bear?"

"He loved it up there. It was isolated, but he really seemed to like it. He learned to paint there. Did he tell you that?"

"Yes." But there was so much I still had to learn about him. *Impossible now.*

Richard let out a long sigh. "He just got back from seeing Reese, too, remember. "That would have taken a toll. Give him time."

"We're done." I gave a shrug.

"Men pull back when they become infatuated."

"Did you?"

"I pulled back the second I saw Andrea. Was a total dick."

"You both worked out."

"We worked out great." He stood up. "Give him some time, please."

I was digesting the painful truth. "Our situation is different."

Standing up, I braced myself to return to the room where Penny and the subs were waiting. I'd have to put on a brave face.

A silken tie lay at the feet of the St. Andrew's Cross. The one I'd misused.

Maybe, just maybe, seeing Reese again had influenced him more than I wanted to believe.

Richard pulled me into a hug. "Shay told me what happened in the Middle East. What Henry did to earn that medal."

"What?" I said breathlessly.

Richard held my shoulders. "Henry refused to leave anyone behind. He led them to safety." Pain flashed across Richard's expression. "Henry went back for a civilian. Their interpreter."

"That's how he got captured?" I whispered. "He was trying to save someone else?"

"Yes. They killed the interpreter and kept him alive."

"Because of his family name?"

"And his rank." Richard's eyes filled with sorrow. "Henry was willing to give his life. And in so many ways, he did."

"I'd gotten through to him." I'd reached him in his darkest hours. "I really believe that."

"There's no helping him, Lotte. He's destined to suffer like this for the rest of his life."

"Why?"

"Cameron says Henry has an aversion to love. I can't see that changing."

I put a hand over my heart, his words of futility cutting deep.

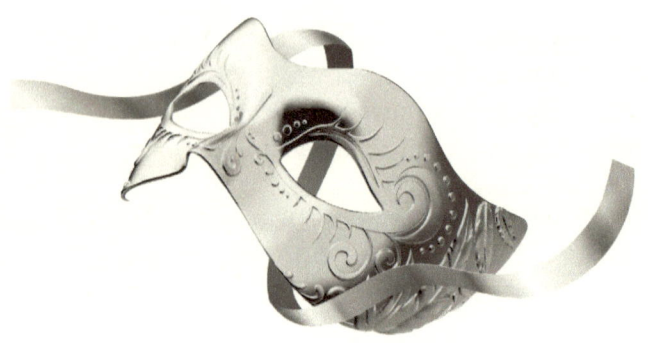

CHAPTER FORTY-ONE

Henry

"I FUCKED UP."

Not the best way to begin a conversation.

I'd downplay how crappy my day had gone and not drag Mia into the mire with me.

Everyone has a person who provides them with a safe harbor. For me, that person was Mia Cole. She had become one of my closest friends.

Standing at the entrance of her Beverly Hills manor, I waited for someone to answer.

This house was a stone's throw from mine.

Mia opened the door. "Henry!" She gestured for me to come in. "How are you?"

"Fine," I lied.

"Cameron's not here."

"That's okay."

No matter how many times I saw her, I'd be struck by her rare beauty, her elegance and her enduring kindness.

My brother was a lucky man. Mia was the best sister-in-law

a guy could ask for. She looked cute wearing yoga pants and one of Cameron's T-shirts.

"Where's the toddler?" I asked, ready to sweep Raif up into my arms.

"Cameron took him to visit Aunt Rose."

"Nice. You still don't have a butler?" I joked. "Want mine?"

"Cameron would never go for that." She embraced me. "How are you settling in?"

"Just about there." Working late at the office had helped keep my mind off the house.

Visiting this manor always calmed me. Maybe because they'd made this big house a home.

"Come have tea." She led me onward into their vast kitchen. "It's Typhoo. Don't tell Cameron."

"What!" I stopped in my tracks.

"I'm joking!" She laughed hysterically.

I chuckled at her shamelessness, which helped remove much of my tension.

She set about making us hot drinks. "I can guess why you're here."

I couldn't hide my surprise.

She flicked on the kettle and turned to face me. "The trip is too risky."

"I'm not going back."

She paused for a second. "What?"

"You didn't mean Florida?"

"Oh, no."

She thought I was here to talk about Cameron.

"What did he tell you?" I asked, not wanting to give anything away.

"He wants me to support his trip abroad."

He'd finally confessed his yearning for adventure.

"He'll respect your concerns," I said.

"He has a baby now."

"After my rogue trip to Florida, I won't wield much sway, I'm afraid."

"Right, how did that go?"

"As well as expected."

Mia poured hot water into two mugs. "You hiked in a preserve?"

"Yes. I had a friend with me."

"That's right, Lotte." Mia mulled that over. "She'd have made it fun." Mia smiled, like she'd guessed my secret.

"You heard why I went?" I watched her reaction.

Her expression turned serious. "I didn't like the way Reese arranged the reunion."

I leaned on the central countertop. "It wasn't boring."

"What was it like seeing her again?"

"Not as emotional as I'd feared."

"How did she act toward you?"

"Cold, but reasonable."

"Were you hoping for a romantic reunion?"

I shuddered. "Impossible."

"I can see why."

I rubbed my brow to ease the tiredness of the last seventy-two hours.

Visiting Chrysalis earlier and treating Lotte the way I had would go down as one of my worst mistakes. I had quite a few to compare it with.

Our brief spark had set off a wildfire that had burned out too fast.

"Let's talk in the sitting room," said Mia.

I raised a hand. "I don't want this conversation shared."

"Of course not."

Mia was the kind of person you could trust with a secret. I'd always loved that about her.

We settled on the plush couch in their tastefully decorated living room. Pastel fabrics covered luxurious furniture. Other sophisticated touches were both homey and intimate, perfect for unwinding.

Mia had been the one to encourage me to leave Big Bear after my reclusive year. I owed her so much.

"Have you and Cameron returned to Chrysalis since you've been married?" I asked.

She set her mug on a coaster on the coffee table.

I read her reluctance. "You don't want to answer?"

"We've attended a few parties."

"You just watch."

"We enjoy the erotic scene, yes."

I'd asked Shay this same question about them back at the Edison when we'd had drinks over a month ago. The loyal bastard hadn't given away anything.

"What was the deciding factor for Cameron leaving Chrysalis?"

"To run Cole Tea."

I flashed a guilty grin. "Until I insisted I take over."

"He wanted that for you," she said. "It's your birthright."

"I was a bastard about it."

"He admired your strength." She lifted her mug and blew on the tea to cool it. "He took his own ego out of the equation. He's happy for you."

"He's a good brother."

"A great dad, too."

"You're great for each other." I narrowed my gaze. "Mia, what's the appeal with BDSM?"

She sipped as she thought on it. "For me, personally?"

"Yes, I suppose."

"Why?"

I mulled over my answer. "I'm trying to grasp why anyone would be drawn to it."

"This is about Charlotte?"

I flinched at being so obvious.

"I watched you at the ball," she said. "The way you were with each other."

"That obvious?"

"You're trying to figure out a way forward for you both?"

"She's a dominatrix." A major concern wrapped up in one pretty package.

"It's so much more than that, Henry."

"Why were you drawn to it?"

"I first learned about it at Enthrall. Cameron used his special brand of psychotherapy on me."

"How did it help?"

"He unblocked suppressed memories."

"With intimacy?"

"For me, yes."

"That trial—you have no regrets?"

"No. We've been through so much together."

"I'm sorry for what happened to you in France."

"We've talked about this, you and me. We've put it to rest." She laid a hand on mine. "I'm fine. We're fine. Now all we want is for you to be happy."

I gave her a heartfelt smile.

"For me, BDSM is about surrendering," she continued. "It frees me. It's also exceptionally arousing."

"What would a dominatrix or a Dom experience?"

"Total control."

"Which makes them feel safe?"

"Having control over another person can give you an erotic rush." She waved her hand. "You'd need to stay longer for me to get into the psychology of it all."

"Right."

She quirked a brow. "Now that you've found her—"

"I broke it off," I admitted.

"Why?"

"I was afraid I'd be torn apart by the press."

"I'm glad you ended it."

"You are?"

"Don't ever see her again."

That made my gut twist. "Did you just pull a Cameron on me?"

"Yes."

I brushed a hand over my face to steady myself.

"You're cute together," she said playfully.

"I went to Chrysalis to see her earlier."

"What happened?"

"I believed she had left that place."

"Careful, it's sacred to us."

"I can see that."

"You've met your match."

I let out a long breath. "What if there are too many broken pieces inside me to be enough for a woman like her."

"You need a session with your brother."

"My history is holding me back?"

"Honestly, maybe your ego."

"Wow, come out and say it, why don't you."

"It's natural to be concerned about how the optics of dating a dominatrix will appear."

"Right."

"There's this brilliant scientist at Enthrall. I met him my first week there. The client was treated by both Scarlet and Lotte. They helped him work through his traumatic childhood. No other type of therapy had helped, and it was his last resort. They gave him his life back. He went on to discover a significant finding in the universe that changes the way we see the solar system."

"Lotte's work is important," I said. "That's what you're telling me."

"Her name will never be associated with some of the world's most important endeavors. But her touch is there, nevertheless. These women are unsung heroes."

Mia had such an innocent way of seeing things.

"Lotte's also forgiving," said Mia.

"She's many things."

"A woman like her might be intimidating, even for a man like you."

There was no denying that her confidence left me spellbound.

I broke Mia's gaze by focusing on the fireplace. "Can you get me into the next party at Chrysalis?"

Mia set her mug down. "You're going to fight for her?"

"I'm going to make it up to her. I'll find a way for us to be together. If that's what she still wants."

"Am I allowed to tell Cameron? About the party, I mean."

"No." I reasoned my foray into their secretive world should remain covert.

She shook her head. "I must tell Richard. He's the boss."

"He's not my biggest fan."

"The more of an asshole he is to you the more he adores you."

"That's strangely comforting."

"Something tells me you still have Richard's masquerade mask."

I smirked. "Might."

Mia gave a nod of excitement. "Lotte's worth it."

"She is," I said. "If she'll forgive me."

She shook her head, amused. "Drink your tea. Let's talk about how to get you in, and what you should expect when you're there."

"I appreciate this."

"Can I give you some womanly advice?"

"Sure."

"Flowers."

My shoulders slumped. Could the answer be that simple?

"Just don't go back to Chrysalis until you've made up," she added. "Women need to see that you respect their boundaries."

CHAPTER FORTY-TWO

Henry

AT NINE O'CLOCK AT NIGHT, THE TEA LAB WAS DESERTED. This is where all the magic happened for Cole Tea—where new brands were concocted and where specialists like Meg Mills and Felix Jones proved their worth.

They'd gone home for the evening leaving me to experiment.

I'd been trying to capture a unique flavor. I had several jars containing the finest ingredients within reach.

There, on the wall, hung a two-hundred-year-old wooden banner from one of my ancestors, my great-great grandfather's merchant tea company. This building may be new but our family legacy went back generations.

The rest of the staff had left the building, except for security and office cleaners. The lights dimmed within the tower.

The lab remained silent.

I didn't want to go home to that big house echoing my loneliness. Working late was the best distraction.

I'd had Griffin take my dog home.

Dex Cole was incredibly spoiled. He'd literally been chauffeured home so he could enjoy playing in the yard.

With my head down, I continued to play around with the assortment of leaves, working hard to discover that elusive addition to what I'd presented to my father in Switzerland—something extra that would seal the flavor and make it a brand that would steal the show.

We were renowned for excellence, creating and selling the finest quality experience. We were also respected for our traditions. The head of the company had personally invented a unique flavor. No small issue to compete with a profound legacy of tea makers.

My mind drifted.

Letting go, becoming Zen, my subconscious led the way as if I were being guided by some unseen force, allowing my imagination to flow.

At the same time, my thoughts were elsewhere. Mia had given me some hope for my future yesterday when I'd visited her. But seriously, having not heard from Lotte, I wondered if I'd totally blown it.

We'd made precious memories together—the two of us sleeping inside the tent. That first time we'd made love beneath the stars.

I tried to recall when I'd last felt that relaxed.

That happy.

Guilt washed over me as I recalled her having to face that stranger in the preserve alone.

Afterwards, after my nightmare PTSD event, she'd again shown understanding. Her soothing words had calmed me, like the way she had given me water to quench my thirst, or handed me a chocolate bar to raise my blood sugar.

Her tenderness had lifted me out of hell.

A spark of creativity hit me as I was reflecting on those moments of serenity.

A brilliant idea flashed through my mind.

I pushed up and searched the stack of bottles containing samples of tea leaves in the endless jars along the wall.

Then I found it—chocolate shavings. I brought back the container and tipped a few into the teacup.

Tiny chocolate droplets melted within the hot brew, the resulting luxurious scent pleasing.

I lifted the China teacup to my mouth and took a sip.

Wow.

I felt a rush of endorphins at its remarkable taste.

This was it.

I scribbled the note to add to the list.

Glancing up, I stared dead ahead, startled.

I saw another blur of movement behind the glass lab door—the shape of a man.

A thousand thoughts flashed through my mind. How did he get by security?

Instinctively, I folded the piece of paper in half with my notes and tucked it into my jacket pocket.

The door opened.

Griffin stood there.

"Hey," I said, faking a calm demeanor.

"I wanted to check on you, sir," he said.

"I told you to go home." I frowned. "Dex okay?"

"Yes, your butler took care of him. Told me he'd feed him."

"That's good."

His focus narrowed on the assortment of tealeaves I'd been playing around with. It would be easy to memorize the names on the jars—if that's why he was here.

It was something our spy might want to do. I turned one of them around making the action appear natural.

"Do you need anything, sir?" he asked, sounding nervous.

"No, but thank you. I'm going to keep going. I'll drive myself home."

I'd not counted on him coming in and sitting down on the other side of the long marble table, like he was now. He'd often shown the confidence to challenge me—both admirable and annoying.

We'd be alone down here and that wasn't terrifying *at all.*

My heart was racing.

"You were in Afghanistan?" he said.

Here it was—the conversation I'd been waiting for.

"Yes."

"It's why I took this job. That and the fact you are who you are."

Good to know, I mused, dark thoughts swirling.

He reached into his jacket pocket, and I leaped up, ready to tackle him or dive behind the table.

He paused, just as startled.

Admittedly an overreaction, but it was impossible to shake that level of training.

His frown deepened. "My phone."

Throat tight, I slowed my breathing.

Hopefully the perspiration spotting my brow would go unnoticed.

"I wanted to show you this." He turned his phone so I could see it.

"Who is it?" But I knew, even from here I could see the man in military uniform had a resemblance to him. "Your dad?"

"He died in Afghanistan. First few weeks of the war."

"I'm sorry to hear that," I said sincerely.

"His buddies told me he was a hero. He saved lives by placing himself in harm's way."

"A brave man," I said softly. "Wish I'd met him."

"He served with the Marines."

"The first soldiers to land in Afghanistan." *So damn brave.*

Griffin seemed troubled. "He never got recognition."

"Why?"

"It's under investigation—someone messed up." His back straightened. "Not my Dad, though. He followed orders."

A familiar sense of camaraderie settled in my gut.

I felt pride mixed with sadness for what his father had given up—his life. Yet the son, too, carried that burden of loss, an unfathomable pain. Griffin wanted what any good son would.

"Your father needs to be recognized for his sacrifice," I said softly.

"Can you help me find out what happened?'"

I gave a nod. "Let me see what I can do."

"I've been waiting for the right time to say something."

"I'm going to call it a day in here. Drive me home. I'd like to hear more about your dad."

His face lit up.

I lifted the jars of tea and set them back in their place to hide my tracks. "I'll just tidy up here a bit. Only take a second."

"Thank you, sir."

I turned to face Griffin. "I'll enjoy the company."

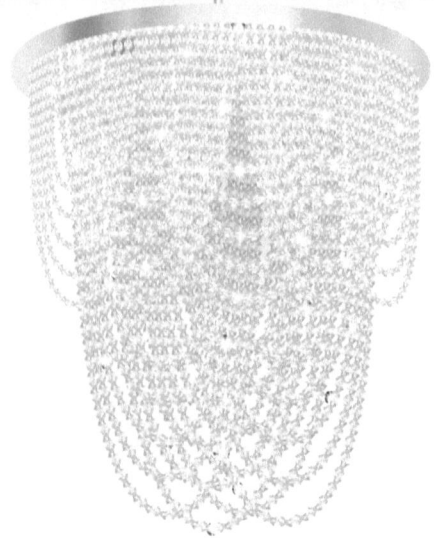

CHAPTER FORTY-THREE

Lotte

A T CHRYSALIS, THEY CALLED THE MAN CURRENTLY
standing in my living room de Sade—and for good
reason. Jake Carrington was a confirmed sadist.

Having a tall, overly fit man who looked pissed off with me
was a distracting sight, especially since he was wearing a black
shirt that stretched across his toned abs and tight designer jeans.

Jake was renowned for wielding pain and merging it with
pleasure—taking kink to an entirely new level. Most of us weren't
into his brand of agony, but a few were.

He got a kick out of dominating with a dangerous edge.

A legendary football player, he was now retired from the sport
and easily worth millions.

He'd long been known as one of the bad boys of Chrysalis.

"No notice," he snapped. "You're just going to quit."

The staff at Chrysalis wasn't over Scarlet Winters exiting the
manor not that long ago. My leaving would be another blow.

Jake moved closer. "Your submissives are relying on you to
see them through."

"There's never a good time to leave."

"You got that right!" He folded his arms across his impressive chest. "You told me this is your vocation."

"It is, Jake, but I'm allowed to change my mind."

"Leave, if you must, but don't give up the scene."

The doorbell rang and we both glanced toward the sound.

"Give me a second," I said, heading down the hallway.

Henry's formidable form could be seen behind the glass front door.

Oh, God, he's going to see de Sade.

I opened the door. "Hey."

He'd seemingly come straight from the office, still wearing a pristine bespoke suit with his hair neatly combed—looking so classy and well put together he could have intimidated a much younger woman.

But not me.

No matter how impressively he towered over me with that domineering stance.

He'd grown a fan base at Chrysalis, all the submissives who had interacted with him. That thought made me smile inwardly.

Henry lifted a takeout bag. "Thought you might be hungry."

"A peace offering after what happened at Chrysalis?"

"These are." He lifted an exquisite bouquet of pink roses.

I quirked a brow. "You'll have to do better than that."

"I shouldn't have visited you at work." He glanced at the bag. "Will poppadoms make it up to you?"

"I'm ashamed to say it will." Gratefully, I accepted the bouquet of at least thirty roses, holding them gently in my arms.

How can I not fall for you?

"Are you going to invite me in?" he asked, frowning.

I spun around to see Jake glaring at us from the hallway.

"He's just a friend," I clarified.

"Bad time?" Henry wasn't convinced.

"Your timing is perfect," I said. "Come on in."

Henry followed me down the hallway to the living room.

I felt self-conscious holding these flowers in front of Jake.

Henry glanced around at the décor, taking in my plush furniture and those unmistakable feminine touches I'd added to make this place feel like home.

His steely consideration summed up Jake. "There's enough food for three."

Though I doubt he meant it.

Jake looked annoyed. "You're the reason she's leaving?"

Henry gave a shrug.

I stared at Jake. "I've thought about becoming a traditional therapist for a while now."

"The fuck you have," he bit out, glaring at the flowers with distaste.

"We've not met." Henry calmly offered him his hand. "I'm Henry."

"Cameron's brother?" Jake cringed. "Another Cole."

"Stop it," I said.

"You're a Dominant, I take it?" Henry walked over to the coffee table and set the food down. "Wild guess."

"I am."

"De Sade?" asked Henry, clearly amused. "As in Marquis de Sade?"

Jake stood proud. "I wield a level of pain you'd never handle."

Oh, shit.

Why did he have to go there?

"Let's continue this tomorrow." I went to guide Jake toward the door. "It was good seeing you."

He snapped his arm away.

"I've learned a thing or two about pain," mused Henry. "The kind there's no safe word for."

I tried to reassure him. "Henry, Jake doesn't know."

"Know what?" asked Jake.

I glared at him to convey this conversation was over.

Jake seemed to be mulling over what he knew about Henry. "You were a SEAL?"

He received a terse nod from the man he'd insulted.

Jake's expression turned fraught. He hung his head in shame as the realization hit him. "I'm an asshole, sorry."

Henry deescalated the conversation with a polite wave.

Jake stepped forward. "You served in Afghanistan?"

"It's great to meet you, too," said Henry and graciously shook Jake's hand.

Jake pivoted toward me. "Will you be in tomorrow?"

"Not sure yet." I refused to make eye contact with Henry.

"We'll talk." Jake gave Henry's arm a pat as he headed out. "The food smells amazing."

"You're still welcome to join us," I offered, and then cringed when I noticed Henry's incredulous flinch.

The banging of the front door signaled that Jake had left and we were alone.

I approached Henry. "After Scarlet left, I became the senior dominatrix. That's why he was here, to talk me out of it."

"What does convincing you entail exactly?" He glared at me.

I wasn't in the mood for an argument. "I'll dish up the food."

"I've lost my appetite."

"Oh, stop it." I picked up the takeout bag and carried it along with the bouquet into the open-plan kitchen. "We're both hangry and need to eat."

I set the food and flowers on the central island.

Henry followed me. "I'm usually not the jealous type."

I reached into the cupboard for two plates. "But?"

"Is he a boyfriend?"

"No." I fished the cartons of Indian food out of the paper bag and smiled when I saw the bread. "Garlic naan is my favorite."

"I thought Chinese is your favorite?"

"I guessed it was yours."

"Why?"

I watched his reaction. "Cameron told me your favorite city is Hong Kong."

"Why would he tell you that?"

"I was fishing for subjects that would impress you." For some reason I had no trouble telling Henry that.

I opened a cabinet and brought out my best vase made of handspun glass. After filling it with water, I arranged the gorgeous roses and set them as a centerpiece on the marble countertop.

"Wow." Henry reacted to a painting on the kitchen wall that had a deep red background with a vintage golden chandelier in the center. The twinkling crystals majestically reflected the light.

"One of mine." I raised a playful shoulder.

"You painted that?"

"I told you I love to paint."

"Yes, but you didn't say how good you are." Impressed, he neared the canvas and studied it closer. "This is spectacular."

"It's my homage to Enthrall."

He thought on that. "Your entire life is wrapped up in that place. And Chrysalis."

"It really is."

His gentle smile revealed that he knew how hard leaving there would be for me.

I changed the subject. "I'd love to see your art."

He tapped the central island. "My possessions just came out of storage and are currently being unpacked at home."

"And your paintings?"

"Those too."

"I'm glad." Hearing he was settling in made me happy. "Tea?"

Henry walked toward the fridge. "How about champagne?"

"I have some."

"You seem like the kind of woman who loves to celebrate."

"I do?"

"You're beautiful and sophisticated. A woman like that has a lot going on."

"Thank you."

"Everything a man like Jake would want."

"He's married. And bi." I studied Henry's reaction. "Shay and Jake were lovers."

Henry blinked at me. "That's him?"

"Yes."

"I only ever heard of him."

"Well, now you've met him."

"He played in the NFL?"

"Quite successfully."

"Still an asshole."

"He means well," I said.

"Jake seemed familiar with my history."

"Cameron and Shay have always been protective of what happened to you in Afghanistan."

"It's public knowledge." He shrugged. "People were curious about Cameron's brother. I get that."

I closed the space between us. "Let's start over."

"In what way?"

"I wanted to give you space," I said softly. "That's why I didn't call."

Henry poured the Bollinger with the panache of a man who wasn't a stranger to expensive brands.

He handed over a flute of sparkling champagne. "I hope you weren't saving it for a special occasion."

"This is a special occasion." *Because you're here with me.*

He took a deep breath. "I've cracked the code to our new formula."

I gasped. "That's brilliant, Henry! Yes, bubbly is called for to celebrate! Can't wait to taste it."

"I should have called before turning up out of the blue."

"That's too formal for us."

"Really?" he said.

"You're passionate. It's what I love about you—"

"Don't worry, you can't chase me away with that word," he said.

"What would scare you away?"

"Betrayal."

"I would never—"

"I trust you with my life." He set his glass down.

Something told me he meant his reputation.

Henry circled the island and came closer. "Are we exclusive?"

"I was going to ask the same thing."

He narrowed his gaze. "You're the one with men visiting."

"De Sade?"

"You leaving that place would hit them hard?" he asked calmly.

"We're a family at Chrysalis."

"Then stay."

"What?" I leaned back a little, trying to read him.

"Don't leave Chrysalis over me."

"Don't flatter yourself, Henry."

He flinched. "We're trying to work through this. Don't make it harder."

I cupped his balls. "This hard?"

He clenched his teeth. "Have you any idea how much you turn me on?"

"Yes, actually."

His cock grew within my palm. "You make me want to do dirty things to you."

"Maybe I'll let you."

"Maybe?"

"You're infuriating."

"I'm working on that."

"Prove it."

"Lotte, dress up as a dominatrix."

"No."

"Why not?"

"Because you don't deserve it."

"Listen, don't give up your career because of me."

"You can't be seen with someone in my profession. I'm under no illusion."

"There's no changing the past." He studied my face. "If we don't work out, you'll still have Chrysalis."

I let my hand slip away from him.

He didn't react, remaining poised. "I can't stay away from you."

My heart sank at his insinuation and yet I said, "Then don't."

The gap between us closed fast. Our lips smashed together, his smile widening against my mouth.

"I missed you." He cupped my face, thumbs firm on my cheeks, pressing his lips to mine, our tongues warring violently to secure equal power, stirring me into a frenzy.

He pulled back. "What do we do about this?"

"We fuck, Henry," I said. "Because that's what we are best at when we're together."

His expression turned serious, chestnut irises darkening.

Despite the silence, I read the truth in his eyes. "You came here to ask me to be your secret mistress?"

His shoulders dropped with humility.

"I can't see any other way," he said quietly.

Reaching up, I pressed my palm to his face. "No."

"Consider it."

"Never."

"Then what?"

I raised my chin with pride. "You may fuck me one final time."

"Don't say it like that," he said, snatching me up in his arms.

He carried me through the house and up the stairs.

"Where?" he asked.

I pointed down the hall toward my bedroom.

Once inside, both of us stripped off our clothes, desperate to be pressing our heated flesh together. I helped him with his shirt and he dragged my jeans off me, tugging them down my legs. Our actions became frenzied as though we were afraid that fate might snatch us apart.

As it soon would.

When we were both naked, he shoved me onto the bed. In a frenzy of need, we lay in a sixty-nine position, me desperate to devour him and his craving for my sex just as passionate—that fixed primal point drawing us beyond all resistance.

With his cock in my mouth and my pussy kissed by his, our

want burned too brightly to deny. In this position, I worshipped him, taking him deeply into my mouth as his tongue flicked my clit, bringing sweeping bliss to that small nub.

I rocked against his firm body, suckling his cock, deep-throating him while he made me forget time and place and everything in between. I was seemingly lost in the cosmos yet somehow found by him.

We made love as though intimacy could defeat what the world thought of us and would help us find our way. Settled between each other's thighs, I focused all my attention upon his rock-hard cock.

I had his shaft so deep down my throat that I struggled to breathe through my nose while my body bucked at the frenzied pleasuring between my legs.

I snatched a breath of air before an orgasm stole it right back.

Captured by this blinding pleasure, I was spinning out of control, out of my mind.

Needing his remarkable erection back between my lips, I stroked fast with a firm palm as I suckled the tip, riding out my own climax, shattered into a thousand pieces, trying to rally, needing his taste, his firmness, needing the certainty I'd been denied.

Finally, when the air returned to my lungs, I focused on him again, driving Henry into a frenzy of pumping hips and cries of desire as he growled his release. His heat filled my mouth and I swallowed him down.

I lay there panting with no use for words.

We broke apart as fast as we'd come together.

Pushing up, I rested my back against the headboard.

Seconds later, Henry was searching for his boxer shorts, and then the rest of his clothes, having discarded his suit in record time. I watched his gorgeous physique move around my bedroom as he retrieved his shoes with a savage casualness, slipping them on calmly.

Cuddling wasn't going to happen.

He came over to me and leaned down to kiss my forehead

like a lover does when an affair is over. His quietness fed the eerie silence, his strong hands dragging up a blanket to cover my nakedness.

Henry walked away from my side and left the bedroom without looking back. Then I heard the sound of his shoes as he descended the staircase.

The lack of his presence was a startling loss.

I listened to the sound of the front door closing behind him. Gone.

It looked as though a tornado had blown through my bedroom. My clothes scattered here and there was the only evidence of his visit.

I put on my silk robe and tied it around my waist as I made my way down to the kitchen.

Settling on the barstool, I ignored the dampness of arousal between my legs. More evidence I'd been beautifully violated by Henry's arrogant yet delicious mouth.

Opening the take-out bag, I fished out a poppadom and munched on the mouthwatering wafer-thin crisp.

Reaching for the champagne, I gripped the bottle's long neck and tipped it to my mouth in an act of rebellion, swallowing gulps of sweet Bollinger as bubbles tickled my nose.

The pretty bouquet in my vase was proof that Henry had tried and failed to seduce me into becoming his secret mistress.

I lifted the bottle again and drank a few more gulps of the bubbly.

Men could be so damn complicated.

But Henry Cole landed in an entirely different category.

What I wanted—and needed—was a man who could love me.

CHAPTER FORTY-FOUR

Henry

FRIDAYS EVOKED WAVES OF HAPPINESS FROM EMPLOYEES eager for time off over the weekend.

Even I anticipated freedom from this office, though my plans had sadly changed.

I'd planned a fun Saturday of sightseeing around the city, seeing more of Los Angeles and hoping Charlotte would join me. That wasn't going to happen now.

I wanted to keep her a secret to protect her. I should have told her that our clandestine relationship would only be temporary until we found a way to be together in public.

The previous night's fantastic sex was probably the last time she'd let me taste her—which made me crave her more.

A knock at the door distracted me.

Jen leaned into my office. "I'm going to grab a bite to eat."

I gestured for her to come into the room, my gut twisting.

Hopefully soon, the nightmare that haunted Cole Tower would be over. The moment that envelope was opened and the contents stolen, and shared, it would be done.

It was down to me to execute the plan. I needed this spy in my rearview.

"Could you take this to the lab?" I asked causally, offering her the envelope.

"What is it?" She walked over to my desk.

"Our new flavor."

Jen looked intrigued. "Does it require FDA approval?"

A question a good employee might ask if they wanted to guess how long it would be before we launched the product.

"Just the packaging." We already had that.

She accepted the envelope. "I'll drop it off on the way to lunch."

"Careful," I joked. "That's a billion-dollar brand in there."

"Thank you for trusting me with it."

"Always," I said. Watching her go, I added, "Jen."

She turned back, her expression full of innocence. "Yes?"

"What are your hopes for the future with Cole Tea?"

Her lips quirked and I saw a glimmer of doubt.

"That's okay," I said. "Have a think about it."

"I appreciate that," she said softly. "I love it here. If you believe I'm ready to take on more responsibility, I'd be willing."

I'd never been one for corporate games.

Shay's department usually handled all those dark deeds needed to keep us safe.

"Is a promotion on the table?" Jen asked playfully.

"Let's talk tomorrow," I said.

She left my office, and I immediately shot off a text to Shay to let him know that Jen was headed for the elevator.

After a minute, I got up and walked through the office door, glancing at her workstation, the place she'd sat for months greeting everyone and guarding my office. She'd gotten close to me.

I'd always believed I was a good judge of character, trusting my employees with so much.

I pushed the button for the executive elevator and when the doors opened, I stepped inside. Turning my back on that incredible city view, I counted down the numbers until I reached the ground floor.

The doors slid open on the foyer and I stepped out and headed toward the corner tea shop. I needed something to soothe my stress so I ordered an Earl Grey.

The barista became flustered, as usual, when I asked them to make my order. I never meant to intimidate them, but this time I couldn't be bothered to rally a smile.

"You, okay?" said a familiar voice from behind me.

I turned to see Cameron standing there.

My shoulders relaxed as some of the tension I was feeling slipped away. He knew I needed company, needed someone who could understand what this violation felt like. Cameron had driven all the way down here to be with me.

"Thank you for being here," I said.

"You know this isn't a personal attack, right?" he said. "It's just about money."

I gave a nod that I got that.

I'd been kind to my staff. I'd given them the time off they requested, been generous with bonuses and listened to their ideas—implemented many of them, too. I'd given credit when credit was due.

Reviewing interactions with our person of interest, I could say with confidence I'd been a great boss to them.

After the barista prepared an Earl Grey for Cameron as well, we sat down in a quiet corner and waited for the suspect to appear. I felt the gut-wrenching reality that an employee's life was about to be ruined. They would even face prison time.

The tea I drank was soothing, but it did nothing to eradicate the bitterness of betrayal.

Cameron lifted his cup and took a sip. "It took Shay just five weeks to find them."

"We knew he would."

"You're welcome," said Cameron.

"Yeah, I'm never going to live that down. Stealing Shay from Enthrall."

"He's part of our family," he said.

"True."

An elevator pinged and Jen strolled out with her head held high. She saw us and walked toward us with her usual bright demeanor. "Hey, Cameron, how are you?"

He beamed back at her. "Doing well."

She had that usual flushed appearance of a woman in Cameron's orbit.

The barista saw Jen and set about making her usual drink. She thanked him and came and sat beside us. "Just grabbing some lunch in the courtyard. Want anything?"

"Lunch is on us today," said Cameron.

"Thank you!" She waved a hand in the air, embarrassed. "You spoil me."

"Today is a good day," I said.

"Because you finally settled on your signature brand?"

Yes, but that beloved formula wasn't in the envelope she'd carried to the lab.

That creation remained locked away in my wall safe.

The elevator pinged and we watched it ascend from the lowest floor—the lab.

Shay led the way.

Behind him, several guards were escorting Felix Jones out of the elevator. They steered him toward the exit.

"What happened to him?" asked Jen.

I studied her carefully. "You handed him the envelope?"

"You told me to take it to the lab." She looked horrified. "I did."

She stared off toward Felix. "What did he do?"

"Allegedly," said Cameron, "he was caught photographing and then texting the brand to Dandelion Diva."

Jen went pale. "I handed it to him. Oh, my God. I thought—"

"Inside was a fake formula," I said. "Felix sent the confidential form to Dandelion Diva."

"He's been spying for them?" she asked.

"Yes," I said. "Sorry to make you part of it. But you're the least suspicious person. We knew he'd trust you."

She sat up straight. "Corporate espionage?"

"He crossed the wrong Cole," said Cameron.

"True," I said. "And we have no choice but to prosecute Felix."

Jen leaned forward to get a better view of the foyer. "He's being read his rights by the police."

"We wanted that done outside," I told her.

We hadn't wanted to alarm our staff.

She turned to face me. "What are you going to do to Dandelion Diva?"

"As from twelve o'clock today," I said. "They no longer have a distributer."

"They can't make tea?" she asked.

"That's the least of their worries," I said.

"Things are about to get interesting." Cameron took another sip of his tea.

Jen stared at him. "Why? What else are you going to do to Dandelion Diva?"

"Wipe them from history," I replied.

CHAPTER FORTY-FIVE

Henry

C AMERON AND I HEADED BACK TO MY OFFICE ON THE 79TH
floor.
He took a seat on the couch in the corner and I set
about making him another cup of tea—only this time the recipe
was mine.

A piece of my soul was mixed in amongst those delicate leaves.
I wanted him to absolutely love my creation, but at the same time
his honest feedback was crucial—especially when it came to his
discerning taste.

He lifted the teacup and took a sip, and then another. "You
added chocolate shavings?"

"Yes."

Cameron sat back as though trying to decipher my inspiration.

"I'm calling it *Reflection*."

He contemplated the name.

"Be honest." I sat down opposite him and braced myself for
what came next.

"Game changer," he said. "The flavor is youthful, fresh and inspiring."

"You mean that?"

"It's remarkable."

My shoulders slumped with relief. I loved it, but knowing that he loved it was just as important.

"It will be interesting to see how Dad reacts," he said. "His taste is sophisticated."

"True."

"This would be an extraordinary addition to our brand." He grinned at me. "Seriously, Henry, I can see myself drinking this all the time. You sure I didn't inspire you?"

"Everything inspires me," I said.

Lotte, for one.

Cameron drank the rest of the tea and then smacked his lips to confirm he liked it. "That trip to Florida was good for you."

Trying to get anything by this man was impossible. He'd probably guessed how I felt about Lotte.

He studied my face. "I hear things are good between you."

He couldn't help himself, always making guesses that were usually astoundingly accurate.

"Listen," he said, "Lotte visited my Beverly Hills practice to check out the place."

I rested my elbows on my knees. "I see."

"She'd planned on becoming a fulltime therapist before."

"Before what?"

"You came on the scene."

"I want to make sure she's making the best decision for her," I said.

"Who abducted my brother and replaced him with an alien?"

We chuckled at the truth in that; I was expressing emotions and he wasn't used to it.

He wanted to protect Lotte, even from me, which was why I sensed he wanted to dig around a little more. More questions were looming.

We heard a knock at the door.

Jen stood there, looking a little sheepish. Cameron was too damn handsome for his own good.

She beamed at us. "Henry, you have a visitor in the foyer. Lilly Vergara."

I swapped a wary glance with Cameron.

"Is she alone?" asked Cameron.

"I believe so."

"Send her up," I said.

Cameron lifted the empty cup and carried it over to the side table. "Want me to stay?"

I got up and walked over to my desk, standing in front of it. "Sure."

Both of us focused on the door. Cameron tucked his hands into his pockets, ready to confront whoever appeared.

"I can't believe Reese has sent her daughter again," he said, his voice terse.

"This is my territory. She won't have the upper hand this time."

"Upper hand?" He shot me a curious glance.

"Back at the preserve, Reese hinted she didn't want us to leave until we had more time to talk."

"Did she make leaving a challenge?"

"They made the motorboat disappear."

"You're just now telling me this?" he snapped.

I gave a shrug. "I had the pleasure of seeing Reese's expression when our helicopter landed."

"She probably had no idea you could arrange an extraction for you and Lotte."

"No."

"We'll discuss this later."

"I'm perfectly capable of dealing with this," I said calmly.

Cameron straightened his back and that served as his answer. He knew it was true but his need to protect everyone set him on high alert.

A few seconds after the elevator pinged, Jen escorted Lilly into my office.

Lilly appeared more confident than the last time she'd confronted me in the elevator.

Jen lingered close behind her, her protective nature for me apparent.

Lilly had dressed casually, wearing jeans and a Harry Styles T-shirt. She was wearing her hair in braided pigtails, which made her appear even younger.

Her style this time was more like her mother.

Cameron flinched as though seeing a ghost.

Neither of us was comfortable with the fact that there was still a woman in our orbit who'd feigned her death and had risen from the fucking ashes like a phoenix.

Consequences—why do people always believe there are none?

Lilly studied Cameron with that familiar fascination of someone who was struck by him. I imagined she'd researched us both online, but seeing Cameron up close had her enthralled.

That word revolved around him in more ways than one.

I only hoped her family hadn't dug around for leverage.

"Cameron." I motioned to my brother. "This is Lilly, Reese's daughter."

Cameron gave her a nod but didn't say anything.

"Jen, can we have tea, please?" I motioned for Lilly to take a seat if she wanted. "Or coffee, if you prefer?"

"Tea's great." She came closer but didn't sit. "May I talk with you privately, please, Mr. Cole? Henry?"

"You can talk freely," I said.

She appeared nervous.

"My brother's a doctor," I added. "He's heard it all."

"It's personal to my mom." She seemed uncomfortable.

"Did she send you?" I asked coldly.

This could be another ruse.

"Cameron." I turned to face him. "I'll call you later."

He hesitated and then gave me a glance that said to be careful. He headed out but left the door open.

Lilly looked from the door to me, conveying she'd rather have it closed.

I ignored that and sat back down, crossing one leg over the other and waiting for her to join me.

My demeanor was harsh, but I wasn't in the mood for games.

Half an hour ago, I'd watched our corporate spy be frog marched out the fucking building.

I was out of patience.

Jen brought in a tray of tea and set it on the table between us. I thanked her and watched her leave. She got the hint we needed the door to remain open.

I poured black tea into two cups and added a dash of milk. Lilly declined sugar and I handed her the drink.

She lifted the cup and took a sip. "I drank Cole Tea growing up."

I didn't need to hear that.

She drew in a sharp breath. "You and Mom got off on the wrong foot in Florida."

"What makes you say that?"

"She told me about your emotional reunion."

I blinked at her, holding back the words to express what I'd really felt when seeing her mom was alive and well and thriving.

The hurt she'd caused was irreparable—so much pain I doubted we'd ever return to any level of trust.

"This is obviously hard on you both," she said.

Glancing at my watch, I made it clear her time was limited.

"I want you to hear what really happened to Mom in Chile," she said softly. "The catalyst."

"How do you mean?"

Tears welled up in her eyes, but she held them back.

CHAPTER FORTY-SIX

Lotte

W E MANAGED TO BEAT THE FRIDAY MORNING TRAFFIC. Richard parked his BMW outside de Sade's impressive home on Mulholland Drive.

We'd just navigated our way up the winding driveway to his mansion, which was situated in a prime location surrounded by a lot of land. The sweeping structure featured glass windows that revealed the interior, so having all those trees made sense.

Jake had bought the property during the years he'd taken a battering as a quarterback in the NFL.

Richard's place in Malibu was just as impressive. He didn't bat an eyelid at the four-story glass palace we'd pulled up to.

De Sade's Lamborghini was parked in the driveway, along with several other flashy sports cars. This was a meeting of multi-millionaires, but Richard's Mercedes-Benz looked modest next to the fancy vehicles.

Richard wore jeans and a black T-shirt and sandals—the uniform of the wealthy. I'd chosen my little black dress and a pair of flats—though my Jimmy Choo Callie purse did add a touch of bling. I was trying to cheer myself up.

Two days ago, I'd chugged champagne because Henry had visited with an indecent proposal. I'd been tempted to say *yes*.

Still, I'd done what every self-respecting woman would and not called him back.

"Well, here we are." Richard unclipped his seatbelt.

"He's trying to persuade me to stay."

Richard shook his head. "Jake told me he's accepted that you're leaving."

I scanned the upper windows of the house for a glimpse of him. "Then why am I being summoned?"

"*We* were summoned."

"Not just us." I glanced over at the decadent Aston Martin and silver Jag, the license plate number seeming familiar.

These cars weren't all his from what I could tell. We weren't the only visitors.

"Let's get this over with." Richard got out of the car and walked around the front to my side to open the door for me. "I like doing it," he said.

Always a gentleman. Over the years we'd cultivated a close relationship. I had grown to trust him and Cameron.

Henry had almost shared that privileged position.

I missed him.

Even after everything.

Maybe I'd stop off at a pastry shop on my way to Cole Tower and bring him something sweet we could have with our coffee, make up with him, perhaps.

The door opened and de Sade motioned for us to enter with a sweep of his hand.

He'd dressed in torn jeans and a tight T-shirt showing off his impressively fit physique. He liked to use his height to intimidate others and he got away with it because of his powerful charisma.

"Looking good, Booth," he said with smirk.

"You too." Richard tapped his arm with affection.

"Lotte." De Sade narrowed his gaze on me and this time his scrutiny felt different.

I found his shady behavior interesting.

De Sade led us through the house's open floor plan. It was challenging to guess whose taste dominated the refined touches of décor—his ex-wife Rylee's or his own masculine leaning. The art was so modern it unsettled me.

Over two months ago, Shay and I had caught him and his ex fucking at Enthrall, proving he was back with Rylee in some capacity.

"Who else is here?" I asked.

"Friends." De Sade's long strides slowed when we made it to an outside balcony.

Richard and I swapped a wary glance before admiring the spectacular view from the second-floor balcony. At night, the cityscape would be beautiful with all those twinkling lights.

Richard let out an appreciative whistle.

De Sade's pad had all the trappings of an L.A. design, including a fire pit below and seating comfortable enough to take long naps outside.

Richard and I sat opposite Jake who'd settled in a high-backed wicker chair. He crossed his legs casually.

A laugh carried from over the balcony, with male voices trailing in conversation. The others had gathered outside on the first floor.

On the glass table sat a bottle of champagne on ice. Beside it were three tall flutes and a small velvet box.

"Drinking before lunch?" said Richard.

De Sade's charisma was off the charts. A man that gorgeous knew the effect he had on women—and men, considering he swung both ways.

That made him all the hotter.

We'd always had an understanding. We'd flirt with each other. Stir each other up. I'd taunt him. But we'd never fucked.

Whenever I was in a relationship he wasn't. Then when he

became serious with someone, I was free. Our timing had always been off.

It didn't stop me from admiring this amazing eye-candy, though.

I placed my purse on the table.

"You're looking gorgeous as always, Charlotte."

I started to reach for the bottle of champagne. I mean, why not? I wasn't driving and having a sip of bubbly might make this mysterious meeting easier.

"No." De Sade clicked a finger. "Relax," he purred.

A petite blonde submissive appeared out of nowhere, like she'd been waiting for that click of his fingers. She looked twenty, maybe, and was pretty in an interesting way. The few strips of latex she was wearing did not cover her breasts or her pussy.

Delicate chains were fashioned around her hips, pulling her labia apart to better show off her clit. It was an arousing view—especially when she moved with elegance and faced us, revealing just how alluring her appearance was.

This submissive wasn't one of ours.

With her gaze lowered, she poured three glasses of Dom Pérignon and then handed us each a flute.

I made eye contact with her briefly, and she seemed nervous.

"Nice to meet you." I waited for her to tell me her name.

"Amelia," said de Sade. "It's her first day." He clicked his fingers again and she went and stood beside him.

"First day as a sub or first day here?" asked Richard.

De Sade's jaw flexed, a lion playing with his food. "First day as *my* submissive."

I resisted asking more—such as who trained her and where she came from.

He was a high-level Dom. Even seasoned subs were shaken after a session with this sadist.

And de Sade wasn't alone here.

It took all my will not to push up from my seat and lean over the balcony to see who was down there.

"Is Rylee joining us?" I asked.

"No." Jake seemingly enjoyed my discomfort.

To make a show of it, he got up from his chair and approached Amelia. "Stand straight," he snapped.

Amelia responded with an obvious arousal, her nipples pert. A delicate shine to her pussy revealed how turned on she was.

Her master's fingers played with the silver chain to pull her folds farther apart. Then his fingertip rested on her clit, slowly moving in a slow circle. Her jaw slackened and her breathing deepened.

A show of control—master and sub harmonious in the way they responded to one another.

Her body began trembling, nipples beaded as her arousal increased, wetting her thighs.

We'd played these games at Chrysalis.

There was no denying de Sade had an edge to his mastery.

A high stakes game she could never win.

She panted and moaned and swooned.

I wondered if she knew it wasn't just us here, that her erotic siren call was rising and falling on the ears below.

"Open the box," said de Sade, whose fingertip hadn't left his ingénue's sex. She trembled, blinking fast and on the verge of coming.

But without his permission she was forbidden to climax.

I snatched up the box and opened it.

Inside was an elegant Rolex.

"Put it on," said de Sade.

"Why did you get me this?" I fished it out of the box and turned it over.

Surprise caught in my throat at the Iced-Out Rolex, set with diamonds and blue Mother of Pearl inlays. It was the prettiest and most expensive watch I'd ever held.

De Sade let go of the sub and she gasped her frustration.

He'd not let her come.

The poor sub left still aroused and trembling in need.

Ignoring her again, de Sade returned to his chair, picked up a football from beside it and threw it over to Richard.

Richard caught it and then turned it over in his hands. "Is this from the last—"

"Super Bowl," said de Sade. "Thought you might like it."

From what I could tell, every team member from the New York Giants had signed it.

Richard set the ball down next to him. "Show's over. We've received our bribes, so what's this about?"

De Sade returned his gaze. "Booth, you're here to see we're not stealing her away from you. Lotte's already planned on leaving."

"We're listening," said Richard.

"What we're offering is generous." He zeroed in on me. "It's way above what any other dominatrix has ever earned."

"You're opening your own club?" I asked.

"It's already open. Has a strong membership. You'd be given full authority. I'll throw in a car. A penthouse. Whatever floats your boat."

"Wow," said Richard. "You really want her."

De Sade leaned forward on his elbows. "Charlotte, what do you say?"

"It's very generous," I said. "But I've already made up my mind. I'm moving over to traditional therapy."

"Because of Henry?" he said.

"No, not because of him," I said softly.

"Wait a second," said Richard, pushing up and strolling over to the balcony. He glanced down and his expression grew tight with concern.

He spun round to face de Sade. "You went in with them?"

De Sade gave a nod. "And a silent partner who will never be known."

That sent a shudder up my spine.

"We will of course continue to visit Enthrall," added de Sade. "This endeavor, this new place, will give us the freedom to indulge in our personal tastes."

Richard stared at him. "Tell me you didn't buy Pendulum?"

CHAPTER FORTY-SEVEN

Lotte

I REACHED OVER TO REASSURE RICHARD, SQUEEZING HIS HAND. Because everyone new Pendulum was bad news. *Everyone.* The club's reputation for favoring Doms and exploiting submissives was legendary.

Not that long ago, Shay had even had to rescue Rue from that dangerous establishment.

De Sade could be a dick, but he wasn't evil. His focus returned to me, his expression serious.

I reached for my glass, lifted it to my mouth and took a gulp of champagne.

He'd just offered me a multi-million dollar position.

At fucking Pendulum.

"Cameron wouldn't approve," said Richard.

De Sade arched a brow. "Cam's invested in his philanthropy. He'll hardly notice."

"Oh, he'll notice," I replied.

"He still wields power over everyone," added Richard, coming to his best friend's defense.

"Cameron encouraged Shay to date you," I told Jake. "He's been good to you."

De Sade genuinely acted surprised.

"I'm not ready to leave Enthrall," I added.

"Hear me out," he said.

Richard sat down next to me, quietly seething.

It was my turn to go peer over the balcony. I held my breath when I saw Greyson Grantchester, that familiar charisma shining bright.

That's where I recognized the license plate from—Greyson's Aston Martin.

Beside Greyson sat the beautiful Atticus Sinclair, his tattooed hands hinting at his darker side. He was a young doppelganger to Marlon Brando—and had the kind of charm that could get him access anywhere.

Two dangerously gorgeous Doms just hanging out with de Sade like them being here wasn't threatening at all.

A trifecta of influence.

They peered up and raised their champagne flutes in a toast like I'd accepted the job.

The allure of temptation.

I'd always lived in Scarlet's shadow.

Enthrall's shadow.

Me, the quieter dominatrix—ruling right alongside Richard, but we all knew he had the final say.

Now I was being given an opportunity to make a name for myself. To honor my profession and stand proudly beside these alphas.

My thoughts raced with how I could protect their submissives. Ensure Pendulum's reputation of respecting a woman's sexual autonomy.

Amongst all these lions, I could be Queen.

"Amelia is from Pendulum?" I asked.

"A gift to me," clarified de Sade, "upon closing the contract."

"A gift?" I said breathlessly.

What kind of a place would they rule over?

"The contract is signed?" said Richard, realizing.

"I'll throw in a sweetener for you," added de Sade.

I wasn't going to do it. Of course, I wasn't. But it was fun to hear what they considered my worth to be.

"I'll throw in thirty million in Bitcoin," said de Sade calmly.

"Jake," said Richard. "She's not bribable."

My throat tightened as I replayed Jake's words.

"Let her think about it," he suggested.

"She doesn't need to," said Richard.

"Of course not," I said. "I'm flattered though."

De Sade pointed to my wrist. "Keep the Rolex."

I slid off the watch and set it back in the fancy box. "Maybe Rylee would like it?"

"What you're suggesting," he said, "wouldn't work. Rylee's not experienced enough. She's too fiery. She'd fucking burn the place down the first week."

Because Rylee didn't take shit from anyone.

I, on the other hand, was more tolerant. Cooler heads would prevail, and all that, which was my reputation at Enthrall. It made sense de Sade would pluck me out of there because he trusted my temperament.

We had always gotten along, and that kind of trust took years to build.

"Will you excuse me?" I pushed up and turned back to the doorway that led inside the house. "Restroom?"

De Sade pointed left. "Three doors down."

"Thank you." I couldn't make eye contact with Richard because I knew he was furious. I'd hesitated a second ago.

Couldn't a girl just fantasize for a minute about making that kind of money? Richard and Cameron were wealthy beyond imagination. They'd never experienced having to deal with student loans or balancing a budget. Never had to worry about coming up with thousands to fix your car if it broke down, along with any other financial crisis.

They paid me well at Enthrall, but not the kind of money de Sade was offering.

Inside the restroom, I admired the continued theme of luxury. The scent of vanilla was probably his sense of humor at play. De Sade's sexual taste was so far away from these shades of vanilla. That level didn't exist in his stratosphere.

Oh, my God.

"Thirty million dollars," I mouthed to my reflection.

And Bitcoin—that currency could double. It wasn't like there was any chance Cameron would be buying me a piece of land anytime soon like he had for Shay, Enthrall's golden boy.

Until now, I had never expected anything from anyone. I was too fiercely independent.

Things were different now. I'd met Henry and we had chemistry.

We were worth fighting for.

As much as I loved being at Enthrall, de Sade's offer was more than generous.

But to give up the chance of love? True, heart pulsing passion? Well, that was just too alluring to turn away from.

Every time I thought of Henry, I grew calm. My adorable, arrogant and impressively smart Henry. So incredibly brave.

That's how I thought of him, even after deciding we were no longer an item.

The moment I took that job at Pendulum, I'd seal the deal on us never crossing paths again.

And that hurt deeply—the kind of agony that sliced through my heart like the sharpest blade.

So, no, there'd be no taking the job.

I left the bathroom.

De Sade stood there leaning against the wall in that masterful pose I knew so well whenever he wanted to speak with me.

Casual but calculated, and so damn sexy.

"I want to ask you something," he said.

"There's nothing you can't say to me in front of Richard."

"Love suits you."

I bristled at his patronizing tone.

"I just hope he's worth it," he added.

"Who?"

"Who." He quirked a lip. "Henry Montgomery Cole. What kind of pretentious name is that?"

"What makes you say that Jacob Scott Carrington?" I snapped back.

"Of the Kentucky Carringtons, no less." He came at me swiftly, locking me between him and the wall, his hands placed on either side of my head, caging me in.

I may be a dominatrix, but he knew I liked *this*.

This rush of dopamine was an easy addiction.

Unruffled, I merely peered up at him.

His cologne wafted around me, trying to break into my mind. Or crack the code to my heart. That's how it felt—an invasion of my senses.

Bringing that familiar arousal a senior Dom brings.

I hated him for it.

What I had with Henry felt sacred and I didn't want my body to betray me.

Jake oozed sensuality. "He can't satisfy your kinky side."

Placing my hands on his chest, I tried to push him away.

He didn't move. "Charlotte, you require a qualified master to bring you to your knees."

"Step back."

"Consider my offer."

"Okay, I will." Though I already knew my answer.

He lifted his hands off the wall. "The others, they want you for this as much as me. We need you. Don't give up this great opportunity."

"I am grateful. Tell them that."

He tipped up my chin and leaned in, his lips dangerously close. "Tell me what you want to make this happen."

"You can step back for a start."

He reached into his pocket and pulled out the Rolex. Grabbing my wrist, he slid it back on roughly, being cruel and yet dangerously compelling. I was unable to pull my wrist out of his grip. He was too damn strong, and too damn controlling as he clipped it in place.

"It looks pretty on you. Keep it."

"Your love language is buying gifts for people," I told him. "You need to be loved for who you are and not what you can do for people."

He flashed a grin, but it carried an edge of doubt.

"De Sade, it's me." These games he played wouldn't fly.

"You have forty-eight hours to decide." He stepped back and walked away. "Then the offer is off the table."

Asshole.

He'd always been the bad boy of Chrysalis.

Cameron had tolerated him because he knew de Sade was willing to go all the way for those who needed it. Cameron could be just as dark, but de Sade had this otherworldly level of cruelty.

Watching him walk away, I admired his butt. Taking what *I* wanted from this moment.

Taking my fucking power back.

If I did accept his offer—*their* offer—I'd have to tackle the trifecta of sinister alphas. Maybe he'd believed I'd say yes. That his offer would be impossible to turn down and right about now I'd be joining Grantchester and Sinclair, all of us downing champagne to celebrate.

Following de Sade down the hallway, I saw him lean over the balcony again. This time he shook his head at his friends, conveying my answer to them.

Richard stood on the balcony beside him. He glanced back at me, his expression reflecting what I'd guessed.

Amelia wasn't in the room.

Didn't take a genius to guess where she had gone. Did I really want to see what de Sade had in mind for her? I wasn't sure.

"Come watch." On seeing my hesitation, de Sade snapped, "Or I'll have them fuck her at the same time."

I glowered at him.

"This is her fantasy," he said coolly. "Come see."

I followed my curiosity, peering over the balcony because maybe, just maybe, I'd see she needed rescuing.

She didn't.

Amelia's contentment reassured me she'd settled into subspace heaven. She was lying on a table, legs spread, with Grantchester leaning between her thighs giving her oral sex. From the way she arched her back and groaned with pleasure, she liked the way his tongue greedily searched her pussy, his firm hands on her thighs to hold her in position.

Sinclair sucked on her right nipple. Both of them were delivering the kind of attention submissives beg for from our senior Doms.

There was beauty here, too.

The way these men interpreted her cries and whispers. The way they zeroed in on her pleasure, checking in with her, sharing her with the kind of desire only close friends can do.

A flash of anger came from Grantchester as he ripped off the latex strips to leave her completely naked. Even with all that access he wanted more of her, wanted that beauty splayed out before him.

Her face was flushing brightly, her legs opening wider as she too demanded more from him, her soaked thighs wetting Grantchester's chin. She was trembling from the blinding pleasure.

The tall trees surrounding the property shielded this exquisite scene.

Richard watched carefully, his brow furrowed as he tried to discern if this was what Amelia wanted.

Glancing at me, he gave a nod to say she appeared to be into the action.

We'd played hard and heavy in our day so there'd be no judging her. Just us making sure everyone consented.

This performance was clearly a show to taunt me.

De Sade's way of saying, *come protect the submissives at Pendulum as only you can, Charlotte.*

Grantchester fucked her now, thrusting hard and deep into her soaking wet pussy, the condom he'd slid on shiny from her arousal. His savage hips were a fierce piston as he entered deep and then withdrew all the way before pushing back in.

Sinclair kissed her mouth with the kind of passion women want. Like she was his everything and love came into the equation. Reaching down, Sinclair played with her clit and that made her go wild. She bucked and pounded Grantchester right back.

These two dazzling Doms were worshipping her.

Moaning rose from below as Amelia reached orgasm, writhing beneath the touches of men who knew how to stun a woman into coming.

My own body reacted to the intensely erotic vision, my clit aching at the vision of the raw and desperate fucking that was equally as controlled as it was unbound.

Grantchester spilled inside her and it made her go weak. He matched her climax with his, thrusting so hard she slid forcefully back and forward over the table.

De Sade had given them his submissive.

And they were honoring that gift by spoiling her.

Afterwards, when Amelia had come several times more, they helped her sit up. She leaned against Sinclair and he hugged her against his chest, telling her how pretty she was. How well she'd performed. The kind of words that would make any woman feel nurtured.

"You're not joining them de Sade?" said Richard tersely.

"Best seat in the house." He chuckled.

I pointed a finger at him. "Watch over her."

"I intend to," he said, leaning over the balcony as though the show had just begun.

"I have to go." I walked back to the table and grabbed my purse.

"Don't forget your gift." De Sade pointed to the football.

Richard waved his hand to decline it and then threw shade my way for accepting the wristwatch.

I waited until we were back in his Mercedes before I said, "He slid it onto my wrist." I smirked. "Sure you don't want that football?"

His shoulders slumped. "She was into it."

"She was."

"I'm getting old," he said as he started the engine. "The darker side of what we do used to be addictive."

"Still is." I elbowed him playfully. "You're just settled now."

"True."

"As long as everyone wants to be there," I reasoned.

"Want my opinion?"

"You'll give it either way."

"The timing of you meeting Henry couldn't be more perfect. The thought of you at Pendulum?" he said, shaking his head. "I'm not sure that's your future."

I let out a long breath. I needed to see Henry one final time. I wanted to talk with him face to face to see if he and I had any kind of chance.

"Can you drop me off at Cole Tower?" I asked.

"I'd drive you to the moon and back if you wanted."

I giggled. "Downtown is fine."

Richard smirked. "I need a fucking cold shower."

We laughed uncontrollably for a while over that eccentric meeting—both of us wound tight from arousal.

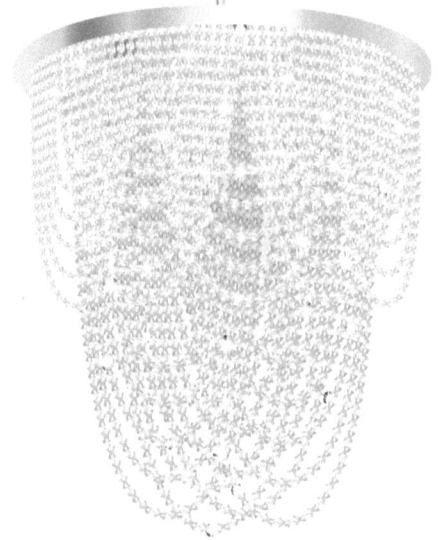

CHAPTER FORTY-EIGHT

Lotte

T HE DRIVE TO DOWNTOWN L.A. WAS SUPER FUN WITH Richard. He was the funniest man I knew, his wit sharp and insightful—the reason why he and Cameron balanced each other out so well.

Whenever I spent time with either of them, I learned something new, their comprehension of current affairs on point.

Much like Henry.

I leaned over in my seat and gave Richard a big hug.

"Henry will drive you home, right?" he asked, glancing at the sidewalk where pedestrians hurried by.

I hoped so. Otherwise, I'd be stranded.

I reached for my door handle. "I can always Uber."

"Go get your guy."

My thoughts rushed back to de Sade's home on Mulholland Drive and that sweet submissive we'd left behind. "She seemed happy, right?"

"Amelia?" Richard gave a nod.

"De Sade told us she came from Pendulum," I said. "I should have talked with her."

"She seemed kind of busy." He arched a brow.

"They're rogues. But they take care of their subs."

"And de Sade's all showmanship," he agreed.

"He's essentially a good person."

Richard held out his hand and tilted it side to side as though to say my assertion was debatable.

"I would have been intimidated by all that testosterone at her age."

Richard smiled. "You?"

"Okay, I'm going. Give Andrea my love. Tell her I want to see her."

"She adores you."

"Love you, baby." I stepped out onto the curb and turned to wave goodbye.

He waved back and then focused on his phone. I imagined he was texting Andrea. On the way here his dashboard had lit up with a slew of incoming texts from her, though he'd not been able to read them.

I guessed he'd been itching to message her.

I'd offered to read them, but he'd told me they could wait. If important, she'd have called.

Richard parked close to Cole Tower.

Peering up at the buildings, I felt humbled by these towering skyscrapers, noticing the glint of sunrays off Cole Tower. It was one of the most impressive buildings in the city, named after Cameron as C. R. Cole Tower. I wondered how Henry felt about that.

Turning slightly, I paused when I caught sight of the most prominent billboard opposite Cole Tower. It featured the sophisticated image of a woman on a sundeck sipping iced Cole Tea as she took in the view of the Amalfi Coast. I recognized the location from the colorful homes and that deep blue sea. Their brand screamed luxury, saying *you deserve the best.* That paying a little more for a superior product reflected how you treated yourself.

I liked that.

I'd grown up poor so any chance to spoil myself was greeted with gratitude. I'd watched my mom put herself second all of the goddamned time.

Living my best life was my way of making her sacrifice mean something.

It wasn't about things, though.

It was about moments.

Passing the businesses, I kept an eye out for a bakery. Now and again, a luxury store popped up. Passing an expensive flower shop I wondered how many people would see this as a saving grace for that last minute gift.

Though flowers weren't right for what I had in mind.

Truffle by Jason Wu was a great name for a restaurant. Glancing through the window, I could see into the packed place. I imagined with this kind of real estate the prices for an entrée would be exorbitant.

The rich red décor and dark wood looked inviting. The tables were occupied by business suit types. It was a convenient place for lunch meetings.

I froze, my gut twisting.

Henry sat in one of the booths—only he wasn't alone. A young woman sat to his left. Reese sat on the other side with her head resting on his shoulder.

His fingers were intertwined with hers.

Reese had ditched the khakis and wore a Burberry vintage dress, her white-blonde hair tumbling over her shoulders. Her rare, earthy beauty emphasized by classy makeup.

He hadn't told me she'd be in town.

My throat felt tight, like I was having an allergic reaction— or like I'd been poisoned. My heart was racing and I had to force the breath back into my lungs.

We'd talked about being exclusive—right up until he'd walked out on me.

We hadn't talked since.

How could it be her?

I couldn't think straight as I stared through the window, taking in the scene that hadn't changed. They were still holding hands, her head still resting on his shoulder.

Her daughter, Lilly, looked on, seemingly glad to see the lovers reunited. Happy her mother's boyfriend was back in her life where he belonged.

No, not where he belonged.

I'd been naïve to believe I had any chance of competing with someone like her—a woman whose disappearance had haunted Henry for so long.

Those old sparks had finally reignited.

Tensions would have been high during their first meeting at the preserve. But after that, when the dust had settled and the words first spoken in anger had cooled, they had realized their love had never died.

If he had been mine all those years ago and I had messed up back then, getting another chance to be together would be vigorously pursued.

I could fight for him.

Reese had seemingly done just that—fought for him.

Our fledging relationship had never stood a chance.

Glad they'd not seen me, I hurried back the way I'd come, tears welling in my eyes, my chest tight with grief.

When I saw Richard's Mercedes still parked at the curb, I let out a sob of relief.

I tapped on his window.

He lowered it to talk. "Hey. He's not in?"

"No."

"Hop in."

"I've already had you drive me all the way out here. I'll get an Uber." That way I could at least hide my emotions.

"I'm not leaving you to hop in some stranger's car." He gestured for me to get in the Mercedes. "Let's stop off for lunch somewhere."

I climbed into his car and pulled on my seatbelt.

"Where do you want to eat?"

"I have period cramps. Can you take me home?" I hated lying to one of my best friends.

"Of course." He pointed to the central divider. "Pain killers. Andrea literally has this car filled with meds for any situation."

"She's the best," I said.

"I wondered why you were pale." He reached over and gave my hand a squeeze. "These things come on fast. Let's get you home. You need a heating pad for your tummy."

I stared out the window so he couldn't see my tears. "All I want is to sleep it off."

Sleep off the memory of seeing them holding hands.

Richard navigated the car back into traffic. "I've got you."

CHAPTER FORTY-NINE

Henry

THE BOX FULL OF FIREWORKS ON CAMERON'S DESK MADE me uneasy. I questioned the logic in this idea—though, ironically, it had been mine.

I'd asked Cameron to get them.

"Desensitization," he said thoughtfully. "I agree this may help." He watched me watching them. "Where are you going to set them off?"

They were inanimate objects—right up until you lit them—and then when those fuckers went off, it was an entirely different situation.

"I'm going to light them at Shay's place," I told him.

"Want me there?"

"No."

Cameron gestured for me to take a seat in the high-backed chair, but I continued to pace. It was generous of him to see me, considering I'd turned up unannounced on his Saturday off.

But after yesterday's lunch at Truffles, I'd been left unsettled. Like a ship lost at sea.

Only my brother could anchor me.

She, too, could anchor me.

Our seeming friendship was impossible.

Cameron was dressed in a T-shirt and jeans to compliment this casual meeting. I'd dressed in my running gear, since I'd probably need a ten-mile run to clear my head after all of this.

We'd left our dogs in the yard to play.

His office theme featured old-world vs. new. Mia had helped him decorate the space in understated luxury, a contrast to our gaudy upbringing. Seriously, you'd have thought Mom had been inspired by the Palace of Versailles.

Which reminded me, why hadn't she insisted he also install those outrageous statues here? We should be treated equally when it came to her over-the-top style.

That made me chuckle.

Reality kicked my butt and my mind returned once more to a swirling, twisting state of confusion.

Cameron sat down in the high-backed chair opposite the one meant for me.

His Beverly Hills home office had been decked out to make it fit for one of his infamous private sessions.

My brother had a thing for Carl Jung and was clearly just as eccentric as that world-renowned psychoanalyst.

Patiently, Cameron waited for me to join him.

"Pacing helps," I said in my defense.

"That's fine."

I jabbed a finger at him. "I don't need a therapist. I need you to be my brother."

He opened his palms in surrender.

"Don't try that weird shit on me."

"No weirdness," he promised like a pro.

I'd been shaken up like a fucking dust bowl.

During lunch yesterday with Reese and her daughter, I'd brilliantly feigned business as usual despite how distressing the charade had felt.

I wanted to go back to earlier in the month when my life felt simpler, when the ghosts of my past weren't haunting me.

My head was all over the place.

"May I suggest meditation?" said Cameron.

"Are you trying to rile me up?" I then stared at him incredulously. "You meditate?"

"Yes."

"I suppose I could try it." I should be polite, at least.

"How have you been lately?" he asked.

Annoyed.

Frustrated.

Angry.

Besotted.

But I went with, "I want you to see this from my point of view."

He steepled his fingers.

"Because?" I hated the madness in his method.

"Because the truth hurts?"

I relented and sat opposite him.

"Psychiatrists make me nervous," I admitted. "When I returned from deployment, I knew anything I mentioned might have me committed."

"I wouldn't have allowed that."

I believed him. "The public never sees what happens out there. They're not meant to. But it means they can't really understand."

"Because your job is to protect them—at your own detriment." He waved a hand in the air. "Can you get to the point, please? This is super boring."

"Don't," I said.

"Don't what?"

"Piss me off like that."

"That emotion," he said, leaning forward, "tell me about it."

"An intense urge to say, 'fuck off.'"

"To me?"

"Obviously."

"You know what I see?"

I gave a nod. "Fear."

"Fear."

My jaw tightened. "I hope you weren't this shitty with Shay."

"Worse."

"Do you find this funny?"

He frowned. "You wanted me to be your brother. Want me to flip to therapist mode?"

"Again, fuck you."

"Your anger is coming out. This is good."

I stared at the ceiling, frustrated with him, with life and with everything in between. "I keep thinking about Lilly's visit at the office."

"Who is she again?"

I clenched my jaw. "Okay, therapist mode it is."

Cameron sat back and crossed one long leg over the other. "Lilly came to see you on behalf of her mom to tell you what really happened out there in Chile all those years ago."

That jolted me, and I tried to discern whether they had spoken.

Yesterday, he'd seen Lilly arrive at my office, but he had left soon afterwards.

He read my concern. "We haven't spoken. They're going for your sympathy. An expected next tactic after the first attempt to get you on their side failed."

"How do you do that?"

"It's a curse and a blessing." He exhaled. "Go on."

"I'm being manipulated."

"What did Lilly say?"

"She asked me to see things from her mom's perspective."

"Do you believe Reese regrets the way she treated you at the preserve?"

"Maybe. Anyway, Lilly told me the real reason her mom decided to disappear off the face of the earth." I tried to swallow the lump in my throat.

I'd become that young man suffering the loss all over again, the same grief capturing me in its hellish thrall.

Cameron got up and walked over to the side table. He brought me back a glass of water and I took it from him, downing the liquid and quenching my thirst.

"What did Lilly say?" whispered Cameron.

I let out a long breath. "Months after arriving in Chile, Reese attended one of their staff parties. She drank too many pisco sours—too much brandy."

"Ah, potent stuff."

I gave a nod. He knew where this was going.

"Reese woke up in this guy's bed the next day. She knew him, he was a local volunteer. There had been some light flirting between them. She says it was consensual, but she regretted it."

"I'm sorry to hear that," said Cameron. "For you and for her."

I sighed. "Reese found out she was pregnant a month later."

"That baby is Lilly?" said Cameron.

"Yes."

"Her pregnancy influenced her decision to disappear?"

I nodded. "She believed I wouldn't want her back after that."

"Did she talk to anyone about the incident?"

"I don't know."

"I see."

"She married a Chilean guy a year later."

Cameron looked sympathetic. "Reese was very young."

"We both were."

"Tell me about lunch yesterday."

"When Lilly came to the office, she brought paper clippings her mom had kept. They were of me. Reese continued to track me. She told Lilly I was her first and only love."

"What happened then?"

He'd passed over the fact her daughter had told me Reese still loved me. That she hadn't forgotten me.

"Henry?" said Cameron.

I blinked. "Lilly told me her mom had invited me to Truffles.

She waited for us there. She'd flown out to see me, just as I'd demanded of her."

"Because you were mad at her," he said. "Understandable."

"I thought she'd forgotten me from way back then. Lilly proved that wasn't the case."

"Why didn't Reese reach out before now?"

"She genuinely needs help for the preserve."

"People change."

"I shouldn't have acted the way I did when I saw her."

"I'd have seen her alive and gotten back in the boat," he said. "You actually took the time to speak with her."

"Would you have, though?" I said. "You wouldn't have wanted to hear why she disappeared?"

He shrugged. "You trekked all that way. Clearly a part of you still has feelings for her."

I sat back, trying to gauge whether he sensed more, if he saw in me any kind of lingering affection I might not see myself.

"How was lunch at Truffles?" he asked.

"Reese became emotional. She apologized for fucking up back then."

"What did you say to that?"

"I told her none of that would have mattered, that I loved her back then and we'd have worked through it."

"Loved." He made a point to use past tense. "How did she react?"

"She cried, right there in the restaurant. I hugged her and tried to stop her from breaking down further in public. I didn't want anyone snapping a photo of me making her cry. I tried to reassure Reese that her coming back pregnant would have been a blow, but we'd have still been together." I shook my head. "I wanted Reese to realize I would have done anything for her."

"Why are you obligated to her?"

I shrugged that off. "I told her I planned to help save the preserve and prevent the construction. I have a few ideas."

"How did she react?"

"She grabbed my arm and wouldn't let go." I brushed my hands over my thighs to self-sooth. "Reese wants to see me again."

"Of course she does," he said with an edge of protectiveness.

A slew of emotions welled up in me at the same time.

Through the window I could see hummingbirds circling a feeder. I hadn't noticed them until now.

Cameron followed my line of sight. "Mia has a thing for hummingbirds."

"You're a lucky man."

Never in my life would I have a love like theirs.

He studied my face. "What are you feeling?"

"Honestly, I'm falling for a woman and it's making me second guess myself."

"Who are you falling for, Henry?"

Leaning forward, I buried my face in my hands, trying to find a way through the confusion and terror I felt over this precious relationship that was so damn fragile. "I can't stop thinking about her," I admitted.

"Ah," he said softly, realizing.

My attention shot to him. "You got me to open up. How the hell do you do that?"

"A whole lot of love for my brother." He winked. "And a dash of fuckery."

I got up and walked over to his desk, resting my hand on the long box. "I'm strangely in the mood for fireworks."

CHAPTER FIFTY

Henry

HIS "DASH OF FUCKERY" I COULD DO WITHOUT.
But seeing my brother this morning at his home had felt impressively inspiring. I had this reputation for remaining closed off, but he'd sliced through that with his uncanny gift.

Finally, I'd also admitted my plan in coming here to him.

He'd given me his blessing.

Tonight, I'd give *Eyes Wide Shut* a run for its money.

I turned the masquerade mask around in my hand to reexamine it. This glamorous disguise would match my bespoke tux, tailored on Savile Row while visiting London.

I wasn't going to call what happened earlier with my brother a session. It was more like a brotherly chat.

I had been heard.

And understood.

His open-mindedness meant I could tell him anything and he wouldn't be shocked and he wouldn't judge. That's what we wanted from everyone, I suppose.

To be seen and loved for who we are, and that was why doing this was imperative.

Lotte deserved someone willing to accept all her colors. This multi-faceted woman reminded me of that spectacular chandelier I had strolled beneath on the way through Chrysalis' foyer.

If she agreed to become my woman, Lotte would have every luxury afforded her, including social status. And love, because for the first time in my life I felt ready for that level of affection.

I felt I was finally closing in on an elusive sense of peace.

Outside this room, music set the brilliant backdrop; I recognized "Angel" playing from the band Massive Attack, majestically setting the scene for the mysterious night ahead.

Laughter carried from down the hallway. Chrysalis' ball was as ebullient as I'd imagined it would be.

On my way in, I'd caught sight of the lavish costumes—and the lack of them, too. Barely clad submissives ran by in their alluring strips of material that covered next to nothing.

I was mesmerized by the sights and sounds of the delicious revelry.

I'd been escorted in by Shay who had brought me into Richard's office. They'd wanted to brief me before I set off into the erotic fray.

I'd been granted permission to attend as a guest for the night.

We'd even walked by the infamous ponies—men with dramatic headdresses trotting along with elegant strides. I'd given them a nod of respect for their showmanship.

Richly textured décor included soft lighting, along with atmospheric fog cloaking the hallways.

The appeal to this place was glaring. You got to be with good friends and eat great food prepared by the finest chefs. You had the freedom to be yourself without judgment.

No denying why I had been drawn back to Chrysalis.

"Well?" I pivoted from the mirror, facing Shay and Richard again, lowering my mask to see them better.

They gave a smirk of approval with warm expressions.

"Love the mask," said Richard sarcastically.

"I'll return it after tonight," I told him.

They both wore flawlessly suave tuxedos. It was easy to imagine the submissives falling at their feet.

"What is it you hope to achieve?" Richard brushed his fingers through his hair, which could be because he was concerned about letting me loose.

Couldn't blame him.

The last time I'd visited hadn't exactly inspired confidence.

"I'm here to have a good time," I said. "Experience this from your perspective."

Shay shook his head. "But why?"

Glancing at my reflection, I wasn't ready to tell them this was for Lotte.

But they'd probably guessed.

I needed her to see that I was willing to explore dating a dominatrix. And tonight, I'd prove that to her. Even though we hardly knew each other, I'd been swept away by my affection for her.

I felt grounded by Lotte's presence in the room and I didn't want to slow down our relationship, didn't want to take time out from seeing her. I wanted to live life in the fast lane.

With her.

I wanted to be myself and let my authentic nature shine.

My being here might appear out of character, but I wanted Lotte to know I was serious about learning more about her specialty.

If she'd invited me to take a trek through hell with her, I'd have followed Lotte into Hades. I was addicted to that woman. The memory of her taste made me harden in my tailored pants.

"Don't go upstairs," said Richard. "Not alone."

I found his comment intriguing.

Last time I'd visited, even the action on the ground level was intense. My mind spiraled with what to expect from the guests who wandered upstairs.

"Ready?" asked Shay.

I put on my masquerade mask and secured it around the back of my head with the strips of silk. One more glance in the mirror at my enigmatic reflection and I knew I'd remain unrecognizable.

My height might be intimidating, but some seemed to like that vibe, from what I could tell.

Shay and Richard led me out into the hallway. Richard slipped on his masquerade mask and walked off in the opposite direction.

Shay and I headed south.

"I can find my way around," I said.

"No doubt." Shay patted my back with affection.

It was the kind of gesture that spoke volumes. He wasn't ready to let me wander off just yet.

"Gonna put yours on?" I asked.

He gave me a devilish grin and then made it disappear behind his plague doctor masquerade mask.

"What's the most extreme thing you've done?" Inquiring minds and all that.

He looked surprised by my question. "The last time I dabbled in kink I had several submissives riding me."

"Taking turns?"

"They can't all fit on me at the same time," he said sarcastically. "I'm a sex god but not that kind of god."

I chuckled at his candor. "You've got some stamina."

His eyes crinkled in amusement.

"Do you still do that kind of thing now that you're with Rue?"

"We dabble together." He elbowed me. "Sign up for full membership and I'll share more."

That would never happen.

"Did Cameron get up to that?"

"Mind your own business." Shay winked.

Probably good advice.

I was only here for one person.

I was trying to be open-minded, but having men fantasizing about my woman? I wasn't sure I could handle that.

"What does the gold pin on your lapel mean?" I asked.

"You have to earn that," he said. "They're given to senior Doms."

I'd noticed one on Richard's lapel, too.

He didn't say it, but the insignia of a curling "C" made me guess it represented Chrysalis' VIPs.

We strolled left down a long hallway.

There were about twenty alcoves lining the way, handcuffs dangling in each one. I imagined these would soon be used by submissives placed on display.

The night was still young.

We entered a ballroom where the music was loud and a half-naked DJ danced behind his turntables in the corner, playing the kind of music you could fuck to.

When I glanced back, I could see we'd come in through a side entrance, the door camouflaged into the wall so that when it was closed it blended perfectly.

Even though I remained masked, Shay was giving me the grand tour with his usual brand of discretion.

I appreciated it.

And I was grateful for the masquerade mask hiding my expression when I scanned the room, seeing a few hundred or so VIPs in black tuxedos. Beside them, there were men and women dressed as submissives. Some were in disguise, like us, and others strolled around confidently showing off their beautiful faces.

In the left corner, one of the Doms had pulled his masquerade mask up and over his head, revealing his face, seemingly to get a better view of two submissives kneeling before him. They were both taking turns blowing him, their hungry mouths lapping his substantial cock, shiny and wet from their saliva.

It was the man who had visited Lotte's home—Jake Carrington, the football player who they called de Sade. He had a VIP pin on his lapel.

A woman walked over to de Sade and I realized it was her. *Lotte.*

I couldn't see her face because of her masquerade mask that

had feathers rising out of the headdress. But I recognized her flowing blonde wig, the one she'd worn the first time I'd met her. She leaned affectionately against de Sade's arm. He gripped her bare butt cheek, fingers digging into her flesh.

Desperately possessive.

With the fingers of his other hand, he stroked her Rolex while saying something to her I couldn't hear.

I was just too far away and the music was too loud.

She wasn't expecting me, so her flirting with another guest shouldn't surprise me. This was her world.

Shay had confirmed back in the hallway the level of kink they enjoyed here. Why would Lotte be any different? She was a beautiful, modern woman confident with her own sexuality.

Everyone here would worship a woman like that.

I started to turn away and Shay tapped my arm. "Let's do shots."

I couldn't look back at de Sade and that decadent act, couldn't watch my hopes and dreams fade after I'd nurtured them like they might save me.

Here, now, Lotte had proven she was lost to me.

"Tequila?" Shay raised his voice above the music.

My throat felt too tight to answer.

He seemed to conjure up two shots out of the air and handed me one. "We're toasting your first time here."

"I've been here before," I said gruffly.

"Not like this you haven't." He lifted his mask and threw back his drink.

I did the same with mine.

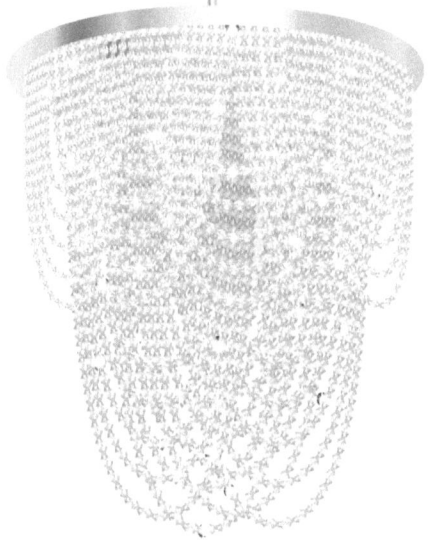

CHAPTER FIFTY-ONE

Lotte

A FEW MINUTES AGO, RYLEE HAD STROLLED OUT OF THIS dark chamber with an elegant sway of her hips.

She'd turned back to me with a look of affection.

We'd always gotten along, which was why I felt protective of her when de Sade went full on with his devilry.

Rylee didn't seem to mind. She encouraged it, for the most part. Both of them were bi and enjoyed all the elements of swapping partners.

I was surprisingly old-fashioned when it came to love.

Before she'd left, I'd slid the Rolex off my wrist and onto Rylee's, giving de Sade's gift back through her.

I couldn't keep it.

Rylee had told me she understood why and that I should take more time to consider joining them at Pendulum—a decision that would be difficult because Cameron wouldn't approve.

Richard handled it well. He knew better, of course. Keeping Grantchester, Sinclair, and de Sade close would be best for Chrysalis.

I'd also loaned Rylee my blonde wig for the evening. Both of us were wearing the same headdress, along with the same bustier and thong—the uniform for a Chrysalis dominatrix. We could be twins.

Only I'd chosen to wear my hair naturally short; no disguise there.

Rylee had spent the late afternoon preparing our submissives, making sure our fifty or so B&D graduates were dressed to Chrysalis' standard.

She'd left me to continue our tradition, all of them waiting for my next command.

They'd had their makeup done, even though many of them might be hiding their faces behind strips of lace. Rylee had also arranged hairstylists for them. They'd experienced a full day of pampering, from massages to assistants to help them dress.

Before they set off into the manor it was my job to inspect them.

Obediently, all the half-naked submissives lined up so I could check each one.

Keeping busy helped distract me from thoughts of seeing Reese at Truffles, draped on Henry's arm yesterday.

I felt my stomach clinch as my mind flashed back to it.

I shouldn't have to fight for a man who wasn't willing to fight for me.

Henry was no different.

If he needed to get Reese out of his system and sleep with her to check his feelings, well, that was a hard *no* for me.

I'd cultivated enough self-respect never to compromise.

But I needed to talk with him about it. I wasn't into condemning a man before he'd been heard.

Communication was everything.

So why the hell had I refused to text him back?

Because in my heart I knew we were an impossible match.

"Mistress Lotte?" came a quiet voice.

The submissives were waiting for me to stop daydreaming.

Strolling along the line, I tipped up the occasional chin of a sub and tweaked a nipple here and there. If I thought the in-génue would benefit from it, I whipped a butt cheek to make them focus.

This erotic vision of our lovelies was an extraordinary gift.

It was a sexual fantasy most would fall over themselves to experience. For us, it was about ensuring our subs were primed to head out into the party, ready to deliver intense pleasure to our guests.

Though our submissives' pleasure always came first.

That rule was sacrosanct.

Maybe my destiny had settled in stone, and I'd carry this tradition over to Pendulum.

I pushed that decision away.

Right now, this wasn't about me. It was about them.

And *for* them—giving my submissives the most wonderful experience they could imagine.

You could see it—their hunger for the extreme, their need for endless orgasms.

Every woman deserved this level of bliss.

Last time I'd run this ritual, I'd had several submissives fall to their knees and work their way along the line of young women. As they'd crawled along, they'd performed cunnilingus to each of their equals, lingering before those shaking thighs as they licked and teased the prettiest pussies.

It ensured that these exquisite submissives were highly aroused when they entered the grand ballroom.

When they joined the party, it truly began.

It was like winding up a perfect sensual doll and watching it play. The scenes that followed would be intensely spellbinding.

Sights and sounds to behold.

All dancing their way beneath the glistening lights of those low hanging chandeliers.

This time, I didn't incite an erotic show.

Henry wouldn't like the idea of me partaking in this kind of kink anymore. While there might still be a chance for us, I had to trust my intuition.

I could still watch over them, so that's what I did. I strolled up and down making sure they all knew their part.

Making sure they were ready for Chrysalis.

CHAPTER FIFTY-TWO

Henry

T WO SHOTS IN AND IT WAS EASY TO IGNORE MY TEQUILA-scorched mouth.

I'd missed the sexual chemistry between de Sade and Lotte when I'd visited her home in Encino.

Like an idiot.

A thousand jealous thoughts raged against this reality.

Then I remembered, he'd dated Shay for a while there, and then left him to return to his ex-wife. I hated the idea of him hurting Shay.

Going over there and punching the bastard wasn't an option. I'd never been into violence off the battlefield. And doing that would humiliate Lotte. Shay and Richard would have me on a rocket and jettisoned out to space before the night ended.

Shay grabbed my arm. "Don't throw daggers."

I'd exposed my feelings. *Can't do this.*

"That's not Lotte," he said, realizing the reason for my anger. "That's de Sade's wife."

"The woman beside him?"

"Ex-wife." He shuddered at that.

A wave of relief hit me, the tension leaving my shoulders.

Blinking through my alcohol-laced vision, I could see the woman clearer. Her breasts were a little smaller than Lotte's, but other than that her figure was strikingly similar.

Taking in the guests, I realized there were a lot of dominatrixes dressed the same.

"I need to find Lotte," I told Shay.

He caught the chain of a submissive and leaned in to ask her something.

Taking advantage of his distraction, I set my glass down on a passing tray.

Strolling casually toward de Sade and his wife, I ignored the two submissives at his feet who were still fervently showering him with oral praise.

I "accidently" bumped into de Sade's shoulder, my hand resting on his lapel for a beat. "Sorry."

"Watch where you're going," he snapped.

"Easy to be distracted," I said. "You okay?"

He checked me out one more time before his attention fell to the angels on their knees before him.

I tucked his VIP pin into my jacket pocket and made my way back to Shay. "Did you find out where she is?"

"What did you say to de Sade?"

"Lotte?" I got his focus back on finding her.

Shay gave a nod. "Abernathy Suite."

He didn't expand on that, but merely led me out of the ballroom.

The place was busier, the music louder, the mood carried on a wave of laughter. The journey to get to Lotte felt as long as eternity, both of us striding fast past partygoers.

This place had a Cirque du Soleil vibe—the erotic edition.

When I glanced through a doorway to our left, I noted men wearing cloaks and masquerade masks, and within their circle knelt a lone submissive.

I shot a glare at Shay.

It made me wonder what act I'd catch my girlfriend in.

I braced myself for when that moment hit.

Shay knocked on a door.

No answer.

I turned the door handle and walked in.

The lighting dimmed to a golden hue, the fog from outside pouring into the room, painting a picture of glamour and luxury and lavish decadence. Velvet drapes. Plush furniture. A burgundy chaise lounge. A classy boudoir for elite submissives.

A remarkable vision played out in the center of the room.

Fifty or so submissives had lined up, their hands held obediently behind their backs, posing like they were being inspected.

Walking before them was a seductive dominatrix with short, raven hair, elegantly dressed in an ornately embroidered bodice, delicate thong, high-top stockings and heeled boots.

She stopped in her tracks. "Gentlemen, this room is out of bounds."

Her sultry voice was unmistakable.

Shay shoved by me and walked a few feet ahead. "He's a VIP."

It was hard to read Lotte's expression through that stunning masquerade mask, her headdress of feathers a glamorous display.

These mistresses were doppelgangers; all striking in their lavish corsets and high-top stockings and heels.

Lotte stepped back and addressed the subs. "You may leave." She waved her whip in the air. "Fulfill your directive. Follow the rules."

The mood of the girls turned gleeful.

"Go!" she shouted.

They hurried by us into the hallway, all of them exuding excitement, leaving a waft of rich perfumes in the air as they flew by like wild sparrows.

My focus returned to Lotte.

Her stride was elegant and confident like the ultimate dominatrix.

She used her whip to ease Shay's masquerade mask up his face. "I will have you punished for your indiscretion."

He nudged the whip away from his face. "Master Booth wants you to escort this VIP."

She turned to me and looked me up and down.

I met her direct gaze.

Her lips quirked for a second and then she slid effortlessly back into her role.

Apparently, the Queen of Chrysalis recognized me.

Closing the gap between us, she pressed her whip against the base of my masquerade mask, just as she had with Shay.

The intensity of her demeanor was exhilarating, her perfume rich and her natural scent hypnotic.

I snapped my hand up and gripped my mask, preventing her from revealing my face.

"Really?" she purred.

That made my heart race.

Being in the same room with her set my flesh on fire. Dressed like this, I had to dig deep not to suddenly reach out for her.

Charlotte was the epitome of a sexual goddess. At some point tonight, I intended on kneeling before her and worshipping her pussy.

I gripped her wrist when she tried to lift my mask again.

She raised her chin with pride. At least that's what I read from her sparkling irises.

Admittedly, some part of me had wanted to see how she'd react to a stranger. My sinister side wanted to see if she'd flirt.

"Leave us," she told Shay without breaking eye contact with me.

"Don't take him upstairs," he said, walking out and closing the door.

Lotte stepped back. "What are you doing?"

Yeah, she knows it's me hiding behind this mask.

"This is a private party," she added.

"I wanted it to be a surprise."

"The last time you were here—"

"Are you going to hold that against me?"

"I'm very protective of my guests."

"How about your VIPs?"

"How did you persuade Richard to let you in?"

"Wanna show me around?"

"Lift your mask."

"No."

She lifted hers off her face first, revealing her intoxicating beauty.

All shadowy eyelids and bright red lips. A few speckles of glitter beneath her lower lashes. Ethereal—a spectacular emphasis of stunning features.

I drank her in.

She had an enduring grace, poised so elegantly, her skin luminescent as though lit from within.

I was instantly jealous of others out there who would get to see her like this.

The tequila I'd downed had lessened my superiority complex. I felt humbled by all this opulence.

Humbled by her.

"You're spectacular," I finally said.

"Why won't you take off your mask?"

"I'm here to play," I said gruffly.

I, too, could deliver showmanship. If she wanted an act of defiance, I would be that man for a night—the dangerous alpha who scared her.

It didn't take a genius to see that's what these women craved—a break from reality, a chance to indulge in their fantasies and delve into their secretive obsessions. Fulfilling their desire for endless pleasure.

In here, beneath the sparkling lights of those brilliant chandeliers, lay an underworld of debauchery unfolding in all its spectacular glory.

It was impossible not to be turned on.

I gave myself permission to savor the sights and sounds and indulge in all these excessive delights.

It was the only way to reach *her.*

I could see the benefit of chasing this high, my pulse quickening, arousal spiking—feeling the need to fuck her hard against the wall.

I stepped forward and grabbed Lotte's throat, my fingers wrapping tight around delicate skin, squeezing her airway.

CHAPTER FIFTY-THREE

Lotte

I REACHED FOR HENRY'S WRIST AND HELD IT.
He'd cut off my air with his tight grip.
I liked it.

His intense gaze through that mask bore into me with an equal measure of control and obsession.

I'd started off as a submissive before that slow glide upward through the ranks had earned me dominatrix status. Here, at Chrysalis, they respected and honored me.

No other man would dare do what Henry was doing.

And yet.

His domination sent me reeling. Like he'd turned back time and I'd become that young submissive again.

Owned.

Possessed.

Willing.

Arousal from his show of power made me wet, a throb of pleasure hitting my clit. My breasts swelled and my nipples became erect as I wished for this to go on and on and on.

I wanted to play out this fantasy.

He looked dashingly distinguished in his tailored tuxedo with silk lapels and his dapper black bowtie.

Finally, he let go.

I caressed my throat, maintaining decorum.

"Take off your thong," he said fiercely.

"No."

I could see that made him curious.

Henry shrugged. "Displease me again and see what happens."

"You don't belong here," I whispered.

"Maybe I do."

"You don't mean that." I tried to read him.

"Show me around."

I refused with a subtle shake of my head. I wanted to protect him from seeing anything he might find too shocking.

His actions shouldn't have come as a surprise. He was trying to find a way to understand my profession—he was trying to understand this world.

Understand me.

This was more than erotic curiosity. He'd come down off his mighty throne to observe us.

He reached into his jacket pocket and withdrew a small object.

My jaw slackened in shock as I watched him pin it to his lapel—a VIP pin that would grant him access anywhere within these hallowed walls.

"Where did you get that?" Richard or Shay wouldn't have handed it to him.

He brushed his fingertips over the pin, that movement reminding me how nimble his hands were when they brushed over me.

It caused me to shiver.

"On your knees," he said quietly.

Another spike of arousal hit me at hearing his command and my body responded with a tremble.

Then came the hurt as I remembered what I'd seen

yesterday—he and Reese sitting in a booth at Truffles, her daughter with them. Recalling Henry's reaction to the way Reese draped herself over his arm.

Their closeness didn't inspire trust.

It made me wonder how much time he had been spending with her, maybe to regain ground on their turbulent friendship.

Were they sleeping together?

Jealousy formed a wedge between my need for him and my heart's desire not to be destroyed.

"Submit," he growled.

"*You* submit."

"That's not who I am."

"Let's discuss this at your place."

Henry walked out, still in character, his Alpha swagger intriguing but also terrifying because he'd set off roaming.

Pulling on my masquerade mask to cover my face, I followed him out into the hallway.

White clouds of fog swirled around his feet, making him look like an eighteenth-century hero heading over the moors.

I'd fallen for him.

I was head over heels for this tall, gorgeous, arrogant man and trancing out at the mere sight of him.

My whip slipped from my hand as I snapped out of this dreamlike state, hurrying after him.

He peered up at the main foyer's chandelier before quickly ascending the central staircase, taking two steps at a time.

At the top, he did a quick pivot as though to see if I was following. Confirming I was, he continued to trek along the second-floor mezzanine.

If he entered any one of those rooms he'd step into high kink.

Holy hell.

He had no idea what he might walk into.

I took off after him up the central staircase, trying not to alert anyone. Each door was guarded by a Dom, but that pin on his lapel would gain him access.

After all, no one entered Chrysalis without the password. If you did manage to get through the main gate, when you made it to the front door, you'd have to pass the retinal scanner to step into the manor.

If you were in here, you belonged.

Which was why the tuxedo-clad guard let him into the most decadent of chambers.

Henry disappeared inside the Highgrove Suite.

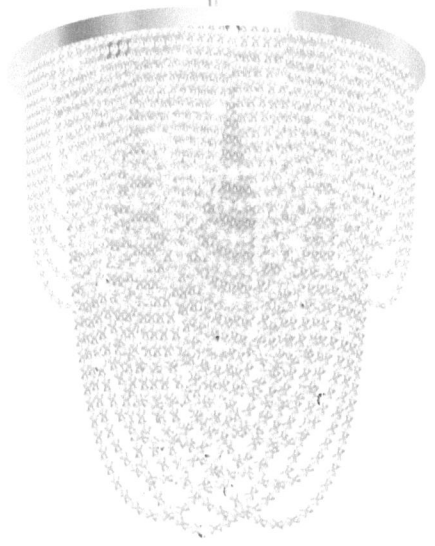

CHAPTER FIFTY-FOUR

Lotte

I ENTERED THE ROOM RIGHT BEHIND HENRY—STEPPING INTO the lion's den.

We were met by the whispers of thirty or more guests dressed to the nines. They'd respectfully gathered for this session. There was a reason this scene had to be well-guarded.

An erotic story was about to be told in real time; a fantasy on the precipice of realization for a young submissive. Her devastatingly handsome master was ready to reveal his unique set of talents. Senior dominant Atticus Sinclair would be showcasing his new submissive to the VIPs.

Heavy green drapes covered the floor-to-ceiling windows to block out the fading light. A chandelier hung above the central four-poster bed with a plush velvet duvet.

What set this room apart from other luxury venues were the chains dangling over the four-poster.

And there was Henry, standing at the back, camouflaged in his black tuxedo and masquerade mask, appearing like he belonged.

A few of the men turned to watch me enter as I strolled elegantly into the room.

With a nod, I feigned there was nothing out of the ordinary going on, that we didn't have an interloper in our midst.

Henry emanated charisma, looking so damn sexy in that gold Venetian mask and suave tux.

He was annoying gorgeous and arrogant enough to believe he deserved to step into this sanctum.

No, that wasn't it at all. I hated him for making me want to say yes to a clandestine affair. I understood his reasoning. He'd become such a hazardous addiction.

Closing the space between us, I walked slowly so as not to arouse suspicion, peering up at this regal stud of a man.

"What are you doing?" I whispered.

His right hand glided down my spine until it rested at the arch of my lower back, the warmth from his palm saturating through my bodice.

If he'd meant to ignite a sense of arousal, he'd accomplished it. The room hushed.

"You can't stay," I whispered.

"Silence," he said sternly.

Cameron is going to fucking kill me.

I drew in a sharp breath at the door being locked by a young submissive.

No one else was coming in.

Or out.

Atticus Sinclair came in from a side door, strolling with his usual arrogant swagger that appeared extra sinister. His tattooed hands complimented his remarkable black tuxedo that reflected a stark sophistication.

He was like a walking pheromone.

And he was exceptionally choosy about which submissive he trained. He had a type. Not necessarily in appearance but more in their ability to be subservient. He loved them to beg. And they always begged him for more.

The young submissive being showcased today was twenty-year-old Olivia Bancroft.

Wearing a filigree mask, she was being pulled along by a fine chain connected to her collar, her large breasts naked. He'd permitted her to wear a thong.

The brilliant Atticus was noted for his level of precision, being a talented surgeon, which was a surprise to those who misread his tattoos. His downtime included expeditions to territories as far reaching as the North Pole. His inked hands threw his patients at first, right up until he showed them the remarkable things he could do, saving the lives of those who would have died under another doctor's care.

He displayed a reckless but controlled vibe.

Olivia was a reasonable match for him. She was a lifestyle blogger who'd made a name for herself on social media as an all-round good American girl.

We were seeing her secret persona.

What we would witness tonight was her passion for kink, her appetite being as filthy as her masters.

Atticus ripped off her thong, leaving her completely naked, other than her collar.

Startled, and then subdued, she remained still as commanded.

He had her climb onto the bed and kneel facing away, showing off her butt with its puckered asshole revealing a sparkling gemstone butt plug and her shiny, glistening pussy. Arousal dampened her thighs.

Standing to the side, Sinclair raised a wooden paddle and began a hypnotic rhythm of slaps to Olivia's ass cheeks. That slow steady flushing of flesh began until that brightness appeared sore, her body rocking with each hit, no doubt releasing endorphins. Olivia gripped the sheets to tolerate the incessant strikes.

I'd almost forgotten Henry stood close by.

His focus was on Atticus.

For those unfamiliar with this scene, there could be an

instinctive urge to rescue the submissive. To be the hero. Guests were expected to respect the art. Stand back and let them be.

I hoped Henry didn't have the urge to save her. She wouldn't want that.

Olivia wanted *this*.

Cycling through the usual components of enticing a sub into a trance, Atticus utilized the chains. Once Atticus restrained her, he set about marking her flesh with a whip, striking her in another dazzling display of control until she stood at the end of the bed naked and subdued in subspace, eyelids heavy, face flushed and trembling with adrenaline.

Atticus sat on the edge of the bed behind her and dragged her onto his lap.

He opened his zipper and pulled out his substantial erection. Olivia followed the order to sit on him, her thighs on either side of his, toes off the ground. She sank onto his cock, plunging herself down so he was buried deep inside her and she was locked onto him with gravity's embrace—her jaw gaping as her sex adjusted to his significant size.

He pulled her thighs farther apart, allowing us to witness the way he stretched her pink pussy with his width, her sex taut and shiny. The pose was familiar to us.

Atticus gave the command for his ingénue to remain still, her obedience witnessed by all. She was only permitted to move upon his order.

Which was why scenes like this were played out respectfully. It was an art form within itself, the couple performing their masterful fuck in a welcome setting.

He pinched her pert nipples and reached between her thighs to part her delicate folds, teasing her clit with an expert circling. She glanced down to see his clever fingers touching her just so. His fingertips were drenched by her arousal.

He whispered in her ear, testing her ability to comply with his commands.

My own arousal spiked, my clit throbbing.

Atticus invited one of the lions to step forward.

The man chosen raised his masquerade mask up a little and knelt before their parted thighs. Leaning in, he began suckling Olivia's cunt with a feverish vigor.

From here, I could see how well he lavished an affectionate tongue over her tautness, flicking her clit with the tip, circling, following the pace set by her master.

Olivia was forbidden to come.

She was merely permitted to rest her head back against her master's chest and endure the intensity of this raw, aching pleasure, a cruel teasing from both men.

One buried deep inside her—Atticus—and the other dominating her pussy, her silky essence creating a shine on his chin.

Her soft moans echoed around us.

Henry took my wrist and pulled me in front of him. His right hand slid around my waist while his left hand moved down toward my pelvis.

"Yes?" he whispered huskily.

"Yes." I would give him this.

Give *us* this.

His hardness behind me pressed into my spine, the succulent sensation of his fingertips sliding along sensitive tissue, mirroring that vision before us. He played me like an instrument of lust, his two fingers circling as he established a brilliant rhythm.

"So wet," he said softly. "Good girl."

I shivered.

How dare he say that to me, knowing the kind of power I wielded? Yet I was made fragile against his thrumming. Reaching behind me, I caressed his cock. It grew harder in my palm.

Before us, the consummate performance was blazing hot upon that opulent bed.

We continued to pleasure each other, me rubbing him through his pants and him flicking me as though needing me to come.

Our connection felt soul-deep.

Olivia moaned softly, desperate to be allowed to orgasm. But she was holding back, obeying her master as best she could despite these dramatic circumstances. Her body shuddered in delight, full of need as they tortured her with her own arousal.

She was so turned on because they'd subdued her.

Atticus was proving his mastery of a new ingénue as he coaxed and praised her, whispered and growled his control. Tattooed hands eased apart her labia, holding that pose for their guests.

Another man was invited to bow before our erotic princess, devouring her sex as though she offered the fountain of youth.

And then another man after that, bowing at her feet to pleasure her with a zealous mouth—each gentleman taking their time to lavish her with affection.

Soon, it would be Henry's turn.

CHAPTER FIFTY-FIVE

Lotte

APPARENTLY REALIZING THE ORDER OF SERVICE FOR Highgrove's chamber, Henry stepped away from me and led the way toward a door on our left.

We slipped into another room.

He used his handkerchief to wipe his fingers clean and then tucked that tell-tale square of white material back into his pocket.

I waited for him to react.

Say something.

Tell me what he thought of us all.

Of me.

Henry met my gaze. "Let's take this to one of your dungeons."

We left the room and hurried down the central staircase, making our way along the foyer to the private doorway.

Briskly, we descended the spiraling staircase.

I glanced Henry's way to see if he might change his mind. He seemed just as eager to make it to our destination—all the way to my favorite dungeon.

The ultimate gentleman, Henry gestured for me to go on

ahead inside the dimly lit, red-walled chamber. Once he was inside, I turned and locked the door behind us.

"Filthy girl," he said huskily. "You deserve to be fucked hard for that."

My body shuddered in response to his harshness.

"I'm going to punish you," he said, "because you are out of control."

Any other man and I'd have been able to rally my power and take charge. But Henry was demanding. *So demanding.*

Dominant and fiercely controlling.

He peeled off his mask revealing an intense expression and a razor-sharp gaze that was impossible to break away from.

After easing me back against the wall, trapping me there, he knelt in front of me.

Tugging my thong aside, he said, "I can speak your language. I'm a 'cunni-linguist.'"

I laughed but stopped suddenly when his mouth met my clit, widening my thighs to give him better access.

The sensation sent pleasure into my core, my body igniting as this blazing passion possessed me. The way he devoured my pussy reflected the oral sex bestowed upon Olivia.

As though all he could think about was *this.*

With a heated urgency, he bewitched my folds, tongue striking up a brilliant rhythm as he flicked up and down, turning me boneless. Pinned against the wall, my trembling fingers gripped his short locks tightly as I moaned like a needy young submissive.

His forceful ways proved he wanted to be my master.

Here, now, I gave myself to him entirely. Being possessed this aggressively lit up the submissive within me.

He eased my thong down and over my hips. I stepped out of the strip of material when it reached my feet and he quickly tucked my panties into his jacket pocket.

"You're desperate to come," he said gruffly.

"Yes."

"Are you going to be obedient?"

I was still trying to read him but, at the same time, I needed this session with him more than I could remember needing anything.

"I should be in charge," I blurted out breathlessly.

"Do I have to repeat myself? Do as you're told!"

"I'm a dominatrix!"

"No. You haven't shown me that's what you want."

"But—" I threw my head back in a swoon.

He sprang to his feet and grabbed the back of my neck, bringing me in close without kissing me. His mouth hovered near mine. "Say it or I'll stop," he said fiercely.

"Do anything you want to me."

"Better."

Henry was full of wrath and lust and alpha-need, and I silently begged him to stay this way. "My safe word is chandelier."

He gave a nod. "I'll remember." His voice sounded deep and throaty, reflecting his arousal.

He led me across the room toward the velvet throne and made me sit there.

Then he made me wait as he went off on a search.

"Let's focus on the pleasure," he said gruffly. "Because I know that drives you wild."

Quickly, he secured my wrists to the armrests with silk bindings and then took another walk along the line of shelves to view the accouterments on display.

"Hurry," I said.

"You will be patient!"

"Yes, sir."

"You will learn respect."

"I will," I whispered, yearning for his touch.

I was mesmerized by this different version of him, set alight by the profoundness of Chrysalis.

Henry brought back a miniature pinwheel and held it to my mouth, my tongue wetting the small tool.

With my nod of approval, he ran it along my jaw line, along

my throat and then down between my breasts, a sting of spikes alighting the flesh it ran over.

"Let me see those tits," he growled.

He yanked down the bustier, exposing me. Placing those blunted blades over my left breast, he circled them around my nipple, causing me to shiver and causing my nipples to bead with the bliss of its pinch. The sensations intensified as he moved it from one breast to the other showing a talent for a sensual tempo.

I was fully aroused and spellbound.

"Open your thighs," he said. "Don't you dare hide yourself."

Leaning back, I spread my thighs for him, feeling strangely self-conscious about how wet he'd made me.

His nostrils flared at the sight of me, and he left me again to find another device.

The wait felt impossibly long.

The small metal wheel was replaced by a pink vibrator—one of the many jewels of this chamber's collection.

As with the wheel, he expertly caressed my nipples with the rubber tip, running it around my areola and causing me to moan and lean forward before teasing my clit with the shuddering vibration furtively pressed to sensitive flesh.

For his grand finale, he ripped off the binds that secured me, lifted me out of the chair and sat down before pulling me onto his lap.

"May I?" I knew well enough to ask for permission.

With hooded eyelids he said, "Yes."

I sat facing him, my thighs spread over his as I eased onto his impressive cock, sinking as far as possible so that he remained buried deep, pussy stretched wide as he impaled me.

"All this time I've been away from you," he said. "Fuuuck."

All I needed was this. *Him.*

"Promise you'll let me protect you," he said.

"If you like."

"Come hard." He sounded like the devil himself.

Already wantonly unhinged, I peered down and watched him press the vibrator against my clit.

I writhed upon him, leaning back and grinding into his lap, my mind going blank as I came, shaking violently as pleasure undulated through my being.

It was a blinding intoxication.

Hips rotating, I pounded him as though crazed, craving an eternal loop that would keep us here.

"I'm going to fill you," he said gruffly.

"Yes, please."

I rode him wildly as he bucked, desperate for his heat.

"Oh, God." I drew in a sharp breath.

Henry's warmth flooded inside me, filling me with his essence.

Grasping his shoulders, I collapsed against him, resting my forehead against his as both of us panted, trying to draw more air into our lungs.

My hand nudged the vibrator away from my sex, and a leisurely smile appeared on his handsome face.

"Hi," was all I could say.

"What do you want?" he asked huskily. "I'll give you anything."

"I want us to be together."

"There's only one way." His fingers pinched the delicate pink skin of my breasts.

"I'll be your secret," I whispered, shivering. "If that's what you want."

If that's all I would ever be. *His mistress.*

"I want to take you home," he said.

I pressed my lips to his, his tongue lashing mine, his hands gently cupping my face.

I climbed off him, sticky and sweat-soaked and filled with joy.

We dressed in silence.

He straightened his bowtie and zipped up his pants. Now and again, he threw me a reassuring glance.

Within minutes, we were speeding away from Chrysalis in his Range Rover, with me wrapped in his jacket to keep warm.

When we reached his home, Henry escorted me in via the side door of the house—because that's how you got your secret lover inside.

"Shush," he said. "Don't wake the dog."

"I can't have the staff see me dressed like this," I said.

"They're not here." He swept me up into his arms and carried me toward his bedroom, placing me gently on the bed.

He ripped off his bowtie. "Time to fuck you again."

"Yes." *Oh, God did I want that.* "Please."

"Let's get that pussy ready." He stood at the end of the bed and stripped the rest of his tuxedo off. "Show me how you like to play with yourself."

Obeying, I opened my thighs and fingered my clit *for him.*

"I'm the only man who gets to see you like this," he said gruffly. "Understand?"

"Yes." I gasped over the fact I had agreed so easily.

"Good, because I lay claim to your pussy. That's non-negotiable."

No more words were needed—no more discussions. The last time we'd fucked at my house, I'd demanded more and he offered no compromise.

I took his offer.

"Come," he ordered.

Arching my back, I surrendered to a blinding climax delivered by my own hand as an orgasmic gift for *him.*

CHAPTER FIFTY-SIX

Henry

I KNEW ENOUGH ABOUT DOPAMINE TO REALIZE THAT EVENTS like last night at Chrysalis could become addictive.

In all honesty, as much as the event enthralled—and it did—I'd found Lotte far more fascinating. The memories of our night there would stay with me forever.

We'd become even closer, this magnetic attraction to her fast becoming an obsession. My passion for Lotte was all-consuming. Every decision I made had me mentally checking to see what Lotte might have to say about it. I trusted her opinion.

Last night, she'd agreed to be my mistress—even though she deserved so much more.

It proved what a complete asshole I'd been to her.

I shook my head to refocus.

Sitting on the patio and sipping coffee by my pool had become a new tradition. I liked it out here. The view was relaxing and I kind of liked the house, too. Dex sat at my feet, having fallen in love with the place a whole lot faster.

Shay appeared in that covert fashion I should be used to by now.

He waved a sheet of paper at me. "Are you sure about this?"

"I've made up my mind."

"Blow everything up for a woman?"

I pointed at my speech for the Gala. "This is how you have your cake and eat it, too."

"Have you spoken to Lotte about this?" he asked.

"Thought it would be a fun reveal."

After all she had endured, this felt like a decent plan—as gentlemanly as it was daring.

He stared at me for the longest time. "Why now?"

"Intuition."

"You and Cameron, you really go out on a limb for us all, don't you?"

I grinned up at him.

"You've gone fucking soft," he huffed, with an amused expression.

The appearance of my butler, Alstead, had us refocusing in his direction. Behind him walked my guests, Reese and her daughter Lilly.

"Jesus," Shay muttered.

"Go brief Kinsley," I told him.

My lawyer waited patiently for us in the conference room.

Shay walked by Reese and Lilly without making eye contact and disappeared inside.

My emotions were locked down.

Understandably, they appeared impressed as they took in the sprawling lawn and in-ground pool. Or maybe the interior had them dazzled—towering statues tend to do that.

I pushed up and threw them a welcoming wave.

Reese brightened. "Not too shabby, Cole."

"It'll do," I joked.

Lilly looked at me wide-eyed. "The pool is big!"

"Did you bring your bathing suit?" I asked her.

"Yes!" She beamed as she watched Diana, my housekeeper, set a handful of plush beach towels on a lounger.

"You really don't mind?" asked Lilly.

"I invited you to swim," I said. "Have fun."

She was easily a younger version of her mom—before life had hardened Reese.

Seeing the charm bracelet on Reese's left wrist made me pause. I'd bought it for her eighteenth birthday. The "R" was missing because she'd placed it in the envelope with the co-ordinates for the preserve.

Reese saw me staring at the bracelet.

"Still fits?" I asked, surprised she thought wearing it was a good idea.

"For old times' sake." She gave me a smile, the same kind that had once haunted my memories.

I snapped my focus back to Lilly. "Your mom and I will be in the conference room."

"Do you ever get lost in there?" asked Lilly.

"Not yet."

Every hallway led to the center of the house eventually. I wondered if that could be a metaphor for my life now—all paths leading me back to Lotte.

"Henry?" Reese touched my arm to get my attention. "Thank you for inviting us. It means a lot."

"Of course."

"You and I are healing old wounds, getting familiar with each other all over again." Reese's expression was full of hope.

I smiled. "How's your hotel?"

"Great."

"Good of you to fly out," I said.

Lilly hurried to the side of the pool and stripped down to her bathing suit. Her being outside would give us more time to talk.

"Forgive me," said Reese. "For everything."

"We have to move forward."

I'd also forgiven myself for pining after her all these years.

Reese was a different version of herself, though her introspection was still lacking.

"There's something I have to tell you," she said.

"Can it wait?"

"I still love you," she blurted out.

Words failed me as I tried to find a reply that would sound kind.

"It might take you longer to come around," she said. "But we can still make up for those years apart."

It was her sadness I couldn't stand.

She'd carried shame when there was no need. Getting pregnant with Lilly had changed the trajectory of her life. It made me imagine how scared and lonely she might have been in Chile, all alone.

Reaching out, I brushed a strand of hair out of her face.

Fate would take care of itself. Everything would work out. I wasn't into sentimentally usually—not with those I didn't trust—but I owed her the kindest sort of closure.

Because she'd not felt comfortable enough to share her pregnancy with me. It was impossible to convince her she'd dated the kind of man you could trust with a secret like that.

"Henry, tell me how you feel about me," she whispered.

Splash.

We both turned toward the pool, hearing Lilly laughing loudly at something. Maybe she, too, felt the tension lift.

"The others are waiting," I said, gesturing towards the house.

As we trekked along the endless hallways, I rested my hand on her shoulder to make her feel welcome.

To break the silence, I said, "I roll calls over to the conference room after work."

"You don't mind it? Working for Cole Tea?"

"I am Cole Tea, Reese."

She'd forgotten how far I'd come.

Several minutes later, we'd taken our seats in the conference room. Shay was already here, sitting beside Kinsley Woo, my senior attorney. He'd been kind enough to attend this weekend meeting.

Once Diana had made sure we all had our chosen beverages, and were comfortable, she left.

And we began.

Kinsley slid a contract across the table toward Reese. "You'll need to sign this before we proceed."

Reese spun the contract around. "An NDA? Is this necessary?

Shay gave a nod. "We need to confirm you won't disclose any private information."

Reese reached for the pen I set before her.

We waited the five minutes it took for her to skim over the document and watched as she applied her signature.

"I hope I didn't just sign my life away," she said.

Shay leaned back. "Community Development is a big donor in Washington. That's how they navigated the state laws in Florida, nabbed the construction contract to build in the center of the preserve. They went around the usual preservation laws and sold their new hotel as an educational center. Then donated to Florida's Senatorial race."

"How did you find all this out?" Reese searched our faces.

"We're thorough," answered Shay.

"How do we fight a company with such powerful connections?" asked Reese.

"We don't," said Shay.

"Don't tell me it's hopeless?" she said.

"We solved the problem," said Woo. "Henry bought them."

Reese sat back. "You bought them! You own Community Development?"

"Yes," I said. "Construction has been halted."

"For how much?" she asked.

"That's undisclosed." I threw a stern glance her way. "We'll find a more positive mission for the company."

"Thank you." Reese sounded breathless as she reached out and rested her hand on mine.

Shay noticed, as did Woo.

Not wanting to embarrass her, I turned my palm around and squeezed Reese's hand.

She smiled at me. "You just saved the preserve!"

Shay pushed back from the table and stood. "That's Henry Cole for you. Always saving the day."

I waved off the compliment. "Let's have lunch by the pool. Kinsley, we'd love for you to join us. Shay, stay for a while, if you like."

In all honesty, I didn't want any more time alone with Reese. It didn't feel right having her here and not telling Lotte about it.

Reese got up. "I'll go tell Lilly."

"Sure," I said. "Go take a swim with her before lunch. I'll have Diana bring out drinks."

Reese remained at the door, her expression a mix of adoration and confusion.

It made me wonder how she'd behave now that she'd gotten what she wanted.

"We have a Cole Gala coming up this Saturday," I said. "You're both invited."

"We don't have anything to wear for something like that," she said.

"We'll take care of it," Shay replied.

"That's amazing of you," she said, face flushed.

Shay had intercepted her with his usual panache.

Reese returned to the terrace.

Shay stood there a bit longer, studying my face, probably wondering why I'd invite her to our annual event. I could see how this would appear.

But that old saying about keeping your enemies closer fit better than Reese would ever sense.

Respecting my decision, Shay gave a nod and followed Kinsley out, leaving me alone in the conference room. I was pondering how smoothly things can go when you have the best team to help solve the world's problems.

The meeting had ended, leaving us aware we had done something meaningful—even if the road that led to this problem had been paved in pain.

I pulled out my phone, my finger gliding to the photo of that adorable baby raccoon I'd taken at the preserve.

"Your cute face just cost me millions," I said out loud. "But you're worth it, little rascal. You're safe now."

CHAPTER FIFTY-SEVEN

Lotte

THE IMPRESSIVE IRON GATE LEADING TO HENRY'S BEVERLY Park Terrace home swung wide for a Range Rover exiting the driveway.

Shay Gardner sat behind the wheel.

I threw him a wave. He threw one back.

I'd given myself away.

Although Henry turning up at Chrysalis yesterday had made it easy for everyone to guess our secret.

Last night had been too much and yet not enough. That man made me tremble in all the right ways.

As Shay drove off, I took advantage of the gate being open and navigated up Henry's driveway.

He had invited me back.

Hopefully, seeing me would make his day better. I could sit on his terrace and play with Dex if Henry had work to do—sad luck on a weekend, but these business tycoons rarely rested.

My body responded as though he was already in my sights.

Last night we'd made love in this house until the wee hours. I'd only left because I needed to shower and change clothes.

Last night. I couldn't have imagined a more perfect evening at Chrysalis that tumbled naturally into an all-nighter.

After our untamed sex was over and I lay on his chest drifting to sleep, I'd realized I hadn't felt this safe in a man's arms for years.

Going anywhere with Henry felt like an adventure. We could be in the middle of nowhere and sleeping in a tent—just being in his presence made me blissfully happy.

Racking my brain, I couldn't recall the last time I'd felt this high from life.

I gently knocked on the front door.

The last time I'd used the doorbell, literally every single staff member had appeared out of nowhere. They had enough to do without having to fuss around me.

I decided to walk around the side of the house, heading toward the noise of laughter and splashing water.

What I saw next caused me to freeze in my tracks.

Reese was swimming in the pool with a young woman who I guessed was her daughter.

Reese noticed me, and I saw the joy fade from her expression. She waded to the shallow end and climbed the steps, walking over to a lounger where she grabbed a towel, wrapping it around her tall, lithe body.

Of course, after seeing them at lunch together at Truffles this shouldn't come as a surprise.

I met her halfway. "Having fun?"

She appeared just as disappointed to see me.

"Lilly needed this." She glanced back at her daughter. "It's been a whirlwind trip."

"Henry told me she wants to study at UCLA," I said, my tone friendly.

"She's applied," she said. "We're waiting to hear if she got in."

"It's a great place."

Reese would want the best for Lilly. UCLA was also

undoubtedly one of the most expensive colleges. It made me wonder how she could afford it.

"I'm here to see Henry," I stated the obvious.

"He's inside," she said.

It was a challenge keeping my expression serene.

She wouldn't realize that I knew she'd hidden our boat at the preserve, blocking our exit. Maybe I was over dramatizing the incident, but Henry being around her made the hairs on my nape prickle.

Her manipulation knew no bounds.

As though reading my mind she said, "Henry wanted us to have fun out here. We just had a lovely lunch."

"Who with?"

"Friends. Shay and Kinsley."

I turned toward the patio.

"He's busy."

My back stiffened. "Are you staying here?"

She went to answer and then glanced back at her daughter. "Lilly, come meet Lotte. She's Henry's friend."

"Girlfriend," I clarified, watching her carefully.

She pouted, dropping her head for a few seconds as though to gather her thoughts. "Henry has been amazing to us both."

"He's pretty special," I agreed.

"He's excited to give *us* another chance," she said, studying my face.

My throat tightened and I had to feign indifference.

I snapped my focus toward the house.

"He wasn't expecting you?" she said.

"Excuse me?"

She nodded toward the patio table with five settings. "He didn't invite you to lunch?"

"I'm surprising him."

This felt like Reese was trying to sow doubt.

"Henry's going to save the preserve," she said. "He promised to do whatever made me happy."

"I'm glad."

"You've been good for him, Lotte." Her expression softened a little.

"We're good for each other."

"How do you get on with his family?"

"I'm close friends with his brother."

"Cameron?" She considered that. "How do you know him?"

"I've worked with him."

"Henry doesn't talk about you, to be honest."

"He's very private."

"Of course, he must protect his reputation."

I lifted my chin. "Right."

I only hoped Henry hadn't shared my profession with her.

She brightened. "I'm sorry you and I didn't have more time together."

"He once loved you, Reese."

She bristled.

I hid my surprise that she might believe they had a chance of rekindling their romance—after everything she'd put him through.

"When do you head back to Florida?" I asked.

"It was going to be later today, but we've been invited to the Cole Gala on Saturday. We'll stay another week."

Henry hadn't mentioned it to me—because lovers were kept in the dark.

"I need to stay in town a little longer anyway," she said. "Help him sort out the details with saving the preserve."

"Sounds intriguing."

"Has his mother taken you aside and had 'the chat' yet?"

There'd been no private moment with his mom because we weren't there yet.

She leaned in as though to whisper. "Me running my father's kabob shop wasn't going to cut it for his mom."

"Did she tell you that?"

Reese nodded. "At a tea party in their New York home, before I took off for Chile. Victoria took me aside and asked me what I hoped to achieve in the future. My dad was there, too. He answered for me. Told her I'd be kept busy running the family business. You should have seen her face. The thought of her daughter-in-law running a kabob shop. My dad seemed to enjoy ruining the evening for me. He could be like that."

Reese had inherited his cruel side.

"I'm sure Henry would have reassured them," I said.

"He would have tried."

"Had you not disappeared?"

"We all make mistakes." She assessed me with her cool blue gaze. "Bet you've made a few."

I couldn't hold back. "Are you really hoping to reconcile?"

"Some things are inevitable."

I tried to find the words, but remained speechless.

She glanced over at Lilly. "It'll be good to have someone watch over her while she's at UCLA."

Her way of saying she'd have more reasons to visit.

Reese fiddled with her bracelet, a beautiful collection of charms dangling off a silver chain—one of them a heart.

She glanced at it. "Henry gave me this."

I swallowed hard, trying not to react. It was the kind of gift you gave someone when you were in love.

Oh, God.

Why hadn't I seen the clues?

This woman right here was the one that got away.

My phone pinged and I stared down hoping to see a text from Henry.

De Sade: We've doubled our offer.

That snagged my attention.

De Sade, Grantchester and Sinclair, along with their silent partner, were coming at me hard. The amount offered probably wouldn't even warrant attention from these billionaires, but for me it was a mind-blowing figure.

Reese drew my attention back to her. "Something important?"

"Job offer."

"That's exciting. Here in Cali?"

"Yes."

You can't get rid of me that easily.

Or maybe she could.

Men like Henry always had more than one woman. I'd been naïve to believe otherwise.

Had I read him wrong this entire time?

My hope for us had blinded reality.

"I have to go." I turned and made my way back around the side of the house.

Once I got back in my car, I sat there trying to calm my emotions. I'd literally interrupted Henry's Sunday afternoon with his old girlfriend.

Maybe someone he'd never stopped loving.

He'd not told me she'd be here today.

It took forever for those tall gates to open and allow me to escape this oppressively wealthy neighborhood.

CHAPTER FIFTY-EIGHT

Lotte

A CLOSE GIRLFRIEND CAN SENSE WHEN YOU NEED THEM—even when you're not quite ready to talk. They can hear it in your voice. They can see the light has gone out of your eyes.

Scarlet's fix for my sadness was us spending time together on a girl's day out.

We'd dressed up, both of us in our little summer dresses thanks to L.A.'s temperate January, her carrying a Prada handbag and me with my favorite Marc Jacobs purse—casual but dressy in the best kind of way.

We dined on salads for lunch at Granville at the Grove, catching up on gossip.

Scarlet shared more about her excitement over the novel she was writing. She'd gone from dominatrix to romance author. It suited her well.

I talked about job hunting. Scarlet was the best kind of listener. Having left Enthrall herself, she was merely consulting now.

After lunch, we visited the Grove's Barnes and Noble, both

of us having fun imagining her books amongst all these amazing novels stacking the shelves.

Then we engaged in a little window shopping.

We came out of Candi's Chocolate Store laughing with a sugar high from eating too many free samples. Not recommended when you're off to buy a gown for a gala. I'd finally received my embossed invitation for this Saturday's event.

I hadn't seen Henry all week.

We'd merely swapped affectionate texts. I'd told him I was too busy with job hunting, that I needed to compare other positions to the prestigious one offered by his brother.

Henry had believed me.

Secretly, I'd needed time to reevaluate our relationship. With Reese back on the scene, I had needed time away from everything and everyone.

I'd almost ripped up the invitation.

Only Scarlet wasn't the kind of friend who'd let me admit defeat. I'd told her everything and, as any best friend would, she'd sided with me against Reese.

I just couldn't stand the thought of Reese hurting Henry again.

He was worth fighting for.

Arm in arm, Scarlet led me into Neiman Marcus to go shopping for a dress. We walked through the handbag section, cooing at all the pretty purses like we didn't have enough already.

We finally made our way over to the designer dress section and we had fun trying on a few different styles.

"You're cutting it a bit close," said Scarlet. "The party's tonight!"

"I wasn't sure I'd even go," I admitted.

I still hadn't recovered from my encounter with Reese the previous Sunday.

Not really.

Reese was probably the strongest woman I'd met. She had a ruthless edge to her.

"Turn around," said Scarlet, using her finger to get me to spin.

"This is the one." I liked this Mac Duggal sequined gown.

"Not feeling it," she said.

"What?" I stared at my reflection.

"You need something sexier."

This was the command Scarlet gave the staff. They brought in more dresses and Scarlet examined them one after the other.

"This one," she said finally.

Minutes later, I faced the mirror, dressed in a silk tulle Paolo Sebastian. The luxurious material fell to the floor with a wispy elegance. The bodice was unique, and barely covered my breasts.

"I can't wear this!" I turned around to admire my butt in the mirror. "Henry will freak out."

"That's the point." Scarlet gestured her insistence. "We need him to see you're all woman."

"Have you met him?" I joked. "He's conservative."

"There's a reason he's with you, Lotte. You're the fun one."

"I'm not sure. Cameron is going to be there."

"When have you ever cared for others' opinions?"

That made me chuckle. "Okay, why not?"

"Yes!" She pumped a fist in the air.

We patiently waited for the dress to be wrapped and boxed as we sat in the store foyer, sipping the complimentary bubbly. Considering the amount I was spending on that dress, I deserved a bloody winery.

A young woman in ripped jeans strolled by the changing rooms. She seemed a little uncomfortable.

Scarlet noticed her as well. She reached over and grabbed my hand as though sensing danger.

The woman turned to face us. "Having fun?"

"Yes, thank you," I said.

She smirked. "I'm from the National Inquirer. We're running a story tomorrow. We need a quote from you."

I swapped a terrified glance with Scarlet.

"You've got me confused with someone else," I said, heart racing.

"Charlotte Chamberlain?"

Oh, God. She must have followed me from my house. She probably stalked us around the Grove.

I felt violated.

What if she'd taken photos of me shoveling salad in my mouth? Or shot other unflattering photos?

"Go away," I said.

She didn't budge. "I'm a photojournalist, just doing my job."

I squeezed my mouth shut, refusing to talk.

"I have what I need." She threw a wave at the shop girl.

She faced us again. "We like to provide a balanced view. Now's the time to have your say."

"What's the article about?" asked Scarlet.

"Henry Cole is dating a dominatrix." She stared at me. "That you?"

I sucked in my breath, panic tightening my throat.

Henry's worst fear was coming true.

"Fuck off," said Scarlet. "Before we call the police and accuse you of harassing us."

Numb from fear, I watched the smug journalist walk out.

"I have to warn him." My hands were shaking as I rummaged around in my handbag and brought out my phone.

"You've done nothing wrong," said Scarlet.

"How did they find out?" I hit his number.

The call went to voicemail.

I was nervous about what to say, how he'd react. *This* would be the end of us.

Henry hadn't answered the call, but those three dots were him texting back.

Henry: PR issue. Don't speak to the press.
I texted back: Shall I still come to the gala?
Henry: We're trying to kill a story. More to follow.

He knew about the Inquirer article.

"I won't need that dress," I said, slumping in the seat.

"Fuck yes, you will," snapped Scarlet.

"I've ruined his brand."

"The Cole brand is fine."

"Cameron's going to kill me." I couldn't swallow this terror. "The Cole Empire might fall because of me."

"Oh, shut up." She pushed to her feet and offered me her hand. "Let's go find your shoes."

"What are you talking about?" I couldn't keep shopping. Not now.

Shaking, I vaguely remembered taking a tall glass from Scarlet and then throwing back champagne.

The solution hit me like an arrow through my heart.

Unless I offered myself as a martyr.

Breaking my own damn heart was a thing I seemed to be exceptionally good at.

I gripped my phone with shaking hands.

"What are you going to say?" Scarlet watched me text, leaning close as though ready to snatch my phone.

Chest tight, I spelled out a message that would get Henry off the hook. My heart smashed into a thousand pieces. "I have to make this right."

"It's not your fault," she said. "Henry knew your profession."

"I encouraged him."

I'd worked hard to avoid drama, yet now found myself inside the center of the worst scandal to hit the Cole family.

I texted Henry explaining what he was going to have to do.

Escort Reese to the Gala tonight. You have no choice.

Then I waited for his answer.

Henry: Fuck.

CHAPTER FIFTY-NINE

Henry

AS THE CAR DROVE ALONG OCEAN AVENUE BRINGING US closer to the Hotel Casa Del Mar, I watched the scenery drift by. Soon we passed by Santa Monica Pier.

Tonight's speech was tucked safely inside my tuxedo pocket. That devilish declaration would set me free.

Shay and Cameron supported my decision to read it aloud to the guests along with the press who sat amongst them.

That story would overshadow the Inquirer.

If you're going through hell, keep going. Great advice from Winston Churchill, a man who knew a thing or two about controversies.

"Do you want to read the article they're going to publish?" Shay offered me the iPad.

My jaw tightened with anger. I knew from the get-go this might be a possibility.

I took the iPad from him and rested it on my lap, bracing myself before scanning what they planned to print. We had twelve hours to provide a quote.

The press was a double-edged sword.

At the event, photographers would be obsessively taking photos of the public figures gracing us with their presence. These men and women who lived in the public eye would draw attention away from us.

I told Reese and Lilly this.

"Use this opportunity to talk about your work at the preserve," I said. "Keep it light."

"I have done this before," said Reese.

She'd lived a full and interesting life despite all of us. She didn't seem to reflect on that. The world would just keep turning around her.

Her chiffon dress softened her features, embraced by the sun over the years. Lilly wore a floral gown. Her temperament was calming. She clearly was a wiser version of her mom.

I'd taken Lotte's advice and invited them as my personal guests. This should throw off the wolves for a few hours.

Shay watched me read the article.

The burn of Reese's stare on the iPad didn't go unnoticed. She'd be reading in the press about my personal life soon enough. Might as well catch the gist.

My team had worked a small miracle and gotten hold of the article to be published in the Inquirer.

I finished scanning the story.

"No comment," I told Shay. "That's what I instructed the team to say."

More than anything, protecting Lotte from this garbage had become my priority.

"Henry," whispered Reese. "Let them believe I'm your girlfriend."

Her saying it made me hate this plan even more. Lotte had seen this as a reasonable solution.

I hadn't expected it to hurt this bad.

She should be here.

"Our PR team's still trying kill the story," I said.

Though we all knew it was poised to be released online.

"What story?" asked Lilly.

Reese rested her hand on her daughter's arm to silence her.

"Nothing of consequence," Shay answered for her.

I missed Lotte—missed setting my sights on her enduring beauty. I needed to touch her soft skin and kiss her tenderly.

"Shit," I mouthed, seeing the crowds.

I wasn't in the mood.

Shay stepped out of the limo first.

Reese and Lilly exited the car behind him. Finally, I withdrew from the shelter of our luxury limo.

Immediately I was met by flashing bulbs and a barrage of questions. Taking the slow walk down the red carpet, I felt loneliness sharpen its blade.

Politely, I addressed the occasional question.

Avoided a few, too.

Though mainly, I stood back and let others enjoy the limelight.

Just inside the hotel foyer, I waited for Reese and Lilly as they scurried off to the restroom, taking this time to check for any new messages.

I was disappointed not to see a text from Lotte. That made me uncomfortable. You don't experience that much intimacy and not feel the loss of someone.

A young man in a bad fitting tuxedo walked up to me.

Shay intercepted him.

"I need to talk to you!" said the guy.

We'd never met, but I recognized his face from the reports I'd read on his company. This was Jasper Green, co-owner of Dandelion Diva.

We'd discovered *his* spy at Cole Tower over a week ago.

Only he didn't know that yet. Or maybe he suspected it.

Our lawyers had struck a deal with Felix Jones, his corporate spy, providing more time to track messages between them. Dandelion Diva had continued to dig themselves into a deeper hole. They were amateurs.

They'd wanted to mimic Cole Tea and in doing so had inadvertently destroyed themselves.

By now, Jasper would have discovered his distributors had dumped his product.

"Did you gatecrash?" asked Shay.

Jasper's face flushed with rage. "Mind telling me why our product is no longer being made?"

I straightened. "You need to get ahead of that."

He glowered. "You overbid for shelf space in every store in the U.S."

"We have a new product coming out," I explained calmly. "My team may have overenthusiastically prepared."

"Bullshit," he snapped.

Shay pressed his hand on Jasper's chest. "Step back."

A wave of security guards appeared around us.

I raised my hand. "Let him have his say."

"Reverse engineering is not illegal," he said.

"But spying is."

He swallowed hard. "Prove it."

"Felix Jones no longer works for us."

"Not heard of him," he said, shaking off a guard.

"He showed us your communications, Jasper," I said. "Proving he worked for you."

"Your fucking life is about to change big-time!" he yelled.

That leak at the Inquirer had come from this idiot.

It hadn't taken those journalists too much digging around to ascertain Charlotte's profession.

Shay had managed to pack one of them back to London. But there were always others in the wings.

"Check out the Inquirer tomorrow." He looked smug.

"I'm more of a New York Times kind of guy," I said calmly.

"Anyone who Googles your name will see that article."

I couldn't be bothered to correct him. Google searches could be controlled. We'd done that in the past and we could do it again.

"I'm aware of the article you're referring to," I said. "We'll face that bridge and all that." My calmness appeared to rile him up more.

I gestured to Shay to get rid of Jasper.

"Wait," he said. "I'm not finished."

Really? He wanted to stay and hear more?

"How old is your company?" I asked.

"A year." His arrogance faded. "Ready to make our mark in the industry."

"Right, well, Cole Tea has been around for centuries. You ignored our legacy. We have decades of experience. When a new company like yours makes a play, you don't stand a chance. Because when we add up all the time we've dedicated to this specialty, that's what makes the difference. We've seen it all. We are a behemoth in this space. Always have been, always will be."

"We are set to take over your space," he said. "You have no vision."

"I am a Cole. This is more than tea to us. It's a movement. A practice for living life. My vision goes beyond your imagination."

Jasper looked smug. "Wait until that story comes out."

I shrugged casually. "Lives will change, Jasper. But it won't be mine."

"How do you mean?"

"Dandelion Diva will be dead in the water."

"Why would you do that to us?"

"Spies leave a bad taste in my mouth," I said. "If you'll excuse me, I have a night of celebrating ahead for all the good work we do."

They dragged Jasper away with a security guard on each arm, our way of inviting him to leave the premises.

Shay made sure he'd left the hotel and then returned to my side. "Bet your heart rate didn't go up."

"What heart?' I said.

Reese and Lilly hurried toward us.

When Reese saw the security guards around us, she asked, "Everything okay?"

"Yes," I said. "Everything is fine."

We walked into the ballroom and soon found our table.

Cameron sat next to me. "Just heard what happened."

"I'm fine."

"You should have reminded him the dandelion root makes you pee."

I chuckled at that. "He's going to be presented with a subpoena. His business will be deconstructed."

Reese and Lilly appeared speechless as they listened in.

"No more discussing business," said Reese.

I ignored that and turned to Cameron. "We have a wake to attend."

Cameron smirked. "Let me guess, Dandelion Diva's?"

Shay approached our table. "Griffin just texted they are close."

Lotte had just missed the drama. "Have her enter through the back entrance, in case Jasper is still out there."

"I can do that," said Shay, texting Griffin.

"Join us for drinks until she gets here," said Cameron, pulling a chair out for him.

Shay sat next to Cameron and accepted a glass of bourbon.

"Watch over her tonight," I said.

"Lotte?" said Reese. "That girl can take care of herself."

"I want her to have a wonderful time," I said. "Even if I'm not with her."

I took a sip of Macallan to wet my throat and take the edge off having to be in the same room as Charlotte without being able to touch her.

"Are you ready?" asked Cameron. "Could be fallout."

We both knew he was referring to my speech.

It would crush one woman and lift the other up to where she belonged—as my girlfriend.

There were always casualties in war.

I drew from SEAL experience.

While training underwater, I'd followed that faint glint of

light to the target until there was none. At the darkest moment of reaching my objective, I'd remained composed.

Then set the explosive.

I'd guessed Dandelion Diva's next move would be an attempt to personally destroy me.

It was why I'd written that speech.

CHAPTER SIXTY

Lotte

H ENRY SENT A CAR TO DRIVE ME TO THE GALA.
The journey in his luxury limo to Hotel Casa Del Mar was quite pleasant. Chatting with his driver Griffin on the way here had been lovely.

I didn't text Henry. I knew he'd be too busy taking interviews on the red carpet and greeting guests.

I couldn't wait to see him.

When the limo pulled up behind the hotel, I felt a wave of doubt. There would be no walking the red carpet.

Still, I planned on having fun.

But I'd have to walk into the ballroom alone.

Rallying my confidence, I checked my makeup in my compact's mirror. *Damn girl,* I mused at my reflection. I hadn't dressed up quite this glamorous since the last Cole party.

I thanked Griffin for driving me here.

My car door opened and Shay leaned in, offering his hand to assist me. I felt relief at seeing his kind expression. He looked suave in his black tuxedo, his beard sexy.

When I stepped out, he blinked at my dress.

"Wow," he said. "You're wearing that?"

Yes, I damn well am.

This sultry dress was beautiful and sensual. A little revealing, but then again, I wasn't with anyone officially so what did it matter?

"Stunning." He smirked. "Well played."

"Scarlet helped me choose it."

"I can see that. It goes with the narrative."

"Narrative?"

A young waiter walked by us carrying a bag of trash. He threw it in the dumpster.

"No expense spared," I joked.

"Keeping you humble."

"I'm coming in the back door!"

"And we know how much you love the back door, Lotte."

I elbowed him.

He laughed trying to avoid another strike.

"Is Rue here, Shay?"

"No, she's working tonight. It's fine. Saving lives at Cedars."

"You're working, too?"

"Try not to over think it." He gestured for me to go inside first.

I walked through the staff entrance and spun around to face him. "I'm being handled. You're handling me?"

He stepped forward and rested his hands on my shoulders. "Henry has this. Enjoy tonight. Trust him."

"I do." *Or at least I wanted to.*

"Have a few drinks. Dance a little—"

"Act like I've never met the Coles?"

He gave an apologetic nod.

"I'm a pariah."

"Yeah, but you're a hot pariah."

Despite being the scandal, the only way to deal with this was to pretend the press had it wrong. I was an acquaintance of the Cole brothers. Our not talking all night would prove that.

It made me wonder if Cameron would ignore me as well.

"Is Henry here?" I asked, sliding my arm through Shay's.

"Yes."

"With Reese?"

He paused and stepped away from me. "We don't need a show—"

"Fuck off."

"You didn't let me finish. Henry's been busy on his speech. It's imperative he owns the story. Play your part."

I was glad I'd worn this figure-hugging gown. My tits looked amazing.

"Scarlet, Richard and Mia aren't here."

I paused for a beat. "Then why am I here?"

"A certain gentleman wouldn't have it any other way."

I could endure an evening of observing Reese flirt with Henry. I was mature enough for any emotional challenge. At least that's what I told myself.

Shay tapped my purse. "Give me your phone."

"Why?"

He took my purse and opened it, pulling out my iPhone. "Here." He held it up to me. The face recognition software granted him access.

Cheeky bastard.

"What's wrong?" I wondered if someone had hacked it.

"I have to hide all messages pertaining to him."

The ones I'd saved from Henry because they made me happy when I re-read them.

Shay's fingers nimbly glided over my screen. "Why don't you have my app?"

"CloudSource?" I frowned up at him. "I don't have anything to hide."

"Other than you're fucking America's most eligible bachelor."

"Don't be crass."

"I've downloaded my app for free. You're welcome."

My heart missed a beat. "Did Henry tell you to do this?"

"Reese is the perfect deflection," he said. "You can be quite the smartass when you want to be."

Right, because me sabotaging this evening had been my idea.

"Henry will catch up with you later and talk to you in private."

Shay was insinuating that Henry planned to have "the talk"—maybe even the one where he dumped me.

Because soon the world would learn he'd banged a dominatrix.

"Get me a drink," I said.

He shook his head. "Don't drink too much."

"I'm good for him," I reasoned.

"Really? Because I recall Richard giving you specific instructions *not* to have Henry investigate the upper floor at Chrysalis."

I wasn't going to be the one to tell him it was Henry's idea to go off exploring, breaking their precious rules. They were the ones who got him into Chrysalis.

I changed the subject. "How did the press find out about me?"

Shay guided me along a bright hallway. "The tabloid article appears to be connected to the corporate spy at Cole Tower."

"Oh, God."

"We have it contained."

"I'm not the breach, though, right?"

"No. They've been tracking Cameron and Henry for a while."

The Cole brothers had been trying to protect me from that nightmare.

"They should have warned me." I cringed at how this evening was already going.

"It happens in businesses." He waved it off.

We walked the same path as the staff.

The moody vocals of Harry Styles singing his heart out met us at the end of the hall and rose to a crescendo as we entered the event.

At least the music sounded upbeat.

The setting was wondrous.

This was my first time visiting the Colonnade Ballroom. The

Cole family had yet again chosen another grand location for their gala.

Guests sat around lavishly decorated tables. Venetian style chandeliers dropped from an ornate ceiling, showering everyone with a soft yellow light.

A devastatingly handsome Henry sat at a corner table, looking relaxed and reasonably happy. He wore that familiar ensemble of formal dinner jacket accented with silk lapels and matching pants, his sophisticated charm emphasized by that bowtie.

His left eyebrow lifted with intrigue in response to a conversation across from him.

I'd kissed that eyebrow more times than I could count. And the rest of him, too—recklessly lavishing affection on that remarkable man.

I should have been the one seated beside him. Instead, I'd valiantly given up my seat to Reese.

Predictably, she emanated an earthy air in that chiffon gown. Her daughter Lilly sat next to her wearing a floral dress. They both looked radiant.

The music changed to a ballad by Lauren Daigle with "You Say" rising over the chatter.

I wasn't going to own those lyrics and admit defeat. I was braver than that.

"Follow me," said Shay.

We went to the bar and I set my purse near me, trying not to glance back. Reaching for a cardboard coaster, I twirled it around until Shay rested his hand on mine to prevent me from fiddling.

The barman poured champagne into two crystal glasses, slipping the bottle of Louis Roederer Cristal Rose 2000 into a silver ice bucket and sliding the cooler toward us.

"Oh, lovely," I said, picking up a crystal flute.

Hmmm.

I enjoyed the taste of the light, crisp drink, bubbles kissing my lips.

I sat on a barstool and people watched. Shay did the same,

both of us staring out at the ebullient crowd. Guests were starting to settle at their tables. Some couples were already slow dancing in the center.

Henry wasn't that far away, but I missed him.

Being in the same room and not talking with him was the hardest thing I'd done in a while. Our chemistry was natural. Our relationship forged during a difficult time.

Maybe I was in denial.

I'd wanted to find a way forward for us.

But now, staring at a table full of strangers sitting with Henry, I questioned everything and it broke my heart.

I made the mistake of glancing over at his table again.

Henry locked his sights on me.

My pulse faltered, heart fluttering.

He looked so regal in his black tuxedo. His gaze met mine and that gorgeous man's face lit up in a smile.

Reese noticed and leaned toward Henry to ask him something, stealing back his attention.

"You're doing great," said Shay.

Externally, maybe. Inside, I felt like a mess.

I noticed one empty seat at their table. Then I realized that they must have reserved it for Shay.

"Go on and join them," I said. "I'll be fine."

"You sure?" He gave me a sympathetic glance.

"Yes, of course. I'll find my table."

He used his chin to point to the table farthest away. "You're over there. I'll eat and come back to check on you."

"Go." I gave his arm a friendly pat.

Then I turned around and signaled to the barman to pour me another drink. I'd have poured it myself, but etiquette ruled in places like this.

Guests would soon be eating a lavish meal served at their tables. I wasn't sure I could even swallow anything other than liquid. My throat felt that tight.

"You're the most beautiful woman in the room," said a deep voice.

Turning, I was surprised to see Jake Carrington.

He sat on the barstool next to mine.

The great de Sade himself was offering to keep me company.

"You're having far too much fun," he said sarcastically.

"How did you get a ticket?"

"I donate a hefty amount to the Cole Foundation each year."

"Why?"

"Because I'm friends with Cameron. What do you mean why?"

"You're the bad boy of Chrysalis."

That made him grin. "We need to spend more time together. You'll really see my dark side."

"What sort of things do you do with Cameron?"

"Fence."

"Does he win?"

"Every fucking time."

"Who is your silent partner?" I pointed at his chest. "I can't work for an enemy of Cameron. And you shouldn't either."

"You're going to have to trust me on that one." He reached for the neck of the champagne bottle and read the label. "May I?"

"Of course."

He quirked a brow. "This is a Louis Roederer Cristal Rose."

I raised my glass for him to refill it. "It's yum."

"It should be. This is a two-thousand-dollar bottle."

I felt a wave of panic. "I didn't order it."

He winked. "You have expensive taste."

Glancing over at Shay, I threw daggers at him for ordering it.

Henry saw me and he raised his glass in a toast. He'd bought that expensive bottle for me.

Feeling better from our brief interaction, I raised my glass to thank him. Then remembered we weren't supposed to know each other.

I refocused on de Sade. "I thought you were breaking away from Chrysalis?"

"You make it sound like I'm committing a heinous act."

"It's Pendulum."

"We're going to turn it around. That's why we invited you to run the place. We want the best for the submissives. It will take a while for the current VIPs to get used to our way of doing things. We're fine with that. Rome wasn't built in a day and all that."

"True."

He finished off his glass. "They need an answer, Charlotte."

"There's been a lot going on."

"You have until the end of tomorrow."

I snapped a quick glance at Henry, who was laughing at someone's funny quip.

A man like that was usually inaccessible.

If this was how my future fell, then giving up the opportunity to run Pendulum might be a mistake—more specifically, giving up that kind of salary.

A job also waited for me in Beverly Hills at that high-class office. They offered pro bono work. There'd be a lot of good I could do.

Why did these kinds of offers all come at once?

De Sade's cologne wafted over me, alpha pheromones promising to subdue.

I was just left wanting one man.

The same man who was easing his bowtie away from his neck. Henry had once spent time in a totally different kind of uniform.

I hated myself for wanting him. How could I have let this happen? Fallen for a man I hardly knew?

I'd literally told him to bring Reese instead of me. From here, he didn't appear to be suffering from the suggestion.

"Why are you at the bar?" De Sade glanced at Henry's table. "What happened? You guys ended it?"

"It's complicated."

He frowned. "I saw you were added to our table."

"Yes."

"Come on, I'll bring your bottle."

We both noticed Cameron strolling toward us with that familiar masterful stride.

"Here comes God," muttered de Sade.

"Jake," said Cameron, acknowledging him before facing me. "Come with me."

"Where am I being shuffled off to now?" I said. "A cupboard?"

Cameron chuckled. "I'm asking you to dance."

"Oh." I slid off the barstool. "Well, in that case."

"By all means," said de Sade. "Steal my girl."

I picked up my purse and set it down on a nearby table.

Cameron took my arm and led me to the dance floor. "Stunning as always."

Having his approval had always been something I needed.

"You're gorgeous," I replied, returning the compliment.

Cameron dazzled in anything, really.

I wrapped my hand around his shoulder and rested my left hand in his palm. "It's good to see you."

"Feeling's mutual."

We slow danced in a circle. There came a familiar sense of comfort of being back in the arms of one of my dearest friends. He had this way of turning off the pain and letting in the light.

He squeezed my hand. "How are you?"

"Did Henry send you to placate me?"

Cameron seemed affronted. "You and I always have a dance at these things."

"True."

"Are you considering de Sade's offer?"

Oh, God. News had reached him.

"Cameron, you have every right to be angry I didn't tell you."

"Angry? No."

I braced myself for his wrath. "It's an interesting concept."

He gave a nod and twirled me around, bringing me back into a hug. "De Sade summoned you to Mulholland?"

"Yes."

Cameron leaned back a little as though to better read me. "Pendulum?"

"Richard told you?"

"As you say, it's an interesting concept." He turned me so that I had a straight view of Henry and the others at his table. "My brother likes you."

"But?"

Cameron frowned.

"I promised to conduct myself professionally," I said.

"I offered you a great job, Lotte. The clinic would benefit from your expertise."

"It's a generous offer."

"You need to stop turning off your phone."

"What?"

He gave a nod. "You tend to run away. We've talked about this. Pain is inevitable at some point. If you keep bolting, you'll miss your chance at something wonderful."

"I'm not taking the job at Pendulum," I said, annoyed.

"That's not what I'm talking about."

"You're upset with me for staining the Cole name? About that article tomorrow?"

Cameron stopped turning. "I still own Enthrall. If anyone is going to take down our empire, it's going to be me."

"But you wouldn't."

"No, of course not. I love tea too much. And we're far smarter than all of them."

A hand tapped Cameron's shoulder.

"We're not done," he told de Sade.

Carrington stood behind him, clearly pissed off. "I'm not averse to stealing her back."

Cameron centered himself. "Do you want to dance with him, Lotte?"

Not wanting to cause a scene, I gave a nod.

Cameron faced me again. "You're being offered great

opportunities. You're spoiled for choice. But only one will make you happy."

Jake pulled me away from him.

Cameron walked off.

When he turned back, I gave him an apologetic glance.

"That was rude," I told de Sade.

"Why are you not sitting with the Coles?" De Sade glowered at them. "Who the fuck is that woman sitting in your seat?"

I tried to pull away. "Dance with Rylee."

He gripped me tighter. "She's not here."

"Go get drunk with your buddies."

"That's no way to talk to your new boss."

The music transitioned into Neil Diamond's "Holly Holy."

Oh, God.

I drew in a sharp breath.

It was the same song I'd danced to with Henry at the preserve. He'd brought it up on his wristwatch after we'd showered together.

He'd chosen this, the beautiful lyrics stirring a visceral response.

"You're shivering," said de Sade.

"I want to go home," I said.

"You can't." He pulled me in tighter. "You're mine now."

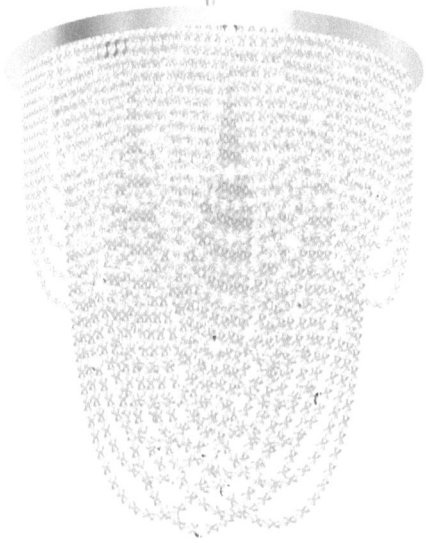

CHAPTER SIXTY-ONE

Lotte

MY HEART SOARED WHEN I SAW HENRY APPROACH THE edge of the dance floor.

I peered up at Jake. "You'll have my answer soon."

Effortlessly, I broke away from him and glided toward Henry's open arms. When his hand touched mine, I felt a spark between us.

He pulled me against his chest.

"You have until tomorrow," said de Sade, walking away.

Henry pulled me in tighter, his cologne flooding my senses, our chemistry electric. Passion ran through my bloodstream, my body weakening in his strong arms as I responded to his firm chest pressed against mine, his powerful hand squeezing mine— his masculine edge.

My thoughts were dominated by all those times he'd made me come. He smelled like sin and love wrapped up in a dangerous spell, rendering me speechless.

I wanted to reach up and brush my fingers through his silky, short hair.

"You chose this song?" I whispered.

Henry nodded. "Us naked in a hut in the middle of nowhere. A bewitching woman in my arms, much like now. Unafraid of anything, as far as I can tell."

Here we were, reenacting our dance to Neil Diamond's heartfelt love song.

Our song.

"I'll never forget that time with you," I said softly.

His thumb brushed along my spine. "Me neither."

"I thought we weren't meant to be seen together?"

"I make the rules." His arm wrapped tighter around my waist. "I break the rules."

Henry's hug felt like home.

Yet both of us knew the fragility of our future.

He gave a friendly nod to someone across the room. "Love the revenge dress."

"Bring on the scandal."

"You're stunning in every conceivable way. Every man in here wants you."

I arched an amused brow.

"Did you wear that so I wouldn't take my eyes off you?" He smirked. "Naked or otherwise, I can't look away—worth remembering."

"I'll try."

"You're a hard person to get hold of."

"I needed time."

"Totally acceptable."

"Thank you for the champagne."

"Of course."

I was trying to play it cool, trying not to show how this man brought me to my knees—working hard to keep my expression neutral so those who observed us would think this was just a dance.

Henry dipped me and then brought me up even closer. "What did de Sade mean when he said you have until tomorrow?"

"I've been offered a position."

"I thought you'd accepted the offer in Beverly Hills?"

"I've been headhunted."

"As a therapist?" He leaned back a little to read me.

A flash went off—the official photographer for the evening had taken our picture.

I bit my lip nervously. "Is that a problem?"

"We have to give the tabloids something delicious." He twirled me around.

"Reese seems happy." I leaned back. "What were you toasting a moment ago?"

"I gave the land back to the preserve. They can't build anything there."

My body stiffened at that remarkable deal. He'd just solidified his connection to her.

Reese had already told me that, but she had apparently failed to mention to him I'd visited his home last Sunday.

Henry started to speak and then reconsidered. "Let's talk later."

"Can't wait."

"You're going to have to trust me."

"How are you going to respond to the article?"

"You'll see soon enough."

"Right."

"You smell amazing. I'm going to bottle that scent and make a tea out of you."

I tried to relax.

His fingers tightened around my hand. "Tell me about this job offer?"

"It's at another club."

Henry shot me a concerned look. "Not like Chrysalis?" He stopped turning. "You told me you were leaving the scene."

I whispered, "I won't make this difficult for you."

"What do you mean?"

"There'll be no public response from me. About us."

"What are you saying?"

"I don't like being shuffled through the rear entrance of a hotel. Forced to sit across the room. Handled by your muscle."

"Shay?"

"I don't like being considered a scandal."

"Not here." He shot a smile to someone at his table.

Probably Reese.

On my reaction he added, "I'm merely escorting her—which was your idea."

"You could have refused."

"You women are complicated."

The husky tones of Neil Diamond faded.

A modern track replaced the song that carried a precious memory.

I sensed there was something he wasn't telling me.

"I have to go," he said. "Will you be okay?"

"More than okay." I beamed him a bright smile and the lie seemed to placate him.

"Eat, please. Enjoy the meal." He leaned in to whisper, "Anything you want is yours."

Just like a mistress.

"Watch out for de Sade." He threw a glance Jake's way. "He's dangerously into you."

"What happens when the article comes out?"

"We'll shoot you off to Mars in a rocket." He grinned.

"I'm serious."

"I'm trying to lighten the mood."

I stepped back, proud of how far I'd come, refusing to be shamed by anyone. A woman soon to be ridiculed in the tabloids with my face splashed on every magazine—my personal life exposed.

"Lotte, I've got this," he said sternly.

"I can see that." I squeezed his arm like a friend would.

Maybe that's what we'd reverted to.

"See you later," I said, strolling away with my head held high.

I felt the stares of all the guests on me as I left the ballroom. I'd just danced with *the* Henry Cole and earned their scrutiny.

The music was muffled inside the restroom. I drew in a sharp breath as soon as I was alone, peering at my reflection and seeing pride.

Right before a fall, I mused.

I played with my hair, though it didn't really need it.

Maybe it had to be me who withdrew from *us.* Protecting Henry was a priority. I could be strong, but I wasn't sure if I could be strong enough to end our relationship.

I wanted to believe I was.

I will not cry.

A familiar reflection appeared in the mirror. Reese stood in the doorway.

I pivoted and headed for the exit, turning sideways to get past her. "Excuse me."

"You're so pretty," she said softly.

"You, too."

She leaned forward. "I'm caught up on what's going on."

My flesh chilled with a surge of jealousy. She'd been permitted to sit with Henry while I'd been ushered away. She'd also arrived with him, along with Lilly.

I stepped out into the hallway and tried to decide which way to go—I'd gotten turned around.

After hearing Reese follow me out, I kept walking and entered the first room I came to, trying to escape her. I found myself standing in an empty ballroom, half the size of the other one.

The door opened and Reese followed me in. "Something wrong?"

"I have to make a call." Only my phone was still in my purse, which I didn't have on me.

She didn't seem to notice. "To be honest, I don't usually mingle with this many people. And this dress cost a small fortune."

"It's gorgeous."

"Henry bought it for me."

I glanced at her charm bracelet, and she noticed.

Looking gleeful, she said, "It's hard to break a relationship off, isn't it?"

"What do you mean?"

"You and Henry are not together anymore."

The blade was invisible, but hurt just the same. "That's none of your business."

"It is."

"How do you mean?'

"On the way here, Shay and Henry were talking about deflecting a major PR scandal. I'm guessing that's you?"

Cruel of you to undermine what we have.

Had.

"Being accepted into a family like theirs comes with expectations," she added.

"I'm well aware."

"Is it true, you're a dominatrix?"

She used it against me like a weapon.

Reese gave a snide smirk.

"You have no idea what it is I do."

"I can imagine." She pulled a face. "Do you wear a skimpy bodice and stuff?"

"Henry is fine with it."

"Then why did they arrange to have you come in through the rear of the hotel?"

"Get over yourself."

"You need to show me respect," she bit out.

The kind of respect reserved for a Cole. She didn't say it—didn't need to.

"You hurt him, Reese. Years later you summon him to Florida without an explanation. That's what disrespect looks like."

"I'm trying to save the planet." She scoffed. "In *my* profession, I'm revered."

"I help with the Cole Foundation. I'm frequently working to

make this world a better place. You're not the only one who dedicates their time for a good cause."

"I've dedicated my *life*." She raised her chin. "In the future, any further charity work you do for the Coles will be done in secret."

"What do you want?" I stepped back, tired of arguing.

"To warn you."

The hair on my forearms prickled. "About what?"

"Tonight, Henry will deny having a relationship with you in his speech."

My flesh turned ice-cold.

She smiled unpleasantly. "He needed an entire PR team to put that fire out."

My breath hitched. I exhaled slowly, not giving her the pleasure of seeing me react.

"We must all play our part," she said quietly, "to protect the Cole name."

"Right," I replied numbly.

"Another good thing came out of this—Lilly has a father again."

I tried to swallow the lump in my throat as I stared at the bracelet on her wrist, that beautiful dress he'd bought her, recalled how she had draped herself over his arm when they sat together and he had not pushed her off.

Maybe this woman wouldn't ruin Henry's reputation like I was on the verge of doing.

I headed for the door. "They'll be wondering where I am."

"Lovely to see you again, Lotte," she called after me.

Back in the ballroom, the lights were softer and the music louder—Adele's perfectly timed lyrics a backdrop to my misery. Laughter and chatter rose from ebullient guests enjoying the party.

No one noticed my return.

I snatched up my purse from the white linen-covered table near the dance floor and made a beeline for de Sade's table, taking the empty seat beside his.

"Looking a bit flushed, babe," he said. "Do I even want to guess?"

"Fuck you," I said.

"Love you too, Charlotte." He smirked and turned back to continue his conversation with the guy next to him.

The moment I say these words, Henry will have no choice but to let me go.

"I'll take the job," I blurted out.

De Sade turned back to me. "Came to your senses?"

"When do I start?"

"Soon." He sat back, looking smug. "My place tomorrow. You can see the contract. Maybe I'll have you naked in my hot tub when you sign along the dotted line."

"Don't push your luck." I got up from the table.

Asshole.

I strolled across the ballroom, glancing over to see Henry watching me, his expression inquisitive. Those beautiful chestnut eyes didn't leave me until I was out of sight.

Cameron's recent warning echoed in my mind, "*Pain is inevitable at some point. If you keep bolting, you'll miss your chance at something wonderful.*"

But he'd never allow a woman like me to become a Cole.

I shot off a text to Griffin, telling him I was ready to go home.

A dry heat hit me when I stepped outside the hotel door. This time, though, I left through the front entrance of Casa Del Mar.

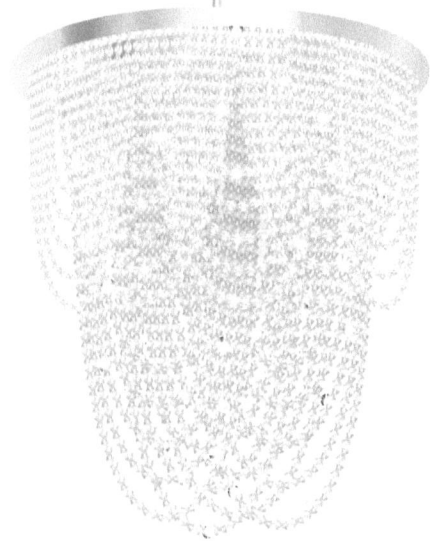

CHAPTER SIXTY-TWO

Lotte

THE LIGHT SUNDAY MORNING TRAFFIC ALLOWED ME TO arrive early.

I parked outside de Sade's Mulholland home, still gripping the steering wheel as though some part of me knew this decision was a mistake.

Yet this felt like my only option.

I'd ditched the glamorous look of last night for jeans and a New York Giants T-shirt, Richard's favorite team. He'd given it to me and wearing it made me happy—usually.

I'd turned off my phone as I'd left the gala and hadn't turned it back on.

I wasn't ready to face the fallout for what I'd done to the Cole family. Wasn't ready to see texts from friends asking me why they saw me featured in the news—or from the Chrysalis staff wanting to discuss why I'd exposed our sacred place.

No way would Cameron let me work at his Beverly Hills clinic after that bombshell dropped. I wasn't naïve. There'd be no tears. I had to surrender to my destiny.

There were too many memories at Chrysalis of Henry, and not enough. His gorgeous face and devastatingly handsome aura were causing me to second-guess myself.

I climbed out of my Jag and walked the short distance to the front door, where de Sade was waiting.

"You're early."

I took a deep breath, accepting the inevitable, and stepped inside his well-lit foyer.

He quirked a brow. "Here to shelve my offer?"

"Why would you say that?"

"I'm surprised no one talked you out of it." He led me farther into the house. "How's your head?"

"I didn't drink that much last night," I admitted.

"We finished off your bottle of Louis Roederer Cristal Rose."

"I'm glad."

"Rylee isn't here," he said. "The others are on their way."

Following him down the hallway, I appreciated the way he swaggered in denim jeans, a far cry from his dashing tuxedo last night.

He hadn't mentioned the news.

Maybe he hadn't heard about my public humiliation—an issue that might affect this job offer.

We entered his kitchen, and I admired the stainless-steel paradise with white marble counters and bright blue tiles—a sunnier theme than I'd expect from a man with his disposition.

And there it was—the contract. It lay on the central island with a pen resting beside it.

Shoving down my roiling emotions, I sat on the barstool and stared at it. Strange how a few papers could drastically change an existence.

It wasn't meant to go this way.

For a moment there, I'd seen another future.

And it had been glorious.

Signing this would steer my life in a totally different direction.

I may even lose my friends—disappoint Cameron, hurt Richard, upset Scarlet and Penny.

I saw no other way.

They'd eventually understand I had deflected the focus off of them; protecting not just Henry, but also my closest friends.

De Sade set a glass of sparkling water before me.

I'd spaced. "I need time to read it."

He sat on the barstool beside me, his expression kind. I wasn't sure whether to trust it or not.

"Have a lawyer read it," he said softly.

"I should, right?"

"I was full of bluster when I told you to come around. This is a major decision. We need you to be sure."

"Tell me what you're offering again?"

"Penthouse."

"I have a house."

"Another house then. Let's move you from Encino to Beverly Hills."

"Henry lives close to Beverly Hills."

De Sade nodded. "Huntington Beach? You'll be closer to work."

Closer to Pendulum.

He squeezed my knee. "Bitcoin. That's a fun option. To be honest, you're in a good position to negotiate. We're billionaires. Ask for the moon."

"We'll shoot you off to Mars in a rocket," Henry had joked.

He'd been kind, at least.

I refocused on de Sade. "What if I bleed you all dry?"

"You'd be worth it."

"I never cared about the money," I said, holding back tears.

"Don't tell them that."

Why the threat of tears?

I should be proving I could handle anything they sent my way. Pendulum was full of arrogant bastards who needed to be reined in. Showing emotions would make me appear weak.

He tapped the contract. "Full authority. Whatever floats your boat."

I reached for the pen and tried to sign my name on the last page. No ink came out.

"Okay, then," he said flatly.

Adrenaline spiking my veins, I let out a howl that his pen didn't work.

He laughed, too, finding it equally funny.

"Read the fucking thing, Lotte." He pushed off the barstool. "We need a dominatrix who proceeds with caution."

"Why me?"

"Why you?" He smiled. "You're the best thing about Chrysalis. You're kind and patient. You'll be respected and adored. You even attracted the attention of America's most sought-after bachelor for a while there. Proving once again, men are idiots. You'll be a fucking queen in our world. We kings at Pendulum will bow at your feet."

"You're high," I said. "No more cocaine."

"I don't do drugs." He lifted his shoulder in a casual shrug. "Unless of course, *you* are the drug."

"I'm not having sex with you."

"It's hard to resist the irresistible." He stepped back, hearing the doorbell. "That's them. Make me proud."

He went to greet his guests at the door.

Picking up the pen again, I ran the tip along a corner of the contract to get it to work. Again, no ink came out. I threw it down in frustration.

A sign from the universe?

This time, I'd take control of my own fate.

I slipped off the barstool and started opening drawers, searching for another pen.

"Here she is," said Atticus standing in the kitchen doorway, suave in a business suit. "And caught red-handed pilfering, by the look of things."

"Funny," I said. "I need a pen."

Greyson Grantchester appeared with de Sade beside him.

"Do you have one?" I asked, holding my hand out to Atticus.

He reached into his jacket pocket and pulled out his pen, offering it to me. This brilliant surgeon was kinky as fuck and predictably organized.

The last time I'd seen Atticus was inside the Highgrove Suite where Henry and I had observed him with his submissive, Olivia.

I accepted the fancy fountain pen. "Thank you."

"I want it back."

"Of course, darling."

"Atticus," said de Sade, "bring the champagne. Grantchester, carry the crystal flutes. We're going down to the pool."

We all gathered the customary items of celebration and moved to the lower-level, me carrying the contract. The view of the city was spectacular.

We set everything on the poolside tables.

"Entertain me while I'm reading." I waved the contract. "All of you strip naked and swim so I can enjoy the show."

"I'm not a fucking stripper," snapped Atticus.

"You are for me." I ambled toward him. "Once I've signed this, you will obey."

He towered over me. "You haven't signed it yet."

Stepping forward, I cupped his balls. "These belong to me now."

He didn't flinch as his erection grew in my hand.

"Very good," I said calmly. "Obedience is rewarded."

"I'm game," said Greyson, pulling his T-shirt up and over his head.

De Sade kicked off his shoes and both men stripped naked before me.

Even Atticus finally gave in to my commands.

It was fun to watch these sophisticated gentlemen reveal their fit bodies. Women obsessed over their firm sculpted chests and taut thighs.

I sat down on one of the loungers, this time reading line by line through the contract—occasionally glancing up to savor the view of them having fun in the pool, laughing and splashing each other. Men really were still boys when it came right down to it.

I suppressed a sob when I thought of *him.*

What is it they say about alternate universes? Perhaps we were together in some other parallel existence.

Pushing up, I walked the short distance to the end of the patio. From here I could see the breathtaking view of the Los Angeles Basin, the San Fernando Valley, and even the Hollywood sign.

Cole Tower loomed large in the distance, rising tall amongst those skyscrapers. A profound reminder of what had been lost.

Fighting back tears, I replayed every interaction with Henry as though I deserved to be this tortured by precious memories.

Many good women had gone before me. Those who'd sacrificed what might have become their greatest love deserved respect. I'd gather strength from that one day.

I went back to my lounger to see this through.

I caught sight of movement at the side gate.

Oh, shit.

Cameron had found out about my meeting. I hoped he didn't ask about Pendulum. I turned over the contract and set the pen down.

Cameron approached, dressed casually in jeans and a T-shirt, looking dashing in designer sunglasses as he strode confidently toward me.

My old boss tucked his hands into his pockets and wandered around the pool, throwing a friendly nod to the guys.

They didn't seem concerned.

Mouth dry, I suddenly saw wisdom in having drinks here.

Cameron came over to where I sat and examined the bottle of champagne, his expression showing approval of the vintage.

Fascinated, I watched him pour bubbly into all the glasses like he'd been invited to the party. I prayed de Sade didn't suspect me of inviting him here.

Cameron offered me a crystal flute.

I accepted the drink and set it down on the side table, not ready to celebrate until he left.

Cameron lifted a glass himself and took a sip. "Very nice."

"I'm guessing the scandal hit the news," I said quickly.

"You're not usually this temperamental."

"I'm not usually a hazard."

"Let's talk about that."

"Who told you I'd be here?" My heart was racing with panic.

He sat next to me on a lounger. "Let's talk, Ms. Chamberlain."

Counting the flutes, I realized we'd brought down five.

CHAPTER SIXTY-THREE

Henry

I DIRECTED GRIFFIN TO PULL OFF SEPULVEDA AND PARK JUST inside Los Angeles National Cemetery—the final resting place of brave veterans.

I'd dressed casually in sportswear, removing any formality that might get in the way.

This place had a way of bringing gratitude back into focus.

After Lotte had walked out of the gala last night, I'd been left to pretend my night hadn't crashed and burned.

I'd still delivered that speech. No regrets there.

The fallout in the press could take care of itself. The Cole family was united. My parents found the increased interest in my love life favorable.

This early Sunday morning was dedicated to a young man who deserved as much of my time as he needed.

I retrieved the bouquet of flowers off the back seat.

"My dad's buried here," said Griffin, turning off the engine.

Our eyes met in the rearview.

"I know," I said. "Let's walk."

We exited the town car and began the long trek toward where Griffin's father had been buried.

I felt humbled by the sight of the endless gravestones marking the resting place of these remarkable soldiers who'd sacrificed their lives.

Respectfully navigating the grass around them, we made our way down to a particular row of tombstones.

To our right, a U.S. Marine in a pristine uniform stood not far away.

I threw him a salute of respect and he returned it.

Griffin led me to his father's grave.

Respectfully, I knelt and rested the flowers at the base of Sergeant Tomlinson's tombstone.

"Such a brave man," I said quietly.

Griffin let out a long sigh. He knew we'd learned more. His eyes studied my face as though searching for answers.

Answers I'd managed to find for him.

"Your father was well respected," I said. "I'm guessing you know that."

He gave a nod. "I was twenty when it happened."

When missions go wrong, people are sought out to blame—but very often no blame should be given.

"What were you told?" I asked.

"His troop was on a mission. Something went wrong. Dad died in the line of duty."

"Your father was involved in one of the most brutal ambushes of the Afghan war. He was one of the military's bravest. I want you to know that."

"Thank you, sir."

"While we're here, Griffin, please call me Henry."

"Thank you, Henry," he said softly.

"The request came in from your father's CO for his men to be extracted. They needed urgent air-support. Chaos ensued—not unusual in these scenarios. They found themselves outgunned. There were casualties. Your dad ran out into the center of the fray and waved an orange panel to flag the rescue helicopter. The extraction began. Your dad began loading the wounded. He went back for the last man, refusing to leave until everyone had been rescued."

I drew in a steadying breath. "As he was helping the last soldier, he took a bullet. They managed to get him inside the chopper and took off, but he died minutes later from his head wound. I'm so sorry, Griffin."

He shook his head. "Why didn't they tell us that?"

"His Captain took the flak for the mission going wrong. The Officer was later vindicated. Details are only now being released."

"Thank you, sir." He took a shaky breath. "I mean, Henry."

"I thought you might like to meet the man your dad saved." I glanced over at Staff Sergeant Palmer.

Griffin stared at the Marine. "That's him?"

"He'd like to meet you, too." I gestured for Andrew to join us. "Your father saved countless lives that day. You should be very proud."

"I am."

"You've got the car. Take tomorrow and the next day off. Take as much time as you need."

He gave a nod.

"Shay has some ideas about you moving over to his team. If that's something you might like."

"Special Ops?"

"Civilian, yes, but it can be interesting. Challenging, but fulfilling."

He brightened a little and I gave him a hug before withdrawing from this private moment. I would let Staff Sergeant Palmer and Griffin—two men connected by the profound actions of one man—have some time alone.

With my head down and heart breaking for him, I made my way back down the pathway. Living without a father would have been a hard cross to bear. He was ours to protect now.

Before leaving, I stood for several minutes facing the cemetery with my hand over my heart, saying a prayer of gratitude to the fallen.

Shay had parked his jeep next to our town car.

After climbing in, I let out a long breath. What I had just done had been even harder than I expected. We both knew the kind of pain a family endures over the loss of a veteran.

For Griffin, the truth had finally come out, leaving some peace to be found amongst the savagery of war.

In silence, Shay drove us away from the cemetery. He no doubt was feeling that familiar guilt I often felt for surviving when our brothers-in-arms had not made it home.

We made it to the rock face in thirty minutes. Though by the time we got there my mood had changed considerably.

As we carried our climbing equipment to the starting point, I kept thinking of how I'd hurt Lotte the night before.

My usual arrogance had driven a wedge between us. I should have let her sit with us at the ball.

My strategy was to get ahead of the press. If they had seen us together on the red carpet, they would have released the story early.

But Lotte had deserved so much better.

I leaned against the rock and gripped the first indent.

"You need your harness," Shay snapped.

"I'm going to free climb."

"No, you're fucking not. If anything happens to you, your brother will dismantle my body and serve me up as chum at Charlie's."

"I need to clear my head."

"There are other ways to do it without risking your life."

Peering up at the rock face, I knew I had this.

Shay stepped closer. "Talk to me."

"It's been a shit weekend."

"I can see that."

"You get it, Shay. Griffin's hurting and that's hard to see."

"And?"

"Last night, I should have done more."

"Call her."

"I'm guessing Reese talked with her?"

Shay set his kit down. "I wonder if Reese misinterpreted what she'd heard in the car on the way to the event and then relayed that to Lotte."

"Which would explain why Lotte left."

"Reese overheard us strategizing with your PR team about how to deal with the leak about you both."

"I went against my PR team's advice. Maybe Reese had told her what she believed the plan to be. The same plan I threw out."

Probably the very reason Lotte didn't stay for my speech.

I clinched my jaw in frustration. I should have protected her.

I peered up at the sheer rock face again. What appeared impossible was made easier by taking one rung at a time.

"Reese's gone?" asked Shay.

"Dealt with."

"Swift and sure."

"Her ruthless side is something to behold."

"She's studied nature, Henry. Reese learned a thing or two. She's dedicated her life to what she believes is important."

"She's doing good work," I said, shaking my head. "But she hurt Lotte."

"Lotte would do anything for you. Her pulling back is her way of protecting you."

"I'll visit her this afternoon."

Tell her she's the only woman I want.

Shay pulled out his phone and read a text. His expression turned dark.

I stepped closer. "What's wrong?"

"It's Cameron. He's on Mulholland at Carrington's place." Shay shook his head. "Lotte's there."

"At de Sade's?" I threw down the climbing gear. "Tell me she didn't accept that job offer."

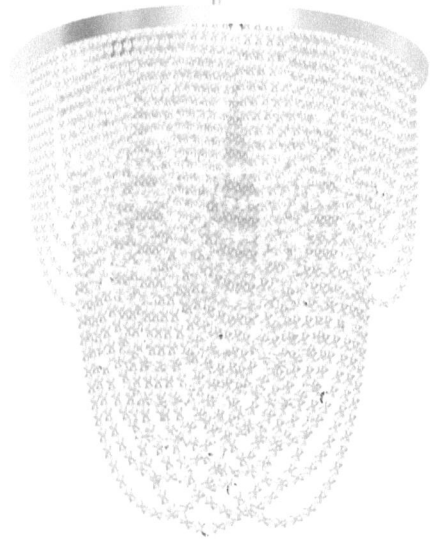

CHAPTER SIXTY-FOUR

Lotte

Q UESTIONS SWIRLED IN MY MIND AS TO WHY CAMERON
had turned up out of the blue.

He was sitting on one of de Sade's loungers, enjoying
the champagne and laughing at something one of them shared—
acting like one of the boys. They didn't seem perturbed.

He called over to them. "How's the water?"

"Warm," said de Sade. "You're welcome to join us."

Not naked though, please. Because having one more naked
alpha here might push me over the edge—especially if that man
was Cameron Cole.

Someone had tipped him off.

Even with his sunglasses on, I could see him eyeing the up-
side-down contract.

De Sade, Grantchester and Sinclair eventually climbed out of
the pool and put some distance between us by soaking in the hot
tub, taking advantage of the Cali sun—three best buddies hanging out while full-on scheming.

Cole's presence was taming the mood.

I needed him gone.

I lifted the glass of champagne he'd put down next to me and took a gulp. "Did de Sade invite you to make sure I'm prepared for what this entails?"

Cameron glanced my way. "Yes."

"Why?"

"I'm here to interrogate you."

I pointed. "That's the contract. I'm ready to sign. I certainly don't need interviewing by you."

They knew my worth.

"Why are you leaving Chrysalis?" he asked.

"I'll draw unwanted attention to Chrysalis and Enthrall—because I'm your brother's harlot."

"That's not good."

"Why didn't you dissuade me from dating your brother? You knew it would end like this."

"You believe I should have done that?"

"You should have protected me."

"I will always watch over you, Lotte."

I set my glass down. "Are you upset I'm here?"

"No, but you seem to be."

I reached for the contract and flipped it to the last page. Pulling the cap off the fountain pen, I signed my name.

Cameron arched a brow. "Hope you didn't do that because of the Cole family."

"I'm disappearing," I said. "Your scandal has removed herself."

"Oh, don't flatter yourself."

I reached for my glass and took another swig to soothe myself. *It was done.*

Cameron's expression softened. "Lotte—"

"You can't interfere," I said. "I've made my decision."

"I can see that."

"You disapprove."

"They own you now," he said. "Is that what you wanted?"

"I can't go back to Chrysalis."

"Well, you could have—before you put pen to paper."

"After that ruckus with me dating Henry, you wouldn't want me at your Beverly Hills office. I imagine that job offer is rescinded."

"Why? Because you're the worst scandal to ever hit the Cole family?"

"It's true."

"You really believe that?"

"I couldn't help myself," I said. "We were right there in a tent in the middle of nowhere. Henry looked perfect. The moment he ripped off his shirt—"

"Yeah, let's not discuss my brother's assets." He cringed.

"He's going to be fine," I said. "I just hope he finally sees through Reese."

Cameron sipped his drink. "You of all people should suspect the truth becomes twisted when motivations are skewered."

"He bought her a charm bracelet. I'm worried about him."

"He did, yes," said Cameron. "When she turned eighteen. He bought her a dress. Nothing more."

I sprung up. "She made me believe he'd just bought her that bracelet."

Reese wanted me out of the picture. I'd delivered myself up like a sacrificial lamb.

"Are you furious with me?" I asked.

"Do I seem furious?" He pulled out his phone and read a text—apparently already bored with my crumbling life.

"I had no choice," I reasoned.

Cameron sat up and leaned toward me. "I thought you of all people understood my brother."

"How do you mean?"

"He purchased the land in the preserve."

"Reese told me."

"For the animal life, not for Reese." He stood and offered me his hand.

"I'm not ready to leave," I said.

"Walk with me."

"I've signed the contract. It's over."

Cameron gave a frustrated sigh. "Reese is out of his life."

For a moment I was light-headed. "How do you mean?"

"He's selling the construction company. He's made sure the preserve is secure for future generations. All the species will continue to be protected. But he's out."

"He's out? But Reese told me—"

"He flew Reese and her daughter back to Florida this morning." Cameron's jaw flexed. "Permanently. Lilly will continue her studies at USC. He gave Reese a contract to sign at his house. Figured she'd be relaxed enough not to question it. He was right. She didn't catch the small print."

"What's in the small print?" I stood up, unsteady on my feet.

"That's confidential," he replied gently.

I shouldn't have left the gala last night.

What have I done?

Cameron reached down and took the contract from me, tucking it into his pocket.

"We certainly hire the best."

I blinked up at him. "What?"

"I'm the silent partner, Charlotte." Cameron pulled off his sunglasses. "Welcome to Pendulum."

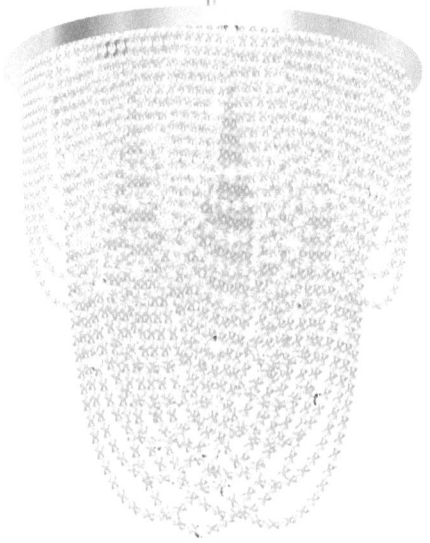

CHAPTER SIXTY-FIVE

Lotte

I WAS HIT BY A SHOCKWAVE OF EMOTIONS AS CAMERON WALKED away.

I kept replaying his words.

"Welcome to Pendulum."

He'd dropped that revelation like it was nothing.

In a daze, I tried to gather my thoughts. Cameron Cole ruled the Pendulum consortium.

With shaky legs, I followed him into the house and up the winding stairway to the second floor, into the familiar sitting room where Richard and I had sat over a week ago—when de Sade had first offered me the job.

Reese was out of the picture. Out of Henry's life.

And I'd just signed my life away.

The bitterly cruel timing was not lost on me.

Henry had asked me to trust him.

Oh, God.

I hung my head as waves of hopelessness washed over me.

"Sit down," said Cameron, sinking into a high-backed wicker chair. "Please."

I plopped down opposite him, feeling defeated.

"Pendulum is a dangerous place," Cameron began. "It always had a reputation for recklessness, but over the years it's gotten worse."

"You purchased Pendulum?"

"We." He pointed over the balcony at Atticus, Greyson and de Sade.

"You're the silent partner?"

"Yes."

"Richard?"

"I told him immediately after you both left here."

"How did he take it?"

"Took it well."

"He's your best friend, why didn't you consult with him on this?"

"I made a decision. I've made it my life's work to honor our specialty. Richard respects this. He'll continue to run Enthrall and Chrysalis. I'll work behind the scenes there, as well as at Pendulum."

"And Mia?"

"She's supportive. As always."

"You chose me as your dominatrix?"

He tilted his head. "Because you are undoubtedly the best."

"But—"

"But now, they own you. I own you. We're all happy, right?"

"You chose me." I repeated the words to find clarity.

"I chose you," he said, smiling. "Glad it all worked out."

"I messed up with Henry."

"That's a shame." He crossed one long leg over the other. "Welcome aboard."

"We could never have been together," I reasoned. "Didn't that scandal break?"

"You shouldn't have left the party, Cinderella."

My chest tightened with grief. "Protecting Henry was the most important thing I could do. No one will ever hear the truth about us."

"We appreciate that."

"It's imperative no one suffers because of the choices I made."

"That won't happen," he said kindly. "The leak to the press about your profession came from our side."

I drew in a sharp breath. "Who?"

"Henry."

"What?"

"He knew the only way for you to be together in public was for him to face the press head on."

"I don't understand."

"He did it his way, controlled the narrative. He hid you from the red carpet so you would be protected until after his speech. He threw down the gauntlet to the press."

"His speech?"

Cameron reached into his pocket, withdrew a piece of paper and unfolded it

"Want me to read it?"

Did I really want to hear how badly I messed up?

"It's long and boring." Cameron smirked. "Just like Henry, not surprisingly."

"Read it."

Cameron pulled a pair of glasses out of his pocket and put them on, converting to his professorial persona. Then he stood and raised the paper as though reading it the way his brother would before a podium.

"I'm going to share something deeply personal. At the last Cole event, I had an episode of PTSD. Something as simple as fireworks set it off.

An experience I wouldn't wish upon my worst enemy.

I have found that it is the darkest secrets that cast the longest shadows.

In case my enemies are gleeful at hearing my admission, I've been working hard on this condition. I'm glad to say, I am making progress."

"Honestly." Cameron shook his head as though unsure whether to continue. "The person who wrote this should be reading it."

"Please, go on," I said. "I want to hear it."

Needed to hear it.

"What if the man who wrote it read it to you?" Cameron asked gently.

"He won't want to see me!" I had sabotaged a perfectly wonderful friendship. The best relationship I'd ever had.

My beloved Henry.

That contract had sealed him off from me.

Turning my head, I saw him and blinked, trying to clear my vision.

Henry was standing in the doorway—here, at de Sade's home.

He stepped into the room as though I'd willed him out of the ether, looking sophisticated even in sportswear and sneakers.

My wonderful Henry.

His expression was surprisingly serene.

I swiped at a tear.

Henry's face lit up with compassion. "Wait 'til you've heard the entire speech," he said with a wink. "It's a doozey."

He accepted the piece of paper from his brother and stepped forward to read it.

"My job is to ensure Cole Tea remains on an even keel—especially in rough waters. Decisions on how to deal with the storms that find us are my own.

An honor I don't take lightly.

On a more personal note, there were reasons I

didn't wish to share my affliction with the public. In all honesty, I once saw it as a weakness. But to believe that is a disservice to my military brothers and sisters.

I didn't get that until *now.*

Not until I met a woman who helped me see my life differently.

Someone who made this man see the light, to envision my condition as a mark of sacrifice for my country—the consequences of putting my life on the line for you.

And of course, you and you.

Proving I am, and always have been, a proud American.

I will always believe in justice and freedom. With every cell of my being, I know it is a worthy fight. To serve in the military was a gift that enabled me to save others.

To fight for peace.

To fight for love.

There's another revelation which I am happy to share with you tonight. The woman who opened my eyes in this way is here."

Henry's gaze met mine.

"This woman came into my life like a sunrise after the darkest night. Lotte Chamberlain.

Lotte is not only exceptionally beautiful, she is also remarkably smart. She stands up to me. Her wisdom surpasses many.

Now, the press savors rumors and drama and juicy gossip. This time, I'm cutting you all off at the pass.

Lotte is a dominatrix.

She hasn't hit my ass yet with a whip, but the night is still young.

Personally, I don't practice BDSM.

I just want you all to hear that I'm really into this remarkable woman and if you write one bad word about her, I'll buy your newspaper. Or magazine. Or TV station. And then I'll personally fire your ass.

This I promise you.

So back off.

Of course, I'm joking, freedom of speech is everything in this country. I fought for that, too.

Still, I am human and will defend her like the knight in shining armor she deserves.

Anyway, I just wanted you to see how lucky I am to have her in my life. And, Lotte, I wanted to tell you personally, in front of all these people, how special you are to me."

He glanced up at me. "You were no longer in the room, so I changed that a little."

"Although it's too early to say those elusive words that convey love, you may find, my darling, that I will whisper them to you sooner than you believe possible."

Henry shrugged. "My speech went like that."

I leaped to my feet and ran toward him, wrapping my arms around his waist. "I'm sorry I didn't stay."

"Everyone was surprised you left," he said. "Considering I'm a hot catch."

"My Henry!"

"I am, Lotte. If you'll have me."

"Yes!"

He kissed my forehead. "I didn't want you to turn down this job if it's what you really wanted."

"I only took it because I didn't believe you and I could be together."

"That was never the case." He pulled me closer.

My face was squished against his firm chest, and I wanted to stay like this forever.

Then I remembered, pushing back from him and turning to face his brother.

Cameron had the signed contract tucked in his jacket pocket. That legally binding document could stop my happiness in its tracks.

"What should I do?" I asked Cameron, pleading.

"Go have some fun," he said. "You guys are way too serious."

Henry flinched when he saw de Sade standing in the doorway naked. "For God's sake, man," snapped Henry. "Go put some clothes on."

De Sade ignored him and zeroed in on Cameron. "Did she sign it?"

"No," replied Cameron. "And I doubt she will."

"Our loss," said de Sade with the shimmer of a tease.

I fell against Henry as he wrapped me in a hug. "You came for me."

"And I always will," he whispered.

CHAPTER SIXTY-SIX

Henry

A COOL BREEZE BLEW OVER LAKE GENEVA.
This time, a month later, we'd flown in during the day, arriving just in time for lunch, which would be served in the luxurious setting of our parent's lawn.

We'd be fine-dining with one of the finest views of the Alps.

The butler greeted us at the front door—straight to business as usual.

Cameron and I took the familiar path along the sprawling hallways of our parent's Swiss home. For Lotte, it was her first time visiting Switzerland.

I knew she'd love the adventure of flying here with us. She'd already been introduced to my parents at the garden party a few weeks back.

Cameron stopped me from entering the room. "You asked for no more surprises," he said. "Dad's going to announce something at dinner."

My back stiffened. "Am I going to like it?"

Instinctively, I wanted to reach for Lotte's hand to protect her.

Cameron lowered his voice. "C. R. Cole Tower is to be renamed the Henry M. Cole Tower."

Lotte gasped her delight.

It took me a few more seconds to process. "You don't mind?"

My brother radiated kindness. "No other name should be on it."

Seconds dissolved as I let that sink in. "Thank you."

Prosperity came in many ways. Today, it found me full of gratitude to be surrounded by the best kind of people.

I'd finally be working in a skyscraper with *my* name on it.

Within minutes, we'd settled into the lower chamber of the house, sealed off, the room temperature controlled to perfect the climate.

Dad was waiting for us.

His stern attitude lightened when he saw Lotte. "We met at the party."

"That's right," Lotte said, relaxing.

"You're the dominatrix?" he added.

"Dad," I said, wanting to protect her. "Please."

"It's fine," she said. "Yes, sir, that was once my profession. I'm now a therapist. I work at your other son's office in Beverly Hills."

"Whip his ass into shape for us, please." Dad pulled out a chair and sat, signaling for us to sit with him.

Inwardly, I cringed. "Thank you, Dad."

Why did parents always extract so much joy from embarrassing their offspring?

Even at this age.

Lotte took it all in stride. Her being here with us proved Dad already liked her. He'd invited her to stay for this.

I poured "Reflection" into a delicate China cup and then carried it over to the man whose appreciation meant everything to me.

"Tell me about the inspiration," he said.

I glanced at Lotte as I returned to my seat.

Up until now, I'd not told her she'd been the reason for this formula's existence.

She studied my face intently, her understanding drawing the truth from my soul.

I answered my dad's question. "Reflecting on my past, I saw more clearly our way ahead."

Charlotte's expression showed her surprise.

My father's assessment of the formula seemingly would take on an entirely new meaning.

Dad tipped the cup so he could observe the deep honeycomb tea as it trickled into the saucer. Taking his time, he stirred the leaves and leaned forward to inhale the aroma, breathing it in as though it was the secret nectar of life.

No reaction.

He sieved out the leaves from the tea and set them aside, then eyed them carefully as he mentally deciphered the recipe. Finally, he lifted the cup to his lips again and took a sip.

Then another, still expressionless.

The silence was deafening.

Sitting back, I realized I didn't care anymore. Not really. Because this was my company. Though I wanted to make him proud—make them all proud.

And anyway, I'd presented to them a great new flavor, totally believing in what I had created.

"I've always been fond of Florida." Dad pushed up from his chair. "See you at dinner, Lotte."

"You too, sir."

"Call me Raif." He winked. "Always good to see my boys. You're staying a few days?"

"Yes, Dad, if that's okay," said Cameron.

And that was it. Dad walked out without saying another word.

Those sieved leaves that lay in the saucer were a precious re-minder of how a delicious flavor can be enhanced with delicate chocolate shavings.

Cameron grinned. "You're taking Cole Tea to a new level of luxury."

Lotte got up from her chair and came to stand behind me, wrapping her arms around my neck and hugging me.

"Bravo," said Cameron.

Leaning in to kiss my cheek, Lotte said softly, "Your dad loved it."

And to prove it, the teacup sat empty.

EPILOGUE

Henry

THE BOAT SWEPT OVER THE FAINT OPAL-COLORED WATERS of Lake Geneva.

Lotte and I had stolen an afternoon away just for us.

I'd sailed luxury motor yachts since childhood; my interest in the Navy inspired by those frequent trips out to sea. This waterway was pleasantly familiar.

We sat on the outer deck, taking in the charming homes and businesses nestled in the hills. Seeing countless restaurants and cafes and sprawling vineyards.

I'd found a quiet place to idle the engine so we could savor this view.

Lotte shielded her face from the sun's reflection as she took in the majestic alpine scenery stretching between the French and Swiss shores.

When she glanced back at me, her face lit up.

"Like it?"

She reacted with surprise that I'd even ask. The view was awe-inspiring.

"I don't recognize my life." She swept her hand through the air. "This is incredible."

"Sometimes that's how it works."

"Thank you for bringing me."

"Thank you for being here."

"It's a far cry from an afternoon clinic in Beverly Hills."

"I hope my brother is a good boss."

"He's a great boss," she said. "He balances work a lot, stays busy with the Foundation."

Cameron dutifully ran the side of Cole Tea that ensures we give back on the grandest scale. He'd also had a hand in the renaming of Cole Tower after me.

He was the best kind of brother, friend, and dare I say, occasional therapist.

"I never thought I'd leave Chrysalis," she said wistfully.

"You're happy?"

"So happy." She let out a sigh.

"I feel like a completely different man."

"How?"

"My emotions were locked down, before you."

She looked at me with a gentle expression, kindness in her eyes.

The rawest feeling of loneliness was lifted.

The Alps were less intimidating compared to the mountains I'd once climbed with my captors, when they'd led me off into the darkness.

In life, when you finally reached the safety of the shore, it was more comfortable to remember the storm that brought you there.

"Tell me what you're thinking?" she whispered.

I pulled her closer until she was sitting next to me. "I see my life in two parts—the time before I met you and the time after."

"I want to make you happy."

"I know you do."

She reached over and took my hand in hers. "Your dad seems to approve of me."

"Don't care if he doesn't."

"It matters. Your mom invited me back."

"Mom's way of showing she likes you."

"I'll be an asset. I hope they see that."

"Already do. You chased away my past when it came back to haunt me."

Reese had returned to being just a memory.

Knowing she'd fulfill her life's purpose brought solace. Her daughter would thrive, too. Their good work would continue.

The state park had been saved.

Whenever I thought of the Fakahatchee Strand Preserve, I'd think of Lotte.

I tipped her chin. "Let's go back to Florida."

"We can."

"I want to see where you grew up," I clarified. "I'll show you Manhattan."

"You spoil me, Henry."

"Get used to it. Favorite memory so far?"

"Dancing to Neil Diamond's 'Holly Holy' both times," she answered, beaming.

"At the gala, I tried blinking in Morse code to tell you all would be fine. You didn't catch it, so I had to bring in the big guns. Diamond always comes through."

"You're really a fan."

I felt comfortable sharing why. "When we were in Afghanistan, one of my men, Sergeant-Major Jack Brown, constantly played Neil Diamond. We used to make fun of him for it, but he loved his music. Had a Neil Diamond tattoo, for Christ's sake."

"Oh," she said softly, realizing the truth.

The words were still hard to say. "He didn't make it."

She exhaled in a rush. "I'm sorry."

"I play Jack's music during significant times in my life. Keep my friend's memory alive. I'm quite the Neil Diamond fan now."

"That's lovely."

"Isn't it interesting, how differently we view the music of our youth? Everything has a deeper meaning."

Her lips turned up. "We're growing older."

"Maybe you'd consider growing older with someone like me?"

She sat back, face radiant.

"Move in with me." I watched her reaction. "If you like."

"I've been staying over at your place every night since you rescued me from de Sade's. I kind of already live with you."

"Officially, I mean. I'll throw out my awkward statues and replace my barren furniture with your beautiful décor."

"That's a big move."

"It's just from Encino to Beverly Hills."

"You know what I mean."

"Anyway, Dex would like it." I grinned.

"Oh, my God, I adore him."

"The first night in the preserve, when we hunkered down in our tent, I watched you sleep, all night long."

"You should have been sleeping."

"You looked so serene. My sleeping beauty."

"That's a lovely thing to admit." She gave me a shy glance. "I kind of guessed you had."

"That night," I said holding her gaze, "was one of the happiest of my life. Watching you sleep beneath the stars."

Her delicate fingers brushed over my hand, her touch soothing me.

"It was always you, Lotte. Never had any doubt you would become mine."

"I was scared to dream of a future."

"You are the air I breathe."

I cupped her face and brought her in for a kiss, our lips crushing, tongues clashing and then softening into a show of surrender—sharing our emotions in waves of tender affection.

"I have something for you." Reaching into my jacket pocket, I pulled out a small square box. "Hope you like it."

Lotte took the gift and lifted the lid, peering inside at the silver locket.

"Open it."

Gently, using her fingernail, she pried open the tiny clasp and saw a miniature cluster of delicate silver stars lying loose within. "Oh, my goodness. They're exquisite."

She was exquisite.

Carefully, she closed the clasp to protect them from falling out. "I'll cherish them." She raised the delicate chain. "Help me." Turning her back to me, she sat still as I worked the catch at her nape and secured the necklace.

"I'll protect your heart forever," she said softly.

"You're the reason it started beating." I pulled her back into a hug.

"That means everything."

"It's a little early to say it," I reasoned. "But lately, I've discovered the joy of not following rules."

"I know what you're going to say," she said softly. "I feel the same."

"This is love."

She leaned against me. "This is love."

We continued toward the French village of Nernier, watching the charming scenery breeze by, letting the silence say everything else as we savored the sacred peace that had found us at last.

My past was shedding its hold.

Back in that war-torn country so far away, my enemy had failed to understand why they couldn't destroy me.

Or break me.

In the shadows of my psyche, I had remained safe within my consciousness with my mind remarkably preserved.

The few therapists who had tried to convince me I *was* broken were right about one thing—a part of me had never come back.

Until now.

Because now, I felt whole.

Once, I had feared I was less than the person who had been

deployed. But that wasn't the truth. The truth is something much different.

Despite all the struggles, all the sleepless nights and all the challenges, despite the once constant fear of losing my life as others lost theirs, the fact is *this*.

The war made me better.

And Lotte—she showed me how to love the man I'd become.

ALSO BY
VANESSA FEWINGS

THE ENTHRALL SESSIONS
ENTHRALL, ENTHRALL HER, ENTHRALL HIM,
CAMERON'S CONTROL, CAMERON'S CONTRACT,
RICHARD'S REIGN,
ENTHRALL SECRETS, ENTHRALL CLIMAX,
ENTHRALL ECSTASY AND ENTHRALL SHADOWS

The ENTHRALL Spin-off series
THE CHANDELIER SESSIONS
CHANDELIER DREAM
CHANDELIER SIN
CHANDELIER ENTHRALLED

THE ICON TRILOGY from Harlequin:
THE CHASE, THE GAME, and THE PRIZE

PANDORA'S PLEASURE
MAXIMUM DARE
PERVADE LONDON and PERVADE MONTEGO BAY
PERFUME GIRL
THE STONE MASTERS VAMPIRE SERIES
THE RAVISHING—With Ava Harrison

ABOUT THE AUTHOR

Vanessa Fewings is the *USA Today* and international bestselling author of the ENTHRALL SESSIONS and THE ICON TRILOGY from HarperCollins along with many additional novels. ENTHRALL has been optioned for film. Her books have been translated into other languages around the world. She now lives on the West Coast with her rescue Foxhound, Sherlock.

vanessafewings.com

www.ingramcontent.com/pod-product-compliance
Lightning Source LLC
Chambersburg PA
CBHW020649110726
47901CB00001B/109